EXIT BEFORE MIDNIGHT:
A Collection of Murder Tales
PATRICK QUENTIN
Introduction by Curtis Evans

Stark House Press • Eureka California

EXIT BEFORE MIDNIGHT: A COLLECTION OF MURDER TALES

Published by Stark House Press
1315 H Street
Eureka, CA 95501, USA
griffinskye3@sbcglobal.net
www.starkhousepress.com

The Jack of Diamonds: copyright © 1936 by Q. Patrick and published by *The American Magazine*, November 1936.
Exit Before Midnight: copyright © 1937 by Q. Patrick and published by *The American Magazine*, October 1937; reprinted as "Murder on New Year's Eve," *Ellery Queen's Mystery Magazine*, January 1950, as by Patrick Quentin.
Another Man's Poison: copyright © 1940 by Q. Patrick and published by *The American Magazine*, January 1940.
The Gypsy Warned Him: copyright © 1943 by Q. Patrick and published by *Short Stories,* October 25 1943.
A Theoretical Reconstruction of the Borden Case: copyright © 1943 by Pocket Books, Inc, New York, published in *The Pocket Book of True Crime Stories* as by Q. Patrick.
The Last of Mrs. Maybrick: copyright © 1943 by Pocket Books, Inc., New York, published in *The Pocket Book of True Crime Stories* as by Patrick Quentin.
The Ordeal of Florence Maybrick: copyright © 1962 by Mystery Writers of America published in *The Quality of Murder: Three Hundred Years of True Crime Compiled by Members of the Mystery Writers of America* as by Patrick Quentin)

Reprinted by permission of the Patrick Quentin estate. All rights reserved under International and Pan-American Copyright Conventions.

"A Collection of Murders: Introduction" copyright © 2023 by Curtis Evans.

ISBN: 979-8-88601-064-0

Cover design by Jeff Vorzimmer, ¡caliente!design, Austin, Texas
Text design by Mark Shepard, shepgraphics.com
Proofreading by Bill Kelly

PUBLISHER'S NOTE:
This is a work of fiction. Names, characters, places and incidents are either the products of the author's imagination or used fictionally, and any resemblance to actual persons, living or dead, events or locales, is entirely coincidental.
Without limiting the rights under copyright reserved above, no part of this publication may be reproduced, stored, or introduced into a retrieval system or transmitted in any form or by any means (electronic, mechanical, photocopying, recording or otherwise) without the prior written permission of both the copyright owner and the above publisher of the book.

First Stark House Press Edition: December 2023

Here's what the critics had to say about our previous Patrick Quentin collection, *Death Freight*...

"["The Laughing Man"] is perhaps my favourite from the collection, and it certainly has the makings of a strong full-length mystery. Both the opening and the denouement have high impact, with the latter being remarkably heart wrenching…"
—Kate Jackson on *crossexaminingcrime.com*

"My favorite is the eponymous and almost-hardboiled, "Death Freight," where murder and greed find a restless writer, Jake Tinker, on a ship voyage across the Indian Ocean. There are stolen diamonds, fisticuffs, tough talk, and even a surprising turn or two."
—Ben Boulden, *Mystery Scene Magazine*

"Each of these short novels is thoroughly entertaining… a solid quartet of mysteries that should please any reader."
—Ted Hertel, *Deadly Pleasures*

7
Exit before Midnight:
A Collection of Murders Introduction
by Curtis Evans

16
The Jack of Diamonds

64
Exit Before Midnight

105
Another Man's Poison

156
The Gypsy Warned Him

218
The Case for Lizzie or A Theoretical
Reconstruction of the Borden Case

234
The Last of Mrs. Maybrick

244
The Ordeal of Florence Maybrick

250
Patrick Quentin Bibliography

Exit before Midnight:
A Collection of Murders
Introduction

By Curtis Evans

Exit Before Midnight, presumably the final volume of murder tales by Anglo-American crime writers Richard "Rickie" Wilson Webb and Hugh Callingham Wheeler, gathers for the mystery reader's deadly delectation four intriguing crime novelettes—"The Jack of Diamonds," "Exit before Midnight," "Another Man's Poison" and "The Gypsy Warned Him"—as well as three thought-provoking true crime essays about a pair of the Victorian era's most beguiling accused murderesses, Lizzie Borden and Florence Maybrick, that should decidedly appeal to all collectors of Lizzieanna and Maybrickabrac. Altogether these tasty morsels of murder in *Exit Before Midnight* should satisfy the most finical of vintage mystery fans.

The four crime novelettes, all of which were credited to Rickie Webb's and Hugh Wheeler's joint pen name "Q. Patrick," smoothly meld mystery, murder and male-female romance, although only in the last of them, "The Gypsy Warned Him," first published in the pulp fiction magazine *Short Stories* in 1943, does a man rather than a woman immediately emerge as the tale's embattled protagonist. Contrarily, in "The Jack of Diamonds," the first of the other three novelettes, all of which saw their initial publication between 1936 and 1940 in the glossily illustrated, female-focused pages of *The American Magazine*, the situation is more ambiguous. As the story opens, six elite New Yorkers are invited by the aristocratic and eccentric Theodore Vanderloon to a weekend house party at Chesham Grove, his ancestral country mansion loftily ensconced in the Berkshire Hills of western Massachusetts (where Rickie and Hugh themselves would soon rent a summer place), in order, it seems, to commit a murder! These lucky, or rather unlucky, individuals are:

- beautiful young opera singer Katharine La Motte
- handsome youthful baronet and clubman Sir Henry Bentley
- post-debutante bridge fiend Libby Hunt Farley
- sybaritic man-about-town John Derwood Thring III
- elderly jurist Homer Rock
- elegant society milliner Baroness Lilli Tresckow

The subject of their fatal attentions is to be corpulent society blackmailer Joseph Starner, who, we find, holds both Vanderlyn and his invited guests in his greedily grasping clutches. However, even with the help of his preternaturally able butler, Bowles, who knows all about the depths to which erring humans can sink, Vanderloon finds that the best-laid schemes of mice and murderers *gang aft a-gley*. There is the snowstorm that cuts off Chesham Grove from civilization, for example, not to mention the inconvenient, unexpected presence of Carmelite, Joseph Starner's pristinely beautiful adopted daughter….

In 1938, a stage adaptation of "The Jack of Diamonds" by British actress Beatrix Thomson (1900-1986), was performed, under the title *Special Delivery*, at metropolitan London's famed Richmond Theatre, with a cast including noted thespian Ernest Thesiger, best known today for his memorably fey performances as Horace Femm and Dr. Pretorius, respectively, in director James Whale's splendidly outré horror films *The Old Dark House* (1932) and *The Bride of Frankenstein* (1935). One assumes that in *Special Delivery* Thesiger played the character Theodore Vanderloon, whose "profile, with its grave eyes and mocking mouth, seemed that of an Etruscan faun rather than that of a twentieth-century American." In addition to her work in stage and film, the fiercely independent Beatrix Thomson, who at one time was married to actor Claude Rains, achieved a certain distinction as the first British actress to obtain an aviation license. Somewhat surprisingly, given Hugh Wheeler's later success as a playwright, "The Jack of Diamonds" is, as far as I am aware, the only collaborative work by Rickie Webb and Hugh Wheeler that has to date ever been successfully staged.

Mystery, murder and romance similarly abound in the second of the tales from *The American Magazine*, "Exit before Midnight," where a woman, attractive executive secretary Carole Thorne ("Blonde, and bothered about love," as the magazine's cast of characters informs us), unambiguously serves as the tale's leading character. The story takes place on the evening of the last day of the year, when Carole has returned after business hours to the semi-deserted fortieth floor of the high-rise Moderna Building, where the offices of her employer, Leland & Rowley Process Company, are located. She is to take minutes at a shareholders' meeting that will vote on the all-important question of whether to merge Leland & Rowley with the Pan-American Dye Combine, thereby subsuming its own identity into that of the larger business entity. As this description suggests, the novelette draws slightly upon co-author Rickie Webb's own executive experience with the Philadelphia pharmaceutical company Smith, Kline and French, which employed him throughout the 1930s.

Upon arriving at her office, Carole finds in her typewriter a menacing memorandum direly warning seven people that voting for the merger will result in their deaths! The threatened individuals are:

- Mr. Rowley, Leland & Rowley's esteemed president
- Peter Howe, Rowley's handsome blond nephew
- Marcia Leland, lovely and brainy heir to her late father's estate, including his whopping block of shares in Leland & Rowley
- Miles Shenton, Leland & Rowley's handsome brunet head chemist
- Mabel Gregg, Leland & Rowley's plump bespectacled treasurer
- Mr. Whitfield, Leland and Rowley's attorney
- Mr. Barber, Pan-American Dye's authorized representative in their dealings with Leland & Rowley

When the vote in favor of the merger goes through in spite of the menacing injunction, these seven people, along with Carole, find themselves trapped on the fortieth floor while their little frightened number is fatally dispatched, one by one. Is the murderer a raving maniac, or is there some diabolical method to his (or her) madness? Will Carole survive to ring in the New Year—just a few mere hours away now—or will a dreadful bell toll for her before she ever gets that chance?

The scenario in "Exit before Midnight" may remind vintage mystery fans of the 1930 mystery novel by Gwen Bristow and Bruce Manning, *The Invisible Host* (staged and filmed under the title *The Ninth Guest*), in which eight people trapped in a New Orleans penthouse are slaughtered one by one by an unknown fiend, not to mention Agatha Christie's altogether more renowned crime novel *And Then There Were None* (1939), which has been adapted to film numerous times. The highrise office building ambience of the novelette may also recall to some Kenneth Fearing's lauded 1946 crime novel *The Big Clock*, filmed two years later in a gripping adaptation starring Ray Milland and Charles Laughton. Unlike "The Jack of Diamonds," however, "Exit before Midnight" seems not, surprisingly, to have been adapted to other media.

In the last of the *American Magazine* novelettes, "Another Man's

Poison," a pulchritudinous woman once again is the tale's focal character. This time it is Rona Heath, "the spunkiest as well as the prettiest nurse" at College Hospital, which becomes the scene of an insidiously clever murder when Thegn Knudsen, the hospital's eminent and idealistic chief surgeon, is slain immediately upon commencing an operation. An autopsy shows that the late, great Thegn was pumped full of deadly hyoscine—and in the coffee he sipped shortly before the operation there was enough of the drug "to kill twenty goats." But finding just whose dread hand administered the hyoscine proves an altogether trickier matter for Lieutenant James Heath of the Homicide Bureau, who conveniently (if improbably) is Rona's brother. Potential suspects in the case:

- Thegn's social climbing, daughter-obsessed sister, Caroline Broderick
- Caroline's second husband, George Broderick, director of College Hospital
- Gregory Venner, Thegn's best friend and an anesthetist of twenty years' standing
- Oliver Lord, a handsome, young, red-haired surgical intern with considerable professional ambition
- Hugh Ellsworth, an "attractive neurologist" (again quoting the cast of characters in *The American Magazine*)

The solution to the murder draws on pharmaceutical executive Rickie Webb's extensive familiarity with medicine and physicians (numbering among his friends was a professor of pathology at Temple University Medical Center in Philadelphia); and it is a clever one indeed, making "Another Man's Poison" the finest tale in this collection from the standpoint of pure detection. That this novelette, in terms of its operating theater scene of the crime, bears some comparison with two classic detective novels, Ellery Queen's *The Dutch Shoe Mystery* (1931) and Christianna Brand's *Green for Danger* (1944), is all to the good.

The final novelette in this killer quartet, "The Gypsy Warned Him," has a male protagonist, although, appropriately enough for a ripe piece of pulp fiction, there are present as well, besides the titular dark-haired gypsy, not one but two elegant and enigmatic blondes—both of whom bewitch, bother and bewilder our ingenuous muscle-bound hero, naval gunner Lew Warren. In a plot reminiscent of "Hunt in the Dark"—a Peter and Iris Duluth crime novelette which Rickie Webb and Hugh Wheeler published in *Short Stories* the previous year—Gunner Warren finds himself perilously enmeshed in an ever-tightening net of wartime Nazi espionage when, "high and happy" with his "white hat perched jauntily on the back of his curly black hair," he fatefully enters the neon lit El Dorado Bar, somewhere in the warren of Greenwich Village....

"What makes you think you can get away with five murders in one night," an incredulous Gunner Warren later finds himself asking a despicable Nazi collaborator holding him at gunpoint, before pointedly and patriotically reminding him: "This is New York. Not Nazi Germany." Will the curly-haired, straight-arrowed American sailor manage to free himself from the nefarious clutches of the Nazis and foil a tangled and dastardly plot? Even more importantly, will he get the girl? And, if he does, just which of the girls will he get?

■ ■ ■

Enigmatic women similarly are the subject of the trio of true crime essays included in *Exit Before Midnight*. The first two of these three essays are "A Theoretical Reconstruction of the Borden Murders" and "The Last of Mrs. Maybrick." Both the formidably titled former essay, written by Rickie Webb and credited to Q. Patrick, and the latter, more succinctly titled one, written by Hugh Wheeler and credited to Patrick Quentin, originally appeared in *The Pocket Book of True Crime Stories*, a 1943 collection of crime pieces that was edited by noted mystery novelist and critic Anthony Boucher. The third essay, "The Ordeal of Florence Maybrick," was first published in another Anthony Boucher edited true crime anthology, *The Quality of Murder* (1962). This essay sees Hugh Wheeler returning, near the end of his crime writing career as "Patrick Quentin" (which he abandoned after Rickie Webb's death in 1966 to concentrate on the composition of mainstream drama for stage and film), taking a final look at the scandalous life and obscure death of Florence Maybrick, a woman who clearly fascinated him.

Together the three essays are suggestive of their respective authors' lifelong contrasting approaches to crime writing. Rickie Webb's "Theoretical Reconstruction of the Borden Case" is, like his crime fiction, analytical and heavily plot-focused, while Hugh Wheeler's matching pair of Florence Maybrick essays are more concerned with questions of character and exhibit finer literary flourishes. However, Rickie's Lizzie Borden piece is itself quite readable and, best of all, it succeeds, in my estimation, in crafting an original and seemingly plausible new candidate for the ghastly double axe slayings of Lizzie's father and stepmother in Fall River, Massachusetts in the summer of 1892.

Despite the fact that at the time he published the essay in *The Pocket Book of True Crime Stories* Anthony Boucher was still a believer in Lizzie's guilt, he nonetheless proclaimed himself delighted with, if stubbornly unconvinced by, Rickie Webb's essay, wryly writing Rickie of the piece, "I am delighted with it and entranced by it and I don't believe a word of it. I wish I'd thought of it and I can't poke a possible finger through its logic, but I still think Lizzie did it."

Rickie Webb opened his "Theoretical Reconstruction" by declaring that he had informed the late noted criminologist Edmund Pearson, the literary leader of the anti-Lizzie brigade, of his own theory of the crimes in correspondence with the latter man shortly before he passed away in 1937 and that Pearson had allowed that Rickie's theory of the case was a "new and original one." Noting that Pearson had "assured me that, so far as he knew, I had in no sense transgressed against facts" and that he had "acknowledged the possibility and plausibility of my argument while tacitly admitting that it did not agree with his own," Rickie cheekily expressed his "forlorn hope" that the late Pearson's "mantle may descend, if but rustlingly, upon me." This never happened, of course, but the essay now appears here in print for the first time in seventy-seven years (one hundred and thirty years after the murders), allowing readers finally to learn just what was Rickie's audacious theory of the case and to judge it for themselves.

Similarly reprinted here for the first time is Hugh Wheeler's pair of true crime essays. In "The Last of Mrs. Maybrick" and its postscript, "The Ordeal of Florence Maybrick," Hugh looks at one of the most notorious of British murder cases, the 1889 trial of Florence Maybrick for the murder of her husband James, which took place just three years before the brutal slaughters at Fall River, Massachusetts. Wealthy Liverpool cotton broker James Maybrick had wed the much younger Florence, a beautiful blonde American belle originally from Mobile, Alabama, eight years previously, after a whirlwind shipboard romance, but the marriage soon proved a dreadful misalliance. The coarse and caddish James kept mistresses (one of whom bore him five children), and Florence with considerable provocation entered into her own extramarital liaisons. Relations between the man and wife continued to deteriorate from there.

When James mysteriously died in 1889, Florence, who recently had fatefully purchased arsenical flypapers for the benefit of her complexion (or so she said), was arrested and charged with murder. After being convicted of the crime and sentenced to hang amid much public outcry—incredibly, in the face of the verdict and sentence, it had not been credibly established just *how* James had died—Florence saw her death sentence commuted to life imprisonment on the theory that she had tried to murder her husband with arsenic but might not have actually succeeded in doing so.

In any event, Florence spent fourteen years in harsh incarceration, returning after her release from prison to the United States, where she ultimately settled, in an increasingly abject state, in the foothills of northwestern Connecticut. In 1941, just a couple of years before Hugh Wheeler's first essay about her was published, Florence Maybrick, now a wizened old woman of seventy-nine years living under an assumed surname, died anonymously at her residence, a tiny three-room dwelling located not far from South Kent School, a private boarding school for boys, where she had resided, with only her cats for company, for the last two decades. To the boys of the school, who delivered firewood to her door, she had been known simply as "The Cat Woman" and "Lady Florence," but with her death the truth came out, even grabbing the attention of a populace preoccupied with the deadly global warfare going on all around it. "Mrs. Maybrick Dies a Recluse," announced the *New York Times* of the notorious accused Victorian era poisoner a week before All Hallow's Eve in 1941, beside disquieting front page tidings about the German advance on Moscow: "Scrapbook in Cottage Reveals Identity."

Certainly to Hugh Wheeler the case of Florence Maybrick held morbid fascination. To Hugh, a gay man who with his partner Rickie Webb shared a life that then was generally deemed criminally unorthodox, Florence's cruel ordeal seemed a textbook case of the unmerited ill treatment which censorious society affords an individual whom it deems—and damns—as too daringly different to live. "Mrs. Maybrick faced trial as an American hussy who had mistreated and deceived a perfectly good English husband, a man, as far as the jury knew, without a blemish on his character," Hugh writes witheringly.

For yet another Anthony Boucher anthology, *Four and Twenty Bloodhounds* (1950), Hugh and Rickie provided a biographical sketch concerning their series sleuth Lieutenant Timothy Trant, in which they divulged that Trant attended not only Princeton University but South Kent School. Why South Kent School? Presumably it was because of the connection of the school to Florence Maybrick. Hugh and Rickie, who in the years immediately before American entry into the Second World War, resided for much of the year together in the Berkshire Hills of western Massachusetts, had friends among the Connecticut educational community, including Reverend Percy Gamble Kammerer, headmaster of the Old Farm School for Boys in Avon, about a forty miles' drive from South Kent.

Seventeen years after he penned his final essay about Florence

Maybrick, Hugh's sympathetic imagination must have been piqued by yet another lost lady, the melancholy character of Lucy Barker in the musical *Sweeney Todd* (1979), for which Hugh wrote the Tony Award winning book. Driven insane by the dreadful indignities inflicted upon her by the sadistic Judge Turpin, Lucy, the blonde, once beautiful wife of Benjamin Barker, aka Sweeny Todd, wanders the streets of London dressed in rags, a haunting shell of her former self, terribly in need of a beneficent protector. She is, indeed, rather poignantly like the real-life Florence Maybrick, whom, Hugh admitted, "intrigues me far more than any fictional lady in distress that I have created myself."

Read on in *Exit Before Midnight* and see in these engaging short works whether murder is stranger—and more engrossing—in fiction or in fact.

—August 2022
Germantown, TN

Curtis Evans received a PhD in American history in 1998. He is the author of *Masters of the "Humdrum" Mystery: Cecil John Charles Street, Freeman Wills Crofts, Alfred Walter Stewart and British Detective Fiction, 1920-1961* (2012) and most recently the editor of the Edgar nominated *Murder in the Closet: Essays on Queer Clues in Crime Fiction Before Stonewall* (2017) and, with Douglas G. Greene, the Richard Webb and Hugh Wheeler short crime fiction collection, *The Cases of Lieutenant Timothy Trant* (2019). He blogs on vintage crime fiction at The Passing Tramp.

EXIT BEFORE MIDNIGHT:
A Collection of Murder Tales
PATRICK QUENTIN

THE JACK OF DIAMONDS
By Q. Patrick

The six invitations were sent by special delivery. The wording of each was exactly the same, and all the envelopes had "Strictly Personal" written on the outside in the exquisite handwriting of Theodore Vanderloon.

Each of the six people to whom they were addressed had met Theodore Vanderloon during one or other of his erratic sallies into New York society. They knew him to be rich, eccentric, and the author of an occasional volume of quasi-philosophical reflections. They knew him to belong to one of Manhattan's oldest families. They knew also that he had long ago shut up the old Vanderloon mansion on Park Avenue and was living in almost complete seclusion on his remote estate in the Berkshires. But not one of those widely differing persons could have called Theodore Vanderloon an intimate friend. Certainly none of them could have expected so intimate—and so unconventional—an invitation....

Katherine La Motte, who was to sing Madame Butterfly at the Metropolitan Opera House that evening, was the first of the six to receive Vanderloon's formal note. She had just stepped out of her verbena-scented bath and looked far more like the Aphrodite of Knidos than the popular conception of an opera singer. As she reached for a rough towel bathrobe, she started to sing with careless perfection.

"Special delivery, Miss La Motte." Her maid handed her the letter.

America's operatic challenge to Europe took the envelope between a damp finger and thumb and opened it unconcernedly. As she read, the Puccini aria soared to high C, hung there a moment—and collapsed. Her smoke-gray eyes clouded. Slowly her fingers crushed the note.

"Cancel all engagements for the weekend," she said to her maid. "I'm going to the country tomorrow."

"But, Miss La Motte, there's the reception at Mrs. Dufrayne's. And then the rehearsal ...!"

"Cancel them." The tone was abrupt, final. "And you can have the weekend off, Marie. I won't be taking you."

Katharine La Motte drew the bathrobe more closely around her superb young body and moved into the bedroom. With a fierce, almost triumphant gesture, she struck a match and held the flame to a corner of the crumpled letter. The creamy paper grew black and limp. It slipped at length from her fingers, twisting and curling to the floor.

Even before the flame had burnt itself out, Katharine La Motte thrust forward her naked foot and ground the ashes until they were nothing more than a gray smudge in the pattern of her thick Persian carpet....

Sir Henry Bentley (Bart.) drank soberly and to schedule. He was fingering his eleven A.M. Scotch and soda at the New York Turf Club while he leisurely turned the pages of the latest reports from his private stables in Maryland and Newmarket.

"Special delivery, Sir Henry."

A waiter handed him a square envelope encrusted with the Vanderloon coat of arms.

As the thirty-four-year-old baronet read through the strange invitation, his plain, rather attractive face lengthened and went grim. Then the flash of steel in his eyes changed to a twinkle. He gulped the rest of his whisky and scribbled Vanderloon's name on the back of the envelope.

"Waiter, send a wire to that address." He tossed a five-dollar bill across the table and then, very deliberately, tore the letter into tiny fragments. "Bring me a double Scotch. Make it smart, man."

"Very good, Sir Henry. And the message?"

"Just the one word— Willingly."

The twinkle still lingered in Sir Henry's eyes as he gazed out of the window at the icicles hanging from the roofs opposite. "And just the weather for it," he murmured....

At society's smartest bridge club, Libby Hunt Farley, post-debutante, took a last overoptimistic look at her hand and went to little slam in spades. In the intoxication of that moment she forgot that she was playing for stakes too high for her; that she had lost several hundred dollars in the last few hours; and that her all-absorbing craze for bridge was strewing her IOU's among the more expensive clubwomen of New York as thick as the frost on the ground outside. She hardly saw the letter from Theodore Vanderloon when it was brought to her.

"Special delivery, Miss Farley."

Libby Hunt's fingers moved absently to open the envelope. But when she glanced at its contents her much-photographed eyes widened with sudden fear. The coated paper crackled as she crushed it swiftly into her pocketbook.

While she played the hand her fingers were trembling with an emotion which, for the first time in her card-playing life, had nothing to do with the game. She made a miscalculation of her opponents' trumps and went three down on her contract.

"Sorry, partner," she said mechanically. "And, by the way, you'll have to count me out at Glenda's tomorrow."

"But, Libby Hunt, darling! I thought nothing short of murder would keep you from your week end bridge."

Libby Hunt Farley started to deal the cards. "Nothing short of murder!" she echoed with a laugh which came a little too quickly and was a shade too high....

A chromium coffee percolator gurgled in the penthouse apartment of John Derwood Thring III. The grandson of the Pious Tract & Treatise Publishing Company gazed at his breakfast-lunch with jaundiced disgust. Opposite him sat a girl with a hard, pink face and hard, yellow hair. Johnnie was trying to remember at exactly what stage of the night before he had met up with her.

The Philippine butler, bringing Vanderloon's letter on a silver tray, interrupted the incoherence of his thoughts: "Special delivery, sir."

John Derwood Thring took the envelope and glanced blearily at its contents. He blinked once or twice, passed a hand across his handsome young face, and whistled softly.

"Let's have a look, Johnnie?" The girl leaned across the breakfast table and snatched playfully for the letter.

"No, you don't." Instantly John Thring thrust the envelope into the pocket of his bathrobe....

"Special delivery, Judge."

Judge Homer Rock sat alone in his office, staring with pouched, gloomy eyes at Theodore Vanderloon's invitation. When he came to the end of the page the color in his fruity cheeks changed from strawberry to plum.

"Preposterous! What on earth …!" He rose heavily, lumbered across the room, and flung the letter into the fire. While it crumpled into ashes he glanced quickly, furtively around him. Then he bellowed for his secretary.

"I intend to be—er—unwell on Saturday and Sunday, Miss Potts. I shall not go to court and I can see nobody." He paused, adding with unnecessary truculence, "And buy me some ice skates when you go out this noon."....

In her expensive millinery shop on Fifth Avenue the Baroness Lili Tresckow gave a rakish tilt to the brim of a chic new model.

"Special delivery, Madame."

As she read, the Baroness's aristocratic face relaxed into a smile. A delicate hand smoothed her hair.

"But it is so comic and so like Theo Vanderloon with his practical jokes," she whispered. "I must of course go."

The assistant removed a pin from her mouth and looked a trifle apprehensive. "Madame is going somewhere?"

"I go tomorrow to the country."

And Theodore Vanderloon's invitation was certainly original, although the Baroness, who knew him best, was perhaps the only one among those invited to have deliberately overlooked its sinister note.

The letter which had called into play such varying emotions read:

> Mr. Theodore Frensham Vanderloon requests the pleasure of your company at Chesham Grove on Saturday and Sunday, February 13th and 14th. A car will meet the train which leaves the New York railroad station at 10:05 A.M. and arrives at Ashford at 12:48 P.M. Mr. Vanderloon further requests you to bring skates, but no automobiles, no valets, and no personal maids.

But the invitation did not end there. At the foot of each note, written in meticulous, ornate capitals, had been added the phrase:

TO MEET AND TO MURDER
MR. JOSEPH STARNER.

At one o'clock the next day Theodore Vanderloon was standing at a bay window in the large living room of Chesham Grove waiting for his guests. The weather bureau had forecast a storm before evening and already there were signs of it in the sky. The whole horizon east of the Vanderloon estate gleamed a dark mother-of-pearl and the unbroken clouds were gravid with the threat of heavy snow to come.

Theodore Vanderloon glanced thoughtfully over the lawns at the large ornamental lake, where the ice shone smooth and firm. In the wan light his elusive profile, with its grave eyes and mocking mouth, seemed that of an Etruscan faun rather than of a twentieth-century American.

"You're sure you'll be able to manage single-handed, Bowles?"

"Yes, sir." The man who had been butler, philosopher, and friend in the Vanderloon family for more than twenty years bent in artistic absorption over a large silver tray of canapes.

"And the ice on the lake, Bowles? It will be—er—dangerous in the right place?"

"You can rely on me, sir."

Vanderloon glanced around him with a flickering smile. The wide room was charged with an atmosphere of well-groomed hospitality. A pile of blazing pine logs spat and crackled on the hearth.

In the distance a car engine throbbed. Gradually the sound grew nearer, steadier. The automobile drew up outside, crunching the brittle ice of the drive. As Bowles went toward the front door, Vanderloon said quietly, "Tell the chauffeur to meet Mr. Starner on the next train. Then he can take the car to Ashford and have it overhauled. We won't need him again today."

As his guests entered the house Theodore Vanderloon moved forward to greet them.

"My dear Lili"—he raised the Baroness's fingers to his lips—"only you could have designed that delightful hat."

He took Libby Hunt Farley's small, nervous hand in his. "Libby Hunt, my dear, still as fascinating and as intricate as the cards you play so well.... And Miss La Motte, the only nightingale who looks beautiful by day and sings beautifully by night."

As Bowles led the ladies upstairs Vanderloon turned his attention to the men: "Well, Sir Henry, the Turf Club's loss is my gain.... And Judge Rock—at last I shall have a guest who will appreciate my 1896 port.... Hi, there, Johnnie Thring, you young scalawag!"

A few minutes later all the guests were gathered in the living room. The conversation was brittle, sparkling as the champagne cocktails, and yet the six guests seemed a little too eager in their nonchalance. Nor could they prevent their eyes from straying occasionally to the door, where at any moment they expected to see Joseph Starner, the man whom they had all met so often—but never before socially.

Theodore Vanderloon moved to the hearth and glanced around him with the ghost of a smile on his sensitive mouth.

"Before our guest of honor arrives," he began, "I feel I should apologize for the somewhat unusual phraseology of my invitation. But then, Mr. Starner is an unusual man, as you all know."

Katharine La Motte was leaning forward with a vehemence that contrasted strikingly with the easy perfection of her clothes. "But I don't understand," she said swiftly. "What—what made you think I knew this man Starner?"

"Do not be alarmed, Miss La Motte. None of us would care to acknowledge the gentleman in public, but here you are among friends and fellow sufferers."

"You mean," whispered Libby Hunt breathlessly, "you mean you are all in the same mess as ...?"

"Yes, my dear Libby Hunt, we are all in the same mess." Vanderloon fingered the clouded crystal of his cocktail glass. "I am going to be frank with you. For the past two years Joseph Starner has been blackmailing me. He is known in New York merely as a successful, if rather unscrupulous, private financier. But he is even more successful as a connoisseur in the indiscretions of others. In fact, his talent in that direction amounts almost to genius. I will not bore you with the details of how I came upon the information, but I have discovered that you, like myself, are all victims of his genius. It is in this capacity that I have invited you here today."

Judge Homer Rock's ripe cheeks had turned a pimento red. He glanced apprehensively at the butler.

"Don't mind Bowles, Judge," put in Vanderloon. "He is completely in my confidence. In fact, it was through him that I found out about Starner's interest in yourselves."

The silence was uneasy. John Derwood Thring was the first to break it. He held out his glass for another cocktail and grinned. "Well, Theo, if you can be frank, so can I. I'll admit that Starner's been fleecing me for a long time. I'm in a hell of a hole. But what are you going to do about it?"

"You read my invitation?" Vanderloon asked. "It was meant in all seriousness. I knew you were sophisticated and—er—unprejudiced people. I thought that the idea I hinted at might appeal to you as much as it did to me."

Once again silence—a silence half of excitement, half of nervous indecision. The Baroness, who was curled in a chair like an exquisite white cat, lit a long Russian cigarette. Sir Henry Bentley glanced at his watch, gulped the third cocktail on his schedule, and said slowly:

"Speaking for myself, Vanderloon, we're none of us squeamish. If we were we wouldn't have come. As it is, we're here."

"Good. Then I can speak freely." Vanderloon's fragile silhouette glowed in the flushed circle of firelight. "For some time I have been thinking very seriously about Joseph Starner. He lives on the indiscretions—or, rather, the misfortunes—of other people, and his demands on those who support him are growing increasingly insistent. It is not merely a question of money. He takes his ample share of that, but, from me at least, he takes a great deal more than cash." Vanderloon's voice faltered infinitesimally. "We all of us have hidden somewhere in our pasts something which is best forgotten. Perhaps it is something we ourselves have done in a moment of weakness. Perhaps it is the—error of someone very close to us. On those particular points we are helpless, defenseless. No one has a right to do what Starner is doing to us."

His thin shoulders were erect now, firm as the steel in his voice. "Obviously, it is impossible for us to obtain legal protection against him."

The Baroness Lili Tresckow gave a tiny shrug. Behind the blue smoke from her Russian cigarette her face was pale. *"To meet and to murder!"* she whispered.

Vanderloon's eyes narrowed. "You have put your finger on the one place where I have been inaccurate, Lili. On your invitation I wrote the word murder, but one could no more murder the Starners of this world than one could murder a rat or a roach. The term I should have employed was *exterminate.*"

His words slipped quietly through the warm atmosphere of the room. Yet behind the casualness of his voice there lurked a strange force. His guests were aware of it, aware of the unsuspected strength of purpose in this man whom they had always thought of as a mere visionary, a philosopher who published his charming theories on life, but who himself took no part in the realities of existence.

Sir Henry's English voice cut through the silence. His lean face creased into a grim smile. "But, murder or extermination—isn't it damn' risky, Vanderloon?"

"Oh, no." His host plucked a petal from one of the jonquils on the mantel and sent it floating to the floor. "This is not going to be murder in the clumsy, conventional sense of the word. There will be no lethal weapon, no complications with the police. Starner is going to die this evening, but when he meets his death it will be by an unfortunate accident.

"You mustn't think that I asked you here to do something which I was afraid to do alone. I am perfectly prepared to kill Starner myself. I think that any one of us would be. But murder implies motives and, sooner or later, motives would involve us all. An accident is far safer, far more satisfactory. And an accident can be convincing only when there are several witnesses."

"This—this is disgraceful!" Judge Homer Rock, who for some time had been listening in speechless indignation, now rose heavily. "I don't know what sort of a person you suppose I am, Vanderloon, but I'm going to tell you right here and now that I think this is the most disgusting, the most degenerate business I've ever come across in my whole life!"

He pressed a silk handkerchief to the damp scarlet of his forehead. "I accepted your invitation as some sort of practical joke. I am going straight back to New York to put the matter in the hands of the police."

"Just a moment, Judge," put in Vanderloon quietly. "You seem to forget that Bowles and I happen to know something of what Joseph Starner—er—knows about each one of you."

"Nonsense!" The Judge's fury had reached a point bordering upon incoherence. "This Starner—who is this Starner? I've got nothing to do with him."

"There again, Judge, I think you're mistaken." Vanderloon turned to the butler. "There was a little matter between the Judge and Mr. Starner, wasn't there, Bowles?"

The butler was untwisting wire from the neck of a champagne bottle. "As I recall, sir, it concerned a certain Falcon Distillers Company. It seems that the Falcon Distillers Company supplied alcohol which is rather far below government standards. They found it wise to have a judicial gentleman on their payroll, sir."

"Have another cocktail, Judge," murmured Vanderloon. "I can assure you that this champagne is not a product of the Falcon Company."

Impatiently the Judge waved away the cocktail that Bowles offered him. His puffy fingers fumbled a tablet from his vest pocket. As he slipped it between his lips he held his left hand to his side. "Go on, Vanderloon. Go on with this farce. But as a man and as a lawyer I can tell you that you'll never trap Starner. He has more shrewdness, more cunning than the rest of you put together. And before you're through you'll find yourselves in a worse predicament than you are now."

Ponderously he sank into his chair. Something in his tone as he had uttered those words had momentarily lent him the dignity of a prophet. It had gone now. He was just an old, tired, and rather ill-looking man.

"If there are no other objections," murmured Vanderloon, "I will do as the Judge suggests and continue with this—er—farce. I asked you all to bring skates. Mr. Starner is bringing some too. He tells me that skating is his favorite form of exercise. As soon as it gets dark I am going to suggest an hour or two on the lake. The ice is at least four inches thick. It is perfectly safe—safe, that is, for everyone except Mr. Starner."

Vanderloon crossed to the window and pointed over frosty lawns toward the gray expanse of the lake.

"You see that post near the eastern bank?" said Vanderloon. "Immediately to the left of it Bowles is going to saw a large, irregular hole in the ice. He will leave the ice block in place and it will be impossible to tell in the darkness that there is danger." Once again there was a hard, menacing quality in his voice. "Should anyone happen to be skating with Mr. Starner at that particular spot, it would not be difficult to take hold of the post with one hand and give a gentle push with the other. Even one of the ladies could do it.

"The water," continued Vanderloon quietly, "is eight feet deep. When the loose block collapses beneath him, the impetus of Mr. Starner's skates should send him forward—under the ice."

"Smart," muttered Johnnie Thring. "But aren't the police going to do a bit of deducting when they find that hole?"

"I don't think so. As I have said, Bowles is going to make it irregular, jagged. With the ice only four inches thick, it is perfectly possible that some spots should be thinner than others. Mr. Starner is a heavy man. What could be more reasonable than that his extra weight should break the ice? Besides, there will be the rest of us to confirm the fact that it was an accident. It is difficult to overlook the unanimous evidence of seven impartial witnesses."

"You have thought well, Theo." The Baroness's delicate face looked older, unusually solemn. "Every leetle detail, it is so carefully planned. But to kill a man, however much one may wish him dead—it is easy to speak of but difficult in the doing. One has scruples, fears …"

"Naturally we all shrink from the idea of making ourselves murderers, Lili." Vanderloon moved back to the hearth and held his pale hands to the fire. "But I think we shall feel different out there on the ice. There are Japanese lanterns along the nearer bank, but the east end will be in complete darkness. Starner will doubtless be eager to have a few moments alone with all of us—especially those whose payments are perhaps overdue. And in the darkness—none of us need ever know who it actually was that—"

"But it all seems so cold-blooded," broke in Libby Hunt in a soft, strangely stifled voice. "Besides, things don't always work out the way you expect."

"Then we have plenty of time to put them right. Ashford, the nearest town, is five miles away. The other servants have developed—er—sick relatives or something, and both my cars have developed engine trouble. The paper forecasts a storm. In the past this place has been cut off from civilization for several days. You can see how easily it could be cut off again—if necessary."

As Vanderloon stopped speaking a clock in the outer hall struck two. Already the light had begun to fade from the room. Shadows slipped but of corners, sliding darkly toward the windows. Then, far away, sounded the faint purring of an automobile.

Vanderloon crossed to the window, gazing over the somber stretch of parkland. "He's coming," he said quietly.

Theodore Vanderloon crossed the room and stood by the door. He gave the impression of any ordinary host preparing to welcome any ordinary guest. But the thoughts in his mind were far from ordinary. Indeed, he, himself, was a little startled at the chaotic intensity of his feelings. This was his first opportunity to meet on his own ground the man he had learned to hate and despise as a symbol of the grasping, insensitive world.

Vanderloon felt the pulses at his temples quickening. And then, close to him in the shadows by the doorway, loomed the large figure of Joseph Starner.

"This is indeed a pleasure, Vanderloon."

In the light from the distant fire, the pink globe of Starner's face and head shone with a cherubic freshness; his massive body exuded a specious benevolence.

He had moved forward and was enveloping Vanderloon's hand in the damp plumpness of his own. "I hope I have not imposed upon your hospitality," he murmured. "I have taken the liberty ... a little surprise ..."

There was an almost imperceptible rustle in the shadows behind him. And then, as Vanderloon realized the nature of Starner's surprise, he felt a sudden alarm.

In a flash he foresaw the elaborate structure of his plan crumbling.

The movement in the obscurity had materialized now into a human form—wraithlike and unreal, yet real enough to be a tangible menace. Consciously or unconsciously, Joseph Starner had provided himself with the only really effective weapon of defense.

He had not come alone.

"Carmelite is so fond of night skating." Once again Starner's voice sounded, smooth and silky. "I did not have the heart to leave her in New York."

It was the girl's aloof composure as she I moved from the shadows which forced Vanderloon to realize his social obligations. Even in that oblique illumination he was struck by her almost breathtaking beauty. Her exquisitely molded face with its dark eyes and grave mouth had the serenity of an early Italian Madonna. Her dress was plain, conventional, the blue-black hair parted austerely and drawn back behind her ears. She seemed the epitome of cloistered innocence—a fantastic contrast to the sleek, middle-aged man at her side.

"Mr. Vanderloon—my daughter, Carmelite."

"How very delightful!" Vanderloon took the girl's hand. "I had no idea you were married, Starner."

"Married!" The blackmailer raised a quizzical eyebrow. "No, no; Carmelite is my daughter only by adoption. She has just graduated from finishing school in Paris, and now I am anxious for her to meet the best people here."

"I am flattered to have your daughter start her career in my house. At least, I can guarantee the charming people." With a slight bow Vanderloon led the way through the long room. For the past few minutes the rest of the party had been chatting with overelaborated nonchalance. Only Judge Rock remained in stony silence. As Vanderloon made the introductions, he was uneasily conscious of the artificial cordiality with which Carmelite Starner was received.

In contrast Joseph Starner seemed the essence of unruffled composure. He moved after his host, according to each guest in turn a pontifical bow. The inscrutable mask of his face gave no hint of surprise or suspicion. His only visible emotion was one of bland, paternal pride at the involuntary admiration which his daughter's beauty had aroused. He laid a possessive hand on the girl's shoulder and looked around the room. His pale blue eyes seemed to envelop the whole party in a comprehensive embrace. "This is particularly delightful for me, as I find myself surrounded by good friends—such very good friends."

Starner's enigmatic words still rang mockingly in Katharine La Motte's ears when, some time later, she stood alone in the dimly lit hall, the first of Vanderloon's guests to be ready for the skating party.

As she waited for the others by the window in her vivid scarlet costume, she suggested a modern Valkyrie or a brooding Clytemnestra. She was peering intently across the twilit parkland toward the lake, where a slight fogginess gave warning of the impending storm. It was as though those smoke-gray eyes were straining to see to the farthest limits of the lake.

Of all the strikingly different types whom Vanderloon had selected as his guests, this young operatic star had perhaps been the most stirred and excited by his scheme. A farm girl from the West who had gained recognition for her talents by sheer forcefulness and hard work, Katharine La Motte, at twenty-nine, had discarded most of youth's softer illusions. Despite her newly acquired success she still thought of life as a continuous battle. At present she was winning. The spoils of fame were hers for the taking. But, even now, Joseph Starner with a single word could send everything crashing around her.

She showed no sign of wavering at the unexpected arrival of Carmelite Starner. She recognized the girl's presence as a menace, but it was also a challenge. Throughout lunch and the subsequent period of strained sociabilities, Katharine La Motte had remained arrogantly apart. She had been impatient for the darkness, impatient, also, for an opportunity to be alone with her host. She was eager to make certain that, in spite of this link with the outside world, he had remained as firm of purpose as herself.

"The first ready, Miss La Motte. You're setting us all a good example." The opera star spun round, to see at her side Theodore Vanderloon in an old shooting jacket, with his skates slung over his arm.

"The girl?" she asked impulsively. "You think she's part of his blackmail game?"

"I hate to be cynical about a Botticelli angel, but Starner's hardly the man to invest in youth and innocence without expecting cash dividends in return."

"But what are we going to do?" put in Katharine La Motte urgently.

"Oh, don't let the exquisite Carmelite worry you. I must confess she gave me some bad moments at first. But now I have made suitable arrangements for her."

"You mean ...?"

"I mean Sir Henry. He is rich, titled, and, apparently, willing—an intriguing bait for a female blackmailer, however neophyte. I've asked him to monopolize her attention, especially while we are on the ice. If he is sufficiently captivating and we are sufficiently careful, we may even turn Carmelite into an asset. A daughter on the party should make an accident sound much more convincing."

Some of the others had joined them now: the Baroness, superbly Viennese with a gray fur cap and a gray muff; Johnnie Thring with a black and white checked scarf tied carelessly beneath his impudent young face. They both seemed gay, almost frivolous.

"Where is she—that Starner girl?" Katharine La Motte's gaze turned instinctively to Sir Henry, who had just come up.

"She'll be down directly." A slight smile flickered over the Englishman's plain, rather attractive face. "And don't worry, Miss La Motte, I'll take dashed good care of her."

There was a momentary silence—a silence which was suddenly broken by the sound of rapid footsteps on the stairs.

They all turned, to see Libby Hunt Farley. She was running wildly down the richly carpeted staircase—running as though to escape some phantom pursuer.

As she saw them she checked herself. Then, with a little cry, she moved dazedly to Vanderloon and clutched his arm.

"*He knows*," she breathed, with a swift, almost furtive glance over her shoulder.

As the others gazed at her in silence, they all felt themselves invaded by something of her panic.

"It's Judge Rock." Libby Hunt's hands fell helplessly at her sides. "I passed Starner's room on the way down. The Judge is in there. I—I didn't hear everything he said. But he's telling—telling Starner about the ice."

It was as though a chill had descended on the dimly lit hall.

"I heard the Judge say, 'They're planning to kill you ... the post at the far edge of the lake.'" Libby Hunt's voice was trembling, almost incoherent. "Don't you see? He knows."

She broke off abruptly. There were footsteps on the landing above. Almost as one the little group swung round to face the stairs, where, slowly, ponderously, Rock and Starner descended toward them. They both wore leather sporting jackets, with their skates slung over their arms.

For the first time that day Vanderloon's guests had no small talk, no sophisticated nonchalance to cover the acute embarrassment of the moment.

Starner had reached the bottom step. He paused there, smiling at them benignly, like an indulgent teacher who had surprised his pupils in mischief and was willing to forgive them. Slowly his gaze focused on the English baronet "I understand you are going to be kind enough to wait for my daughter, Sir Henry."

He turned serenely to his host. "I am glad you're ready for the ice, Vanderloon. The Judge and I were afraid the coming storm might make you change your plans."

For a moment the others looked at each other in amazement and indecision. Then, one by one, they passed out into the darkness of the February evening.

Only Sir Henry remained behind. As he stood looking after them, he heard Starner's voice outside, brisk and cheerful.

As Starner's voice trailed in through the open door, Sir Henry felt a reluctant admiration for this man whom he had every reason to wish dead. His admiration, however, was tinged with perplexity. Starner knew of their plan to kill him and yet he was deliberately walking into the trap. It was crazy—it didn't make sense. But, first and last, the English baronet was a sportsman. And now his sporting instinct at least was satisfied that Starner had been given a fair chance to defend himself. The Judge's disaffection had evened up the odds. What had been planned as a covert attack was now a battle in the open, a battle which must inevitably be fought to a finish.

But Sir Henry loved danger. He was one of those normally phlegmatic men to whom excitement is a tonic. And things were really exciting now. There were excitement and danger in Carmelite, too. A smile hovered around the baronet's mouth as he thought of the strange situation which had precipitated this intimacy with the adopted daughter of his enemy. The smile had not faded when, a moment later, Carmelite herself descended the stairs.

"Thank you so much for waiting."

She was very simply dressed in a white jersey and skirt which accentuated the youthful lines of her body. Beneath a cap of white fur her face was dark and secret as a flower. Without a word Sir Henry took her arm and they passed out.

When they reached the lake they paused a moment by the small boathouse. In front of them the scene was animated and colorful. The night air and the smooth strength of the untrammeled ice seemed momentarily to have dispelled all fears and uncertainties. Vanderloon's guests appeared excited, almost hectically gay; they swooped in circles, pirouetting with laughing chatter. And in their midst, calm and benign as ever, there glided with incongruous grace the heavy figure of Joseph Starner.

Vivid colors, the hissing of skates, red cheeks, and the nodding Japanese lanterns. In spite of himself Sir Henry was caught up by their magic. Here were all the superficialities of a carefree weekend party. And yet, somewhere outside the glowing circle of light stood that post—that solitary post with its warning of invisible death.

"Allow me to help you, Miss Starner." Bowles had materialized from the darkness and was bending over the girl's skating boots. Swiftly Sir Henry slipped into his.

The others, as if gradually gaining assurance, had started to move farther away now. They were to be seen less and less frequently near the light bank. Soon they had all melted into the shadows, and there was nothing to betray their presence but the ringing of skates and the high singing of the ice, fainter … fainter …

With their departure, the deserted circle of light lost its innocent blandness. It had taken on a sinister, almost eerie quality. Sir Henry felt his pulses beating quickly as Carmelite slipped her gloved hand in his and they moved in silence onto the lake.

"I'm afraid we're going to have a storm." Polite, detached, Carmelite's voice broke into his thoughts. "I love skating and there won't be much time. Will you excuse me if …?"

Almost before he realized it, she had slipped her hand from his and was gliding away into the shadows. For one moment of intense anxiety he thought she must have guessed the reason for his constant presence, that she was deliberately eluding him. Then, to his relief, he saw her again, circling around him.

And then, suddenly, she was back at his side, so near that he could hear her breathing—rapid, excited. He gazed at her in silence. From the beginning he had known she was dangerous. And yet he did not care. Against reason he found himself yielding to the spell of her nearness. He heard his own voice speaking as from some half-remembered dream: "I never thought it would happen like this—here on the ice, in America."

She did not move or speak, but somehow he could not check the stream of his own words: "I've often wondered where I would find her—the most beautiful girl in the world. I imagined her lying on the moonlit beach in Tahiti; moving behind a lattice window in some yellow house in Toledo or Cartagena; in the Tyrol, perhaps …"

"Why are you saying these things?" Carmelite's voice cut sharply through the darkness, strangely real in contrast with his own.

"Because I mean them—because I'm—"

"You're lying!" Her eyes gazed unflinchingly into his as they stood there together, alone and dangerously close in the darkness. "You're lying, and you're trying to fool me. I know what you really think about me—about us. I …"

She broke off, catching her breath in a little gasp. Somewhere in the obscurity beyond them Katharine La Motte's superb voice had risen, flooding the lake with the sudden melody of a Puccini aria. It was as if the voice of Madame Butterfly herself were coming to them, now tragic, now triumphant, now near, now remote. To Sir Henry it seemed the very essence of all the elusive dreams of youth, all the nostalgic longings which had been brought back to him by the slim girl at his side.

Carmelite, too, seemed to have been caught up in the magic of the singing. In the half-light he could see the line of her parted lips, the fringe of her lashes, dark as the reeds at the lake's edge. They had been very close; and now, as if moved by the rising wind of the storm, they drew closer. He felt her soft hair brush his cheek. Then, suddenly, she was in his arms. Her lips were pressed eagerly, fiercely against his.

As they clung together, the singing faded, and with it seemed to fade the enchantment of the moment. The following silence was deathlike and from life it turned Sir Henry's thoughts to death. Even Katharine La Motte's voice seemed ominous now in retrospect. It was as though its very strength and beauty had deliberately been used to drown some other more sinister sound.

Carmelite was still in his arms, but she, too, had undergone a subtle change. She was no longer warm and responsive. Her lips were cold and her young body had become tense, resistant.

"What is it, Carmelite?" he asked softly. "You're frightened."

She did not reply. With a fierce, impulsive gesture she broke away from him. And before he had time to stop her she was skating off into the darkness.

For a moment Sir Henry stood irresolute. And then, sudden and capricious as Carmelite's departure, the full force of the storm struck the lake. He felt himself enveloped by the icy wind. It seemed to crush him, almost to throw him backward. On the bank the Japanese lanterns had started a crazy dance.

Then, like the violence of the storm, came the realization that Carmelite had skated away from the bank, away from those hectic lights. She had vanished toward the east end of the lake. And she alone knew nothing of the invisible death trap in the ice. Struggling against the wind, he started to skate forward. He did not care now that he had betrayed his trust; that the others had relied upon him to keep this very thing from happening. He could think only of Carmelite.

Snow had begun to fall in thick, blinding flakes. He was vaguely conscious of voices calling anxiously from different parts of the lake. The others all seemed to have lost their sense of direction.

"Make for the lanterns," shouted someone.

And then, as if in mockery, those tossing gloves of light vanished.

Sir Henry urged himself forward, although he seemed to be making no headway against the wind. Now and then dark figures passed him, disappearing as swiftly as they had come. At length, as he peered through the whirling chaos of the storm, he caught a faint gleam of white—Carmelite's white costume.

"Carmelite!" he called hoarsely.

The figure checked itself, turned and skated away toward the boathouse. As Sir Henry plunged after her something loomed out of the darkness ahead of him. He tried to swerve, but the collision was inevitable. He felt a crashing blow on the side of his head. His hands flew out to steady himself and he found he was clinging—clinging desperately to the post.

Half stunned by the impact, he could not piece things together for a moment. Then he was brought violently back to consciousness. From the darkness at his side came a low, strangled cry. And almost instantaneously the beam of a flashlight was thrown blindingly onto his face.

"Are you hurt, Bentley?" It was Vanderloon's voice, soft and toneless, scarcely audible above the howling of the wind.

"I'm all right. But—did you hear that cry?"

Vanderloon did not answer. The circle of light from his torch was moving slowly over the snow-covered ice.

"Look!"

Sir Henry's eyes followed that pointing beam. At the far side of the post a dark patch of water broke the lake's white surface. And in its center, tilted upward like a miniature berg, floated an irregular block of ice. Sir Henry saw it, but only vaguely. His whole attention was fixed on the other thing thrust up from the water.

It was the arm of a man, and the fingers were clutching frantically to catch a grip on that shifting, slippery ice block.

Instantly Sir Henry moved forward, urged by some primitive instinct far stronger than reason. He flung out a hand to help. But he was too late. The fingers had loosed their hold, stiffening in a mute gesture of despair. There was a momentary agitation on the pool's dark surface. Then swiftly, inexorably, the arm disappeared....

Libby Hunt Farley had heard that cry, too. She was alone on the ice—lost in the angry swirl of sleet and snow. Before the storm broke she had wanted to be alone, had wanted to shake off Johnnie Thring, who had stayed with her so persistently. But now that he was gone her loneliness only added to the nightmare quality of those moments. She was passionately eager to find the others. And yet, something in her dreaded them more than this solitude. She dared not think what they might say, what they might have found....

From somewhere ahead she caught the confused sound of voices. Then, like the pale ghost of the extinguished lanterns, she detected the beam of a flashlight. Hesitantly she started to skate toward it against the buffetings of the wind. Gradually the light grew stronger. She could make out figures, see them gesticulating excitedly.

As Libby Hunt approached, they drew aside, revealing Vanderloon. He was shouting rapid instructions to Bowles, who was on his knees peering down through a hole in the ice. As she watched, the butler picked up a long boat hook and thrust it into the water.

"What—what is it?" She heard her own voice, strangely remote.

"It's happened—in spite of the Judge's warning." It was Katharine La Motte who answered. "Starner's down there—drowned."

Libby Hunt felt a moment of faintness. "It's all right, darling." A gruff young voice sounded in her ear, and she felt Johnnie Thring's arm slip comfortably around her. In the pale light from the torch she could trace the outlines of his handsome face. The customary mocking droop had left his lips. He looked older. "He's dead. There's nothing more to worry about, Libby Hunt. But they've got to find the body—act as though they'd done everything they could, for the police."

The silence was intense—somehow by the wailing of the wind and the sporadic knocking of the boat hook against the ice. And then Bowles's respectful voice: "There's something here, sir." Vanderloon turned to Lili Tresckow. "The ladies better go back to the house." Vaguely, Libby Hunt was conscious of the Baroness's hand on her sleeve. Katharine La Motte turned almost with reluctance, and the three of them moved across the ice toward the boathouse.

"That girl—his daughter? What has become of her?" The Baroness's voice; and then Katharine La Motte's indifferently: "I saw her skating back toward the house some time ago."

Libby Hunt heard these words faintly. She was absorbed with her own thoughts—absorbed with the immense feeling of relief which was welling up within her.

There would be no more trouble from Starner, no more of those suave telephone calls, no more of those carefully worded solicitations which during the past months had rendered her half sick with helpless panic. She had already paid dearly enough for her passion for cards, but that was not all....

She shuddered when the memory of that afternoon at the Junior League rose up once more in her mind. She had not taken that other woman's pocketbook on purpose. It was not until she reached home that she had realized the mistake. It had been wrong of her, criminally wrong, to have used the money in it for her more immediate debts and to have gone to Starner for a loan on that diamond bracelet. But she had always meant to redeem it—to send it back anonymously.

Starner had guessed from the beginning; unwittingly she had put her head under a yoke which was far more crushing than a mere weight of debt. She had been weak, foolish. But he had had no right to make her life miserable, to threaten exposure and prison, to bleed her white for that one impulsive action.

Libby Hunt Farley was hardly conscious of removing her skates and slipping on the shoes and cape which Bowles had left for her in a neat pile in the boathouse. Instinctively she followed the others to the house, through the hall and upstairs to change her sodden clothes. Soon they were all in the living room again, where now the electric lights were blazing.

Katharine La Motte was tossing logs onto the dying flames. Somehow Libby Hunt found a chair and stretched out her numb hands.

And then, without warning, the lights in the chandelier flickered and faded, plunging the room into darkness. She gave a little cry and Katharine La Motte exclaimed sharply, "What's happened?"

"The electricity—it has failed." The Baroness's voice trailed calmly from behind the bright point of her cigarette. "Often it happens in Theo's house in a storm. There is nothing to worry about."

She rose, the glowing cigarette revealing her passage to the window. Libby Hunt followed with Katharine La Motte, and the three women stood there together, gazing through the swirling snow toward the lake. Far off, Libby Hunt could see the flashing of the torch. As the clock on the mantel ticked away the minutes, the light grew nearer.

"They've found him," whispered Katharine La Motte. "They're bringing him back."

Soon that macabre cortege became faintly visible. It paused a moment at the boathouse and then moved forward again over the snow-blanketed lawns. Gradually Libby Hunt could see more detail—see those four male figures walking in rhythm, see the vague burden that they carried.

"The end of Starner!" The words came impulsively from Katharine La Motte. Once more there rose in her that involuntary exultation—then suddenly her heart missed a beat. She had heard nothing—nothing but the faintest creaking, yet she knew as certainly as though that dark room had been drenched in light, that something was moving in the shadows behind them, something malignant, evil. She wanted to cry out, to warn the others. The creaking sounded again—nearer and nearer.

And then, as though breathed insidiously in her ear, a voice slipped out of the darkness—low, silky: "Well, ladies, there seems to have been an unfortunate accident—a little miscalculation."

Libby Hunt screamed—a long, hysterical scream. Her hand shot out and gripped the Baroness's arm. The older woman was standing by her side, tense and rigid. Against the windowpane Katharine La Motte's silhouette was frozen into startled immobility. Libby's scream sank to a strangled sob. At first she had thought that she must be mad. Now she knew that the others had heard it and that they too shared her blind, overwhelming panic.

The voice which had come to them out of the darkness was the voice of Joseph Starner....

Outside, in the tumult of the storm, John Derwood Thring heard Libby Hunt's scream. But it glanced off his consciousness; his whole mind was absorbed by the fact that he and his companions were carrying a dead man. In his twenty-five easy years, Johnnie Thring had seldom stumbled upon reality. This violent encounter with it had shocked him from delayed adolescence into maturity.

Starner was dead—and gone with him was the forced remembrance of those indiscretions which Johnnie had taken so lightheartedly at the time, but which, with the entrance of Starner, had become menaces to his present peace of mind and his very existence in the future. Starner had acquired letters—letters that could have led to divorce court scandals, breach of promise suits, and other unsavory publicity which would not only have cut him off from his inherited interest in the Tract & Treatise Company, but which would also have alienated him forever from his puritanical family.

During the past months, with Starner's threats of exposure hanging over him, Johnnie had lived even more wildly, more recklessly. He was a dog who has been given a bad name and he did not care if he hung himself. But now he would be free to start over again, to try and pick up the dissipated fragments of his life. Maybe he could get in with a better crowd, mix up with decent girls like—like Libby Hunt....

These reflections had jostled each other in his mind as he had stood there. He had felt exhilaration even at the climactic moment when Bowles called out that the hook had made contact and three of them had pulled together—pulled in grim silence while that grisly burden moved nearer and nearer the surface of the hole.

He could still see that scene with acid clarity. First the dark water had rippled; there had been the glimpse of a sodden jacket; a limp male arm; and then, awkwardly, unnaturally, that figure had reared up like some grotesque, half-human monster of the lake.

He and Sir Henry had gripped the wet, slippery shoulders and somehow had heaved until the body lay sprawled face downward on the ice. Vanderloon pointed the torch so that its light gleamed on the matted hair at the back of the head. Bowles and Sir Henry were turning the body over.

Johnnie saw the face first in profile; then gradually the bloated cheeks came into view, the staring eyes, the blue, swollen lips. As he watched, the elation drained away, leaving him defenseless before a sickening wave of disgust and panic.

That dead, distorted face was not the face of Joseph Starner. It was the face of Judge Homer Rock.

And it was Judge Rock whom they carried now past the house toward the stable buildings.

A *mistake*, Johnnie's mind was chanting in rhythm to the slow progress of their footsteps, a *horrible, ghastly mistake*....

They had entered a small, dark shed that smelt of wood shavings. They set the body down on a bench and Bowles covered it with a horse blanket. Johnnie saw Vanderloon's slim figure move through the obscurity; heard the click of a switch and then his host's voice muttering, "Light's gone ... must be the storm. Well, there's nothing more we can do."

"I'll see to everything, sir. Don't worry." Bowles's voice was reassuring. It was an immense relief to Johnnie to be able to leave that lifeless body there with the butler and to return with the others to the house. Somehow, as he went up to his room, the sight of his own familiar clothes spread out on the bed helped to bring things back to normal. But when he, Vanderloon, and Sir Henry descended to the living room, something of the nightmare atmosphere of that small, musty tool shed came rushing back.

The long room was in darkness except for a little circle of candlelight around the hearth. And leaning against the mantelpiece in the very center of that flickering illumination, stood the large, placid figure of Joseph Starner. Grouped around him, like actors holding a pose before the curtain drops, were Libby Hunt Farley, Katharine La Motte, and the Baroness Tresckow. They were staring at his smooth, benign face in fascination.

As soon as he saw the men, Starner half turned his head and smiled. "Ah, Vanderloon, I was just commiserating with the ladies."

Vanderloon did not reply. Johnnie could sense the tension in the atmosphere, sense how completely Joseph Starner was now master of the situation.

"Won't you all be seated?" he was saying, as though already he had taken possession of Chesham Grove and become its lawful master. "Baroness—allow me."

With a slight shrug Lili Tresckow took the chair he was holding for her. One by one the others followed, making a stiff, unnatural tableau in the uncertain candle beams.

"And now," said Starner briskly, "let us be businesslike. I suppose it is too late for a doctor. But at least we can call the police."

"The police!" The word came from Libby Hunt like a cry. "You're—not going to ..."

"My dear Miss Farley, you would not have us shirk our responsibilities." Starner's benevolent gaze settled on Vanderloon. "If you would tell me where to find the telephone, I could take the routine matters off your shoulders."

Vanderloon tapped reflectively on his chair arm. "There's a telephone in the hall."

"Good."

As Starner moved toward the door, a low, respectful cough sounded from the threshold. Through the gloom Johnnie could just make out the impeccably neat figure of Bowles.

"Excuse me, Mr. Vanderloon. I have just looked at the power plant, sir. I'm afraid it will take some time to restore the lights. And I think I heard Mr. Starner mention the telephone. That, I regret, has also been put out of commission."

"It has, eh?" Starner paused, and his voice held a trace of mockery. "I might have expected it. Then we must take a car to the nearest village. Or is that impossible, too?"

Bowles had slipped unobtrusively forward and was laying two logs on the fire, neatly parallel to each other. "I'm afraid there is no car available at the moment, sir. Mr. Vanderloon told the chauffeur to leave them in

Ashford to be overhauled. And then, these dirt roads are dangerous in a storm—almost impassable, in fact." He whisked a brush over the coppery glaze of the hearth tiles and moved silently from the room.

During the pause that followed, Johnnie Thring crossed to Libby Hunt's side. She smiled swiftly, but she did not speak. It was Starner's voice which finally cut through the silence:

"Well, Vanderloon, as the elements and your excellent butler seem to have conspired together to maroon us, I feel that the only thing to do is to discuss this matter among ourselves with absolute frankness." He turned his paternal gaze on Libby Hunt. "I can see why Miss Farley is reluctant to have the police brought into this. It is all very awkward. In fact, I cannot help sympathizing with you upon the unfortunate miscarriage of your plan." His smile embraced them all now. "And it was an excellent plan, Vanderloon. The mechanics were ingenious and you chose your—er—collaborators with great intuition. But, unluckily, you made one initial mistake."

"I would be interested to hear it," said Vanderloon with ominous control.

"You overlooked the fact that one of your guests had a very serious heart disease; that he was under sentence of death from his doctors. No man with only a short time to live would be anxious to strain his conscience by conniving at murder. That is why he came to me."

Johnnie Thring's hand touched Libby Hunt's. He felt her fingers grip his.

"Yes," Starner was murmuring, "perhaps you are wondering why two condemned men, one condemned by the doctors, the other by your own good selves, should have ventured onto the lake this evening. Frankly, with me the motive was curiosity. I was eager to see that hole in the ice which had been destined to receive me. I persuaded the Judge to take me down there." He paused, and added slowly, "That is why I am able to appreciate how he met his death."

"You're being rather academic, aren't you?" cut in Vanderloon. "Or is it just heroic?"

"Oh, no. I was not at all heroic, I assure you." Starner beamed. "As soon as the storm started I went straight back to the house. Poor Judge Rock was left at his post. Presumably one of you saw him there and pushed him into the hole, believing him to be me. We were both of a similar build. It was a natural, though rather exasperating mistake. And, if it is a salve to anyone's conscience, whoever killed Rock merely hastened a death which would inevitably have occurred soon."

There was an undercurrent of storm and uneasiness in the silence that followed. It was as though the oil in Starner's voice had been the only check on the turbulent emotions of the others. At last Sir Henry leaned forward, his face pale and his manner truculent: "Perhaps you're right, Starner. Perhaps it was a mistake—and a darned unfortunate one, too."

"Most unfortunate!" Starner's smile was gently reproving. "But it won't help any of us to lose our tempers, Sir Henry. After all, we are cut off here together. Things are bound to become rather unpleasant unless we behave like civilized beings."

"Civilized beings!" Katharine La Motte sprang to her feet, her hands clenched fiercely. "Why should you expect anyone to treat you like a civilized being? You think you've got us where you want us. Well, you're wrong. There are six of us …"

"I was expecting that point to come up, Miss La Motte, although I had not imagined it would be expressed quite so forcibly." Starner's voice was cool, almost indifferent. "And, if any of you are still foolhardy enough to consider another attempt on my life, I would like to draw your attention to a small detail which you overlooked in your ingenious plan. I refer to Carmelite. Not only is she a potential witness; she is also sole testatrix to all my property—including certain papers which I don't think any of you are particularly anxious to have made public."

"That girl you call your daughter!" exclaimed Katharine La Motte scornfully. "You think you can scare us with her?"

"In spite of your contempt for civilized beings, Miss La Motte, you would hardly consider murdering Carmelite as well as myself. In fact, I should have thought that you of all people would have respected the feelings of a parent—especially of an unorthodox parent."

Katharine La Motte took a swift step forward, but Starner continued imperturbably:

"And even if you were to kill both myself and my daughter, Miss La Motte, I would have made arrangements for the facts to come out. Your public would be interested to know you have a most romantically unmarried mother. It would be overcome with excitement when it discovered that the child's father is a famous bank robber now serving life sentence in Alcatraz, and that, in your less profitable days, it was his money which financed your career. And then there is the future of the child himself …"

While he spoke the color had drained from Katharine La Motte's cheeks, leaving them chalk-white. She made no attempt to reply. Slowly she moved to a chair and, dropping into it, buried her face in her hands. The Baroness crossed to her side, laying sympathetic fingers on her shoulder. Her aristocratic profile was contemptuous as she exclaimed, "This, Mr. Starner—it is unpardonable! It is vulgar!" Joseph Starner's small eyes narrowed. "Yes, I may be vulgar and I may be unpardonable, Baroness. But I have my uses. I was useful to you when I saved you from being sold out on that optimistic margin account of yours and rescued the speculative securities which you had bought with the profits of your delightful hat shop. It is too much to expect so artistic, so charming a lady as yourself to be anything but muddle-headed in business, but at least you must realize how useful I was in saving you from embarrassing explanations to your backers. I, myself, was chivalrous enough to believe you when you told me you thought the money was entirely your own. But others might have used an uglier word for your innocent little flutter. Embezzlement is always—embezzlement."

Starner's gaze moved leisurely from one to the other of the strained, hostile faces in front of him. A trifle of the benignity had left his cherubic countenance and there was a dangerous glint in his pale eyes.

"Talking of titled foreigners," he said musingly, "we Americans are almost childishly hospitable to them. But we cannot forgive them if they abuse our hospitality. For instance, in your case, Sir Henry. Of course, I personally could never believe that a well-known English sportsman would have ordered his jockey to hold back a popular horse in so important a race as the Westover Stakes. But the man in the street is not so sympathetic. And there is the inalienable fact that I do possess a sworn statement from your jockey on the matter. It is those little details which prejudice our foolish American public. I'm afraid it might ruin even your international reputation to be warned off the American turf."

Sir Henry had risen and was pouring himself a drink from the whisky decanter on the sideboard. It was too dark for the others to see that the nails pressed against the glass had gone a livid white.

Starner was shaking his head sadly as though pondering on the world's follies. "It is extraordinary how our sports and recreations can get us into difficulties. Now Miss Farley, for example—I'm sure that she would agree with ..."

"Lay off that!"

Johnnie Thring had sprung to his feet and was standing squarely in front of the girl, his face dark with anger and disgust.

"What you say may be true, Starner—every damn word of it. Perhaps we *would* be too scared to murder you. But there's no law that can stop me beating you up. You get a kick out of sticking pins in us and watching us squirm like—like insects. Well, if you go on with this mudslinging, I'm going to get a big kick out of taking a poke at you that'll knock you this side of hell."

The two men stood very close together. Johnnie's jaw was thrust forward and his eyes were gleaming. For a second the smile left Starner's lips, but almost instantaneously it returned—mild, tolerant.

"The young are so impulsive, Mr. Thring. So careless how they fight and—how they love. But, even so, I must thank you for giving me fair warning of your intentions. And in return I will be frank with you. I am warning you that I have a gun with me to protect myself not only against murder but also against any physical violence."

Slowly Johnnie moved back to Libby Hunt and, as he did so, a calm, expressionless voice broke the silence:

"I thought the ladies might like some refreshment, Mr. Vanderloon."

Bowles had moved into the room, carrying a tray neatly loaded with cut-glass tumblers and a silver bowl of ice. He paused as he reached Starner's side. "I think I heard you mention a gun, sir," he murmured deferentially. "I'm afraid I took the liberty of removing it from your suitcase shortly after your arrival, sir. Mr. Vanderloon does not approve of firearms."

Before anyone had time to comment, Bowles had vanished.

It was impossible to judge the precise effect of the butler's words upon Starner, for when he spoke again his voice had resumed its normal suavity: "The perfect servant, Vanderloon. Not only can he control the weather, the lights, and the telephone. He can also control your guests. But, now I come to think it over, it is much more sensible to have the gun out of the way, and far more desirable that the police should be ignorant of what has happened—at least for the moment. In fact, I am prepared to make a gesture." He raised pontifical hands as if to pronounce a benediction.

"I am willing to say nothing of your little plot against my life. You will doubtless appreciate my tactful silence and show your gratitude accordingly." He smiled again. "That should cause none of you grave inconvenience. You are all comparatively wealthy people." He moved from the mantel, making his way slowly through the darkened room. "I am willing to subscribe to the theory that the Judge's death was accidental, Vanderloon. But, as a precaution, I do think our host should make an effort to find out who is responsible for the accident, just in case the police chose to be—er—difficult. I will leave you alone now so that you can discuss this matter more freely."

As he reached the threshold the door was thrown open and a slim white figure moved into the room. Starner turned.

"Carmelite, my dear child, what are you doing here?"

"It was dark up there in my room. I was frightened."

"Frightened? What of—ghosts?" Starner's laugh was indulgently paternal. "Well, you'd better go back, my dear. These people want to be alone."

The girl hesitated. Her gaze had focused on that corner of the room where Sir Henry was seated.

No one spoke as the Englishman rose and moved toward her. He stood at her side, his eyes fixed upon hers as though hypnotized. Then, as Carmelite turned to the door, he pushed blindly past Starner and followed her out of the room. Sir Henry's mind worked with British slowness. During the past hour things had happened too swiftly for him yet to grasp their full significance. But, as he felt Carmelite's arm warm against his, he was conscious once again of that exciting sense of danger.

"I don't want to go back to my room," she was saying. "Not alone."

Bowles had left a single candle in the hall. As Sir Henry turned to pick it up, he caught a glimpse of Joseph Starner, who was watching the two of them from the living room door. The round, pink face was gleaming with strange satisfaction.

The baronet drew Carmelite away. They passed through an old-fashioned, formal drawing room and came to the conservatory. Sir Henry set down the candle and for a moment they stood there very close together without speaking.

Carmelite had changed her skating costume, but she was still dressed in white. She looked a mere child, and yet there was something elusively mature about that grave, Madonna face.

"What you said on the ice?" she asked abruptly. "Did you mean it?"

The fragrance of the flowers invaded Sir Henry's senses like an opiate. "I said you were the most beautiful girl in the world, Carmelite. I meant it."

Her expression had changed as he spoke. In the candlelight her eyes were shining eagerly.

"Then take me away," she cried impulsively. "I'll live with you. I'll do anything. Only take me away from here—now."

Her breath was fragrant against his face. He felt her young arms glide around his neck and she was clinging to him, kissing him passionately. Her words came urgent, incoherent: "I … I don't care … I want you … I want you to take me away … anywhere … now …"

"But, Carmelite, I don't understand …!"

"Understand!"

She moved away and he could see her face, pale and intense, tilted up to his. "You think I'm a blackmailer," she said fiercely. "Well, what if I am? What difference does it make?"

And as Sir Henry looked down at her he realized that it did make no difference: Nothing seemed real except the quick beat of his own heart and this girl, remote as a sheathed flower, yet warm and vibrant with life. He drew her nearer again and held her in his arms. "Carmelite, darling, I worship you … we'll leave tomorrow … we'll get marired …!"

"Married!" Instantly she turned her face away so that his lips could not reach hers.

"You don't mean that—you don't mean anything you've said." She swung round to face him. "You don't want to marry me. I can see now you're—you're just playing an act like the rest of them."

Sir Henry moved closer; his hands went out toward her and then fell to his sides. "You know that's not true, Carmelite," he said gently. "And you know I mean it when I say I love you—that I want to marry you. Of course, it's crazy. We've only just met—but I can't help myself."

"But your name, your family, everything … and, well, you know what I am. I'm just—nobody."

"But I'm nobody, too," said Sir Henry wryly. "As for the proud ancestral family, my father was a wholesale green-grocer who hogged the potato market during the war. The Bentley baronetcy was bought on the proceeds of his profiteering."

As they stood there together there were soft footsteps close behind them. They turned to see Joseph Starner, his small eyes narrowed in a shrewd smile.

"You must excuse my interrupting," he murmured, "but your friends are having an important conference, Sir Henry. They will be needing you."

Sir Henry drew swiftly away and swung out of the conservatory. In the darkened drawing room he paused a moment in indecision. Suddenly he could not bear the thought of leaving the girl alone there with Starner. He started to retrace his steps, but the sound of the blackmailer's voice checked him:

"You have made a very promising beginning, my dear." There was a soft, satisfied chuckle. "An entrée into the English—er—market should prove extremely profitable for us both."

After Starner's departure from the living room the others sat around the fire in silence. No one had touched the tumblers which Bowles had brought. Outside, behind the patterned brocade of the drawn curtains, the storm had abated little of its violence.

Theodore Vanderloon looked old and tired as he rose and assumed his place in a front of the mantel. The dominating forcefulness of the morning had left him. When at length he spoke, his voice was diffident, uncertain: "One should know more about life than to try to shape it to one's will. I tried to solve our problem. I have succeeded only in making it far worse. I apologize."

"There is no need to apologize, Theo." The Baroness had lit another of her Russian cigarettes. "We have done our best."

"And our best is rather pathetic, Lili. So far we have achieved the doubtful advantage of depriving Judge Rock of his last few weeks of life. Incidentally, you have just heard Starner suggest that it is my duty to find out which of us was responsible for the Judge's accident. I suppose no one feels like helping me to do my duty?"

There was no reply. Questioning glances met each other and flicked away. It was Katharine La Motte who finally voiced the thought uppermost in every mind.

"Let's forget the Judge," she said harshly. "It's Starner we've got to think about. He made life hell for us before; now, with this hanging over us, it's going to be a thousand times worse. We've got to get rid of him."

"And have the lovely Carmelite blackmail us in his place?" asked Johnnie Thring with forced flippancy. "Of course, that might be more romantic. Or are you figuring on bumping the girl off, too?"

While he was speaking the door had opened, and Sir Henry Bentley stood motionless on the threshold. "If you do decide to kill Starner," Sir Henry said quietly, "I don't think you need worry about his daughter."

The others stared at him in eager surprise. There was a long moment of silence followed by a spurt of rapid sentences:

"... but she's his heir ... his accomplice ... might easily be more dangerous than Starner himself ..."

"I don't think so," broke in Sir Henry softly. "At least, I don't think she would be if she were married to me."

"Married to you!" The words came incredulously from Katharine La Motte.

"Yes. That should remove Starner's only real weapon of defense. And now that we have his gun ..."

"But, Bentley!" cut in Vanderloon. "You really mean this?"

"Certainly, and congratulations are quite in order." The baronet's smile was humorless. "In spite of my caddishness on the turf, in spite of the fact that Starner possesses the framed statement of a discharged jockey, I am none the less considered an extremely desirable match by my future father-in-law."

Johnnie jumped up and gripped him by the hand. "Let me be the first to wish you joy," he said with a grin. "And if you mean it and it's all true, bring on that gun, Vanderloon, and I'll take great pleasure in disembarrassing Sir Henry of the least attractive of his family connections."

"Johnnie! You mustn't!" exclaimed Libby Hunt instantly.

"Libby is right." Vanderloon glanced at the boy's flushed young face. "Things are not as simple as that. And, incidentally, you must all remember that Starner is here in the house and liable to come in at any minute." He paused. "Sir Henry's—er—gesture has made the situation much more promising, but we must not be rash. We've got to think."

"Think! We've done too much thinking—and too much talking," said Katharine La Motte sharply.

As she leaned forward into the light the sculptured lines of her face had somehow coarsened. The glamorous veneer of the prima donna was cracking, revealing glimpses of the unscrupulous farm girl who, in her fierce struggle for fame, had used even gangsters for her own ends.

"We came here to kill Starner, and a darn good job we've made of it! We've argued, theorized, done everything but act. But we've got the perfect setup now. We're cut off here in the country; we have that gun; Sir Henry can keep the girl's mouth shut; and, best of all, Starner thinks we're too scared of him to do anything. All we have to do is to shoot him with his own gun—and make it look like suicide."

"Excellent, my dear Katharine!" murmured Vanderloon, his eyes steady on hers. "I might as well have two dead guests as one. But who is to have the honor? Shall we apply for volunteers? Or shall we be Biblical and cast lots?"

Once again there was no reply. Johnnie moved, but Libby Hunt's hand touched his arm.

And then, cool and clear as spring water, the Baroness's voice rose: "Many years ago when I was a little girl in Vienna," she murmured, "we play a game." Her eyes smiled with amused recollection. "It was like, so like to this. One of us she had to be the Wolf. We used the cards." Lili Tresckow leaned back in her chair. "I remember so well the rules. One of us children, she was to try to catch the others. She was the Wolf. But first we chose who was it to be. We took the cards and dealt them. She who get the Jack of Diamonds ..." She broke off with a slight shrug.

"The Baroness has an idea there!" exclaimed Johnnie excitedly. "We can deal cards and no one will know who has the Jack except the lucky fellow himself."

"We had a pleasant little game in England that might be adapted, too," put in Sir Henry grimly. "It was called Cry in the Dark. After we've drawn the cards, we could leave the gun somewhere in the room and put out the candles so that the man with the Jack of Diamonds could get it without being seen. How about it, Vanderloon?"

"Slightly theatrical, Sir Henry." Vanderloon answered. "But Aristotle maintained that it was through melodrama alone that one could achieve complete catharsis. I will get the cards, the gun. And we three men can make our bids for the role of protagonist."

"Men?" exclaimed Katharine La Motte. "Do you mean we're not going to be in on this?"

"It is more or less a man's job, isn't it?"

"A woman can pull a trigger." Katharine La Motte's eyes were shining with fierce intensity. "We'd all be under suspicion anyway, so why not ...?"

Libby Hunt's face had turned very pale. Her hands were clenched together in her lap. But softly she whispered, "I agree. It's awful—beastly. And I never thought I could feel this way. But I see we've got to go through with it now. It isn't only us. If Starner went on, there would be dozens of other people, too."

"Very well." Vanderloon smiled again. "I had overlooked the progress of feminine emancipation. We will let the ladies play. But we cannot afford another mistake." His eyes had hardened and the old strength rang in his voice. "After this initial childishness, I propose that we adopt Starner's suggestion and behave like adult, civilized beings. We will dress, dine as usual; and then divide up so that Starner will not suspect a conspiracy. I will have Bowles put candles in every room—but not too many. Some time during the evening the opportunity will arise. That will be the business of one person. The rest of us will come back to this room as soon as a shot is fired. We will ask no questions, and when we are all assembled we can go in a group to discover the—er—suicide. It is all rather crude, but I'm afraid the situation demands it."

"And Carmelite Starner?" breathed Libby Hunt.

"Whatever happens, I think I can manage her all right," muttered Sir Henry.

"Excellent." Vanderloon squared his lean shoulders against the mantel. "But remember that Starner must commit suicide. I am no expert, but I have a vague idea that a gun should be fired at very close range. There must be powder marks ..."

Slowly he moved from the mantel. His guests watched in intense silence as he crossed the room and fingered a bell rope. And then from somewhere in the distance, hollow and strangely ominous, sounded the faint ringing of the bell....

"You rang, sir?"

Vanderloon's guests stirred uneasily as the butler appeared on the threshold.

"Yes, Bowles. You have seen Mr. Starner?"

"He and Miss Starner went upstairs to dress for dinner some time ago. Do you want him, sir?"

"No." Vanderloon crossed back to the hearth. "I want a pack of cards,

Bowles, and Mr. Starner's gun."

"Very good, sir."

There was no change in the butler's expression. Quietly he left the room. When he returned he held out to Vanderloon a silver tray on which lay a small automatic and a morocco cardcase.

"Keep the gun for a moment, Bowles." Vanderloon's gaze circled the tense faces in front of him, resting finally on Libby Hunt. "And give the cards to Miss Farley. I think you should shuffle for—er—luck, Libby Hunt."

The butler slipped a deck of cards from the case and handed them to the girl. Her fingers trembled as she took them and laid them on her lap; but they moved with instinctive efficiency when she cut the pack and flicked the cards together. She shuffled once, twice.

Johnnie Thring had been leaning forward, watching the girl with strained eyes. Now, suddenly, he whispered hoarsely, "You've got to keep out of this, Libby. You're only a kid ...!"

"It's all right, Johnnie. If you do it, I'm going to." Libby Hunt's voice was soft but determined. She handed the deck of cards to Vanderloon.

Quietly Vanderloon explained the situation to the butler. The two of them moved to an oak table which stood near the window. One by one the others followed until they were all grouped around it.

"I think we have everything straight," Vanderloon said. "The—er—significant card is the Jack of Diamonds. We all look at our hands and then lay them face downwards on the table."

His long fingers slid the top card from the deck. It fell in front of the Baroness. There was a soft swishing as he sent the others gliding over the polished wood in front of each of his guests in turn.

Bowles had set two candles on the table. The light radiated outwards, throwing into bright illumination the silent circle of faces. Each expression was different. The shadow of a smile hovered around the Baroness's eyes. Sir Henry's face was set in a hard, wooden mask. Katharine La Motte's chin was thrust aggressively forward, her lips tightening as the cards piled up in front of her. Libby and Johnnie stood close together, looking very young as they stared downward with fixed intensity. Vanderloon himself was impersonal.

When the pack was two thirds gone, his fingers paused. "We have overlooked one thing," he said. "There are six of us and fifty-two cards. That means that four will be left over. What shall we do?"

"If I might take the liberty, sir." Bowles stood respectfully at his elbow.

The guests glanced up from the table, their eyes momentarily losing their glazed absorption.

"Thank you, Bowles. I appreciate your willingness to share our obligations."

He completed the deal, handing the last four cards to the butler.

There was a fragmentary pause. Then hands moved over the surface of the table; some eager, some reluctant, some deliberately casual. For a second each pair of eyes fixed on the fan of cards in front of them. Deep silence; then a rustle as the hands were tossed face downwards again on the table. Imperturbably Bowles leaned forward between the candles and gathered the cards into a neat pack.

No one spoke until after the butler had snapped the clasp of the morocco case. Then Vanderloon murmured, "Now for the gun. It is loaded, of course, Bowles?"

"Yes, sir."

Vanderloon's eyes scanned the room, settling finally on the grand piano which stood near the door. "Perhaps you would put it on the piano, Bowles. We can screen the fire, but, even so, it should be as far as possible from the light."

The butler picked up the silver tray and carried it to the piano. Returning to the hearth, he lifted a beaten brass screen from a corner and set it in front of the fire.

Vanderloon's voice rose again: "We can extinguish the candles now. Johnnie, you take those on the table. Bowles and I will attend to these on the mantelpiece."

Hurriedly Johnnie crossed the room, his shadow following him, vague and grotesque. Brass snuffers were raised, and one by one the small flames vanished, plunging the room into blackness. The darkness was tense, vibrant.

"I suggest we all move around for a few minutes," said Vanderloon. "That will make things easier. When I give the word, we might leave the room singly and go upstairs to dress for dinner."

The Baroness Lili Tresckow heard these words with a strange excitement. Slowly she started to move through the darkness. Without seeing or even hearing them, she was acutely conscious of the others around her. Once she brushed against the rough tweed of a male arm—Sir Henry, she thought. Once a sharp intake of breath betrayed Libby Hunt. Instinctively she strained her eyes, trying to make out her position in the room. Was she near the door—the piano ...?

And then she heard another noise. It came from outside the door—the muffled tread of heavy feet on the staircase. The footsteps grew nearer and stopped. There was a faint click of the turning handle and the door began to open.

Fascinated, the Baroness watched that widening strip of light. The door was fully open now, and looming black against the faint illumination from the hall was the broad silhouette of Joseph Starner. She was aware of a white shirt front and the coruscation of two diamond studs.

"Is anyone here?"

There was no answer. Interminably Starner seemed to linger on the threshold. The Baroness could feel the subtle change in the atmosphere, could sense the stillness of her invisible companions.

Then the light behind him narrowed and was absorbed once more into the darkness. The door had been shut. Starner was with them in the room.

When it sounded again, his voice was amusedly benevolent. "What is this, Vanderloon? Hide in the dark? Or has the candlepower gone back on you, too?"

"I'm sorry, Starner." Vanderloon's answer was immediate and steady. "We were just going up to dress for dinner. As we don't know how long we're to be cut off, we have to be a bit economical with the candles."

The Baroness could hear her host's footsteps, soft and regular, as he moved to the door and threw it open. She saw his erect figure passing out into the hall. The others followed in silence, while Starner stood by the threshold, his hands in his tails' pockets, his pale eyes questioning but untroubled.

Lili Tresckow was the last to move. She felt her heart beating rapidly as she drew nearer the door and the dark shadow of the piano.

The Baroness was opposite the piano now. Swiftly her glance flashed over the polished surface of the mahogany. She felt a moment of exquisite reassurance. The silver tray was empty....

The long living room of Chesham Grove was empty—warm and securely closed against the storm outside. Bowles had set new candles on the mantel. Eight ... eight-thirty ... eight-forty-five ...

Dinner was over now. Occasional footsteps sounded in the hall; footsteps and voices, some soft and hurried, some loud and unnaturally cheerful; the only indications that there were still guests, still life in Vanderloon's house. The hour hand of the clock was abreast of nine, when the door opened and Bowles appeared and piled more logs on the fire.

From then on people drifted in and out, first Sir Henry and Carmelite Starner, the baronet pale and preoccupied, the girl exquisite as a Lalique glass figurine. Vanderloon himself came in for a moment; Katharine La Motte, the Baroness. But none of them stayed for long. They were all tense, on the alert, as though with every second they expected that falsely tranquil silence to be cut by a gunshot. They talked feverishly or moved restlessly about, charging the atmosphere with their own uneasiness and, only by their departure allowing it to settle back into placidity.

Once the door opened to reveal Joseph Starner. He was alone and brought with him the aroma of an expensive cigar. But he, like the others, seemed unwilling to remain for long in any one room of the dimly lit house. Humming under his breath, he strolled out into the hall.

After him, no one broke the warm quietness of the room. With invisible rhythm the clock hands moved on …

And then, splintering the fragile silence, a shot rang through the house. As though in imitation, a log crashed in the grate, sending up a tiny geyser of sparks. A burning chip of wood sprang out onto the thick carpet. It glowed there, grew dull, and winked into nothingness.

Then, like a delayed echo, a second shot sounded.

Silence again—punctuated faintly by the precise ticking of the clock....

At length the living room door opened unhurriedly, and Katharine La Motte entered in a trailing saffron gown which seemed to light up the room like an extravagant candle flame. She moved to the piano with studied composure. It was as though she were taking the concert stage at Carnegie Hall. Drawing her long train aside, she seated herself and ran her fingers caressingly up and down the keyboard.

And then she started to sing.

The opening notes of the *Liebestod* flooded the quiet room. Gradually they mounted to a heightened ecstasy, made fierce and triumphant by the impassioned beauty of that voice. The whole house seemed to be filled with music. Even the sporadic sounds of the fading storm outside became somehow absorbed into that defiant dirge with its undertones of victory, love, and death.

Vanderloon's other guests had begun to assemble. One by one they moved silently to the piano, caught up in spite of themselves by the spell of the music. Katharine La Motte herself seemed hardly conscious of them. Her head was tossed back and the Grecian profile glowed with a new, strange beauty.

No one noticed the door opening. No one was even aware of the slim, intense figure of Carmelite Starner until the girl took a step into the room. Then the singing faded; Katharine La Motte rose from the piano; the others swung round, staring.

Carmelite Starner stared back at them, her eyes dark and strained against the startling pallor of her skin. Then, with a little sob, she stumbled toward Sir Henry.

"He's dead!" she whispered hoarsely. "He's been shot—in his room!"

The others stood motionless as the baronet's arm moved to support her. "Carmelite, *please!*" His voice was very gentle. "Please, let me take you up to your room."

The girl's face was dazed and expressionless as Sir Henry led her out into the hall.

Vanderloon shut the door behind them and stood with his back to it. There was a faint gleam in his eyes as he glanced around him. "We'd better go up and see," he said slowly.

"All of us?" The words came from Libby Hunt, low and stifled.

"No! The women are out of it this time!" Johnnie Thring moved forward determinedly. "Come on, Vanderloon. You and Bowles …!"

Without a word the two other men followed him into the hall. Bowles took a candle from a table and lighted the way up the heavy oak staircase. They passed down a dark corridor toward Starner's room. The door was shut. Vanderloon opened it and the three of them hurried across the threshold.

The room itself was in darkness. There was nothing but the light from Bowles's candle to illuminate the grotesque scene in front of them. The massive figure of Joseph Starner sprawled, face upwards, on the brightly patterned carpet. Overturned at his side was a small wooden table; and lying across his white shirt front was a silver candlestick. The flame was extinguished, but it had left a broad black smudge on the starched cotton.

The candlelight revealed a dark stain on the carpet near the head; the wound above the right ear was ringed with burnt hair and marks of powder. And, clutched in his right hand, Joseph Starner was gripping his own gun.

Johnnie Thring's eyes darted about the room. He seemed to be taking in every detail of that gruesome tableau. At length he gave a low whistle. "I'm no expert," he muttered, "but I'd say that was the perfect suicide."

"Yes, indeed." Vanderloon turned away in distaste. "Someone appears to have done a very efficient job. There is, of course, the question of fingerprints. But you can attend to that later, Bowles."

"Yes, sir."

"Now we'd better lock the room and discuss our next move with the others." As they went out into the corridor, Bowles turned the key in the lock and handed it to Vanderloon. Without speaking, they hurried downstairs to the living room.

The women were grouped around the piano in the living room. Instantly they glanced at Vanderloon, their eyes apprehensive, questioning.

"Well …!" asked Katharine La Motte.

"It looks at present," said her host tonelessly, "as though the suicide will satisfy the most meticulous of experts."

Nervously Libby Hunt fingered the folds of her evening gown. "But, Theo, there's such a lot we haven't—haven't thought about. There's Judge Rock … and then Starner's motive for suicide … what are we going to say?"

"I have already given some thought to that matter, my dear." The smile that hovered around Vanderloon's mouth was humorless. "And you have in part answered your own question. Obviously it would be difficult to convince the police that this day has brought forth both a fatal accident and a suicide. But I think that the two tragedies might perhaps be combined. I suggest that for official purposes, Starner committed suicide because he murdered Judge Rock and found out that we suspected him."

"But what reason can we give for his killing the Judge?" broke in Katharine La Motte sharply.

Vanderloon shrugged. "Starner himself helped us there. He told us the Judge knew he was doomed by his doctors; that he had nothing left to live for. We might hint to the police that Starner had been blackmailing Rock and that the Judge had threatened to expose him. That supplies the motive, since exposure would have meant a long prison term for Starner."

"But mightn't that mean exposure for us all, too?" asked Johnnie. "I'd rather swing for murder than have the Tract & Treatise Company know some of the things Starner had on me."

"I don't see why we—er—survivors should be involved except as witnesses," replied Vanderloon.

"But the hole in that ice?" breathed Libby Hunt. "How can we explain that?"

"You will all be witnesses of how I warned you that the ice was dangerous near the post." Vanderloon's voice was casual. "That strengthens the theory of premeditated murder on Starner's part. It should be quite convincing."

"So darn convincing," cut in Johnnie enthusiastically, "that I'm beginning to believe that's what really happened. I never thought much of the accident theory anyway. What do you others think?"

"It does not matter what we think." The Baroness's velvet gown rustled softly as she moved to a chair. Her voice was calm and quiet. "Now it is best for us to forget everything except what it is the police must know."

"Yes, Lili." Vanderloon's eyes twinkled. "I suspect that we learned a fundamental truth about life. Of course, everything depends on Sir Henry's ability to convince the girl. But if we can be certain of no trouble from her I think we may safely notify the police of Joseph Starner's suicide."

For the first time that day the tension in the atmosphere slackened. Faces lost their expression of strain and uneasiness. "All's well—if it ends well," murmured Johnnie Thring.

And then, as he spoke, the silence was broken by a sound from the hall—a sound familiar and simple, yet terrifying in its very simplicity.

It came again, sharp, urgent—the shrill ringing of the telephone.

Katharine La Motte was the first to find her voice. She swung round to Bowles and whispered dazedly, "I thought you said it was out of order … the storm …!"

"But the storm is over now, madam," replied the butler quietly. "And it was only for Mr. Starner that the wire was disconnected."

Once more the insistent clamor of the bell, bringing with it all the potential danger of the outside world.

"What—what shall we do?" moaned Libby Hunt.

Everyone was staring at Vanderloon as though he and he alone could make a decision.

"Shall I, sir …?"

"No, Bowles, I'll go myself."

Slowly Vanderloon turned, passed through the door, and closed it behind him. As the telephone rang again, they could hear his footsteps moving through the hall outside.

At last the door opened.

"Who was it? … What did they want?"

Vanderloon did not leave the threshold. He stood there, his shoulders stooped, his ascetic face pale and worn. "He's beaten us again," he muttered hollowly. "Even now he's dead, Starner's beaten us again."

Never before had Vanderloon's guests seen him lose control. But now there was a faint note of panic in his voice—a panic which infected them all.

"I might have guessed it," he murmured; "might have guessed that Starner would not accept my invitation unreservedly. Before coming here he left instructions with a Mr. Wenz, who appears to be his secretary. He told him to telephone this number at eleven and, if he was unable to get in touch with Starner, he was to inform the nearest police station that there was the possibility of foul play."

"What did you say?" asked Johnnie breathlessly.

"I could only temporize and prevaricate." Vanderloon's smile flickered uncertainly. "And the net result of my prevarications is that, unless Mr.

Wenz is reassured by twelve o'clock, he intends to notify the Ashford police."

"But is that so terrible?" The Baroness glanced around the circle of pale faces. "We were going to call the police ourselves. It makes no difference that this secretary, he call instead."

"And have him tell the local police that Starner came here suspecting foul play?" cut in Katharine La Motte. "Do you suppose they'd believe our suicide story then?"

"Even the localist of police wouldn't be quite that dumb," said Johnnie.

"I'm afraid you're right. The whole situation has taken a—er—distinct turn for the worse," agreed Vanderloon wearily. "If that man calls the police we must be prepared for them to suspect murder."

"And if they do, what is it we say?" asked the Baroness.

"There are plenty of courses open to us, Lili." Vanderloon threw out his hands in a little gesture of resignation. "But none of them is particularly attractive. We can deny everything and risk a most embarrassing investigation. We can admit everything with a certainty of charges for criminal conspiracy. In both cases we would all be involved. The least of the evils would be for one person to take the entire blame. And, being prime mover of the whole business and the most logical suspect, I willingly offer my services as the symbolical Knave—the Jack of Diamonds."

"The Jack of Diamonds!" Libby Hunt's voice rose shrill, almost hysterical. "But you can't do that, Theo. I've got to tell you—" She broke off, looking wildly around her. "It was I who had the Jack of Diamonds. It was—"

"Stop it, Libby!" Johnnie Thring gripped her arm fiercely. His young face was defiant as he glared at the others. "You mustn't listen to her. She's hysterical. She didn't do it. I looked at her cards. I knew she had the Jack of Diamonds. But when the lights went out, I saw to it she couldn't get the gun."

"You mean you took it yourself, Johnnie?" put in Vanderloon quietly.

"No, Johnnie didn't take that gun!"

Everyone started as Sir Henry Bentley moved calmly into the room. The baronet was tapping a cigarette on his cuff. "Why all the excitement anyway?"

Swiftly Vanderloon told him what had happened. "So you see there is adequate cause for excitement, Bentley," he concluded ironically. "And it's such a pity. The suicide seems to have appeared quite convincing."

"Thank you," murmured the Englishman with a mock bow. "I seem to be in the market for congratulations tonight. I thought it was a pretty good job myself."

The others looked at him in astonishment.

"You mean—?" began the Baroness emphatically.

"Yes. Libby Hunt may have drawn the Jack of Diamonds, and Johnnie may have chivalrously prevented her from getting the gun. But he needn't have bothered, because I took it myself."

"Henry …!"

The Englishman swung round at the sound of his name. Carmelite Starner stood in the doorway. She was still pale, but in the candlelight her young face was calm and strangely composed.

The baronet moved swiftly to her side. "Carmelite, you promised—you said you wouldn't come down."

But the girl paid no attention. She brushed past him as though lost in some reverie of her own. The others watched in silence as she crossed the room and sat down, erect and childlike, on the edge of a ladder-back chair. "I don't know what you were talking about," she said at length, "but I heard Sir Henry say that he took the gun. Well, he didn't. None of you did. It was my father who took it. He saw it lying there on the piano when he came in here before dinner. He had it in his tails' pocket the whole evening."

"But, Carmelite," broke in Sir Henry anxiously. "What is the point …?"

"What is the point of lies?" The girl turned to him almost angrily. Then her eyes moved back to the others. "I don't know what you've all been thinking about me," she said steadily, "but I expect you imagined I was just some little nobody that Starner picked up for his own purposes. Well, you're right. I'm just that."

"There is only one thing that concerns these people, Carmelite." Sir Henry's English voice was suddenly pompous. "And that is the fact that you have done me the honor to promise to be my wife."

"But that's the very reason why they have to know, Henry." She did not turn to him as she spoke. Her delicately molded chin was set and determined. "After all, they're your friends. They have a right to know that the future Lady Bentley was rescued from a slum orphanage by Starner. And there are other things they've got a right to know, too…. I wonder if someone would please give me a cigarette."

Johnnie Thring jumped up from the couch and proffered his case. Vanderloon glanced quickly at the clock on the mantel.

"Thank you." The girl inhaled deeply, gazing unseeingly through the haze of smoke. "As my adopted father told you, I returned from Paris only a few days ago and this is my debut in American society. But there's something he didn't explain to you, something he didn't explain to me until today. I knew, of course, that I was under deep obligations to him, but I did not know exactly how I was expected to repay his generosity.

Mr. Starner told me this morning. He hinted at his methods of extorting money and suggested that I would be just the person to help him."

The room was silent as she crushed her cigarette in a bronze bowl. "I'm not going to pretend that I was horrified or shocked," she continued quietly. "The first and last lesson I learnt in the orphanage was that charity must be paid for with obedience. But I received no instructions until after we got here. Although I did not understand why at the time, Starner seemed very much amused when he saw all of you. Immediately after lunch he told me he had the ideal job for me. I was to do my best to become Lady Bentley.

"That didn't shock me particularly, either. I tried to obey orders, but I'm afraid I wasn't very good at it." She turned swiftly to the baronet. "I couldn't go through with it, Henry. Besides, I felt certain that you'd guessed, that you were acting a part for some reason of your own. That's why I left you on the ice." She turned back to the others. "And that's how I happened to see Judge Rock being murdered."

The atmosphere of suspicion seemed heightened for a moment. Then it broke into a torrent of eager questions: "You mean … you actually saw …?"

"Yes. I actually saw it." The girl nodded her head gravely. "When I left Sir Henry, I skated away alone. Of course, I knew nothing about that trap in the ice. But just after the storm broke I heard voices. The sleet was almost blinding but I made out two men by that post. One of them was the Judge. As I watched, the other man deliberately gave him a push and I saw him fall. Then, to my horror, the ice seemed to crack, to collapse …"

"But the other man," broke in Katharine La Motte. "Did you see who he was?"

"I did." Carmelite's voice was still flat, expressionless. "It was my—er—father."

"Starner!" exclaimed Johnnie. "Then at least we've figured out one thing right."

"But why should he kill the Judge?" asked Libby Hunt.

"I went to see him as he came off the lake. He explained quite calmly that Judge Rock had threatened to expose him unless he destroyed all his blackmail papers. Starner promised to do it if the Judge would tell him the real purpose of this house party. When he heard of your plan Starner seemed to think it all very amusing; and it was even more amusing that he'd been able to persuade the Judge to show him the trap you had set for him in the ice and then make use of it himself. It was one of his strange, perverse jokes."

"And the cream of the jest," commented Vanderloon sardonically, "was that he could accuse us of it and use his own crime to extort more blackmail."

"Yes. He told me he was going to do that," said Carmelite slowly. "I think he guessed that I didn't share his sense of humor, but—" She broke off and for the first time she seemed to lose something of her almost superhuman composure. Her eyes had involuntarily turned to Sit Henry's. "I—I didn't know what to do. I was frightened—bewildered. Then the lights went out. I lay on my bed in the darkness trying to make up my mind. I owed Starner so much, and yet ... At last I couldn't bear it anymore, being up there alone. I was desperate when I came down here. I was desperate when I begged you to take me away, Henry. But I don't think I'd have ever told about Starner if you'd just done what I asked you to—but you asked me to marry you."

She turned defiantly to the others. "I don't care whether you believe me or not, but something happened then which made me realize I could never be on Starner's side. It all made me feel cheap and dirty."

Vanderloon's eyes had turned once again to the clock. The hands were moving toward midnight.

Carmelite seemed to sense his uneasiness, for her words came more swiftly now:

"After dinner I made up my mind. I went to Starner's room determined to have it out with him. He was still in one of his humorous moods. He told me how he had found you all in the dark and how he suspected he had spoiled another of your plots against him by taking his own gun. I did my best to keep cool, but when he started talking about Henry I told him I was through. I said that if he didn't give it all up I'd go straight downstairs and tell everyone how he had murdered Judge Rock. He forbade me to leave the room."

"But you disobeyed him," put in Sir Henry swiftly. He turned to the others. "From now on I'm telling the story. Carmelite came down and told me. And I went straight up, fought with Starner, and shot him. You've already congratulated me on a deuced efficient job."

"If I'm going to be your wife, Henry," said Carmelite, with the shadow of a smile, "you must let me have the last word. I didn't go down right away, because Starner tried to hold me there by force. He'd always banked on his knowledge of human nature and at first he could hardly believe that I'd turned against him. When he saw I was really serious he started to call me filthy names. At last he pulled out the gun and said that if I left the room he would shoot."

She looked down at the silver points of her slippers. "Before I knew what was happening we were struggling. It was quite dark in the room, with only the one candle on the mantelpiece. Then he stumbled and"—she paused, passing a hand across her forehead—"somehow I had the gun. I saw him lying on the floor. I heard him laughing at me. It—it was horrible. But even then he didn't seem afraid. He dared me to shoot ... Something must have snapped in me, for I did it deliberately. I wanted to kill him."

"Carmelite, there's no need," protested Sir Henry.

But the girl paid no attention. "I heard the shot, saw his face. And then—well, I don't know what happened next. I must have fainted or something. When I came to and found myself on my own bed I just couldn't believe it had really happened. But I went back to Starner's room and saw him—well, you know the rest." Her hands fell limply to her sides.

Katharine La Motte's gray eyes were strangely soft as she held out her jade cigarette case. "After all, you only did what any one of us would have done," she said quietly. "We'll stand by you."

"But I don't want you to stand by me." Carmelite's voice was steady. "I've told you all this and I don't mind telling the police. I feel justified in what I did, and a few years in prison—that wouldn't be so bad compared with the orphanage or the kind of life I'd have led with Starner." As she sat there, straight, erect, with her dark hair drawn austerely from her forehead, her air of conventional simplicity was even more marked. She was like a novice, ready to renounce the world and to welcome penance.

"Listen to me, Carmelite." Sir Henry moved to her side and laid his hands on her shoulders. His eyes as he bent over her were caressing and faintly amused, but in his tone was the authority of a typical English husband. "You say that orphanage taught you obedience. Well, you're going to obey me now. You are never, never going to repeat outside this room what you have told us. When the police come you will say that your father committed suicide because we had found out that he killed Judge Rock. You can leave all the details to us."

There was a general murmur of assent. Slowly Carmelite's mouth moved into a smile. Her grave eyes were smiling, too, as they gazed up into Sir Henry's.

"Perhaps you're right," she whispered. "I suppose the future Lady Bentley ..."

"Damn the future Lady Bentley!" exclaimed the baronet with gruff tenderness. "I'm thinking of the present Sir Henry Bentley and his friends, who will all be absolutely in the soup if Starner didn't commit suicide."

"Unfortunately, the soup seems inevitable," put in Vanderloon quietly, as his slender finger pointed toward the clock. "It is almost midnight, and the vigilant Mr. Wenz is doubtless getting ready to spoil our story by calling the Ashford police."

"Wenz! You mean Starner's secretary?" Carmelite had sprung to her feet. "Good heavens! I'd forgotten all about him! Of course ..." She broke off, glancing around her at the faces which had suddenly clouded with apprehension. "But the telephone, isn't it out of order?"

Swiftly Vanderloon explained what had happened. As he spoke the girl's lips parted in a fleeting smile.

"There is one advantage, Mr. Vanderloon, in being the daughter—and the heir—of a blackmailer," she said. "One inherits not only his property but also his hold over other people. I think I can prevent Mr. Wenz from calling the police."

"But, even so," put in Libby Hunt anxiously, "he will know what Starner suspected. He can make trouble for us."

"We shall have no trouble from Wenz," replied Carmelite firmly. "Starner made a point of picking his assistants from people who might have had difficulty in finding employment elsewhere. I shall call Mr. Wenz and tell him that Starner has committed both murder and suicide. I shall hint that there may be an investigation into his blackmail activities and remind Wenz that I alone have access to my—er—father's private papers. By tomorrow, I'm sure, Mr. Wenz will be many miles from New York." Her lips were still curved, but her lovely eyes were fixed gravely on the baronet. "After that I might prove how obedient I can be, Henry. Someone's got to call the local police and report the suicide. I think that I'm the most appropriate person to do it."

For a moment she stood there, motionless. Then slowly she turned and moved toward the hall. As they heard her calm, controlled voice asking for New York on the telephone, Johnnie Thring turned to Libby Hunt.

"What a girl!" he exclaimed enthusiastically....

The hands of the clock in the living room pointed now to four. The Ashford police had come and gone, taking with them the bodies of Judge Rock and Joseph Starner. The forces of the law had been confronted with a unanimous story, politely but firmly reiterated by each person in the house. Since the town of Ashford, five miles distant, had itself been paralyzed by the blizzard, the police appreciated the fact that the temporary dislocation of the telephone, the absence of automobiles, and the bad state of the roads had made it impossible for them to report the Judge's death earlier. A routine but thoroughly efficient examination revealed nothing to arouse suspicion. No embarrassing questions were asked. And Carmelite's demeanor alone would have been sufficient to convince far more skeptical probers. There had been a murder, and the murderer had committed suicide. The case was open and shut.

The living room was very quiet now. Vanderloon's younger guests had gone to bed. Only the Baroness remained downstairs with her host.

"Well, Theo," she murmured, "it is over. The police believe us and plainly they respect you. There will be no more trouble." The smoke from her Russian cigarette curled lazily toward the ceiling. "It is strange—strange and rather amusing. All the time we plot and scheme, we become emotional, we lose our heads—and what is the outcome? We achieve nothing. It is the others—the ones we feared, who really act."

"And it is strange," said Vanderloon reflectively, "that the three people who we thought would make trouble were the ones who really removed our troubles: the Judge—Carmelite—Starner.... As a dilettante philosopher I should consider that a profound commentary upon life."

"I am no philosopher, Theo, but so often I see the same thing in my shop." The Baroness gestured with her cigarette. "Life, it is just like the hats. Days and nights I work to create a model. It is superb. It will take New York by storm. But what happens? People—they turn up the nose, and then the simple little hat I make up in five minutes, everyone want to buy her. You cannot plan. You can only expect the unexpected."

The Baroness smiled sympathetically at his tired, drawn face. "You must not regret it, Theo. This day, with all its violence, its stupidities, it has been good. All of us, we have been brought face to face with reality; we have seen ourselves as we are; and that happens so seldom. And then, the young people, they have not only found themselves, they have found each other. I think they are going to be happy."

"You have a charming talent for making a fool forget his folly, Lili. And great intuition, too."

"But my intuition, she cannot probe so very far, Theo." Lili Tresckow looked at him curiously. "Even now, there is one thing I do not understand. I thought I knew you well—and yet this whole thing, it is too hard and ruthless. It is not my idea of you. What made you do it?"

Vanderloon's face had gone very pale. "It was because of Leon," he said quietly. "He's coming out the end of the month."

"Theo ...!"

"Yes. Now Starner is dead, you and Bowles are the only two people to know I have a son who spent five years in a French penitentiary. Possibly you are the only two who know that I married and had a son at all. It's almost twenty years since Henriette left me and took Leon back to France with her. But, now that she is dead, I think he'll come home and be a Vanderloon again." He gave a slight shrug. "The boy didn't have much of a chance with Henriette; he would have had no chance to make a fresh start with Starner alive. You see now, Lili, why

I had to step out of my egoistical seclusion to make a gesture."

The Baroness's eyes were shining as she rose. "So your son, he comes back to you," she whispered. "Oh, Theo, I am glad, so very glad. But now it is late. I say good night." Her fingers pressed his arm; and then, with a gentle smile, she moved away, fading from the pale sphere of candlelight like a charming memory.

After she had left, Vanderloon crossed to the hearth and leaned his thin shoulders against the mantel. The house was very still. Only an occasional movement from upstairs indicated that there were still guests at Chesham Grove.

Vanderloon did not look up as Bowles slipped into the room. Slowly, ritualistically, the butler moved across the thick carpet, emptying ash trays, plumping out cushions. At length he paused. "Well, sir, it's all over."

"Yes, Bowles; tomorrow we shall be alone again."

A frown of remembered dissatisfaction rippled the butler's forehead. "I must apologize for dinner, sir. I'm afraid the sauce Hollandaise was not all it might have been. But I did not have as much time as I could have wished."

"You've had a busy day, Bowles." Vanderloon's mouth moved wryly. "No one but you could have managed so well."

"Thank you, sir." Bowles had reached the hearth now and was carefully brushing fragments of ash from the carpet.

Vanderloon watched him with an amused smile. "You're a remarkably tidy fellow, Bowles."

"Thank you, sir." The butler glanced up. "Miss La Motte was kind enough to tell me this evening that I was as tidy and efficient as Sir Henry Bentley."

"What did she mean by that?" asked Vanderloon indifferently.

"I imagine everyone took it for granted that it was Sir Henry who went in and tidied up after the young lady, sir. Miss Starner was obviously far too upset at the time to give such a very convincing appearance of suicide." Bowles had moved away from the hearth and was collecting together a number of stray tumblers. "But, personally, I wouldn't say Sir Henry was such a tidy man, sir," he murmured. "He's made a stain on this lacquer table with his glass and I noticed a small burn in the rug where he dropped a cigarette." He shook his head thoughtfully. "And I know these Ashford police, sir. They're a thorough lot. You'd have to be a tidier man than Sir Henry to satisfy them."

"Good heavens, Bowles! You seem to be quite a detective. Do you mean you are dissatisfied with the present version of what happened?"

"In a way, sir."

"Well, I'd like to hear your views. But I think I'll have a drink first—

some of that Napoleon."

The butler brought a brandy decanter.

"And help yourself, too, Bowles."

"Thank you, sir, if it isn't a liberty …"

The butler fetched balloon glasses, and for a moment the two men stood together near the dying embers of the fire. Bowles fingered the stem of his glass reflectively.

"I was surprised that no one mentioned that second shot, sir," he said at length. "It might have been awkward for Miss Starner if it had been proved that two shots were fired."

"So you thought of that, too!"

"Yes, sir. And then there was the burn on Mr. Starner's shirt front. Of course, the police thought the candle fell on him when he knocked over the table. But Miss Starner happened to mention that it was on the mantelpiece while she was struggling with her father. I just wondered why anyone should have wanted it to look as though the candle had been on the occasional table that was overturned."

"You're being distressingly like one of those omniscient butlers in fiction, Bowles," said Vanderloon, as he twirled the amber liquid in his glass. "I really believe you have a theory. Let's hear it."

He moved to a chair and sat down, nodding Bowles to follow his lead. Stiffly the butler seated himself on the edge of the divan.

"Well, sir, I gather that Mr. Starner was a very cautious man and his profession was one in which threats were often more effective than weapons. Of course, I examined the gun after I had taken it from his bag, but I know so little about firearms that all I could tell was that it was fully loaded."

"Psychologically sound, Bowles," said Vanderloon. "And perhaps you're going to explain why a sensible man like Starner should have defied that angry girl to shoot him when she had the gun and he lay helpless on the floor. It was just a ruse of his to get a stranglehold on her, eh? He knew she was the type who would shoot only once; he also knew that the first—er—cartridge was a blank."

"That's exactly what I was going to suggest, sir."

Vanderloon drained his glass and held it out to the butler. "Thank you, Bowles, I think we're both ready for another. And while I drink mine you can give me what I believe is popularly called—the reconstruction of the crime."

There was a fragrance of old French vineyards as Bowles measured out two equal portions of the brandy. Vanderloon watched as the butler moved back to the hearth and resumed his seat on the divan. "You mustn't expect too much of me, sir," murmured Bowles solemnly, "but

I could give you my idea of what happened. I think Miss Starner told the truth, but I also think there was someone who did not obey your orders about coming down to the living room as soon as a shot was fired. That party hurried to Starner's room and found things very much as the young lady had left them. Starner was lying on the floor, possibly dazed by the blank explosion, or possibly even pretending to be shot, for reasons of his own."

"And then—?" put in Vanderloon.

"Only an eyewitness could tell you what happened next, sir. But this same party must have seen the gun lying on the floor, snatched it before he could be stopped, and shot Starner in the temple at close range. Then, of course, he did everything he could to make it look like suicide. The only really difficult matter must have been the powder marks on the shirt front caused by the explosion of the blank. That overturned candle was a clever idea, sir. Covering fire with fire, as you might say."

"So you don't think Sir Henry would have done such a good job, eh, Bowles?"

"Well, in a sense, sir, he might have done a better one. Being a sporting gentleman, Sir Henry would most certainly have searched first of all for the only thing which was completely overlooked by the other party. I mean the empty shell of the blank cartridge fired by Miss Starner."

The butler's hand went into his pocket and brought out a small metal object. "Luckily, I was able to retrieve it when I took a last look round the room before the police came.

"Admirable, Bowles!" Vanderloon took the discharged shell and fingered it thoughtfully. "I must confess I would never have thought of that. I suppose this would be what they call a clue, Bowles. And I suppose it proves that Miss Starner was not responsible for her father's death."

"That would be my guess, sir."

"As I said before, you've had a busy day, Bowles. You've been butler, cook, electrician, detective, and philosopher. Now I am going to ask you to play the role of ethical adviser, too. Do you think that the—er—party you refer to should ease Miss Starner's conscience by telling her what really happened?"

With the appreciation of a connoisseur Bowles inhaled the aroma from the last drops of brandy in his balloon glass. "In my opinion, sir, that is a question which only you can decide. But I would like to suggest that you seem rather tired. You have had a hard day, too, sir. You had better not worry about anything like that until tomorrow."

Vanderloon looked at him quizzically. Once again the faunlike smile was hovering around his lips. "From your excessive emphasis on the personal pronoun, Bowles, I gather you have known all the evening that it was I who finally killed Starner."

"Well, it wasn't exactly deduction, sir." The butler lowered his eyes modestly.

"In any case, you were quite right, Bowles. When I went to Starner's room after hearing that first shot, I never dreamed that I would have the honor. I merely went there to see if there was any tidying up to be done after the—er—Jack of Diamonds."

"Exactly, sir," said Bowles with an apologetic smite. "And I had the same idea myself. In fact, I did take a look in Mr. Starner's room. If I hadn't seen you there I should probably have taken the liberty of doing—er—exactly what you did."

The End

EXIT BEFORE MIDNIGHT
By Q. Patrick

It was quite unreasonable to feel afraid. There should, Carole Thorne told herself, be nothing alarming about returning to one's office after business hours. And yet, as the tower elevator let her off at Leland & Rowley's, she felt an odd moment of apprehension—an instinctive desire to get into the elevator again, to let it carry her down those forty floors of the Moderna Building away from this lonely, darkened office.

Carole stamped the snow from her overshoes and told herself she was a fool. Business buildings were always a bit spooky at night, anyhow. Besides, to Carole a dark office brought back uneasy memories of Christmas Eve, of that disturbing encounter with Miles Shenton. In fact, it had been partly to avoid seeing Miles when he came for the stockholders' meeting tonight that she had slipped out to the hairdresser's an hour ago.

"Miss Thorne!" She started at the sound of the elevator man's voice behind her. "You're not forgetting the tower elevator service stops at six. If your meeting isn't through by then, the stockholders will have to walk down to the thirtieth floor and take the regular night elevator from there." The man grinned. "Good night, Miss Thorne. Happy New Year!"

The doors slid shut. The elevator whirred downward.

Happy New Year! Carole had almost forgotten it was New Year's Eve. Appropriate that the last day of the old year should be the last day for the Leland & Rowley Process Company. Already the office looked deserted and abandoned. The desks and chairs seemed strangely unfamiliar.

There was no sound of life except the faint drone of voices from Mr. Rowley's office, where the stockholders were probably in the very act of voting away the company's corporate existence. Carole took off her hat and coat and moved toward her desk outside the president's office. She could hear Peter Howe's voice now, pleasant, reassuring. He was telling the stockholders how rich the merger with the Pan-American Dye Combine would make them.

It still seemed incredible that Peter Howe, the company's vice-president and boss's nephew, was actually in love with her, Carole

Thorne, who had nothing much to recommend her except rather nice blond hair and a very real appreciation of Mr. Howe. But it was exciting, too ... exciting to think that she would soon be having dinner with Peter, discussing the possibilities of their own matrimonial merger. Perhaps with Peter she would be able to forget what a fool she had been about Miles Shenton ...

She had actually sat down at her desk before she noticed the sheet of paper slipped into her typewriter. It must have been put there during her brief absence from the office.

Curiously, she pulled the sheet from the machine. She read:

MEMORANDUM TO:

Mr. Rowley   Miss Leland
Mr. Howe   Mr. Whitfield
Mr. Shenton   Mr. Barber
Miss Gregg

The blood drained from her cheeks as her gaze moved to the actual message:

This is to warn you that the merger with Pan-American Dye is not going through. Of course, you're planning to have it carried at the meeting by an overwhelming majority. *But it is not going through.*

Remember—it cannot become legally valid until midnight, anyhow. If enough of the largest stockholders died before then, fifty-one percent of the stock could change hands, couldn't it? The heirs of the deceased would undoubtedly demand a new vote. Think it over when you turn in your ballot slips.

Because, if the merger is carried, I have decided to murder several of you—and, if necessary, all of you.

You'll have plenty of time to consider whether you want to—
EXIT BEFORE MIDNIGHT

Carole stared dazedly. A threat of murder! Could this just be a practical joke? Or ...?

"So you're staying to be in at the death, Miss Thorne?"

Carole spun around. Little Mr. Whitfield, the company's lawyer, had slipped out of the president's office. His thin, birdlike fingers were picking up his briefcase, which had been lying on her desk.

"Mr. Whitfield!" Carole threw out a hand to detain him. But the little man had scurried back into the lighted room.

For a second Carole hesitated; then she made up her mind that she couldn't risk the responsibility of keeping this to herself. She would have to go in—interrupt the stockholders' meeting at once.

When she pushed open the door of the president's office, the large room was portentously silent. Grouped around in chairs, the score or so of stockholders were bent over ballot slips, signing their names. So it was too late to do anything about it anyway, she thought. The vote was actually being taken at this moment!

Carole noticed Mr. Rowley's gaze on her, inquiring, annoyed. Some of the stockholders had looked up, too. To whom should she take this mad memorandum? Not to Mr. Rowley—the shock might bring on one of his heart attacks.

Peter Howe, of course.

The young vice-president was sitting at the far end of the room next to Mr. Barber, the representative from Pan-American Dye. There was something reassuring about Peter's athletically square shoulders and blond, forthright face.

Carole hurried to his side and slipped the note into his hand. "I just found it, Peter. In my typewriter."

His gray eyes went very grave as he read. He glanced at her; then, with a quick "You'd better stay, Carole," he passed the paper on to Mr. Barber.

Carole dropped into an empty chair at his side. Miss Gregg, the company's plump, bespectacled treasurer, was bustling officiously around, collecting the ballot slips. The merger was going to be carried, of course. Carole knew that this hastily summoned meeting was a mere formality.

The names on the memorandum kept repeating themselves in Carole's mind. Miss Gregg was one of them, little Mr. Whitfield, the lawyer, Mr. Rowley, and Peter. And Mr. Barber from Pan-American, the stocky man with the alert, bushy-browed eyes who was bending over the note with Peter.

Then there was Miles, too. He was on the list. Although she deliberately did not look at him, Carole was acutely conscious of Miles Shenton, Nathaniel Leland's erratic but brilliant young protégé, who had inherited the old man's unfinished work and his position as head research chemist for the company.

Carole could sense the maddeningly amused half smile on his dark face with its high cheekbones and its slanting, insolent eyes. He had smiled that way when she had found him in the office on Christmas Eve after he had broken their date for earlier in the evening. He had smiled that way when he had started to make violent love to her in this very room. He had smiled that way, too, when he had casually let her know he was going out after the wealthy Marcia Leland as a "permanent meal ticket."

And his future meal ticket, Marcia Leland, was sitting there at his side. Slim, young, exquisitely dressed. Like some sea nymph, thought Carole, with her dark hair cut to her shoulders and those green, strangely observant eyes. And yet Marcia had inherited twenty thousand shares from her father, Nathaniel Leland. That fragile girl would logically be the murderer's first victim.

Miss Gregg's brisk fingers had counted through the ballot slips and proxies now. Her spectacles flashing, she whispered something to Mr. Rowley. The president rose, his thin fingers twisting the long, steel paper knife which always lay on his desk. "Ladies and gentlemen, the merger has been carried by a ninety percent majority. The papers which Mr. Barber and I will now sign are dated as of tomorrow, January first. The merger will legally go into effect at midnight."

Amidst a flutter of approval from the stockholders, Mr. Barber crossed to Mr. Rowley's side. The two men were signing their names. Carole glanced anxiously at Peter.

"Peter," she whispered, "what are you going to do?"

"Barber thinks we should ask the people threatened to stay behind afterwards. Don't want to make a fuss in front of everyone."

"You—you don't think it's serious?"

She could tell from the expression in his eyes that he was worried, but he smiled reassuringly. "Probably just a crank. You and I are going to exit before midnight anyhow. We're going to Longval's to knock the old year for a loop."

The documents were signed. Slowly Mr. Rowley leaned over his desk and speared with his paper knife the final sheet of the old year's calendar. He held it out with a little dramatic flourish. "December the thirty-first, ladies and gentlemen. The end of an old year, the end of a fine company, and the end of my own business activities. As you know, I retire with the signing of the merger. There remains nothing but to wish you a happy and a prosperous New Year."

As the stockholders prepared to leave, Peter rose and asked those mentioned on the memorandum to stay behind. The others moved out into the main office. Almost immediately Carole heard the elevator doors clang shut behind them. She glanced at her watch. Exactly six o'clock. With a queer pricking of alarm, she realized that the tower elevator had made its last trip for the night.

Mr. Rowley's large office seemed austere and empty now that the majority of the stockholders had left. The people whose names had been called were grouped apprehensively around the desk. Peter had started to read out the crazy message.

When he had finished, there was a moment of unbroken silence. Then he said, "I thought you all ought to hear it." His mouth moved wryly. "Personally, I don't think these formidable threats will be put into action. But if anyone is nervous …"

"Certainly I'm nervous," snapped Miss Gregg, the treasurer. "We must consult the police at once. A threat of murder! Disgraceful!"

"But ingenious." Miles Shenton was standing at Marcia Leland's side, an ironical smile in his dark eyes. "Killing off major stockholders to get a new vote on the merger! If he wants fifty thousand shares to change hands before midnight, he'll have to be pretty wholesale."

"We cannot afford to treat this lightly," broke in Mr. Rowley. "Mergers always cause bad feeling. This was probably written by some employee who's losing his work. He may conceivably be desperate enough to attempt something—er—rash."

While he was speaking, Mr. Whitfield, the company's lawyer, had been moving jerkily to and fro the zipper of the briefcase which he had taken from Carole's desk. Now he gave a sudden exclamation. "Wait a minute!" he cried. "I think I understand—I think I can explain."

Everyone turned to stare at him. His eyes were bright with alarm.

"This threat *is* serious—terribly serious. Some of us are in very real danger. We—" His voice was high, breathless. "As Mr. Rowley's lawyer, I have no right to make a statement. But I can see no alternative. This is a question of life or—"

He never finished his sentence … for suddenly, without the slightest warning, the lights in the president's office went out, plunging the room into swift, blinding darkness.

Voices called out; arms brushed against Carole. Instinctively she groped her way to the light switch. When she reached it, someone else was already there. She heard a click and her fingers touched the rough material of a coat.

"The switch doesn't work." It was Miles's casual voice, close to her ear. "Fuse must have gone. If it has, all this side of the floor will be in darkness. And the main office, too."

"Better move over to my office." Peter's suggestion was calm and steady. "It's on the other circuit."

There was a general movement toward the door. In an uncertain little procession, they all passed out into the main office which separated them from the group of private offices on the east side of the building. Miles had been right. All the lights in the main office had gone, too. It was profoundly dark.

Peter had hurried ahead. In a few moments a beam of light filtered toward them from his office. Shortly, they were all hovering anxiously around his desk, blinking at the unaccustomed brightness.

"Well, Mr. Whitfield"—Peter's voice was abrupt, jerky—"you had something very important to tell us and—" He broke off.

Carole looked around quickly and saw what was wrong. The lawyer was not in the room.

There was a murmur of startled comment. Mr. Rowley glanced at the open door and then at Carole. "Perhaps you would ask Mr. Whitfield to come here, Miss Thorne," he said curtly. "I have no idea what he was going to say, but it's getting late and …"

She moved to the door, the president's voice trailing impatiently after her as she hurried out again into the main office, away from the beam of light. It was somehow uncanny being in the darkness alone. As quickly as possible she retraced her steps to Mr. Rowley's office and paused at the door. "Mr. Whitfield." Her voice sounded oddly cavernous.

There was no sound. She crossed the threshold.

"Mr. Whitfield!" she called again.

She was a little frightened now. Mr. Whitfield must be here. He couldn't have slipped away. She tried to keep back the crazy thoughts that were invading her brain. They were absurd, ludicrous. And yet, there it was, that phrase from the memorandum, writing itself across the darkness in front of her: "… *exit before midnight* …"

"Mr. Whitfield!"

Step by step, she moved forward. Her foot touched something lying on the carpet. Instantly she froze. The darkness around her seemed to stir.... She forced herself to bend, to touch that thing with her finger. It was hard, slick—the leather of a shoe. Her hand moved, groping through the darkness.

It touched something else, something soft—limp. She knew what it was—knew with absolute certainty. Her fingers had touched a human hand.

At first she just stood there, numbed by the shock. Then she heard her own voice. She hardly recognized it, it sounded so small and lost. She was calling, "Quick—Mr. Rowley! Come quick!"

She could hear footsteps, faint and then nearer—hurrying. In a few seconds there were voices, rustlings, movements all around her in the darkness.

A hand gripped her arm, and Peter's voice, low, urgent, was asking, "Carole, what is it? What's the matter?"

"It's—it's someone," she faltered. "Lying there in front of me. I felt his hand. I—I think he's—"

Someone struck a match. It was Miles. Carole could see his dark, high-cheekboned face, the only illuminated thing in that room. Then another match was struck, and another. The little troop of flames lighted up the carpet in front of her. Mechanically her gaze moved downward.

Mr. Whitfield was lying there, slumped beneath the desk—looking pathetically small and unobtrusive, with his fingers still clutched around his briefcase. The match light cast strange little rays across his face The match light caught something else, too. Still adorned by the crumpled sheet from the calendar, the shining steel handle of Mr. Rowley's paper knife protruded from the lawyer's vest, just above the heart.

Matches flashed and lingered like slow-motion fireflies. Carole caught stray images of people around her—Mr. Rowley's haggard face, blank and horrified; Mr. Barber's wide, bright eyes.

Peter had dropped to his knees and was bending over the body. Carole waited for him to speak, but she knew before he said it what it would be.

"Dead."

"Murdered! And—and he was one of the largest stockholders." Miss Gregg's tone was oddly strangled. "So he actually means it—the man who wrote the letter."

A fresh sputter of matches. And then Peter's voice again, suddenly different: "Look!"

Rapidly his fingers were smoothing out the sheet from the calendar which, still impaled on the knife, was half thrust into the wound. With the others, Carole peered down in the uncertain matchlight. She saw at once what he meant.

The date which the president had speared during the meeting had been December 31. Now, glaring up at them in bold black print was:

JANUARY
1

At the farthermost edge of the arc of light Carole could just see the loose-leaf calendar for the new year on the desk. It showed January 2.

"You see"—Peter's voice rose again, steady but very grim—"he put it there, the murderer. Number One. He meant us to know that Mr. Whitfield was the first—that there will be others—"

Gradually Carole's mind began to take in the full implications of this appalling thing. The person who had typed out that memorandum must somehow have fused the lights on this circuit and crept into the room in the consequent confusion. He was carrying out his incredible threat.

Mr. Whitfield had owned ten thousand of the hundred thousand shares outstanding. He had been the first to go.

The last match had flickered out now and no one seemed to think to light another. There was a long, helpless silence. Then Carole heard the familiar clatter of the telephone receiver and Mr. Rowley's distracted voice at the desk, shouting: "Hello, hello! Give me the police station at once. Hello …"

"You won't get any reply, Mr. Rowley," Carole said. "The operator left the switchboard at five."

"Operator?" echoed the president. "Oh, yes, of course. Well …"

"I'll try and work the switchboard."

"Yes, yes. Thanks, Miss Thorne."

"You're not going alone, Carole," cut in Peter's voice. "I'm coming with you. None of us must touch anything," he ordered. "We've got to leave everything exactly as we found it for the police."

Somehow Carole found Peter and they were groping their way together out into the main office. His arm was around her, strong, protective.

"Oh, Peter, isn't it ghastly? What—what are we going to do?"

"Call the police," he said grimly, "and get away from this place as quickly as possible."

The switchboard was in a corner of the main office, close to the elevator shaft. They found their way to it with nothing to guide them but the faint light emanating from Peter's distant office. Carole sat down at the board, struggling to remember the little she knew about it. She put on the earphones and started to push in plug after plug.

"Hello … hello …"

One plug after another. She worked with growing anxiety. But it was no use. The instrument seemed absolutely dead.

The others had left Mr. Rowley's office now. They were all crowding around her in the darkness.

"I'm sorry, Mr. Rowley," she said at length; "I'm afraid I can't work it."

There was a spurt of light. Carole saw Miles Shenton with a cigarette lighter cupped in his hand. He was bending forward, peering behind the switchboard. He gave a low whistle. "I'm not surprised Miss Thorne can't work it. The wires are cut—all of them."

"Cut!" echoed Miss Gregg weakly. "You mean deliberately?"

"Deliberately and most competently." Mr. Rowley's voice rose, hoarse, uncertain: "Then we must use the elevator. Go down to the ground floor, Peter, and tell the night watchman …"

"I've been ringing the buzzer, Uncle. Nothing happens."

"It's no use, anyway," said Carole faintly. "The tower elevator stopped running at six."

"But—but what can we do?"

"The fire stairs," said Carole. "We'll have to walk down to the thirtieth floor, to the main building, and take the regular elevator there."

Her words galvanized the others into action. They all started to hurry back through the main office, stumbling over chairs and desks. Carole felt herself pushed along with the rest of them. They reached the door to the stairs. Someone struck a match. Miss Gregg gripped the handle and pushed. Nothing happened. She pushed again, and then gave a little sob. "It's locked."

"But it can't be." Marcia Leland's cool voice. "A fire escape door can't be locked. It's against the law."

More matches. Peter tried. Then Miles. They all pushed together feverishly. But it did not give. "It must be wedged," Peter said. "Wedged from outside. We'll never open it."

For the first time Carole felt real panic invading her. This was all part of the plan then—telephone cut, door jammed. They were to be shut up there in the half-darkness until the murderer had achieved his crazy purpose.

"But the fire alarm." It was an unfamiliar voice—Mr. Barber's—"There must be a fire alarm."

Carole answered, "It's outside the door—on the fire tower. We can't get to it."

They were standing absolutely still now in the darkness—stunned by the ruthless and cold-blooded deliberation that underlay this dreadful scheme.

"Cut off!" It was Mr. Rowley's voice, shrilling to a crescendo. "It can't be true."

But Carole knew it was. Locked in at the top of the tower, with a dead body, in an office that was less than half lighted. Cut off in the very heart of Manhattan! She stood there, her arms limp at her sides. In her mind she conjured up the image of the Moderna Tower as it must look to the people in the streets, forty floors below. A gigantic dagger thrusting up into the cold December sky. And the offices of the Leland & Rowley Process Company impaled, helpless and lonely, on its tip.

It was Peter who finally said, "There's no use standing around here. Better get back to my office."

To Carole it was an immense relief to return to the brightly lit room. The broad desk, the shiny chairs—they were so essentially a part of normal business routine, so essentially part of Peter. And it was to Peter, instinctively, that the others looked for the next move. Mr. Rowley had sunk into a chair, his eyes fixed unseeingly on the floor. He, obviously, had been crushed by the successive shocks of the past half-hour.

Peter stood by the window, his blond face very grave, his chin thrust forward grimly. "Well," he said, "we're up against it, all right. But we've got to keep our heads."

"There must be some way out," exclaimed Mr. Barber. The representative of Pan-American Dye had sat down behind the desk. "A modern office—cut off! It's impossible. Surely we could do something—drop a message out of the window."

"Unfortunately, we are in a tower, and the message would only fall onto the roof of the main building ten floors below," said Miles. "It stretches all around. You couldn't get anything down to the street from here."

"Then we must shout for help," exclaimed Miss Gregg brokenly.

"Forty floors up? New Year's Eve? Try and do it, Miss Gregg." Miles said, unemotionally.

Mr. Rowley looked up with a harsh, bitter laugh. "So we've just got to wait here and let ourselves be killed off one by one—like poor Whitfield!"

"But there must be a night watchman," persisted Mr. Barber.

"There is," said Peter. "He's due to plug in here about midnight."

"If he's sober," added Miles. "He has a marked tendency toward celebrating holidays. I very much doubt whether he'll attain to the top floor for a long time."

"So we *will* be here." Miss Gregg's voice rose to a stifled little sob, "We *will* be here until midnight."

In the sudden shock of finding themselves shut in, they had not thought of that—had not thought how long it would be before they could hope for release. Carole's heart sank. Shut in all night. What couldn't happen? What ...?

And then she remembered something. "The cleaning service!" she exclaimed. "It works at night. They'll be here soon."

"Good for Miss Thorne." Miles grinned. "Saved by the scrubwomen. When do they get here?"

"I think somewhere around nine."

Marcia Leland glanced at her watch. "It's nearly seven now. Only two more hours."

Only two more hours! Somehow those words made all the difference between sanity and insanity.

"Well, it's obvious what we've got to do." Peter's voice was steady. "Stay together in this lighted room. No—er—danger can come to us here."

"But this—this maniac who killed poor Mr. Whitfield!" The treasurer was twisting her plump fingers together. "How do we know he's not still somewhere in the office?"

"Exactly, Miss Gregg." Peter's glance moved to Miles. "Shenton and I had better make sure. We'll turn on all the lights that work on this side of the office and search the place thoroughly."

"Quite a tricky proposition—searching for a murderer in the dark," murmured Miles. "I'm sure you were a boy scout, Howe. Don't you carry a revolver or a flashlight?"

Marcia Leland had been sitting apart as if absorbed in her own thoughts. Now she pushed the dark hair back from her face and said, surprisingly, "You could use paper spills. I'll make some for you."

She rose, moving to the desk. Swiftly she twisted pieces of paper into tapers. She gave some to Peter, some to Miles. "That ought to be better than nothing."

"The superwoman!" Miles's smile was amusedly admiring.

He and Peter set matches to the spills. Cupping them in their hands, they slipped out of the room, out into the darkness of the main office.

With their departure, the rest of the group started to talk feverishly, to plan, to speculate. Who could be doing this? Was it an employee of the company or some unknown maniac? How could he have killed Mr. Whitfield and escaped?

Carole moved to the door and peered out, following with her eyes the little flickering lights that marked the two men's progress away through the office. What if they did find this—this person lurking somewhere in the darkness? He had already murdered one man. He would be desperate, probably armed. What could they do against him without weapons—anything?

Peter and Miles! How absurdly trivial her own problems seemed now. She had been worrying about whether she could bring herself to tell Peter the truth: that she liked him more than anyone she knew; that she respected him; that there was nothing to stop her growing to love him if only it hadn't all happened so suddenly, if only she could shake off those maddening memories of Miles.

And how absurd that even now she felt that tingling excitement when she thought of Miles; that burning anger when she remembered Christmas Eve, the broken date, his kisses, and his cynical remarks about Marcia as a "meal ticket."

"... I knew we should have called in the police as soon as Miss Thorne brought us that terrible note." Miss Gregg's emphatic voice broke into her thoughts.

"But we never had a chance." Marcia Leland's answering tone was cool, imperturbable. "Don't you see, Miss Gregg? Everything was worked out beforehand. Probably the telephone was already cut and the door jammed before the note was put in Miss Thorne's typewriter."

Carole glanced curiously from one woman to the other. It was strange, she thought, how shock and danger brought out characteristics one would not have guessed. Miss Gregg had been the company's treasurer ever since anyone could remember. For years she had bullied the girls, harassed the executives, and kept her ledgers with machinelike accuracy. Miss Gregg, Carole would have thought, could have stood up against anything. But now the treasurer was obviously on the verge of a collapse. She looked old and helpless.

And it was Marcia Leland who had risen to the occasion; Marcia Leland, the young, fragile girl just out of college, the woman whom the merger was to make a millionairess. Carole had been jealous of Marcia, antagonistic because of Miles. She admitted that to herself. But she could not help admiring her now.

But then, of course, she had already faced death that year. Carole remembered how, at the time of his final attack six months before, Nathaniel Leland had been alone with his daughter, working in a makeshift laboratory in Florida, where he had been sent by his doctor. The old man had guessed he was marked by death and had been desperately eager to complete his new chemical processes which were going to revolutionize the industry and restore the prosperity of Leland & Rowley. But death had cheated him. He had died, leaving behind him only a few worthless notebooks. And this slight girl had given up a brilliant career as a physicist to take care of him. She had nursed him to the very end. Peter and Mr. Rowley, who had flown down to Florida when the news of Leland's death came through, had returned full of admiration for Marcia's courage.

Footsteps outside in the main office deflected Carole's attention. She turned and saw the vague light of tapers, quivering in the darkness. Miles and Peter were back.

"Well?" asked Miss Gregg sharply. Peter moved to Carole's side, giving her a brief, fleeting smile. "We've searched everywhere. There's no one there."

"Impossible!" exclaimed Mr. Barber. "How could this man have got out?"

"Simple." Miles dropped down on the couch next to Marcia, his eyes resting for one moment on Carole. "He must have got the wedges all ready and kept them outside on the fire tower. After the murder he just had to slip out of the door and jam it behind him."

"But I can't believe that." Marcia Leland leaned forward. "He's trying to kill off the major stockholders before midnight. If—if he really means that, he'd never leave us all locked up here and go away."

"He would," explained Miles slowly, "if he intended to come back."

"Come back!" echoed Miss Gregg.

"Why, of course. He's bound to enter before midnight again." Miles's smile was slightly mocking. "Several times, in fact. After all, Mr. Whitfield owned only ten thousand shares. Our friend has to kill off at least thirty-one percent more if he wants a new vote on the merger."

"Then if the murderer's not here at the moment," Carole said quickly, "we've got to think out some way of stopping him from getting back."

"The efficient secretary speaks!" Miles gave her a mock bow. "In spite of Howe's scornful comments, I have already contrived a burglar alarm, an ingenious device of my own invention: three chairs piled against the door, with a glass water cooler perched on top. If anyone opens that door we'll hear it."

"Provided your theory's correct."

Carole started at the sound of Peter's voice. She glanced at him quickly. There was a strained look in his gray eyes.

"Does anyone really believe the murderer ever left the office?" he asked.

"But you searched," cried Miss Gregg. "And you didn't find anyone."

"We didn't. But does what Shenton says make sense? Could anybody have fused the lights in some other room and then crept into Uncle's office and committed the murder? How would he have known where the paper knife was … or the calendar? And how could he tell in the darkness where Mr. Whitfield was?"

Mr. Rowley stared blankly at his nephew. "Peter, what are you driving at?"

Peter looked down at his strong, capable hands. "If I'd been clever enough to have staged all this, I would certainly have been clever enough to have added my own name on that memorandum. It would have been easy to jam the door, go down the fire stairs, and come up again in the elevator before six, when it stopped running."

Carole leaned impulsively forward. "Oh, Peter, you can't think …"

"Yes." He shrugged almost apologetically. "I'm afraid it's far more likely that the murderer of Mr. Whitfield is one of us here in this room."

Carole could hear the quick beat of her own heart. Of course, what Peter said made perfect sense. The murderer had shut himself in with them here, pretending he was as much a victim as they.

She glanced dazedly around the room.

Those pale, familiar faces! Against her will, suspicions began to stir in her mind. Mabel Gregg. was losing her job through the merger, the job she had held for twenty years. Neither she nor Miles was being taken on by Pan-American Dye. And Mr. Rowley—this transaction was forcing him into a retirement which was only half voluntary.

And the others? Peter was getting a big job with Pan-American. The merger meant everything to him; as it did to Marcia Leland, whose great holding of stock would be trebled in value at midnight. And Mr. Barber, the representative of the company that was taking over. Surely none of those three could have a motive for fearing this merger.

"There's something else," Peter was saying quietly, "that makes me pretty certain the murderer is one of us. We've been forgetting that Mr. Whitfield was trying to tell us something when ..."

"You mean he had it figured out?" cut in Miles swiftly. "He suddenly realized it was one of us and was going to let on?"

Peter nodded. "That would explain why the murderer fused the lights at that moment—to stop him. Only one of us in the room could have done that."

There was a long, uneasy pause.

Mr. Barber shot a swift glance at the president. "Rowley, just before the lights went out, Mr. Whitfield mentioned your name. He acted as if you knew what he was going to say."

"Yes," added Miles curiously. "He said something about having no right to make a statement because he was your lawyer. What did he mean?"

They had all focused their attention on the president. He stirred uneasily in his chair. "I haven't the slightest idea," he said weakly. "Not the slightest idea."

Suddenly Carole remembered that Mr. Whitfield had been in conference with Mr. Rowley all that afternoon. During the past few days, too, the lawyer had been coming in regularly. And while he was there the door of the office had invariably been shut, a sure sign that they were discussing something very confidential.

Impulsively she turned to her boss. "It wasn't anything to do with those conferences you've been having with Mr. Whitfield lately?"

Mr. Rowley started. There was an almost angry gleam in his eyes. "Really, Miss Thorne, my private business with poor Whitfield has nothing whatsoever to do with this. We were discussing a purely personal matter—purely personal."

Another awkward moment of silence followed.

It was Marcia Leland who spoke first: "I've just remembered something." Her voice was brisk. "Just as the lights went out I heard a very faint spluttering sound."

Peter took a quick step forward. "The fuse going?"

"Yes. Don't you see? That means it was blown from the room where we all were. That would prove it was done by one of us. And if we can find out which outlet was fused, we might be able to remember which of us was standing near it."

"An excellent idea, Miss Leland." Mr. Barber was gazing at the girl admiringly. "One of us had better go right away and look at those outlets."

"I'll do it," volunteered Miles.

"No, Miles." Marcia Leland rose. "Let's all go together. We'll have to use spills again."

Marcia Leland had moved to the desk. Carole joined her, and together they folded sheets of paper. They were running short of matches, so Carole was given charge of those that were left, as well as Miles's lighter.

Keeping close together, the little group moved out into the main office. With uncertain fingers Carole lit a spill.

When they reached the door of Mr. Rowley's office Carole held the taper up so that its rays shone as far as possible into the office. In the fitful light there was something horrible about this dark, deserted room. Only one thing seemed real—vividly real—the huddled body of the little lawyer, lying beneath the desk.

"Miss Thorne, perhaps you know where the outlets are." Marcia Leland moved into the center of the room.

"Yes. There's one by the window." Carole joined her, and the others followed. While Carole held the taper low, Marcia stooped to inspect the plug in the wainscot. "No. We can't tell anything from that. Some sort of insulated gadget must have been used. I don't think the murderer would have been foolish enough to keep it. I imagine we'd find it left by the outlet. Is there another plug?"

"Yes, there's—there's one right by my desk." Mr. Rowley's voice was rather hoarse. "I had a desk lamp for a time." He pointed to a plug in the wall a few inches from the desk and on the same level as its surface.

"A very convenient place," mused Marcia. "Anyone could have pushed something in there without having to bend and attract attention."

"And here it is!" Miles's voice rang out excitedly "Clue number one!"

They all spun around. From beneath a sheaf of papers on the desk, he had produced a small, two-pronged kitchen fork with a wooden handle.

"Of course!" Marcia took it and slipped it into the outlet. It fitted perfectly. "The ideal thing for fusing a plug. The murderer must have brought it in with him."

"But who ...?"

Pale faces gleamed faintly in the taper light. Eyes moved uncertainly to eyes.

"Yes, who?" echoed Marcia. "Who was standing there to the left of the desk?"

Carole was wracking her memory. Hadn't Miss Gregg been standing just there while Mr. Whitfield began his extraordinary speech?

"I thought it was you, Miss Leland." It was the voice of the treasurer herself. "Weren't you standing there?"

"I," said Miles softly, "thought it was Howe."

Mr. Barber's eyes were intent on the president. "Didn't you move over there, Rowley, just after you'd been speaking?"

"No, indeed. No." Mr. Rowley's voice was crisp. "I was on the other side of Mr. Whitfield—to the right."

"Well, one thing's definite," Peter's voice broke in dryly. "We're not going to get anywhere from this angle. In thirty seconds we've accused three different people. To be perfectly frank, I haven't the slightest idea where anyone was."

"I'm afraid I agree." Marcia inclined her head. "When something startling happens, like the lights going out, you don't remember what went before."

"We might as well go back to Mr. Howe's office," Carole suggested. "After all, the cleaning women ought to be here soon. There's not much longer to wait."

She turned. As she did so, the light from the spill struck fanwise across the surface of the desk. She gave a little gasp. "Look!" she exclaimed. "Look!"

The others swung round.

Carole was pointing at the loose-leaf calendar for the new year. When last they had been in this room, the calendar had shown January 2. Now the light of the taper revealed:

JANUARY

4

Miles gave a low whistle. "The second and third—someone's taken them."

"And it must have been one of us." Mr. Barber's voice was sharp with incredulity. "That definitely proves that the murderer is here—here in the room."

In the uneasy silence, Marcia Leland moved forward. "It also means," she said, "that the danger isn't over yet. Number 2 and Number 3. Apparently the murderer has decided to kill two more of us."

"Come on. Let's get back to my office," said Peter brusquely. "You lead the way with the light, Carole."

Shielding the taper with her hand, she moved quickly to the door and out into the darkness of the main office, the others behind her.

She passed the fire stairs door with chairs piled bizarrely against it and a heavy glass cylinder gleaming dully on top. The burglar alarm! They wouldn't be needing that now, she reflected grimly. She was almost halfway to the safety of light, when she heard behind her an ominous rattle. Almost immediately it was followed by a crash that resounded like thunder around the invisible walls—the heavy crash of chairs falling and the splintering crash of broken glass.

The trap on the door had been sprung! The murderer had not been one of them. He had been waiting out on the fire stairs and now he had slipped in through the door. At that very moment he was somewhere there in the darkness around her … somewhere …

The taper slipped through Carole's fingers. In horror she watched the flame flicker a moment on the floor and then wink out. Some remote part of her brain was conscious of the others. They had burst into hectic life. She could hear them stumbling against desks and chairs, calling out to each other, shouting for lights.

And then one voice rose above the vague babel around her, loud and authoritative. It was Peter and he was shouting, "Get back to the lighted office—all of you!"

The lighted office! Safety! Carole ran toward the faint radiance ahead. When she reached Peter's room she sank into a chair. Her hands were trembling and she could not stop them.

There were hurrying footsteps outside. Someone else dashed into the room. It was Peter. "Quick, Carole! The spills, and some matches! Quick!"

Shakily she gave them to him, and he was away again before she could speak.

The others were entering now: Mr. Rowley, a frail, ghostlike figure; Mr. Barber; Miss Gregg, her graying hair falling loose and disheveled over her forehead. None of them spoke. They just stood by the open door, gazing out.

Carole crossed to join them. At last Miles and Peter appeared. Their faces were very grim.

"We were fooled," said Miles curtly. "No one came in through that door. The trap was knocked over from inside."

"By one of us?" exclaimed Mr. Barber.

"Yes." Peter's eyes were moving rapidly around the room. "It was a false alarm. The murderer must have done it to—" He broke off. "Where's Miss Leland?"

"Marcia!"

Miles dashed out into the darkness Peter followed instantly, lighting a taper as he went.

"Marcia, Marcia …" Miles's voice trailed back to them.

Carole's gaze flickered helplessly from one face to another.

"She's been murdered!" screamed Miss Gregg suddenly. "I know it! In the darkness, she ..." Her voice rose to a high, hysterical laugh.

"For heavens sake, stop it, woman!" barked Mr. Barber. He spun round, gripping her arms. "Stop that noise!"

From the door, Carole had been able to follow Peter's progress by the lighted taper in his hand. Suddenly he stopped, somewhere near the elevator shaft. For a second he stood absolutely still. Then he stooped and shouted, "Quick, Miles!"

Carole drew in her breath. The light of the downward-pointing taper had revealed the prostrate figure of a woman.

The spill burnt out almost immediately, and darkness swallowed up what Carole had seen. Behind her, in the lighted office, Miss Gregg had stopped sobbing now. As Carole peered urgently forward she saw figures approaching. Peter first—then Miles. In his arms Miles was carrying a vague, slim form.

"Miss Leland," exclaimed Mr. Barber. " Is—is she—?"

"No." Peter crossed to the couch and piled the cushions up at one end. "Looks as though someone tried to strangle her. But she's still breathing!"

Miles carried the unconscious girl to the couch and very gently set her down.

Carole moved forward. Marcia's eyes were closed, her lips half parted. On her throat were long, inflamed marks.

Mr. Rowley was fluttering helplessly around. "One of us attacking Miss Leland! I can't believe it."

"On the contrary, she's the ideal victim. Twenty thousand shares." Miles's voice was sardonic. He had brought water and was bending over Marcia. "Poor kid, I'm afraid I'm developing an intense dislike for someone in this room ..."

He broke off with a little grunt of surprise. Carole saw his fingers slip down the front of Marcia's dress and bring out a crumpled piece of paper.

"What is it?" asked Mr. Barber sharply. Miles rose from the couch, smoothing out the sheet. The upward slant of his eyes was dangerously accentuated. "A very methodical murderer."

The crinkled scrap of paper showed:

JANUARY
2

The others were crowding around, gazing in mute astonishment at the leaf from the calendar.

Peter glanced down at Marcia. He exclaimed suddenly, "She's coming to!"

The dark head against the cushions was stirring. Marcia's eyes half opened.

"What happened?" Miss Gregg had sprung forward. "Tell us what happened, Miss Leland."

"Give her time." Peter's voice was curt.

With an effort, the girl pushed herself up against the cushions. Her lips parted in a faint smile. "I'm sorry. It was foolish of me to faint."

"Foolish!" echoed Miles. "My dear, you were half strangled."

Marcia's fingers moved slowly over the dull red wales on the delicate skin of her neck. "But the trap on the door was sprung. What ...?"

"Just a blind," exclaimed Peter. "The door hadn't been opened."

"I see." Marcia's impassive gaze scrutinized each of them in turn. "So it was one of you six that tried to kill me."

"But you must be able to remember what happened," broke in Mr. Rowley. "Surely you know who it was that ..."

"I remember what happened. Perfectly." Marcia pushed the dark hair back from her forehead. "But it won't help."

"You haven't any idea who attacked you?"

"None at all. You see, when—when the water cooler crashed, I ran toward it. I don't know why. I suppose I had some crazy notion of trying to catch the murderer. Then I heard Mr. Howe telling us all to go back to the lighted office. That made me more sensible. I turned and started back in this direction."

"Yes?" put in Miss Gregg.

"Then I felt a hand on my arm. It was quite a gentle grip. I felt myself being drawn along." Marcia shrugged. "I wasn't frightened. I thought it was probably Miles or someone taking me under their wing. The hand dropped from my arm. It moved over my dress. Before I had time to realize it, both hands were closing around my throat." She gave a little shiver. "I tried to cry out, but I couldn't. I remember stumbling backward, feeling myself choking. That's all."

"But it must have been a man," urged Miss Gregg. "You must have known it was a man."

Marcia glanced at the treasurer quickly. "No, Miss Gregg; as I said, the grip was very gentle at first. It—it was never particularly violent. It might just as well have been a woman." She was glancing at her watch. "Twenty-five minutes to nine," she said. "If Miss Thorne's right, the cleaning women will be here in about half an hour. What are we going to do?"

"Half an hour," said Peter suddenly. "I think it's about time we started to consider the really important question—which of us is doing all this. It's not exactly pleasant. But presumably the police will be in charge soon. Everything's going to be a lot simpler if—if we can get some points cleared up before they come."

"Precisely." To Carole's surprise, it was Miss Gregg who spoke. The treasurer seemed miraculously to have reacquired her normal brisk manner.

"I suppose we all agree," continued Peter quietly, "that this terrible business concerns only stockholders and employees of Leland & Rowley. Whoever arranged this trap must have known everything about the office. I can't understand why Mr. Barber was included on that memorandum. But, as the representative of Pan-American Dye, he obviously has nothing to do with these—these crimes. I suggest we give him absolute authority and let him cross-examine us."

"Excellent." Miles brought lighter and cigarette together. "Of course, a lurid imagination could conjure up a case against Mr. Barber. Pan-American may have got cold feet about the merger and sent him over to murder us all." He grinned. "Still, I'll second Howe's recommendation."

In a vague murmur, the others agreed.

Mr. Barber was gazing rather angrily at Miles. Apparently he was not used to being treated flippantly. "I agree with Mr. Howe," he said. "We should do our utmost to clear the dreadful matter up. And I think it should be fairly easy."

"Easy!" echoed Mr. Rowley.

Mr. Barber nodded. "We have to look for the criminal among those of you who stand to lose rather than gain by the merger."

Mr. Barber had the situation formidably under control now. His voice was sharp, unemotional. "If the murderer has so strong a feeling against the merger, it is reasonable to suppose that he voted against it. I should like to see the ballot slips. They may give us a clue."

"Not a bad idea," cut in Peter.

"They're in my office," offered Miss Gregg. "I took them in with some other papers after the meeting."

"Before anyone gets them," broke in Mr. Barber slowly, "I have another suggestion to make, one which we should already have thought of. The murderer took both the second and third of January from the calendar. We found the second on Miss Leland. Presumably, this—this person is planning a third attack. If so, the calendar slip should still be in his possession. I suggest that each one of us should let himself be searched."

"Searched …?" began Miss Gregg.

But she broke off at a strangled little exclamation from Mr. Rowley. He had half risen, his cheeks the color of cigarette ash. "I … someone

"... a glass ... water ..." he breathed hoarsely.

His hand moved jerkily to his heart. With a gasp, he sank back into his chair, doubling forward with an expression of acute suffering on his haggard face.

"Mr. Rowley!" Carole knew her ex-boss had a weak heart. She had seen an anginal attack like this only a week before, after Mr. Barber had come to the office to discuss the final arrangements for the merger. She hurried to the cooler, poured a cup of water, and crossed to Mr. Rowley. Peter was already at his uncle's side. "Pocket!" Mr. Rowley was whispering. "Right-hand pocket."

Peter's fingers slipped into his uncle's pocket. He produced a small ampule and crushed it swiftly beneath Mr. Rowley's nostrils. Carole hovered close with the water. As she did so, she noticed, to her astonishment, that Peter was concealing something in his left hand— a small piece of paper. He saw her looking at it and shot her a warning glance.

"Give me the water, please, Carole," he said.

She passed him the cup. He tilted it to his uncle's lips. Then, swiftly, he slipped the crushed piece of paper into the empty cup and handed it back to her.

In one blinding second, Carole realized what had happened. Peter had found the third calendar slip in his uncle's pocket; he was trying to conceal it, mutely asking her to help him protect Mr. Rowley.

The others were clustering around anxiously. The president's breathing was becoming more normal now. He forced a pallid smile. "So sorry," he muttered. "The heart's been acting up lately."

No one spoke for a long moment. Then Mr. Barber said, "I must ask all the men to empty their pockets. Perhaps, Miss Thorne, you'll look through the ladies' coats and handbags."

The search seemed to take hours. At last Mr. Barber seemed satisfied. "He must have anticipated the fact that we would make a search, and disposed of the sheet from the calendar. Now, perhaps someone will get those ballot slips."

"I will." Hurriedly, Peter slipped his handkerchief, pen, and change back in his pocket. Casually he picked up the cardboard cup from the table where Carole had placed it.

"Perhaps you'll come with me, Miss Thorne," he said. "It's only next door." Carole knew what he wanted to tell her.

"Yes," she said. "Of course I'll come."

Miss Gregg's office was next to Peter's. Neither he nor Carole spoke as they hurried to it. Peter closed the door behind them. His gray eyes looked down at her seriously. "You guessed, Carole? I couldn't let Uncle see it. I was afraid the shock might be too much for him."

Slowly he pushed open the crushed cup and took out the piece of paper. Staring up in that heavy, horribly familiar type was:

JANUARY

3

"You found it in Mr. Rowley's pocket?" Carole said dully.

He nodded.

"Peter, how awful. But how—how did it get there?"

"I suppose the murderer must have planted it on him." Peter's voice was hesitant. "But I don't see how Uncle …"

"You can't think Mr. Rowley was the one who took the sheets from the calendar?" cut in Carole suddenly.

Peter moistened his lips. "No, it's absolutely impossible for him to have done anything like that deliberately," he said softly. "But I have been worried about him—about his health. He hasn't been well for some time. The idea of the old company having to break up has been preying on his mind." He crushed the slip into his pocket. "Listen, Carole, you're his secretary. You're as close to him as anyone. Has he done anything at all strange lately?"

He broke off. Carole knew how beastly this must be for Peter—to have in his mind even the vaguest doubts about the bachelor uncle who had always been like a father to him. But, as she thought back over the hectic events of the past weeks, she felt a slow suspicion stirring in her.

"I hate to say this," she began impulsively. "But he—he has been rather odd lately. And then, just after Mr. Barber came here to the office the day before Christmas, he had a heart attack like the one he had tonight."

"Mr. Barber!" exclaimed Peter blankly.

"Yes. Just after Mr. Barber left, the buzzer went and I found your uncle doubled forward over the desk. He managed to tell me about the ampule, and he was all right again in a few minutes. But I had a feeling he'd heard something that had given him a shock."

Peter's eyes were anxious. "That was the day Mr. Barber came round to discuss the final arrangements for the merger, wasn't it?"

"And it was the next day that Mr. Rowley started to have those long conferences with Mr. Whitfield."

"You don't know what they were talking about?"

"No. They kept the door shut. But this afternoon they sent for me to witness a signature and …" Carole paused. "Oh, Peter, I've just remembered. When I went in there this afternoon, Mr. Whitfield had borrowed my typewriter. He was sitting there—typing."

"Typing!"

They stood perfectly still, staring at each other. That memorandum. *Exit before midnight.* Had—had Mr. Rowley and Mr. Whitfield somehow compiled it together?

"What are we going to do, Peter?" Carole asked quietly.

"Whatever we think, it's only theory. We've got no proof." Peter's voice was taut. "Carole, we can't tell the others. It's not fair to Uncle, now he's sick. The police will be here soon. If—if they find out anything, well, they find it out, but …"

"All right," murmured Carole.

Suddenly she felt terribly tired. Peter's fingers were still warm on her arm. She was very conscious of his nearness, of his comforting strength. Maybe some good had come out of this nightmare evening, she thought. It had taught her to appreciate Peter—sane, loyal Peter …

"New Year's Eve!" She looked up at him with a little grimace. "Just a few hours ago I was having my hair fixed and planning to dazzle you with my new black velvet. Rather absurd, isn't it?"

He did not reply for a moment. The light gleamed down on his head. Slowly his arms went around her and drew her toward him. His lips met hers, warm, passionate. "Carole, darling," he whispered, "I know it's a crazy time to say it, but I've—I've got to tell you how crazy I am about you."

His hand moved caressingly over her soft blond hair. "I guess I'm not used to explaining the way I feel. I'm not like Shenton and those fellows who know the phrases. It's—all the evening, with all these ghastly things happening, I've just been able to think of you—of how I might have been alone with you …"

He broke off, gazing down at her, his gray eyes anxious, uncertain, like a boy's. "Carole, darling, will you marry me? I want you so much."

She let herself relax in his arms. Life with Peter would be so safe …

"Pardon a most untimely entrance."

Carole spun round at the sound of a quiet voice behind her. Peter turned, too. They stood very close together, staring at the door. There, his hands in his trouser pockets, his dark, mocking eyes fixed on Carole's face, was Miles Shenton.

"I had no idea this remarkable evening was breeding romance." He drew a hand from his pocket and examined his nails. "I'm sure the ex-employees of Leland & Rowley will take great pleasure in organizing a wedding shower for the almost ex-Miss Thorne."

Carole felt sudden anger. She hated him for coming in; hated him for staring at her with those insolently amused eyes, for being so—so disgustingly handsome.

Peter still had her fingers in his. He was glowering at Miles. "What did you come here for, Shenton?"

"For the same reason as you, Howe. I was hoping for a little private talk with Miss Thorne. I wanted her to refresh my memory on a certain detail of our *tête-à-tête* here on Christmas Eve."

Carole felt the blood flooding her cheeks. How exactly like Miles to bring up Christmas Eve! She swung round to Peter. "Mr. Shenton was kind enough to ask me out to dinner on Christmas Eve," she explained acidly. "Unfortunately, he discovered at the last moment that he had a very important business engagement. He called up and broke the date."

"Oh, I wasn't referring to that." Miles grinned. "I meant our little encounter here afterward." He glanced at Peter. "I happened to drop into the office around half past ten that night. And who should appear but Miss Thorne herself? We had a very pleasant session together."

Pleasant session! Carole remembered vividly every moment of that pleasant session. When Miles had stood her up she had gone back to the office, after a solitary dinner, to retrieve some Christmas packages she had left behind. She had found him there, alone and in tails for his "business engagement." He had kissed her, made love to her. For some mad reason she had let him. And then he had suddenly broken away, saying, "*Well, Marcia Leland's waiting for me downstairs. A practically unemployed chemist can't afford to keep his potential meal ticket waiting.*"

Pleasant session!

The two men were gazing at each other. "Your office is down at the laboratories," said Peter quietly. "What were you doing here at ten-thirty on Christmas Eve?"

"Robbing the safe." Miles's smile was less humorous than usual. "As a matter of fact, I was on a very innocent mission. That afternoon your uncle called me up at the laboratories. It was the first time, incidentally, that I'd heard about the merger. He wanted me to send him all the unpatented processes and the notebooks old Leland kindly but quite unprofitably bequeathed me in his will. I sent them up." He took out a cigarette. "As Miss Thorne told you, I had a business engagement. Marcia and I happened to be passing, and I wanted my notebooks back. So I came up here to get them … But we seem to be wandering from the point I intended to bring up with Miss Thorne."

"There's no need to bring up any other points now," cut in Carole curtly. "We'd better be getting back to the others."

"Miss Thorne is probably right—as usual." Miles held his lighter to the cigarette. "As I remember, you two were sent here to collect the ballot slips. You seem to have become sidetracked from your original purpose." He crossed and picked up the ballot slips. "O, careless love," he murmured.

When they rejoined the others, Miles took the ballot slips to Mr. Barber. The executive from Pan-American Dye glanced through them, his eyes widening. "Well," he said briskly, "the murderer has voted in favor of the merger—presumably to avert suspicion. Every one of you present in this room voted aye."

Surprised murmurs stirred the group. "But, even so," continued Mr. Barber's level voice, "I think we may reasonably eliminate those of you whose interests are obviously bound up with the carrying of the merger." He glanced at Peter. "Mr. Howe is to have a very remunerative position with Pan-American. I fail to see how he could have the slightest motive for committing these crimes."

Mr. Barber's gaze shifted to Marcia. "And Miss Leland, too. Even if she had not been brutally attacked, she owns twenty thousand shares, and the merger will greatly enhance their value."

Marcia inclined her head. "As a matter of fact, I'm very anxious for the merger to go through. I need the extra capital badly. You see, I'm planning to endow an institute for noncommercial research in—in memory of my father."

"I can confirm that," put in Miles. "The proposed Leland Institute is Marcia's sole passion. Cross her off the list."

Mr. Barber's thick brows lowered as he glanced at Carole. "Miss Thorne, I understand, is losing her job through the merger."

"It's absurd to suspect Miss Thorne," broke in Peter. "Besides, she has an alibi. When the trap on the door was sprung, she was at the other end of the office. You could tell that by the lighted taper."

"That is true," Mr. Barber said. "We may eliminate Miss Thorne."

The atmosphere in that small room was increasingly electric. Suddenly Miss Gregg leaned forward in her chair. "There's no need to suspect me," she said calmly. "I know what some of you are thinking: Poor old Miss Gregg, who's been with the firm practically all her life—maybe she couldn't stand the idea of having to start all over again; maybe she's just an old spinster driven crazy by the idea of the merger—driven crazy enough to commit murder."

She snorted. "Well, you're wrong. The merger is going to treble the value of my shares; give me a big enough income so's I won't have to work anymore. And I'm through with work. I want to have a good time—I want to travel before I'm too old to enjoy it."

She crossed her hands in her lap and looked around her defiantly. "You can cross me off, too."

Miles smiled wryly. "That's the spirit. Good for you, Miss Gregg."

Mr. Rowley had been listening with rather tense interest. Now he lifted a hand. Carole thought of the calendar slip they had found in his pocket.

"As Miss Gregg has explained her point of view," began the president quietly, "I might as well explain mine. Some of you, I know, realize that my heart wasn't in the merger. Perhaps I was sentimental, but, with my old friend Nathaniel Leland, I started this firm—it meant everything to me. In the back of my mind, I hoped that we would be able to struggle along without losing our corporate existence." He smiled faintly. "But that was only a sentiment. As a large stockholder I have as much to gain as anyone by the merger. Besides, like Miss Thorne, I have an alibi." He threw out his hands in a small gesture of finality. "Only my nephew, Peter Howe, knows this, knows why I could have no motive for interfering with something which no longer concerns me. Last week my doctors gave me less than three months to live. My alibi is—death."

There was a calm dignity on his face.

There ran through the group a spontaneous ripple of shocked and sympathetic comment. They lapsed into silence, until the sharp click of a lighter drew all attention to Miles. He was leaning back against the cushions of the couch, a faint trail of smoke issuing from his nostrils.

"I seem to be the only suspect left," he said. "I might as well save you all the trouble and give you the case against myself. The merger is removing my job. I happen to be in fairly desperate need of money. Mr. Leland, who was so generous to his other dependents, failed to be generous to his protégé. He left me no shares in his will, only a few and regrettably sketchy notes of the experiments he was working with at the time of his death. So I am the only one who has any kind of logical motive for committing murder to stop the merger from going through."

He grinned. "As defense, I merely state the fact that I did not murder Mr. Whitfield. I certainly did not attack Marcia, to whom I am very devoted. And my motive is not quite so strong as it appears, since Marcia has offered me a job with the proposed Leland Institute."

"That's true," broke in Marcia swiftly. "I want him as head research chemist. And I know he's as excited about the Leland Institute as I am. It's ridiculous to pretend he could have any motive."

Carole felt an overpowering sense of relief. Of course, Miles didn't mean anything to her. Why should he? But …

"So"—it was Miles's voice that broke in calmly—"we have proved that none of us has the slightest motive for inaugurating this mass exit before midnight."

"But," blustered Mr. Barber, "there must be some mistake. We …"

"Why don't we give up being detectives for the time being?" asked Miles. "Besides, I have a rather uneasy suspicion which I feel I must share with you all." His eyes moved gravely to Carole. "Miss Thorne and I happened to meet here in the office on Christmas Eve—quite accidentally, I might add. The time was about ten-thirty, and, I may be wrong, but I don't remember noticing any signs that the cleaning women had been here."

Carole stared at him, her eyes gradually widening. "You're right," she breathed. "The scrubwomen hadn't come."

Miles nodded. "From which I can draw only one conclusion: Christmas Eve was the day before a holiday. So is tonight. Scrubwomen don't put in an appearance on the eve of holidays. They won't come till tomorrow night."

Miss Gregg gave a little horrified gasp. "So—so we won't be let out! We *will* be here until midnight!"

"Undoubtedly," said Miles gravely. "And even then we shall be at the mercy of an alcoholic night watchman."

"But we've got to find some way of getting out." Miss Gregg voiced the thoughts of them all. "We can't let ourselves be trapped here—let the murderer do what he wants with us."

"There is a chance—just a chance." Miles's cool voice broke in. "We can always revert to the most primitive method of attracting attention. *Fire*."

"Fire?" echoed Mr. Barber. "How?"

"By making people in the street think the Moderna Tower is on fire. By having smoke pouring out of all the windows." Miles's face was very serious. "I've got a fairly workable plan. There are some samples of one of our specially processed dyes here in the office which smokes like hell when you set fire to it. Each of us gets a metal scrap basket stuffed with paper. Each of us takes a window. I've got some lighter fluid in my desk. We can make little individual bonfires and put up quite a convincing impression of fire. Some New Year's Eve reveler might turn in an alarm."

"Yes. We could put the scrap baskets on the sills." It was Mr. Rowley speaking, quickly, excitedly. "There are seven rooms and just seven of us. Excellent."

"But the darkness!" cut in Miss Gregg. "It means going out again—out there in the darkness."

"Leave that to the most stalwart of us, Miss Gregg." Miles rose. "You ladies can share the lighted offices."

The next ten minutes were hectic. Seven scrap baskets were stuffed with paper, sprinkled with the dye and lighter fluid.

Finally everything was ready. Marcia Leland was to stay behind to look after the window in Peter's room, while Miss Gregg was to take charge of her own lighted office. The rest of them started out in silence through the semidarkness.

Carole had been allotted the central window in the main office. She felt a little twinge of fear as the four men slipped away from her into the deeper obscurity, leaving her alone in that large, silent room. A faint shaft of illumination took the edge off the darkness. She moved toward the window, and pushed it up. A little gust of chill air rushed in.

The snow was icy against her hands as she banked it up on the sides of the sill to make room for her scrap basket. She fumbled for a match in her box. Then she stiffened. From the darkness behind her had come the soft sound of footsteps.

She could hear soft breathing, feel the presence there behind her. For a second she could not move. Then she spun around blindly. "Who's ...?"

Her voice faded. An arm had slipped purposefully around her waist. She felt breath warm on her cheek and then lips pressing against hers. As soon as he touched her, she knew it was Miles. It was a strange, intoxicating sensation—part anger, part relief, part excitement. She tried feebly to break away from that long, aggressively male kiss.

Gradually his arms relaxed around her. He drew back. And with the moment of his moving away, she felt anger rising to swamp all other emotions. "Miles ..."

"I had to kiss you to stop you from screaming." The vague light from the Manhattan sky struck in through the window, softly accenting his bright eyes and the ironical curve of his lips.

"What are you doing here?"

"I thought it would be a good opportunity to have a talk with you alone."

"And what is there to talk about?"

"Your future." Miles twisted his warm fingers around hers. "Carole, you're not going to marry Howe, are you?"

"I shouldn't have thought it mattered to you what I did. There'll always be lots of other girls to neck in dark offices."

"Listen, Carole; you're being a fool and you know it." His arm had slipped around her again. His face, very close to hers, was dark, earnest. "Christmas Eve was all a mistake. I'd have explained it days ago if I'd ever realized what you were thinking. I went out with Marcia because she called me up to offer me this job with her Leland Institute. It was a business engagement. Heaven knows, there's nothing more emotional between Marcia and me than the mutual respect of two scientists and a brotherly-sisterly friendship—never has been." He gave a little laugh. "Maybe you misunderstood my remark about a meal ticket. Anyway, you're not going to marry Howe. I'm not going to let you."

His lips were moving softly over her hair. She tried to cling to her anger, tried to fight against a feeling of elation.

"If you've got any sense, Carole, you know I'm crazy about you. I—well, when I heard about the merger I knew that my job was on the skids. I didn't exactly feel like asking you to be the wife of an unemployed chemist. But I'm going to have a job now with Marcia—a good one." He gripped her arms and gazed down at her. "You don't want to marry a stuffed shirt like Howe. You'd be bored in a week, and you know it. Of course, I'm not much of a catch. I don't inherit the Rowley fortune, like Howe, but—you'd have a better time with me, Carole. You'd have fun."

Still Carole could not speak.

He kissed her again almost fiercely. Then he gave a short laugh. "Two proposals in an evening—you *are* in demand." Abruptly he turned away. "Say, you haven't lit your bonfire yet."

While she stood there, breathless, he struck a match and bent over the scrap basket. A trail of smoke curled up.

"Which just goes to show that you can't get on without me." He touched her arm. "Make up your mind, dimwit, and don't mess up your young and beautiful life."

She heard his footsteps growing fainter as he disappeared into the shadows. She was alone again. For a moment she stood still, her lips numbed by the harshness of his kisses, thinking dazedly of what he had said. He had explained Christmas Eve; his explanations were perfectly reasonable. Probably she had made a fool of herself. But—but could she believe him? Did she want to? Only a few minutes ago she had decided that life with Peter would be safe, sane ... and now Miles had come along and complicated things again.

She wouldn't think about it now. She forced herself to concentrate on the moment. The paper in her scrap basket had been too closely packed, and the snow had dampened it. The flames which Miles had started were dwindling. She cupped her hand to shield them from the breeze. And, as she did so, she noticed her own name on one of the crushed sheets.

She looked more closely. It was her signature: *Carole Thorne*. And then, above it: *Samuel P. Whit* ...

The flames shivered and died out.

Stooped as she was over the sill, she could see the smoke streaming from Mr. Rowley's office. She caught a glimpse of the president's pale, lined face bent intently over his scrap basket.

Suddenly it all seemed so pitifully inadequate—these frail strands of smoke trailing out of office windows forty floors above the street. What chance was there that anyone would notice?

The snowflakes fell, crystal cold, against her face; the chill night air tugged at her hair. She could still see the smoke eddying slowly from the president's room and the dull glow of burning paper.

And then, suddenly, the smoke curled crazily. She saw Mr. Rowley's scrap basket lurch forward, topple, and crash from the sill, falling like a miniature comet down the dark side of the tower. While she watched, her nerves tense, an arm was flung wildly out through the window next to her. Another arm. Then the figure of a man was poised there over the sill.

She screamed, but her voice seemed to dissolve without sound into the night air. The figure had jerked forward. She caught one blinding glimpse of Mr. Rowley's pale, distorted profile. His legs and arms were flaying helplessly. Then he too was hurtling downward, downward ...

Carole never quite knew what happened next. Somehow, she found the others, told them of the dreadful thing she had seen. She remembered Peter's face, pale with shock. She remembered thinking, "Peter and I were wrong, then. That slip was in poor Mr. Rowley's pocket because he was the next victim—not the murderer."

They were all back again—a shaken, silent little group—in Peter's office. No one seemed to have spirit enough left to talk.

They had played once more into the murderer's hands. Mr. Rowley was dead. There seemed nothing to do now but to wait—to wait in the safety of light for midnight, and to hope that the watchman would keep to his regular schedule,

After what seemed like hours, Mr. Barber was speaking again, his voice dry but with some semblance of composure. "Surely," he said, "this can't have happened without—without anyone seeing anything. Whoever killed Mr. Rowley had to leave his own window, go down the corridor past the rooms where the others ..."

"Did you notice anything, Mr. Barber?" cut in Marcia Leland quietly.

"I? Well, no. I was attending to my scrap basket and ..."

"Exactly. We all were."

"But I still can't believe it," murmured Miss Gregg shakily. "Just before it happened we'd proved that none of us could be guilty."

Marcia looked up. "We'd only proved that none of us had a motive for wanting to stop the merger, Miss Gregg."

"That seems very much the same to me," said Miles.

"But it isn't." Marcia's voice was slow, deliberate. "We all benefit by the merger, and yet we know one of us has been committing these crimes.

We must have been working on the wrong motive."

"But that memorandum!" exclaimed Miss Gregg. "It said exactly what the motive was."

"Why should we believe what the memorandum says?" asked Marcia. "The murderer's clever. Why couldn't he have deliberately given the wrong motive to put us off the scent?"

"But what other motive could there be?" asked Carole, perplexed.

Peter Howe glanced up, a faint, almost bitter smile on his lips. "In the case of my uncle's death, I suppose I have the most obvious motive. It happens that I was terribly fond of him; he—he had always been like a father to me. But—well, so far as I know, I inherit his estate."

"But that isn't a motive, Peter," cut in Carole quickly. "No one could possibly believe you—you killed your uncle because you're his heir. We—all of us heard Mr. Rowley say that you, and only you, knew he was a dying man."

"Exactly," agreed Marcia Leland. "It's absurd to consider that. Besides, we've got to think of a motive that includes Mr. Whitfield's death, too." Her tranquil eyes stared straight in front of her. "If the merger and the memorandum really were an elaborate blind, it's obvious that the murderer had a reason for killing both Mr. Rowley and Mr. Whitfield. Miss Thorne tells us they had been having private conferences together lately. Mr. Whitfield tried to tell us something just before the lights went out and he was killed. Isn't it possible that they had found out something which had given the murderer a motive for having to kill them both?"

"But you, Miss Leland," cut in Miss Gregg sharply. "You're forgetting you were attacked, too."

"But I wasn't killed. And if he'd really wanted to, the murderer could easily have killed me. He had plenty of time."

"So you think you were attacked to throw us off the scent?" asked Peter.

"I do. If the murderer had wanted to make us believe he was trying to kill off the major stockholders, I was the obvious person to pretend to attack."

Miles gave a low whistle. "Maybe you have got something, Marcia. Mr. Whitfield, Mr. Rowley, and those conferences!" He turned to Carole. "Do you have any idea what they were talking about?"

Carole shook her head. She outlined what she had already told Peter, how she had seen Mr. Whitfield typing a document when she had been called in that afternoon to witness a signature.

"Typing a document!" broke in Miles. "If there's anything in Marcia's theory, those papers would probably have something to do with it. Mr. Whitfield didn't go back to his office before the stockholders' meeting, did he?"

"Why—no."

"Then the documents are probably still in his briefcase."

Miles dashed out of the room, only to return a few seconds later. He was gripping the lawyer's briefcase in his hand. He shrugged. "False alarm. It's empty."

"Empty?" echoed Carole, glancing at him doubtfully. "But—but I know there were important papers in it. Mr. Whitfield forgot it and left it on my desk. He came out of the stockholders' meeting especially to get it."

"He did?" Quick, confused glances were exchanged.

Marcia Leland exclaimed, "Then we are on the right track. Don't you see? Mr. Whitfield and Mr. Rowley must have been killed because of those papers. And the murderer's stolen them."

"Stolen them? But …"

"Of course," exclaimed Peter. "That's what must have given Mr. Whitfield the clue. When we were all discussing the memorandum, I remember now that he was moving the zipper on his briefcase to and fro. He must suddenly have noticed the papers were gone and connected up the theft with the murder threat."

"But what could the papers have been?" exclaimed Miss Gregg.

"Wait a moment," broke in Carole. "Mr. Rowley had a heart attack last week just after you'd been to see him, Mr. Barber. I had a feeling then that something you'd said had given him a shock. What did you talk about?"

Mr. Barber looked rather flustered. "I—er—I merely came around to discuss a certain aspect of the merger."

"What aspect?" demanded Peter.

"As a matter of fact, it concerned the unpatented processes which had been turned over to our company with your patents, trade-marks, and other official documents. Our head chemist was very much excited about certain of them. He asked me to make sure from Mr. Rowley that by the terms of the merger they were to become the property of the Pan-American Dye Combine. Mr. Rowley assured me that they were."

"Unpatented processes?" Peter's face was blank, "But—Shenton is Leland & Rowley's head chemist. He can tell you we didn't have any unpatented processes that were valuable."

Miles nodded. "Howe's right. They weren't worth a damn—any of them."

Mr. Barber looked even more agitated. "I do not understand. Of course, I am no chemist myself. But I was assured that certain processes for the artificial manufacture of aniline derivatives of indigo which Mr.

Leland left at the time of his death, were extremely valuable."

"But—but the notes for those processes were left to Shenton personally," persisted Peter. "And they were worthless."

"That's so," agreed Miles. "Mr. Leland hadn't finished them. They were far too sketchy."

"We must be talking at cross-purposes," spluttered Mr. Barber. "Our head chemist had seen the processes himself. He told me they had been worked out down to the last detail."

Marcia Leland rose, her cheeks flushed.

"I always thought so," she exclaimed. "Just before he died in Florida, Father was working desperately to get his results down on paper. I know Father. He'd never have given in until he'd finished his job." She turned to Miles. "Don't you see what happened? Father *did* complete his experiments. We always thought it was strange he'd left you nothing in his will He'd actually left you the records of his most important and revolutionary work."

"And—?"

"And you received only the few useless notebooks, because someone stole the ones that had the valuable data in them."

Mr. Barber cut in crisply: "They must obviously have been taken by someone in Leland & Rowley's who was financially interested in the merger going through; someone who knew the firm was losing ground; who knew our company would never consent to a favorable merger unless we were offered those particular processes as an additional inducement. He not only cheated Mr. Shenton. He also cheated Pan-American. He persuaded us into this merger under false pretenses."

"That makes sense," added Peter slowly. "Uncle must have realized something was wrong after Mr. Barber had brought up the subject of the unpatented processes on Christmas Eve."

"And that's why he called me that same day and asked to see the notebooks I had down at the lab," added Miles. "He figured out what had happened. He discussed it with Mr. Whitfield—"

"And that was why they were murdered," broke in Miss Gregg her face creased with dawning understanding. "Because they were the only ones who knew there'd been a fraud."

Since Marcia's initial suggestion, developments had followed one another so quickly that they were all left breathless. Peter was the first to speak again:

"But, if my uncle knew about the theft of the processes, why didn't he realize they were the real motive behind the murder threat? Why didn't he tell us we were on the wrong track as soon as Mr. Whitfield was killed?"

"Probably because the murderer had gone to a great deal of trouble to fool him," explained Marcia. "Perhaps that was the real reason why I was attacked, why the murderer used that theatrical device of the calendar slips. It was partly to confuse all of us, but mostly to throw Mr. Rowley off the scent."

"But where does that get us?" Miles lit a cigarette a trifle too jauntily. "Presumably, it eliminates me. I would hardly have stolen processes which were legally my own. But, so far as I can see, any one of you could have taken them when Mr. Rowley brought them back from Florida."

"But how could an unscientific layman have realized the value of the processes?" asked Mr. Barber.

"Anyone who knew Mr. Leland could have made a shrewd guess that they'd be commercially profitable." Miles looked from one face to the other. "I wonder which of you did pull that particularly dirty trick on me." He glanced at the treasurer. "It would have taken a keen financial mind like Miss Gregg's to realize how those processes would increase the value of her stock holdings." His eyes moved to Marcia. "Or an earnest young physicist who wanted money for pure, noncommercial research. Or"—his ironic gaze rested on Peter—"a farsighted and ambitious young executive like Howe. One might build up a very good case against Miss Thorne, too, who, as Mr. Rowley's secretary, had easiest access to the papers and who, as the prospective wife of one of the people financially involved, had a motive." He was looking at Mr. Barber now. "The case against you, Mr. Barber, is obvious. Those processes are going to make you and your company even more famous and prosperous."

"Supposing we stick to facts," snapped Mr. Barber. He turned to Carole. "That paper you say you saw Mr. Whitfield typing—is there any way we could find out what was in it?"

Carole looked up quickly. "There's just a chance. I rather think Mr. Whitfield was using a carbon. If so, the copy may be in Mr. Rowley's private safe. The murderer couldn't have taken it, too, because I'm the only person who knows the combination."

Peter rose. "Come on, Carole. Barber and I will go with you and have a look."

Carole followed the two men to the door, and together they hurried through the main office back to Mr. Rowley's room. Carole's fingers were trembling as she spun the handle of the safe. If there were any papers inside, she knew they would be the ones they were searching for. All Mr. Rowley's private documents had been removed the day before.

The door swung open. Peter's flickering match gleamed on a single sheet of paper. "Looks as though you're right, Carole." He took the paper out, and the three of them hurried back to the others.

The room was absolutely quiet as Peter crossed to the window and stood there, bending over the document. At length he looked up, his eyes very grave.

"Well," asked Mr. Barber, "what is it?"

"I'll let you see it for yourself in a moment." Peter's voice was dangerously quiet. "For the time being, I'd rather not name names—because I think this paper explains who took the processes and exactly who is responsible for what has been happening tonight." His level gaze moved around the little group. "We were right. The motive did lie in those discoveries of Mr. Leland's. Someone did turn them over to Pan-American Dye to insure our getting good terms on the merger. I believe I can guess who that person was."

"You mean …?" breathed Carole.

Peter glanced at her almost apologetically. "I hate even to have to think this. But I believe my uncle was the man who took those processes."

"Mr. Rowley?"

"And I think I can understand the way he would have felt. Ever since Mr. Leland's death, the company had been slipping. Uncle realized that. He would also have realized that there was only one way by which he could possibly save the interests of the stockholders. That was by exploiting those processes. I won't try to justify him. But I do see what a great temptation it would have been."

His words were followed by a flat silence. At length Marcia said, "Do you mean that paper is a confession? Surely, Mr. Rowley couldn't possibly have killed Mr. Whitfield and then committed suicide."

"Of course not. My uncle wasn't a murderer." Peter tapped the paper in his hand. "But this document gives us a clue which would explain the murder both of Mr. Whitfield and my uncle. Suppose someone found out what Uncle had done and planned to blackmail him. Suppose that person went to Uncle, told him that he would expose him if he didn't change his will and leave all his property to him. Uncle was in a very nervous, overstrained condition. It would have been easy to scare him. Suppose he did agree to change his will in favor of this extortionist and brought Mr. Whitfield in to draw it up." The others were listening now with rapt attention.

"Suppose, then, that this person was satisfied that Uncle had changed his will. He would have known that it was very unlikely that Uncle would have let the will stand that way indefinitely. If he was going to get Uncle's money, he would have to act quickly—and kill him before he changed his mind. He realized he had a perfect opportunity to shield his real motive behind the merger. He wrote that crazy note; he got us here, planning to kill Uncle and throw us off the scent. But Mr. Whitfield, as Uncle's lawyer, knew about the will. Tonight he guessed about the blackmail." Peter shrugged. "He had to be killed, too."

"But are you actually accusing someone?" cut in Mr. Barber.

"I am. I'm accusing the person who is named in this document." Very slowly, Peter crossed and handed Mr. Barber the paper they had found in the safe. "Perhaps you'd like to read it out," he said.

The representative of Pan-American Dye bent over the document. When he looked up, his expression was very stern. "This," he said, "is the copy of a short will drawn up this afternoon in which Mr. Rowley bequeaths his entire estate to one person." He paused a moment and then continued, "To a person who is in no way connected with him either by blood or by sentiment."

His bushy-browed eyes fixed on Miles. "Mr. Shenton, I presume you know that you are Mr. Rowley's sole heir."

The others turned sharply to Miles, was lounging back on the couch.

"No," he murmured. "I wasn't aware of it. But I'm grateful for the information. I'm also grateful for Mr. Howe's implied information that I'm both a blackmailer and a murderer." His eyes moved with sardonic hostility to Peter. "But I'm rather confused on one point, Howe. Since those processes were legally my own—why wouldn't it have been simpler for me to take legal steps to recover them from your uncle instead of descending to extortion and—extermination?"

Peter moved, so that he stood in front of the other man. "Just because you didn't find out what had happened until after the processes had been shown to the Pan-American chemists. You were shrewd enough to realize that, since they were unpatented, their value to you was considerably lessened."

"Ingenious and rather ingenuous," drawled Miles, rising to his feet. "But not so ingenuous as you're trying to make me out to be. Perhaps you can explain why I should have gone to the risk and trouble of murdering your uncle for my inheritance—when I only had to wait three months for it."

"For all you knew, you might have had to wait for years." Peter's voice was ominously low. "Everyone in this room heard Uncle say that no one except myself knew he was a dying man."

In the silence that followed, Carole stared at the two men: Peter, large, unshaken, and unshakable; Miles, lithe and studiedly casual. She was struggling with the confused speculations that swirled in her brain. Then, suddenly, one single thought emerged from the confusion to banish all others—a thought more horrible than any of the ghastly events of the evening. What a fool she had been! All the time she had really had the clue …

Before she had realized what she was doing, she had risen to her feet. "Wait a moment, Peter. You've got to let me say something." She moistened her lips. "It—it sounds crazy to bring my own private life into this, but I see now that it's all linked up with what's been going on. Tonight"—her voice sounded very remote—"two men asked me to marry them. I'm afraid I was conceited enough to think both of them had been overwhelmed by my brains or my beauty, or both. But I was wrong. One of them, I believe, was quite sincere. At least, I—I hope so. But the other—the other asked me to marry him because he's afraid of me."

"Carole …" broke in Miles, but she did not seem to hear.

"One of those men," she went on, "did arrange this trap; he did write that mad memorandum to throw us off the scent because he wanted to kill Mr. Rowley and Mr. Whitfield—the two people who knew about the stolen processes. But there was someone else who had to be reckoned with: Mr. Rowley's private secretary."

Her fingers gripped tightly to the back of her chair. "How could he be sure she hadn't overheard something damning during those conferences? How could he be sure she wouldn't gradually put two and two together?"

She laughed rather bitterly. "Being a gallant gentleman, he didn't actually murder her. He made love to her, presumably on the theory that her dumb head would be so turned that she wouldn't know whether she was coming or going—let alone give any thought as to whether the wonder man might be a double murderer. He was so gallant that he was even prepared to marry her to keep her mouth shut."

Her eyes flashed sparks of amber as she gazed from Peter to Miles. "The funny part of it is, he needn't have bothered to try and fool me. I didn't know anything about the stolen processes or the new will; I was utterly harmless. But I'm not so harmless now. And I'm going to be perfectly shameless, too, I'm going to trot out something that all girls have to trot out at some stage of their careers—feminine intuition. Both those men kissed me tonight, and my feminine intuition's just getting around to realizing which of them kissed me because he meant it."

She broke off, looking rather wildly at the tense faces in front of her. "And I've got something more tangible than kisses and intuition to offer. We know the murderer, my prospective husband, stole those documents from Mr. Whitfield's briefcase. Well, he thinks he's destroyed them. He was very smart, he stuffed them in with the rest of the paper in my scrap basket and took it for granted I'd burn them.

"But I'm a very poor fireman. I let my fire go out and I noticed my signature there—on a document. That was the paper I was called into Mr. Rowley's office this afternoon to sign."

There was a crooked smile on her lips. "I rather think," she said, "that we'll find what we want in that scrap basket."

Impulsively she turned and ran out into the darkened main office. She could hear exclamations, shouts from the others. Vaguely she was aware of hurrying footsteps, following her. But she was blind to all thoughts of her own danger now, carried away by a burning indignation against the man who had made a fool of her. She hurried on, stumbling against desks and chairs. At last she reached the window. Swiftly she snatched up the scrap basket and slammed down the sash.

As she did so, she felt herself gripped from behind. She spun around, dropping the basket, and started to struggle, beating with her fists at the face of her invisible assailant. But the steel strength of the arms around her relentlessly pushed her backward—back against the closed window.

She tried to scream, but a stifling hand was pressed over her mouth. There was a mocking tinkle of glass; a gust of snowy air rushed in through the broken pane. Although she fought desperately to keep her balance, she felt her feet losing hold of the floor. She was being lifted ... Oh, God, any second now, she too would be hurtling downward, falling, as she had seen Mr. Rowley fall.

And then, suddenly, miraculously, the viselike grip loosened. She felt herself being jerked forward away from the window. As she staggered against a desk for support, she realized that another shadow had loomed out of the darkness just in time to save her. Ahead of her, there in the obscurity, two men were fighting—fighting savagely.

Everything began to blur. She heard the dull impact of a blow, a little cry, and a heavy thud as one of the men stumbled to the floor. That was the last thing she knew before she lost consciousness.

When she came to, Carole was lying on the couch in the lighted office. She turned her head. A man was bending over her.

"Nothing serious, darling," he was saying softly. "Only a cute little cut here and there where your gentleman friend tried to throw you out of the window with the scrap basket."

"But what ...?"

"It's all over now." The mockery in Miles Shenton's eyes had changed to tenderness. He sat down on the edge of the couch, his fingers slipping over hers. "Quite a close shave, Carole. He knew you'd figured out the solution and he knew the game would be up if we found those papers from Mr. Whitfield's briefcase which he had so ingenuously hidden in your scrap basket. I think he was just about desperate enough to have thrown you out of the window. But luckily my unpredictable left hook was in form."

"But where—where is he?"

"Out very cold at the moment. He hit his head on a desk."

Painfully Carole pushed herself up against the cushions. She looked around her. Marcia Leland and Miss Gregg were standing together by the desk, gazing solemnly down, while Mr. Barber, with pieces of stout cord, trussed the unconscious figure of Peter Howe.

"You were one hundred percent right," Miles was saying. "We've got all the evidence the police'll need from the papers in the scrap basket. One was the signed copy of Mr. Rowley's new will, rather charred but quite legal. The other was a personal note to me explaining exactly what kind of a skunk his nephew is."

Carole was still staring down in fascinated horror at the man who had just done his best to kill her.

"So—so it was Peter himself who stole those processes when he and Mr. Rowley went down to Florida."

"Exactly. And it was Howe who showed them to the chemist at Pan-American and made sure the merger would involve a fat job for himself. Mr. Rowley knew nothing about it until Mr. Barber came around, in all innocence, the day before Christmas to talk about the unpatented processes. Rowley realized then what had happened. But Pan-American had already seen the processes, and the damage was done. I imagine he'd have exposed Howe if he hadn't known he was, himself, a dying man. That gave him the opportunity to make amends to me without having to drag the family name in the mud. This afternoon he made that new will cutting Peter out in my favor—the will you and Mr. Whitfield witnessed."

"It's easy to see why Howe arranged this elaborate exit-before-midnight party," Miles went on. "He found out about the new will and realized Mr. Whitfield wouldn't be going back to his own office before the stockholders' meeting. If he could destroy the new will and murder his uncle and the lawyer before anyone else knew about the will, the old one in his favor would still be valid. He'd also have killed off the only two people who knew he was a thief."

"And the stockholders' meeting gave him the ideal opportunity."

"Of course. We all knew he had everything to gain by the merger. But his uncle knew he was a thief; that's why he had to build up such an elaborate bluff. The attack on Marcia, the calendar slips, were used as false trails to throw Mr. Rowley off the scent and fool him into believing there really was an imaginary bogeyman who was determined to stop the merger. At first he probably hoped we would think it was all being done by some crazy maniac who kept coming in and out of the fire tower door. But my burglar alarm spoiled that and he had to change his tactics. Which he did admirably. He was the first to point out that the murderer was one of us. And he took care to lead the investigation, so that his fingerprints on the knife wouldn't be suspicious."

"It was incredibly clever," said Carole.

"Horribly. And I really believe he'd have gotten away with it if there hadn't been a carbon copy of the will in the safe, where he couldn't get at it and—if you'd been a better stoker."

"If my feminine intuition hadn't been dampened by Christmas Eve," murmured Carole, "he wouldn't have gotten away with as much as he did. I should have realized he was putting that calendar slip into his uncle's pocket instead of taking it out. I should have guessed when he kissed me that he was less interested in me than in finding out just how much I knew. If you hadn't broken in on us, I expect he'd have persuaded me into opening Mr. Rowley's safe for him."

Her nose crinkled delightfully. "The whole thing only seeped through my thick skull when he accused Mr. Rowley of stealing the processes and tried to get too smart by turning that will into a case against you. I guess he was desperate by then."

Miles leaned over and kissed her hair, "Darling, I'll never forget how gorgeous you looked when you went into that denunciation. A blond fury. But I wasn't listening to a word you said—not after you'd hinted that one of your two prospective husbands wasn't repulsive to you. Carole, did you really mean that?"

She glanced up at him, her eyes smiling. "Dimwit," she said.

"I seem to be quitting the old year in style." Miles's lips moved ironically. "Despite battle and murder, I rake off an inheritance and the heroine of the hour."

The others were moving over to their side now.

Mr. Barber gazed down at her, his face grave and worried. "I'm glad to see you are all right again, Miss Thorne. This is terrible—terrible. But there is no question about Howe's guilt. I am sure, too, that he hoodwinked our chemist at Pan-American. I know he would never have been party to a fraud." The bushy-browed eyes turned to Miles. "Well, Mr. Shenton, we always have a vacancy at Pan-American for a man of your caliber."

"No, Mr. Barber," broke in Marcia's soft voice. "Mr. Shenton has promised to work with me, and you're not going to lure him away." There was a twinkle in her clear green eyes as she turned to Carole. "I warn you, Miss Thorne, I'm going to get all the work out of him I can—and as much of his money as possible for the Leland Institute."

Miles groaned. "So I'm going to be a meal ticket for two unscrupulous women."

Marcia glanced at her watch. "Almost midnight. Any second now the merger will go through—and the New Year begins."

As she spoke, there was a faint sound—a sound coming from somewhere outside in the darkness of the main office.

"It's somebody singing," exclaimed Miss Gregg weakly.

They could hear it louder now—a male voice raised in alcoholic melody.

"*'Sweet Adeline'!*" cried Miles. "The night watchman—God bless him!"

They all dashed out into the main office, ran to the door to the fire stairs and started to bang wildly. There was no mistaking it now. The singing drew nearer. Within a few seconds they would be free.

And then, as they stood there, another sound joined in the chorus of Sweet Adeline. From forty floors below in the streets of New York, came a distant throbbing, the blaring of myriad car horns and toy trumpets, welcoming in the New Year. Somewhere a clock boomed out the opening chime of midnight.

With one hand Miles was beating on the door. The other arm was around Carole's waist. Very gently, his lips met hers. "Happy New Year, darling," he whispered. "After all this, we deserve it."

The End

ANOTHER MAN'S POISON
By Q. Patrick

Tension was growing in the large operating theater of the College Hospital. Rona Heath sensed it as a definite, almost palpable presence. It was in the expectant immobility of the medical students waiting in the raised gallery above her; it was in the curiously strained stance of Dr. Oliver Lord, the young intern, as he stood, shrouded in mask and gown, by the instrument table.

And it was in Rona, too—a tension and a vague feeling that something was wrong.

Everything in the theater was ready, and Dr. Knudsen should be here. It was quite a long time since she had heard the chief surgeon go into his private office beyond the scrub room, where it was his habit to snatch his frugal lunch before the afternoon work. But now the theater clock showed twenty minutes past two, and he had not even come out to start sterilizing his hands.

Never before, during many months of service as his chosen operating room nurse, had Rona known Dr. Knudsen late for a case—and this emergency abdominal case was serious.

Voices and a faint moan sounded from the anesthetizing room to the left of the scrub room. A grayish, unobtrusive man appeared in the doorway, followed by a white-coated orderly.

"We've just brought the patient up, Dr. Lord." Gregory Venner, Dr. Knudsen's anesthetist of twenty years' standing, looked worried. "He's having considerable pain. Oughtn't I to start putting him under right away?"

"Better wait. There's not a peep out of the Chief yet. Can't imagine what's keeping him." Oliver Lord's blue eyes, turning to Rona, showed unmistakable anxiety. "Go get him, Rona. Say it's rush or—rupture."

Obediently Rona hurried toward the scrub room door. She had been worried about the Chief all day. Throughout the morning operating session, he had been as impersonal and efficient as usual. But, from the tiny creases around his eyes and his almost hostile taciturnity with Venner and Lord, she had judged that something was wrong.

As she crossed the white tiles of the scrub room floor toward the door of Dr. Knudsen's private office, a woman's voice sounded from inside the room. That was odd, too. The Chief followed a strict routine, and it was unheard of for him to allow any visitor to interrupt his brief lunch hour seclusion.

Near the door Rona started at the words she heard: "Of course, it's blackmail, Thegn...."

She recognized that hard, assertive voice. It belonged to Caroline Broderick, the Chief's immensely wealthy sister, who had recently made a second marriage with the director of the hospital and had become its most influential nuisance.

The voice sounded again with almost savage vehemence: "But you wouldn't understand! You, with your cold-blooded ideals, wouldn't realize that I'd far rather be blackmailed than have anything interfere with Linette's happiness!"

Rona had knocked, but there was no reply. Not wishing to eavesdrop, she pushed open the door. But, as she stood on the threshold, no one paid any attention to her The chief surgeon, lean and ascetic, was sitting behind his desk. Opposite him stood Caroline Broderick, handsome, smart, and almost too youthfully streamlined,

"It's my problem, not yours, Thegn. You've got to keep out of it."

Dr. Knudsen rose to his feet. "But you have made it my problem now, Caroline," he said, with slow deliberation. "I have made an agreement, and I shall not go back on my word. You must do as you wish about the grant; you know my point of view regarding it. But I shall most certainly see that this entire matter is exposed at the Board Meeting this afternoon and that all moneys are returned to you."

As Rona moved forward, both he and Mrs. Broderick turned sharply to face her.

"Ah, yes, Miss Heath. The operation." The Chief's voice was clipped. "I will be with you as soon as I have sterilized. Tell them they can start anesthesia immediately."

"But, Thegn ...!" insisted Mrs. Broderick.

"I am sorry, my dear. There is nothing more to say." Dr. Knudsen's shrug was final. "As it is, you have made me late for an important operation. You have also made me miss my lunch."

As Rona hurried out of the room, she caught a last glimpse of the chief surgeon. He had picked up the coffee cup from the tray of lunch in front of him and was lifting it impassively to his lips.

Rona had no time to dwell upon the implications of that remarkable scene. She had just delivered the Chief's instructions to Venner and started to re-sterilize, when Dr. Knudsen came into the scrub room and took the basin next to hers. Before he began the routine process of washing his hands, she noticed that he was nibbling at a lump of sugar. She had seen him do that on several other occasions, and he had explained that sugar was the best source of quick energy, especially in any emergency which caused one to miss a meal.

That afternoon, as he tossed the remains of the lump into the container for soiled linen and plunged his hands into the soapy water, he made no attempt to talk. He was still silent later when Rona helped him into his sterile gown and tied on his mask. Feeling vaguely uneasy, she preceded him into the operating room.

The patient had been wheeled in. Dr. Oliver Lord, his red head bent over the prostrate form, was preparing the abdominal field. At the end of the table, Gregory Venner was taking a blood pressure reading with his usual fussy precision.

As always before an important operation, an expectant silence filled the large theater, stretching up to the cluster of students in the gallery. When Dr. Knudsen appeared, all attention focused on his thin, white-gowned figure as it moved toward the table.

Only his eyes and forehead were visible above the gauze mask. But, with a twinge of anxiety, Rona noticed that the skin of his temples had turned a grayish white.

The Chief had taken his place by the table and was nodding to her. Immediately she handed him a scalpel. For a second Dr. Knudsen stood in silence, carefully scrutinizing the field of operation. Then, with a caution that was almost too meticulous, he made the initial incision, cutting through the outer layer of epidermis.

Dr. Lord hovered by the table, ready with the artery clamp. Rona held out a sterile sponge on long forceps. Her eyes, trained to watch every movement of the surgeon's hands, were intent on the knife, which should now be probing deeper into the wound.

But it was not. It had been withdrawn, and hung uncertainly poised in Dr. Knudsen's fingers. Rona's startled gaze traveled upward to the surgeon's face. He was staring fixedly in front of him with a dull, almost vacant look.

"Dr. Knudsen, you're not well. You—"

She took an instinctive step toward him. But, as she did so, the surgeon lurched backward with a little groan. The scalpel fell from his hand.

"Look out!" A sharp voice rang from the spectators' gallery above. "He's fainting."

Gregory Venner moved swiftly from the end of the table, but before the anesthetist reached him, Dr. Knudsen staggered away, one rubber-gloved hand clenched against his heart.

"Lord—you—carry—on." His voice came jerkily through the gauze mask. For a moment he stood motionless, keeping himself steady with an obvious effort. Then, suddenly, he fell, his thin, white-robed figure sprawling grotesquely at the side of the operating table.

Some of the medical students had started to clatter down from the gallery. Rona felt a moment of blind panic. But Oliver Lord's incisive voice steadied her: "Miss Heath—Venner. Don't touch him. You've got to keep sterile—got to go on with the operation immediately. Do you want the patient to bleed to death?"

Two students had run up to Dr. Knudsen and were lifting him from the floor. Lord rapped, "Take him into his office. Get Dr. Broderick—anyone." The young intern picked up a fresh scalpel. "Miss Heath, another sponge. Quick!"

Rona obeyed. But, as she did so, she could not keep her eyes from moving to the door of the scrub room, through which the students were carrying Dr. Knudsen. The chief surgeon's body was sagging and limp—almost like a dead man's....

Rona forced herself to concentrate on her duties as Dr. Oliver Lord continued with the operation. It was an extremely difficult case and one that normally would not have been entrusted to a relatively inexperienced intern. This was going to be an acid test for Oliver Lord, she realized, and he would need every ounce of cooperation from his assistants.

The long, careful minutes of the operation ticked by. Thirty ... forty ... fifty.... Rona knew enough to realize that Oliver Lord was doing an extremely dramatic and efficient job.... At last the final sutures were in place. The intern gestured, and the patient was wheeled away.

Oliver looked exhausted, but his eyes beneath the thick red hair showed a certain grim satisfaction. "Well, I always wanted a cholecystectomy, but I didn't want it wished on me quite as suddenly as all this." As Rona untied his gauze mask and he peeled off his rubber gloves, he grunted, "Hope nothing's badly wrong with the Chief."

The two of them moved toward the scrub room, but Gregory Venner pushed ahead of them, his face creased with concern. They saw him disappear into the Chief's office, and then come hurrying back.

"He—he isn't there, Dr. Lord!" he faltered. "They've taken him away. It must be serious."

Gregory Venner, Rona knew, centered his entire life around his devotion to the Chief and made the ideal stooge for the aloof, arrogant Knudsen, who gave intimacy to no one and who accepted the anesthetist's unquestioning loyalty as his right. For twenty years the two bachelors had spent their vacations together, mountain climbing in various parts of the States, and the anesthetist's chief pride lay in the fact that it was Knudsen and not himself who had won a reputation as one of the country's most expert climbers. Venner, himself, had always modestly avoided the limelight, even on the much-publicized occasion five years before when the iron man, Knudsen, had collapsed high up the flank of a remote peak and the little anesthetist had trekked miles to procure the medical aid which had arrived just in time to save the Chief's life.

"What can have happened?"

Venner broke off as the heavy double doors of the theater swung open and Dr. Broderick came in, accompanied by Dr. Hugh Ellsworth, the young head of the Neurological Clinic, where Rona had worked before she had switched to the surgical side. With a quickening of concern she watched the two men move toward them. Hugh Ellsworth looked very grave; Dr. Broderick's handsome, rather florid face wore the expression of someone bringing serious news.

The Director did not speak, however, until a gesture of his hand had banished the few remaining medical students from the spectators' gallery. When the door above had flapped shut for the last time, his portentous gaze moved from Rona to Gregory Venner, resting finally on Oliver Lord.

"I'm afraid I have a very tragic announcement to make," he said. "Dr. Knudsen is dead."

"Dead!" The word came bleakly from Gregory Venner. "Dr. Knudsen dead! It's—it's not possible."

It did not seem possible to Rona, either. The Chief had taken an almost fanatical pride in his iron constitution.

And now he was dead.

The Director was saying, "He died in his office almost before I reached him. Ellsworth and I had just arrived at the hospital from lunch and were able to go to him almost immediately. But there was nothing we could do."

"But what was it?" Oliver Lord's voice was incredulous. "A heart attack?"

Dr. Broderick hesitated. Then, giving each word careful emphasis, he said, "It is too early yet to be certain, but both Ellsworth and I are of the opinion that my brother-in-law died from acute poisoning through an overdose of some drug such as atropine, or more probably hyoscine. It must have been ingested very shortly before his collapse."

"Hyoscine! But why the hell should he have been taking hyoscine?" Oliver stared blankly. "He wasn't ill, was he, sir?"

"Not that I know of, Dr. Lord. My brother-in-law was very—ah—

uncommunicative. Especially so on personal matters. As for drugs"—Dr. Broderick shrugged—"you know his reputation. He hardly ever prescribed internal medication and was most unlikely to use it himself."

"In any case, he'd never have taken an overdose of a dangerous drug like hyoscine by mistake. It's absurd." Oliver's lips had gone very pale. "You're not implying he committed suicide?"

The Director shot him a rather pained glance. "There was no conceivable reason for his wishing to kill himself. Even if there had been, he would not have taken poison while faced with the responsibility of performing a major operation."

"It wasn't an accident! It wasn't suicide!" Gregory Venner's voice trembled. "You don't—you can't be trying to tell us that someone poisoned Knudsen?"

Dr. Broderick replied heavily, "Under the circumstances it seems extremely probable that Dr. Knudsen has been deliberately murdered."

"Murdered!"

Oliver Lord and Venner were watching the Director in stunned silence. Rona felt as if the whole world had suddenly gone mad. A great surgeon murdered in a great life-saving institution. Things like that just did not happen.

And yet Dr. Broderick was discussing it as an established fact. He was saying, "A terrible thing for us all, for my poor wife, and for the hospital, Newspaper publicity ... questions ... the police."

The police! Rona could think more clearly now, and her thoughts turned instantly to her brother on the police force. Jim Heath, as lieutenant in the Homicide Division, was known and respected around the hospital. She said, "Dr. Broderick, Lieutenant Heath, of the Homicide Bureau, is my brother. If you could get him to investigate this, I know he'd be as considerate as possible."

"A brother on the force, you say?" The Director's smooth face registered interest and relief. "That may prove most fortunate." He whispered a few words to Ellsworth, and then said, "Miss Heath, will you be so kind as to ask your brother to come around immediately?"

Feeling rather dazed, Rona went to the telephone and called Headquarters. Jim's voice over the wire sounded strangely unfamiliar, clipped and official. He would be around at once, he said.

The prospect of the police's imminent arrival seemed to spur the Director into flustered activity. "The—ah—poison was probably administered in Knudsen's office. You, Ellsworth, and you, Miss Heath, I can rely on you to see that the room is locked up immediately." He turned to Oliver Lord. "Dr. Lord, were any other operations scheduled for today?"

"No, sir. Dr. Knudsen had put off all except emergency cases until tomorrow. He told me there was a very important directors' meeting this afternoon."

"Ah, yes. The meeting. It will have to be postponed, of course." Dr. Broderick turned to Gregory Venner: "Venner, go and tell my secretary to make the necessary arrangements and explanations.... Dr. Lord, you had better come with me, to be there when the lieutenant arrives."

In a few seconds Rona and Hugh Ellsworth were left alone in the operating theater. For Rona there was a certain embarrassment about being alone with Dr. Ellsworth in those first confused moments. The year before, when she had worked for him in the Neurological Clinic, she had developed a strong admiration for this dark, attractive young man, with his uncanny insight into the human mind and his fierce absorption in his work. Her association with him had been exciting—too exciting, in fact.

That had been one of the main reasons why she had applied for a transfer to surgery and the secure dullness of Dr. Knudsen. She was far too levelheaded a girl to let herself do anything so futureless as fall in love with a young man for whom women were either problems in psychiatry or impersonal automatons to promote the efficiency of the clinic.

"This isn't so good, is it, Rona?" Hugh Ellsworth's dark eyes met hers with grave sympathy.

"It's incredible. Do you really think it was murder?"

"Hard to see any alternative."

"But Dr. Knudsen, of all people! He was so conscientious, so unselfseeking. It's fantastic to think he had any enemies."

"Sometimes you can be too conscientious and too unself-seeking for your own safety." Ellsworth's voice was thoughtful. "Knudsen was a fighter for his ideals. He would willingly have sacrificed himself for them. He wouldn't have hesitated to sacrifice anyone else, either." His lips had gone rather tight. "It's not hard for me to see how he might have had enemies."

He was right, of course. Dr. Knudsen's stubborn code of ethics had often antagonized Dr. Broderick and the other more practical members of the staff.

Suddenly, for the first time since Dr. Knudsen's collapse, there came flooding back to Rona memories of the extraordinary conversation she had overheard in the Chief's office. While she was trying to make up her mind whether she should tell Hugh Ellsworth about it, his quiet voice broke through her thoughts:

"Well, Rona, we're supposed to see that the doctor's office is locked up."

Together they moved through the scrub room into Dr. Knudsen's private office. It was sparsely furnished with the desk, a glass-fronted drug cabinet, a closet where the Chief had kept the white coats which he wore when making his hospital rounds. At the far end a second door led to the main corridor.

"That door was always locked on the outside," Rona explained. "Dr. Knudsen was the only person who had a key."

"So no one except Knudsen could get in here without coming through the anesthetizing room or the scrub room first?"

Rona nodded. "And the key to the door from the scrub room's on a shelf of the drug cabinet. Dr. Knudsen kept it there where I could get it to lock up after work in the theater finished for the day. The cabinet's always locked. But I keep an extra key."

They crossed to the small drug cabinet and Rona unlocked it. As Ellsworth picked up the door key which lay on the bottom shelf, Rona glanced swiftly through the drugs, wondering if there might be some sign of the poison which had killed the Chief. But the supplies all ranged neatly in order told her nothing. Dr. Knudsen had kept there only drugs that might be needed in an emergency during operations. On the shelves in their customary places were the rolls of adhesive, bandages, three hypodermic syringes, a stethoscope, iodine, adrenalin, morphine tablets, a package of insulin ampules, alcohol, and digitalis.

Rona locked the cabinet and they both turned to the desk. The tray of lunch still lay there in front of Dr. Knudsen's empty chair.

"Looks as if he didn't eat anything," said Ellsworth quietly. "But he must have drunk some of the coffee."

With sudden vividness Rona remembered the last glimpse she had caught of Dr. Knudsen in his office, standing with the coffee cup raised to his lips. "Yes, he did." Shakily she added, "You don't suppose the coffee could have been pois—?"

"That's something for your brother to find out." Hugh Ellsworth's mouth was grim "I'll see he gets it down to Peters for analysis right away."

For a moment they stood there in silence, staring at the half-empty coffee cup. Then they moved out into the scrub room, Hugh Ellsworth locking the door after them.

"Your brother's probably here by now," he said. "I should get down to Broderick's office. Are you coming?"

"I think I'd better wait till I'm called for. It's one of my jobs to keep the operating room ready for any emergency case that may come in. You never know when it'll be needed." Rona gave a little shiver. "It's pretty awful having to work in there, now the Chief's dead. But I guess hospital routine must go on."

Hugh Ellsworth watched her for a second with faintly amused admiration. Impulsively he took her hand and squeezed it. "That's the kid. You're not going to let this get you down, are you?"

In spite of herself Rona was very conscious of the warm strength of his fingers. It was rather frightening to find that she could still feel the old excitement at being with him. She said awkwardly, "I can bear up, all right. It's no worse for me than the rest of you."

The young doctor's smile came and went suddenly. "I always thought you were the spunkiest as well as the prettiest nurse in the hospital, Rona. Now I'm sure of it."

Before she could speak, he left her.

It was cold and cheerless in the empty operating theater. The daylight was fading quickly. Rona switched on the heavy arc light above the table, drew up a high stool, and mechanically started her work, cleaning the instruments and slipping them into the sterilizer. The minutes seemed interminable as they limped by in the great, silent room. At one stage she heard voices from Dr. Knudsen's office. Some of her brother's men probably, sent up on Hugh Ellsworth's advice to take away the lunch tray for analysis.

Her mind, clear again now, reverted to the half-overheard quarrel she had interrupted between the Chief and Caroline Broderick. She struggled to remember the exact words that the Chief's sister had used: *... Of course, it's blackmail ... but I'd rather be blackmailed than have anything interfere with Linette's happiness....* And later Dr. Knudsen had said: *You've made it my problem now.... I shall see that the whole matter is exposed and that all moneys are returned to you....*

Could that be the explanation? Could someone actually have been extorting money from Mrs. Broderick? And, if so, had that person found out that Dr. Knudsen was planning to expose him at the Board Meeting that afternoon? Found out and murdered him?

Mrs. Broderick, who had inherited a huge fortune from her first husband's patent-medicine business, was, of course, a lucrative subject for any kind of extortion. But to Rona, the Chief's sister, with her social ambitions and her hardboiled determination to obtain a blue-blooded husband for her daughter, had always seemed far too close-fisted to allow herself to be victimized.

And yet ... *Linette's happiness ...*

If there was one weak spot in Caroline Broderick's hard, social armor it was her devotion to the beautiful and talented daughter of her first marriage, Linette Clint. Rona had learned that only a short time ago, when she had acted as nurse for Linette after the girl had undergone a minor operation. During Linette's convalescence in the hospital, Caroline Broderick had been an institutional menace, with her almost hourly visits and her constant complaints that her daughter was not getting the attention she rated.

Yes, if Linette's happiness were at stake it was perfectly credible that Mrs. Broderick would go to any length to try and save it.

But blackmail ... Linette ... how were they tied up with the other thing Dr. Knudsen had mentioned—that he would *express his point of view* to the directors about Mrs. Broderick's grant?

What grant?

She was trying to piece it all together as, her fingers working with efficiency, she sat in the operating theater, alone.

Suddenly the double doors were thrown open, and Oliver Lord strode across the threshold. His face was dead-white under the fiery red mat of his hair. "I thought surgeons, anesthetists, and nurses were supposed to be angels of mercy," he said bitterly. "Apparently one of us three is an angel of death."

Ever since she had first known him as a redheaded kid of an intern who had tried in a rather clumsy way to rush her, Oliver Lord had overdramatized everything. But Rona had never before seen him look so shaken.

"What are you talking about, Oliver? Which three of us?"

"All three of us. You and Venner and me, of course. They've traced Knudsen's lunch tray and that darn coffee cup from the diet kitchen. It was sent up on the dumbwaiter direct to Knudsen's office, and it arrived just before he went back there after his morning rounds. The outside door was locked. The only way anyone could have gotten at it was through the theater or the anesthetizing room; and the only people who would have done that were you and me and, I guess, Venner."

"Then the coffee on the lunch tray was poisoned?"

"Poisoned!" He snorted. "Peters, in the analytical department, gave a couple of drops to a rat and it died within two minutes. Typical atropine-hyoscine reactions."

"And they really think one of us three must have done it?"

"What else can they think?—unless one of the dietitians went haywire and whipped up a little coffee-and-hyoscine cocktail."

Oliver Lord swung himself onto a stool, running agitated fingers through his hair. "Knudsen must have drunk the coffee just before he went in to scrub. Couldn't have taken it earlier, or he'd have died before he'd got through sterilizing." He twisted around to face Rona. "That policeman brother of yours is damn polite and cagey, but I could tell all the time he half suspected me. Suspected me! As if I would have killed the Chief!" He got up and started pacing back and forth across the tiles of the floor. "You know how I felt about Knudsen, Rona. He was swell to me, picked me out of a dozen of us to be his assistant, gave me every break. It's hellish funny I've got to be the one suspected of murdering him."

Trying to keep calm, Rona said, "I don't suppose you're suspected any more than Venner or I, are you?"

"You!" he echoed. "Lieutenant Heath's hardly going to suspect his own kid sister. And, as for Venner, everyone knows he's just a dried-up old dodo who's worshiped Knudsen for twenty-odd years. Venner, with his anesthesia and his fussy little side job of filing the records—no one in their sane mind's going to suspect him."

He stopped in front of Rona, thrusting his hands into his trousers pockets. "That leaves just one honest-to-goodness murderer, sweetheart, and that's me. Of course, I didn't go into the Chief's office before he got there; but there is no one to prove I didn't."

"You're crazy to pretend you're the only suspect," Rona said. "Even if you do count Venner and me out, there's Mrs. Broderick. She was in the Chief's office just before the operation."

"Caroline!" Oliver's mouth dropped open. "What the hell was she doing here?"

"I don't know. But they were having a pretty violent argument about something."

The young intern stared at her. "You're not implying that Caroline poisoned her own brother?"

Rona was cynical enough to know what lay behind the indignant incredulity in his tone. A few months ago Oliver would never have leaped to the defense of Mrs. Broderick. But it was very different now that the Director's wife had taken him up socially as one of the attractive young men whom she used to swell Linette's stag lines.

In the past Rona had thought a great deal of this aggressive, hard-headed boy from a hick town who had worked his way through medical school and who had spent every minute of his spare time on his thyroid research. They had been good friends, indulging themselves occasionally in a supper and a forty-cent movie. All that and some of Rona's respect for him had vanished before the new, social Oliver Lord, who danced attendance on Linette Clint and her mother.

He was repeating, "You really think Caroline murdered the Chief?"

"I'm only pointing out," Rona snapped, "that she had as much of an opportunity as the rest of us."

"But it's crazy. She was his sister; she—was fond of him."

"I never noticed it. I never knew Caroline Broderick cared about anything except her own money and the chances of pulling a husband for Linette out of the *Social Register*. But of course you would stand up for a woman who pours champagne into you by the quart."

Oliver gazed at her, his face blank. Then he gripped her arms roughly. "It's about time we had this out. Why the hell shouldn't I go to Linette's parties? She's a swell girl."

"I'm glad you like her."

"I like Caroline Broderick a lot, too. She shows a darn intelligent interest in my thyroid research."

"So that's the idea, is it? You're hoping she'll come across with a big, fat grant. Well, you're wasting your time. Mrs. Broderick may be rich and she may throw thousand-dollar parties, but she's as tough and as tight as they come when it's a question of giving money away to impecunious young men." She added wildly, "And if you're figuring on marrying Linette Clint...."

She broke off, and they stood staring at each other.

Finally, with savage sarcasm, Oliver said, "Thank you for your invaluable warning, Nurse Heath. But I haven't the slightest intention of trying to marry Linette Clint. Even if I had, there wouldn't be the remotest chance for me, because she happens to be very much in love and almost engaged to Governor Drayton's son."

"So you go to her parties purely for the love of research," flared Rona.

"I go to her parties because I decided it was about time I started to have some fun. I'm through with mooning around after a girl who's too damn stuck on herself to realize I exist."

"Just what do you mean by that?"

"Figure it out for yourself. Or do I have to scribble sonnets to you all over the hospital walls?"

"To me?" echoed Rona incredulously.

"That's what I said. Have you been too dumb to guess the way I've always felt about you?"

His face, with its firm mouth and intensely blue eyes, was very close to hers. For one crazy moment Rona thought he was going to kiss her. She tugged herself away. "I haven't the slightest idea how you've always felt about me," she said. "But I'm beginning to see how you feel about me now that you're in a spot and you know I've got a brother on the police force."

Oliver's lips parted, showing strong white teeth. "That's a pretty filthy thing to say."

"Is it?"

"It is. Just because you've always been crazy for the high-souled

Ellsworth you're about as conscious of the way other people happen to feel as a patient under ether." He gave a harsh laugh. "You say I'm wasting my time on Linette Clint. Well, I can tell you you're wasting a hell of a lot more time on Ellsworth. If ever he falls for a girl it'll be one with a pile of dough to sink in neurology. Shouldn't be surprised if he hadn't tried for the Clint millions already and ..."

"That's a lie," cut in Rona heatedly. "Hugh Ellsworth's never been interested in Linette. He's—he's just her doctor and ..."

She broke off sharply as the doors rolled and Gregory Venner appeared on the threshold. The anesthetist looked so broken, so pathetic, that she forgot her indignation at Oliver and moved toward him with a gesture of sympathy.

"I'm terribly sorry for you, Mr. Venner. Dr. Knudsen was your friend, and ..."

"Thank you, thank you, Miss Heath." Gregory Venner shook his head dazedly. "Yes. I can hardly believe it. I shall miss him. He was very good to me. I was at his apartment for dinner last night, you know. He seemed so well and happy. We were making plans to go to Switzerland this spring. It's been the dream of my life to climb the Jungfrau, and now, when everything was almost arranged at last ..." He broke off, turning away his face.

Oliver Lord relaxed the stiff line of his shoulders and said with unconvincing casualness, "At least, I hope you haven't been all but accused of murdering him the way I was."

"I do not feel anyone would accuse me of murdering Dr. Knudsen." The anesthetist looked up at him with sudden dignity. "Lieutenant Heath did question me about my movements, but he says it is not possible for me to have figured in the case anyway. He says the poison must have been put in the coffee. At the time when the tray was sent up to Knudsen's room I was out to lunch with Peters, and when finally I came up here Dr. Knudsen was already in the office with—er—Mrs. Broderick."

"So you knew Mrs. Broderick was there, too?" said Rona.

"Why, yes. She has a very penetrating voice. Both the orderly and I heard it through the wall of the anesthetizing room." Gregory Venner fingered his watch chain. "Although it was most embarrassing to have to mention it in the presence of Dr. Broderick, I could not very well have kept the fact back from the lieutenant."

Rona was relieved that the anesthetist should have taken on his shoulders the responsibility of telling Jim about Caroline Broderick's visit. And yet she felt sorry for him. Gregory Venner's almost idolatrous respect for the Chief was equaled only by his fear of Dr. Broderick. She realized what an ordeal it must have been for him to have to tell Dr.

Broderick that his wife at least had an opportunity to commit the crime.

She realized too, now that Dr. Knudsen was dead, Gregory Venner was completely at the mercy of Dr. Broderick's reshufflement plans. In his ruthless drive for hundred percent efficiency in all departments, the Director had decided some time ago that Venner was inadequate to act the dual role of Dr. Knudsen's anesthetist and keeper of hospital records. On several occasions the Director had tried to ease him out, and would have succeeded if it had not been for Dr. Knudsen's stanch support of the man who had once saved his life. Now it looked as if this day might well deprive Gregory Venner not only of his old friend, but also of his position in the hospital.

The anesthetist had been looking at her in what seemed like nervous hesitation. At length he said, "Miss Heath, I—I have a very awkward question to ask you. There is something I thought I overheard Mrs. Broderick say. I did not tell the lieutenant, because I was not entirely sure and—and it is not the sort of thing one should mention unless one is completely certain of the facts."

"What was it?"

"You must have heard something of the conversation that was going on in Dr. Knudsen's office when you went in to tell him we were ready for him to operate. Did"—he coughed—"did you by any chance hear Mrs. Broderick mention the word *blackmail?*"

For a moment Rona hesitated. Then, impulsively, she passed on to them exactly what she had overheard in the Chief's office.

The two men stared at her, Oliver incredulous, Venner moistening his lips. "So—so I was right," murmured the anesthetist at length. "Your brother told me that he wanted to see you in Dr. Broderick's office right away. You must tell him all this, Miss Heath. We cannot hold it back."

"Of course we can't," agreed Rona.

"But this gives the murder motive!" Oliver had swung round to her. "Why didn't you tell me before?"

"I was going to—but we got sidetracked being—rude to each other." All Rona's indignation against him had faded.

"This is swell for me, isn't it?" he exclaimed in a hard, grating voice. "Your brother's alibied Venner out of the picture. Mrs. Broderick would hardly have been extorting money from herself. That leaves me as the only person who could have put the poison in that coffee and who could have had a motive. Everyone knows I've been doing my darnedest to get her to finance my research." He gave a sharp laugh. "When you see your brother, Rona, why don't you tell him to arrest me straight away?"

Lieutenant James Heath, of the Homicide Division, was in the Director's office when Rona entered a moment later. She had never seen her brother at work on a case before. Somehow it did not seem real for him to be sitting there so very solemn and official.

Dr. Broderick drew up a chair for her and gave her an uneasy, rather forced smile. "We are grateful to your brother for promising to do his best to keep this terrible thing as quiet as possible, Miss Heath," he said. "He is also prepared to let all of you who are involved continue with your regular duties."

Jim was looking at Rona across the desk, square hands playing with a pencil. Concisely he checked with her on the lunchtime movements of the operating team and on the events immediately preceding Dr. Knudsen's death. He concluded: "We've got the physical setup fairly straight. What we want is a motive. You were close to Knudsen. Have you anything to suggest?"

It was an awkward moment. Rona started to say something, but broke off with a glance at the Director.

Dr. Broderick interpreted that glance, and said stiffly, "If you know anything you will pass it on to your—ah—brother. There must be no question of concealment or sparing people's feelings."

"All right."

Very conscious of the effect her words produced, she told them exactly what she and Venner had heard pass between the Chief and Mrs. Broderick.

In the long silence that followed, her brother stared at her without speaking. Finally he shifted his steady gaze to the Director. "Would you be able to throw any light on this, Dr. Broderick?"

"I don't understand it at all—not at all. All I know is that my wife came to the hospital this afternoon for a sinus treatment. She is still here. I think it far better for you to take the matter up with her."

He rang for his secretary and told her to ask Mrs. Broderick to come there as soon as possible.

Jim was still watching him, slightly skeptical. "It really means nothing to you, Dr. Broderick—not even Dr. Knudsen's reference to expressing his point of view toward some grant at the Directors' Meeting?"

"Oh, ah, the grant! Yes. I am conversant with Knudsen's point of view toward the grant. We had discussed it several times. But I cannot see how it could have the slightest bearing upon what has happened." Dr. Broderick passed a smoothing hand across his hair. "You see, my wife is a very rich woman in her own right. Last week she generously offered to donate a quarter of a million dollars to the hospital to be divided among certain—ah—specified departments."

"The matter was going in front of the Board this afternoon?"

"That is correct."

"And Knudsen was planning to oppose it?"

"Why, yes." The Director had picked up a pencil and was tapping with it on the desk. "My brother-in-law was an unusual man in many ways, He had a—well, a very strict code of ethics, Lieutenant. And I'm afraid his exacting conscience sometimes conflicted with what I consider the practical interests of the institution.

"My wife's money is inherited from her first husband, who made a large fortune as manufacturer of the Clint Home Remedies. While these products are harmless in themselves, they cannot be said to conform to the highest standards of medicine. Although he was Caroline's brother, Knudsen was opposed to our accepting the grant, because he felt that, by doing so, we would seem to be endorsing remedies that militate against the ethics of our profession by advocating—ah—self-medication in disease."

"You feel he was being too squeamish?"

"I—ah—" Dr. Broderick coughed pompously. "Of course, a great hospital like this cannot afford to be associated with the Clint Remedy Company. But we are sorely in need of funds, and I see no cause to refuse a grant which comes from my wife as a private individual and under the name of the Broderick Foundation."

The lieutenant's eyes were very alert as asked, "If the grant is accepted, how is it to be divided?"

"The larger part is to go to—ah—my own special department of gynecology and to Dr. Ellsworth's Neurological Clinic. There is also a third endowment in my brother-in-law's own department. It was to establish a fellowship to assist young Lord in thyroid research."

Rona stiffened in her chair. So Oliver *had* got what he had tried to get out of Mrs. Broderick. He *was* benefiting by the grant.

Jim Heath asked, "If the grant was not accepted it would be a very big disappointment to you people who stood to benefit by it—you, Ellsworth, and that young man Lord, wouldn't it?"

"Naturally. And to many others, also." Dr. Broderick was rather injured. "But it is not my wife's intention to distribute money to us for our own personal use. It is purely for the general good of the hospital."

"But Knudsen was going to oppose it." In a voice which concealed the challenge implied in his words, Jim added: "In a way he was standing between certain people and a lot of money, wasn't he? Lord, for example—there he was in Knudsen's own department, knowing that Knudsen was going to do his best to keep him from getting a fellowship. That wouldn't have made him feel any too friendly, would it?"

Rona's fingers were digging into her palms as she waited for Dr. Broderick's reply.

"I think Knudsen's attitude would have alienated Lord just as much as it alienated the rest of us," the Director was saying frigidly. "But I might tell you that our directors are already familiar with my brother-in-law's overscrupulousness on financial matters. As a single member of the Board he could never have brought the other eleven around to his point of view."

"Then you mean Knudsen couldn't have stopped the grant being accepted?"

"Not possibly."

"Not even," asked Lieutenant Heath softly, "if he could have shown that it had been extorted from your wife by blackmail?"

There was a long, vibrant moment of silence.

Dr. Broderick opened his mouth to speak, but closed it again as the door was thrown suddenly open and Caroline Broderick came into the room.

Dr. Knudsen's sister was deathly pale; her face was completely without expression. She crossed to her husband's side.

"Hugh Ellsworth's just—just been telling me about Thegn," she said. "It's terrible—it's fantastic, completely incredible. But before we do anything we've got to see the news doesn't come out in the papers. While Linette's staying at Drayton's house, with her engagement hanging in the balance, it will be appalling if all the headlines blaze the fact that her uncle has been murdered."

She swung round fiercely to Jim. "You're the policeman, the lieutenant in charge or whatever you call it, aren't you? Please, please see that this is kept quiet."

Lieutenant Heath was looking at her with calm steadiness. "I'm afraid I'm rather more interested in finding out who murdered your brother than in worrying about your daughter's convenience or inconvenience at the moment, Mrs. Broderick. Perhaps you'd take a chair. I have a few questions to ask."

This unexpected counterattack had a deflating effect upon Mrs. Broderick. Without another word she dropped into a chair.

He said, "You were in your brother's office this afternoon just before the operation, weren't you?"

"I was." Mrs. Broderick's voice was defiant.

"When you went into the room with your brother, did you notice his lunch tray?"

"Why, yes. It was on the dumbwaiter, and Thegn took it over to his desk. He was planning to eat it, but—why do you want to know?"

Without replying, Jim continued, "You were with your brother up to the time he went into the scrub room, weren't you?"

"Yes. I—I stayed on. Then I went out through the anesthetizing room."

"And all that time no one came in?"

"No one at all. We were entirely alone. That is, until Miss Heath came to tell Thegn the patient was ready for the operation. Why are you asking all these questions?"

Caroline Broderick looked at him rather wildly, and then, as if light had dawned precipitously, she flashed a glance at Rona. "I see what you've been trying to prove. Miss Heath told you Thegn and I were quarreling. You're—you're suspecting me of killing him, my own brother. That's absurd." She threw out a hand imperiously to Dr. Broderick. "George, this is disgraceful."

Dr. Broderick looked uneasy but made no reply.

The steely note still in his voice, Lieutenant Heath asked, "What were you quarreling with your brother about, Mrs. Broderick?"

There was a fraction of a second before Caroline Broderick answered. Rona thought she saw a flicker of fear in her eyes, and when the woman spoke it was with incoherent swiftness: "We were just arguing about the grant I am offering the hospital. My husband must have told you about it and about my brother's pigheaded objections."

"You're sure that was all you talked about, Mrs. Broderick? I think it's only fair to tell you that two different people overheard you use the word *blackmail.*"

"Blackmail!" Caroline Broderick's tongue came out to moisten scarlet lips. "Maybe I did use that word. I don't remember." She added hurriedly, "It is blackmail in a way, in any case—doctors getting money out of a rich woman for their wretched hospital! They know you can't very well refuse and have everyone think you're not—not performing your civic duty. They do hold you up at the point of a gun. Yes." She nodded vigorously as if she felt she had a good point. "That's what I mean. In a sense the whole grant has been blackmailed out of me."

"And that's what you said to your brother?"

"Yes, yes."

"And his only objection to having the directors accept the grant was the fact that your money came from the Clint Home Remedies?"

"That's right. That was his only reason."

Jim took a shot in the dark: "Mrs. Broderick, listen to me carefully. I understand that your daughter was here in the hospital recently for an operation. A great deal about a person is liable to come out when she's in a hospital. I've been thinking about it, and there's a possibility that someone threatened to expose something damaging about your daughter if you didn't give the hospital a quarter-million dollars. Isn't that what you meant by blackmail, and isn't that the real reason why Dr. Knudsen was going to see that the grant was refused and that all moneys were returned to you?"

While she listened with staring eyes, Caroline Broderick's cheeks had turned from white to a dull, ashen gray. "That's not true. It's ridiculous. I haven't given the hospital any money yet—how could it return any moneys to me?"

Unsteadily she rose to her feet, and once again she turned distractedly to her husband. "George, tell him it's all a lie. Tell him I won't answer any more preposterous questions. The shock of the news—and the pain of my sinus treatment … I'm not myself … I think I'm going to faint."

Her voice faded. With a little sigh, she swayed and crumpled sideways to the floor.

While the Director hovered ineffectually, Jim sprang forward and picking Caroline Broderick up, carried her to a couch. "Quick, Rona. Water."

Rona brought some from the cooler.

Dr. Broderick seemed completely nonplussed by this sudden collapse of anyone as strong-willed as his wife. He stood absolutely still, staring, while Jim tilted the water to Mrs. Broderick's lips and Rona sent the secretary running for Dr. Ellsworth, who was the Brodericks' family physician.

The moments of waiting were tense. Rona's mind was keyed up, oddly undecided. Had this faint been genuine? Or had Mrs. Broderick used it as a device to forestall any further questioning?

Soon Hugh Ellsworth arrived, was told what had happened, and made a swift, expert examination of the prostrate woman.

"Nothing serious," he said at length. "Just a faint. But all this must have been a big shock to her." He turned to Dr. Broderick: "I think it would be better if we put her to bed here in the hospital for a while "

"Yes, yes," assented the Director. "Miss Heath, tell my secretary to have a room prepared for Mrs. Broderick in the Ives Wing."

Within a few minutes they had taken Mrs. Broderick away. Ellsworth and Dr. Broderick followed, leaving Rona alone with Jim.

Lieutenant Heath said, "Well, Ro, you certainly gave me a break overhearing that conversation."

"You really think she was blackmailed into giving that grant?"

"Either into giving the grant or into giving cash to someone."

"And Dr. Knudsen got killed because he was planning to expose the blackmail?"

"Seems that way." Jim tapped on the desk. "Doesn't look as if we've got many suspects to pick from, either. Mrs. Broderick's obviously keeping back a whole raft of evidence; but I don't see how the motive could be twisted around to her. I've checked up on the rest of them. Venner's alibied up to the last minute. Broderick and that guy Ellsworth were both out of the hospital when the operation was being performed. We've got to believe Knudsen was killed by that poisoned coffee." He paused. "And there isn't anyone who had the physical chance of doing it except Lord—and you."

Surprised by her own indignation, Rona said, "You can't seriously think it's Oliver Lord. It's absolutely fantastic!"

"Fantastic for him to kill a man who, if we're right, was going to expose the fact that he'd extorted money out of Mrs. Broderick?"

"That's what I mean. Oliver couldn't have blackmailed Mrs. Broderick. I'm not a fool. You know that. And I tell you it's just not in his character." She added: "Anyway, you suggested just now that Mrs. Broderick had been victimized by someone who'd found out something about Linette when she was here in the hospital. Well, Oliver had nothing to do with that case. I was the nurse in charge and I know."

Jim's eyes showed interest. "What was the girl operated on for?"

"It was just a small brain operation to correct an injury she'd received some time ago. It wasn't serious."

"I see. And who had anything to do with that operation?"

"Hugh Ellsworth diagnosed the case and recommended the operation, of course. But it was performed by a brain surgeon with his own team—people quite different. I was working in Ellsworth's Neurological Clinic then. That's why I nursed Linette afterward." Rona added stubbornly, "Oliver Lord knew nothing about it—not a thing."

Jim was watching her with a faint smile. "You don't happen to be stuck on this guy Lord, do you?"

"Me? Don't be ridiculous!" Rona felt the color flooding her cheeks. "He's a perfectly nice person but he—he makes me madder than anyone I ever knew. I just can't have you suspecting him, when he couldn't possibly have killed anyone."

"Redheaded young surgeons can kill people just as well as the next guy, probably a great deal better." The smile was still in Jim's eyes, but it was a smile without humor. "You say Lord had nothing to do with Miss Clint's operation. But he knew her and Mrs. Broderick socially, didn't he?"

"He went to several parties at their house."

"Was he chasing money for his research or chasing Miss Clint?" Jim asked suddenly. "I hear she's an attractive girl. I also hear she's going around a lot with Governor Drayton's son. Suppose Lord hoped for an heiress, felt mad when he lost out, and figured the least he could do was to get a little gravy out of the mother and ..."

He stopped as the door opened and Hugh Ellsworth reappeared.

"Mrs. Broderick's come round all right, Lieutenant. But she's still pretty shaky and we've decided to keep her in the hospital until tomorrow. Wouldn't advise you to try and get any more out of her until she's quieted down a bit."

"Okay," said Jim. "I guess I can leave her lie a while until she's got her story straight."

Ellsworth smiled. "I'll go and tell ..."

He had moved to the door, but Jim's quiet voice called him back: "While you're here, Dr. Ellsworth, I'd like to ask you a couple of questions. Do you know anything about this grant Mrs. Broderick was planning to give the hospital?"

"Do I know anything about it?" Ellsworth crossed back to the desk. "I ought to. We're hopelessly in the red here, you know, and we've all been doing everything short of murder to get Mrs. Broderick to crash through with that quarter-million."

"And which of you was finally successful in persuading her?"

"I don't want to boast. But I think I take most of the credit. Broderick did his part. Young Lord even went so far as to dress up in evening clothes and dance, when he wanted to stay at home with his thyroid researches. But I think I probably worked the hardest and the longest."

"I see." Jim's tone was very alert. Suddenly changing his tack, he asked, "Mrs. Broderick is fond of her daughter, isn't she?"

"Psychopathically so."

Lieutenant Heath looked down at the polished surface of the desk. "You said the bunch of you around here did everything short of murder to get that grant. I'm interested in that remark, interested to know how far you'd have gone. If, for example, one of you knew something damaging about Linette Clint, would you have used that for a lever on Mrs. Broderick?"

Hugh Ellsworth's smile faded. "You don't seem to have a very high opinion of the medical profession, do you?"

"I can't afford to have a high opinion of anyone."

"Well, maybe you're right. But if you're wondering whether I personally blackmailed Mrs. Broderick into giving us that grant, I think I can put your mind at rest." He moved a little closer.

"Perhaps you don't know a great deal about the work we neurologists do. By the time we're through with a patient, we know absolutely everything about him and his friends and relations, and often what we know isn't any too savory. Right now, for example, I have under treatment a dozen, twenty, fifty people who come from the wealthiest and most respectable families in town. Some of them are drunks, some of them are moral wrecks, some of them—I needn't run through the more intricate features of mental unbalance. But, if I went in for blackmailing my patients and my ex-patients, I'd never have to waste my time worming a paltry quarter-million dollars out of Caroline Broderick."

Jim said, "Thank you for making your point so clear, Dr. Ellsworth."

"On the contrary. Thank you."

Jim rose. "Well, since Mrs. Broderick has gone into retirement, my next job is looking through Knudsen's papers. Come on, Rona. I guess you're the best person to show me the ropes."

Rona moved to follow him, but surprisingly Ellsworth stepped in front of her. He said to Jim, "Rona may be your sister, but she's paid by the hospital, not by the police force. And, since I'm planning to try to get her back into my clinic, I take a paternal interest in her well-being." He smiled. "Rona's had a very tough day and it's long past dinnertime. She's coming out to eat with me."

Lieutenant Heath hesitated by the door, watching both of them. Then, the grim line of his mouth relaxing, he said, "Okay. Give her some food. I'll take Knudsen's papers back to Headquarters with me." He left.

Hugh Ellsworth, watching Rona, looked suddenly serious. "Tell me, does he really think someone's been extorting money out of Caroline and that she's holding back on him?"

Rona nodded. "Yes. That's what he thinks."

"I see." There was a curious curve to his lips. Then he patted her arm and said, "Go get yourself out of that starched prison uniform into something gay. We'll find a place downtown for dinner and forget all this business for an hour or so."

And, when finally they were settled in a little French restaurant, Rona found that she could almost forget that the real reason for her sitting there with Hugh Ellsworth was that Dr. Knudsen had been murdered.

Ellsworth talked with infectious enthusiasm about the clinic and his plans for its future. For Rona it was as if the clock had been turned back to the exhilarating days when he had been her boss and she had been an essential part of his plans.

They were sipping their coffee, when he broke off with an odd expression, half mocking, half affectionate, on his face. "Well, Rona, I meant it just now when I told your brother I was planning to get you back into the clinic." He hesitated, and added suddenly, "But I want you to tell me something. Why did you walk out on me last year?"

"You really want to know?" Rona asked.

"Very much."

"It's all very simple. You see, I have no illusions about my fatal fascination. I started getting too—too interested in you as a person, and I had enough sense to see it was a stupid thing to do. I quit while the quitting was painless."

"You were a smart girl, my dear." His mouth moved slightly at the corners.

"To realize I was wasting my time?"

"On the contrary. If you'd stayed any longer, I would probably have asked you to marry me and you might even have accepted."

"And would that have been so terrible?"

"Frightful!" He grinned. "Frightful for you, that is. A psychiatrist may make a passable boss, but he makes the worst husband in the world. He's seen far too much of what goes on in the human mind. To him love's just a compulsion neurosis that marriage aggravates, and a wife's just someone who'll bring a whole new raft of complexes into the family." He leaned across the table and patted her hand. "You ought to be eternally grateful you didn't wait around in the clinic for that marriage proposal."

"Oliver said you'd never marry," Rona told him. "At least, he said you never would unless you found a girl with a lot of money to sink in research—a girl like Linette Clint."

"So that's Lord's analysis of me, is it?" Hugh Ellsworth's smile was still amused, "Nice, healthy reaction, too. He's the sort of person a smart girl should marry, Rona—a young man with a lot of muscle and a lot of masculine contempt for human textbooks like me." He added, glancing up at her, "As for Linette Clint, she's another smart girl. And she's going to make a darn good wife for that boy of hers."

While he spoke, a newsboy came into the restaurant with a sheaf of late-night papers. Ellsworth signaled him and bought a copy.

As he unfolded it and looked at the front page, he said, "I guess the time has come when the world's to be let in on the little secret I've been sharing with Linette. Yes, here it is, plastered all over the front page."

He handed Rona the paper, pointing at a column.

She read:

DRUG HEIRESS IN RUNAWAY MATCH WITH GOVERNOR'S SON

Linette Clint, heiress to the Clint Home Remedy fortune, and Charles Gormley Drayton, III, Governor Drayton's son, slipped across the state line and were privately married last night. The young couple eloped from the Governor's mansion itself, where Linette Clint had been staying as a house guest. As yet neither the bride's nor the groom's families have made a statement but …

When she put the paper down Ellsworth was watching her as if he were intensely interested in her reaction.

"Your brother thinks Caroline's holding back on him," he said slowly. "If he's right, I have a very good hunch this news will make Mrs. Broderick reshuffle her plans."

"You mean she doesn't know anything about the elopement?"

Ellsworth shook his head. "Nothing. It's just a little something worked out by Linette, Charlie Drayton, and myself."

As he paid the check and they went out of the restaurant, he added enigmatically, "I wish to hell all my patients' problems were as easy to solve as Linette Clint's."

Ellsworth left Rona at the main entrance of the hospital and went to take the news of her daughter's elopement to Caroline Broderick. Rona hurried to her room in the nurses' quarters and changed into uniform.

When she returned to the main building, the loudspeakers in the corridors were calling, "Miss Heath wanted in Dr. Ellsworth's office."

When she reached the neurologist's room, Hugh Ellsworth was waiting for her. He said, "I had the right idea about Caroline. I never saw a patient respond to treatment the way she responded to that account of Linette's marriage. In two seconds she switched from the bereaved sister to the delighted mother—and she's eager to unburden her soul about something."

"To the police?"

"No. She says she wants to see you."

"Me? Why me?"

"I don't know. But it's you she wants."

"All right."

As Rona hurried along the corridor, she passed the open door of the record room. A voice called her name, and Gregory Venner bustled out. "Miss Heath, may I speak to you a minute?"

Rona stepped with him into the small room whose walls were lined with the filing cabinets where Venner kept the hospital case histories in meticulous order. He closed the door portentously behind them. He looked very pale and tired.

"I've been so worried, Miss Heath," he said. "I can't concentrate on my work, can't do anything, thinking about what has happened to Dr.

Knudsen. Tell me, has—has Mrs. Broderick been able to help the police? Were we right about what we thought we heard?"

Rona told him how Mrs. Broderick had denied that there was any kind of blackmail. "But Jim believes she's lying," she concluded. "And she's just sent for me to tell me something important. So maybe we'll hear the truth now."

The anesthetist's face lightened. "I hope so, indeed. It's about the only thing left for me—to try to find out who killed Thegn." He threw out his hands in a rather forlorn gesture. "You see, already Dr. Broderick has sent for me and told me I won't be needed any longer to administer anesthesia." He hesitated. I always hoped that I had done my work satisfactorily. But you know how Broderick is—all for young people."

Rona thought it typical of Dr. Broderick—typical and entirely inhuman. Venner, who had worked for the hospital so long and who had devoted his life so completely to Dr. Knudsen—it was tragic to think of him thrown out into the world with nowhere to go just because the Director had this fanatical passion for superefficiency.

Gregory Venner seemed to read her thoughts, for he gave a pale smile and said, "Please don't worry about it, Miss Heath. I have a little money saved. I'll be all right. I may even be able to go to Switzerland, after all—before I get too old."

Impulsively Rona squeezed his hand. "We'll always remember you here," she said. "And if I find out anything about—about Dr. Knudsen, I'll let you know. Now I'd better get to Mrs. Broderick."

Hurrying down the passage, Rona took the elevator to the second floor and made her way to the Ives Wing, where Mrs. Broderick had been settled. As she moved down the long central passage, the door of one of the private rooms opened and Oliver Lord came out, followed by the night nurse. Oliver gave the nurse some rapid instructions and she hurried away. As soon as she was out of sight, he gripped Rona's arm and drew her roughly into one of the vacant private rooms. "I've got to talk to you," he said, his blue eyes very steady and stubborn. "And this is going to be the moment."

"What do you want to say?"

"I want to say a hell of a lot but I'll try and keep my language adequately censored." He moved closer, his strong hands crushing the white cotton of her sleeves. "You made some pretty raw cracks at me in the operating room this afternoon. In fact, you're a rude, ornery little piece, but I've got to know where I stand with you."

Rona tried to pull her arms away, but his grip was too tight. She said, "For heaven's sake, stop mauling me about, Oliver. I'm supposed to go to Mrs. Broderick."

"I'll stop mauling you about when I'm good and ready." He was looking at her with a kind of angry intensity. "And Caroline Broderick's as good a place to start as any other. I did go to a couple of her parties. I went to them purely and simply because I wanted her to crash through with the grant. That doesn't make me a gigolo, does it?"

"I haven't any idea what it makes you."

"Well, whatever it makes me, it tars your high-minded boyfriend, Ellsworth, with the same brush. The hospital had to have money, and Mrs. Broderick was our one hope. He worked on her as much as I did."

"Why bother to explain all this to me?"

"I don't know. I haven't the slightest idea why I bother about you at all." His jaw was thrust out aggressively. "I think you're badly stuck on yourself; I think a lot of things. But for some godforsaken reason I'm stuck on you, too. I told you that this afternoon, and you paid about as much attention to it as one of my experimental frogs. But I've been that way for a long, long time, and I don't give a hoot whether you do any reciprocating or not. I just want you to believe me when I say that for better or worse—largely worse—I think you're swell."

Rona could not help smiling. "Oliver, you're being utterly ridiculous."

He was not smiling. Suddenly his arms slipped around her. He pulled her toward him, and his lips met hers in a long, rough kiss. In spite of her indignation the touch of his mouth on hers was warm—exciting.

"That's better," he said at length. He pushed her away and gazed at her from blue eyes that were still very belligerent. "Now run and tell your brother I'm trying to make up to you because I murdered Knudsen and want a good police connection."

"I'm sorry I said that to you this afternoon," said Rona sincerely.

"So you take it back, do you? That's grand. It'll give me something pleasant to think about when I'm behind bars waiting trial for Knudsen's murder."

"Trial? Oliver, what on earth are you talking about?"

"What are you looking wide-eyed about? You know perfectly well that brother of yours is all set to arrest me any minute. You talked to him, didn't you? So far as I can tell, he's built up the perfect case against me. Peters did a Vitali test on the coffee. He's proved the poison was there—hyoscine, and enough to kill twenty goats." He added savagely, "And, according to your brother, I'm the guy who put it there." For a moment he stood in silence, looking at her fixedly. "Rona, tell me something," he said. "Do you think I murdered the Chief?"

"Of course I don't."

A grim smile spread over his lips. But his eyes showed a queer sort of excitement. "Okay, Rona. If you're back of me it's worth taking a fighting chance. Things are going to be tough as hell. If Knudsen was poisoned by that coffee, I don't see that I have a hope. But"—he paused, adding quickly—"it sounds crazy, Rona, but I'm going to try and prove that he wasn't poisoned by the coffee at all."

"But, Oliver, you've just said Peters proved the coffee was full of hyoscine."

"That's one of my points. I think the coffee was a lot too full of hyoscine. Rona, tell me, the Chief didn't take sugar in his coffee, did he?"

"He never took sugar in anything."

Oliver's excitement was increasing. "Then explain this. I've just thought of it. It's not easy to tell how hyoscine's administered, you know—even with an autopsy. It gets into the bloodstream almost immediately. But there's one very definite thing about it. It has an extremely bitter, unpleasant taste. If Knudsen had nothing to sweeten that coffee, how the hell could he have gulped down more than half of a cup without realizing something was wrong?"

"Oliver, you've got something there."

"You think so?"

"Yes. He surely would have noticed something was the matter if …" She broke off, adding lamely, "But the coffee was poisoned, and I myself saw him lift the cup to his lips. How can you explain that?"

Oliver looked suddenly tired and crestfallen. "I guess that's something I can't explain. I guess the whole idea was just one of those things. Forget it."

"Forget it! I certainly won't forget it so long as you're in a jam and there may be some way of getting you out of it."

"You really mean that?" Oliver's eyebrows tilted upward. "You're actually being nice to me? I can't believe it." He leaned forward and kissed her again on the lips. "I never dreamed," he said, "that one perfectly ordinary Wednesday could produce the best and the worst moments of my life."

Feeling exhilarated against all reason, Rona hurried to Mrs. Broderick's room, which was just a few doors down the passage. She found the Director's wife sitting up in bed, looking very handsome. "I'm so glad you've come, Miss Heath. I told Hugh Ellsworth I particularly wanted to see you."

Rona sat down on the chair by the bedside, watching her expectantly.

"Well, my dear"—Mrs. Broderick's smile was affable—"I'm going to confess I lied this afternoon to your brother. That is, I held back some of the truth. You mustn't blame me, because I was in the most embarrassing position."

She leaned forward. "I am confiding in you, my dear, because you are

Lieutenant Heath's sister and because you were very kind to Linette when you nursed her.... I knew absolutely nothing about her elopement until Hugh Ellsworth brought me the news. If I'd known about it earlier I would have acted very differently with the police."

Rona asked, "You mean it all somehow centered around Linette and her marriage?"

"Yes, my dear. Linette and her health." Caroline Broderick lowered her voice to an intimate softness. "It began some years ago when she was still a sub-debutante. She suddenly started having fainting spells—rather like fits. You can imagine how I felt! I took her to a very famous neurologist in Chicago. After he'd studied the case he told me that Linette suffered from—epilepsy!"

"Epilepsy!"

"He took a very gloomy view and was doubtful whether she should ever get married. I was desperate. A short time later, however, when I came East, I took her to Hugh Ellsworth for a second opinion. A fine doctor, a wonderful man! He sent for the entire case history, kept Linette under observation for a long time, and—it was the happiest day of my life—he told me he was almost sure the diagnosis was wrong. He believed that the whole trouble came from an accident Linette had had as a child—that there was something pressing on the brain and that it could be corrected by a minor operation."

Mrs. Broderick leaned back against the pillows. "You know the rest. They did operate. And there've been no attacks since. Although Hugh Ellsworth says it's too early yet to state officially that the Chicago doctor was wrong, he's sure there was never any question of epilepsy at all."

Rona was beginning to understand now. "So you—you were being blackmailed. Someone was holding the epilepsy rumor over you to …"

"Yes, yes. But you can see why I was terrified of mentioning it even to the police. The Draytons were naturally ambitious for their only son." Mrs. Broderick said frankly, "I'm not much socially, and certainly money means nothing to them. I knew that if ever they had even a suspicion that something was wrong with the stock, they'd prevent Charlie from marrying Linette."

She nodded emphatically. "But now the dear young things have taken the matter into their own hands. Hugh's just told me. Linette went to him as her doctor and asked him if he really thought it was all right for her to marry. He assured her it was, and said that just so long as Charlie knew everything there was no need for the Governor to be told. Charlie had known all along, of course, and it made no difference to him. So they eloped."

Now that she knew the truth Rona could see just what Hugh

Ellsworth had meant when he had referred to the ease with which Linette's problems had been solved.

Mrs. Broderick, still in a confidential mood, went on, "I can explain now the conversation you overheard between me and my brother. About two weeks ago I received an anonymous letter. Whoever wrote it just stated that he knew everything about Linette and would pass it on to the Draytons unless I deposited $25,000 in a certain place here in the hospital."

Rona broke in, "So it wasn't the grant that was blackmailed out of you!"

"The grant?" Mrs. Broderick looked indignant. "Of course not. I offered that money to the hospital entirely of my own free will in gratitude for what Hugh Ellsworth had done for Linette. This was something entirely different—a disgraceful piece of private extortion." She picked up the flimsy sleeve of her negligee and dropped it again. "I was horrified when I read that letter. Although I, myself, was sure the epilepsy diagnosis was wrong, I realized it could do almost as much damage with the Draytons as if it had been true."

She shrugged. "I deposited the money at the hospital in a suitcase, and hoped against hope it would keep the person quiet."

"But it didn't?"

"No. A second note came, and that time it asked for even more. By then I felt I had to confide in someone. I didn't want it to be my husband, because we haven't been married very long and I never discussed Linette with him. But Thegn, my brother, he knew, and I thought I could trust him. Last week I told him everything and pleaded with him somehow to find out who was responsible."

"And he did?"

"He promised to. I didn't hear from him again until last night. He told me then that he had found out who had been doing it."

"And he told you the person's name?" asked Rona urgently.

"No." Mrs. Broderick shook her head. "You know how Thegn was. Whatever he did, he was always scrupulously fair. It seems that he had forced a confession out of this man and had made a bargain with him. If every penny of my twenty-five thousand was returned to me by today, he said he would take no action. If the money wasn't returned, he was going to expose the whole thing at the Board Meeting this afternoon."

"And the money wasn't returned?"

"It wasn't. That's why I came to the hospital this afternoon. I was simply desperate. I thought the whole idea was stupid from the start, and the very last thing I wanted was for Thegn to bring everything out into the open just when, as I thought, Linette's chances of marrying Charlie Drayton were hanging by a thread. I pleaded with him to let the whole thing drop. You heard me. But he was as obstinate as ever. The man had been given a chance to redeem himself and had failed, he said. Whatever embarrassment it caused, he was going to see that the whole thing came out and that the man was handed over to the police."

"But even then he didn't tell you the man's name?"

"Not even then. It's tragic that he didn't, of course. But it was absolutely typical. The Board Meeting wasn't until five-thirty, and there was just a flimsy chance that the money would still be returned. He was going to keep his side of the bargain right up until the last minute."

She added firmly, "You see now why I've told you all this. You've got to promise to let your brother know everything. I would rather not speak to him myself until I've had some rest tonight."

"Of course I'll tell Jim. And I'm sure he'll consider it absolutely confidential." Rona added, "You're sure you haven't any idea who this person could have been?"

"None." Mrs. Broderick returned her stare with a steady gaze. "That's something for your brother to find out. But certain people can be eliminated, can't they? Hugh Ellsworth told me they thought something on Thegn's lunch tray was poisoned. Who could have got at that tray?"

Rona said awkwardly, "No one but—but you and me and Oliver Lord."

"Oliver Lord!" echoed Caroline Broderick. For a moment she did not speak. Then, very softly, she said, "You don't think it would be Oliver Lord, do you? I hate to suggest it; he's always seemed such a nice boy. But then he is in need of money."

Rona said stubbornly, "I know Oliver didn't poison that coffee."

"The coffee! What do you mean?"

"Didn't you know it was the coffee on the lunch tray that poisoned Dr. Knudsen?"

"The coffee on the lunch tray." Mrs. Broderick was staring at her now, the pupils of her eyes very wide. "No one ever told me that. There—there must be some mistake."

"But how could there be? Dr. Knudsen drank some of it, didn't he?"

"Yes. Not much, but he did sip some of it." Mrs. Broderick was still staring in amazement. "But he couldn't have been poisoned by it. You see, after he left, I was still very upset and angry. I wanted something to steady my nerves before going for my sinus treatment." She paused. "Thegn had left practically all the coffee in the cup. It was quite cold but—I drank it."

Rona stared at Mrs. Broderick, her thoughts swirling. "But Peters analyzed what was left in the cup and found enough hyoscine still there to kill several people!"

"Well, I'm not dead," said Mrs. Broderick reasonably. "And I drank from the same cup that Thegn did."

The truth suddenly screamed itself to Rona. Of course, there was only one explanation. Mrs. Broderick had drunk some of the coffee after Dr. Knudsen and had suffered no ill effects. Obviously, the coffee could not have been poisoned at that time. The hyoscine must have been slipped into the dregs later. In other words, the coffee must have been poisoned *after* the murder! Dr. Knudsen must have been killed by hyoscine administered in something else.

As soon as she realized that, the whole plan and its purpose took logical shape in her mind. The murderer had wanted to make it look as if only the three on the operating team could have had an opportunity to commit the crime. Sometime after Dr. Knudsen's death he must have slipped into the office, seen the half-drunk coffee, taken it for granted that Dr. Knudsen himself had drunk it, and planted the hyoscine in the cup.

Mrs. Broderick's sharp voice cut into her thoughts. "Miss Heath, can you make any sense of this coffee business?"

"Yes, yes. I see it now. Dr. Knudsen was killed in some other way."

"What way?"

What way ...? Dr. Knudsen had eaten nothing from the lunch tray. That was certain. And yet hyoscine was a quick-acting drug; the Chief could not possibly have stayed alive as long as he did if the poison had been administered before he came up to the operating room floor.

How then ...?

In a vivid flash of memory there came to her a picture of Dr. Knudsen as she had seen him just before the operation that afternoon when he had joined her in the scrub room. He had been nibbling a lump of sugar!

Until that moment the incident had completely slipped her memory. Yet now it showed itself by far the most significant fact in the entire case. On several occasions Dr. Knudsen had told her of his habit of nibbling sugar to supply sufficient energy for any emergency task which involved missing a meal. If she knew of that practice of his, surely the murderer could have known of it, too. It would have been easy for him to substitute a poisoned lump of sugar for the one the Chief must invariably have carried.

If that was really the way it had happened, if Dr. Knudsen actually had been killed by that lump of sugar, Oliver need be suspected no more than anyone else. The murderer might easily have been miles away from the hospital at the time when the Chief died.

Excitedly she said, "Of course, we were all wrong, Mrs. Broderick. I understand now. Dr. Knudsen must have been poisoned by a piece of sugar. I—I saw him eating it just before he started to scrub."

The Director's wife looked at her rather skeptically. "Have you told Lieutenant Heath about this?"

"No, no. I'd forgotten. I never thought of it until just this moment."

"Then I think you'd have difficulty in getting the police to believe you," said Mrs. Broderick sagely. "That brother of yours is smart. He'll think that you're just making up a story to throw suspicion off Oliver."

Rona's heart sank. That was true, of course. Coming so belatedly, anything she said about the sugar would sound pitifully unconvincing—particularly since Jim had made up his mind that she was rooting for Oliver against all comers. But again memory came to her aid.

"If I could produce some of the sugar and prove it was poisoned, Jim would have to believe me then," she said.

"If you could do that."

"But I think I can. You see, Dr. Knudsen threw part of it into the linen basket. It—it might still be there. I could get it. I'll go get a flashlight from my room."

Mrs. Broderick called, "Don't be in such a hurry, child. If you really think you know something, you had better tell your brother and let him look."

"No. Jim's not here now. I've got to try to get it right away before—before anything can happen to it."

Mrs. Broderick protested again, but Rona paid no attention. Her mind definitely made up, she hurried out into the passage.

As she hesitated on the threshold she had the queer impression that the door of one of the empty rooms opposite was moving—closing infinitesimally, as if someone had just that moment slipped through it. She felt her pulses tingling slightly. Was it possible that someone had been listening to their conversation? And had then darted behind the door opposite, so that he should not be seen? The idea seemed altogether too fantastic. Dismissing it, she hurried down the passage toward the stairs.

The operating room, she knew, would most certainly be locked at this time of night. But, as Dr. Knudsen's special nurse, she had an extra key to the door which led through the anesthetizing room.

Hurrying to her room in the nurses' building, she found the key and a flashlight, and then sped back to the hospital. Tense with excitement, she climbed the long stairs to the top floor. In the dim corridor light the great double doors of the theater reared in front of her. She slipped past them to the small door which led into the anesthetizing room. At night this was the most deserted part of the hospital. Everything was still as death as she slid the key into the lock and opened the door onto pitch-darkness.

Closing the door carefully behind her, she switched on her flashlight. She didn't dare risk attention by turning on the brilliant room lights.

Vaguely wishing she had not come, she forced herself to penetrate into the scrub room, where the gleaming white washbasins reflected her light. One ... two ... three ... Dr. Knudsen had used the third basin from the door.

She reached it and, with a sudden stab of excitement, saw that the towel basket had not been emptied. She bent over it and groped swiftly among the soiled towels. Almost at once her fingers touched something small and hard. She picked it up, holding it in the beam from her torch. Yes, it was a half lump of sugar, with one end jagged and uneven where Dr. Knudsen had bitten it. She stared at it, lying in her palm.

Then, suddenly, she stiffened and plunged the piece of sugar into the pocket of her uniform. What was that sound coming from the direction of the anesthetizing room? Had it been her imagination? Or was it a footstep—a light, cautious footstep?

She killed her flashlight. In the thick darkness she stood there straining her ears, every nerve in her body alive. The sound came again. She knew then that she had been right. There were footsteps in the adjoining room. Someone was moving, slowly, furtively, toward her.

Stubbornly she fought against a rising flood of panic. It might easily be someone with a perfect right to be there. One of Jim's men perhaps. Or the night watchman.

But, if that were so and this person's mission were innocent, why had he not turned on the lights by now? Why was he moving through the next room so stealthily?

For one paralyzed moment she stood motionless, pressed against the cold porcelain of the washbasin. Every instinct warned her then that the invisible presence beyond her in the thick darkness was the murderer of Dr. Knudsen. She had been right. He must have been listening to her conversation with Mrs. Broderick, must have slipped into the room opposite, waited while she went to the nurses' home, and then deliberately followed her here—followed her to stop her from getting that lump of sugar.

It was only then that she began to realize just how important it would be for the murderer to see that the true method of death were never brought to light. If this were really he, he would be desperate; he ...

She cut her train of thought. She must not lose her head. She had to work out a plan. Should she switch on her flashlight? No. That would only give her position away. The safest chance was to stay perfectly still, to hope against reason that this person would not be able to trace her in the darkness.

The next moments were agony. The footsteps grew steadily nearer, but slow, shuffling, and uncertain. Then they stopped.

Gradually, as she became more accustomed to the obscurity, she found herself able to distinguish a form, a misty outline, poised on the threshold of the door which led from the anesthetizing room. It was impossible to distinguish height or features. But the complete immobility of that figure was terrifying. There was something about it that reminded her of an animal of the night, watching, trying to gauge the exact position of its prey before it sprang. Then slowly it started forward again, veering toward her in her pathetically vulnerable position against the gleaming white of the washbasins.

Rona held her breath, struggling to check the convulsive trembling that had invaded her limbs. His progress toward her was so steady, so deliberate. He had seen her. She was sure of it.

Suddenly she could bear it no longer, the suspense, the stifling darkness, the relentlessly moving presence. She cried, "Who is it? What do you want?"

Absolute silence followed, far more horrible than any reply could have been.

"Tell me. Who is it? Why don't you speak? Why ...?" Her voice broke into a little strangled cry. The figure was almost on top of her now, hemming her in. She could hear low, quick breathing.

And, hanging poised in the darkness in front of her, catching illumination from some unknown source, she could make out a faint gleam of steel. She knew what it was. Even then, in the confused panic of that terrible moment, she recognized the cruel blade of a surgical knife.

There was only one thing to do. Mustering all her strength, Rona plunged forward straight at the amorphous figure which grasped the knife. She felt hot breath on her face. A hand grabbed at her sleeve. But with a desperate effort she wrenched herself free, swirled round, and ran blindly into the operating theater.

Something loomed in front of her—the sterilizer. Instinctively she slipped behind it, crouching in its shadow. For a while she could do nothing but try to silence the spasmodic sobs that shook her. She was free for the moment but—she realized it at once—she had only run into a trap. The operating theater was a dead end. The heavy double doors of the main entrance were locked on the outside. The door upstairs in the gallery was locked, too. There was no exit except the door to the scrub room through which she had just come. And now, as she peered through the gloom, she saw the figure of her unknown assailant, blurred and indistinct, standing there directly on the threshold.

Wildly Rona looked around her. It was slightly lighter here in the operating theater than it had been in the scrub room. She could make out the white tiles stretching away on all sides, and, beyond, the little staircase that led to the spectators' gallery.

The spectators' gallery.... Suddenly, as all hope seemed gone, she remembered a window in the gallery. It was seldom used. But—yes, she was sure—it gave onto a fire escape.

To reach the stairs leading to it she would have to run across half the operating room, have to expose her whereabouts to that dim, motionless figure standing by the door. If she were not quick enough, if she stumbled, if, when she reached the gallery, she could not open the window, then she would be caught, hopelessly cut off from all chance of escape. But it was her one slender hope.

Stealthily she slipped forward, easing herself around the wall to the stairs. For a moment the figure by the door stood immobile. Then it swung toward her. He had seen her. That knowledge sent all caution spinning. Crazily, making no effort to conceal herself, she dashed across the theater toward the small stairway.

Somehow she reached it. She was running upward. She was in the gallery, speeding down its narrow length to the window at the far end. Her pulses were drumming in her ears. There was the window, its pane shining faintly. It was shut. Her fingers felt for the catch; turned it, and tried to push up the sash. It did not move.

There was a creak on the stairs, and then footsteps on the wooden floor of the gallery, coming toward her.

With the strength of despair she gave a last tug at the window. It opened, and the cool night air rushed in. Vaguely she could make out the spidery rails of the fire escape. She was through the window. Her feet were on the iron steps. She was running downward, downward....

Not once did she look back; nor did she pause until she caught sight of a heavy door, half open, with the light streaming through. She pushed it full open, to find herself in one of the main corridors. There were bright lights ... people ... safety. Shutting the door behind her, she swiftly shot the bolt.

Her mind was clear enough to realize that she should get in touch with Jim at once. Without giving a thought to her disheveled appearance she hurried to the nearest telephone. When at last she got through to her brother, at Headquarters, she poured out a broken account of her talk with Mrs. Broderick, her theory of the coffee, and everything that had happened subsequently, "I've got the piece of sugar, Jim," she concluded, "but the murderer knows I've got it. What am I to do?"

"Exactly as I say." Lieutenant Heath's tone was very stern. "Take the sugar to that fellow Peters for analysis right away. He's doing some work for the police, and you'll find him in his lab."

"All right. But—but you're coming over, aren't you?"

"Of course. I'm coming immediately. And it looks as if you've got something really important, Ro. Nice work." His voice was edged with anxiety as he added, "But for God's sake take care of yourself. Don't wander around the hospital alone. I'm not going to have my sister murdered to amuse anyone." He rang off.

The laboratory was in the farthest wing of the building. Rona hurried down the almost deserted corridors toward it, still feeling the vague dread of being pursued. Once, to her horror, she did hear footsteps far behind her. But when she looked back she saw that it was only Hugh Ellsworth. He waved to her and turned off into another corridor.

It was with relief that, as she went through the high archway which led to the wing, she saw ahead of her the tall, redheaded figure of Oliver Lord. She called, "Oliver!"

He spun round and hurried toward her. "What on earth's the matter, Rona? You look as if someone had been trying to murder you, too."

"They have," Rona said excitedly. "But I've done it, Oliver. I've proved that Dr. Knudsen wasn't killed by the coffee."

"You—what?" His mouth dropped open.

"I can't explain now. I've got to go to Peters in the analytical lab. Come with me."

They found Dr. Peters busily watching a beaker where a violet liquid was turning to brown above the flame of a Bunsen burner, Rona gave him the sugar, with her brother's instructions for an immediate analysis.

When they were out in the passage again Oliver gripped her arm. "You're not crazy, by any chance … talking about sugar and analyses and …?"

"No, I'm not crazy." Breathlessly she told him everything. "So you see, Oliver," she concluded, "if we can prove it was the sugar that killed the Chief, anyone could have slipped it into his pocket at any time—anyone could have committed the crime."

"The little detective gal!" There was grim admiration in his eyes. "And you almost got yourself murdered trying to save me from the shadow of the death chair! That's the second very nice thing you've done for me today." His smile faded. "But something's crazy, Rona, If the murderer chased you to the operating room, how the hell did he know you were going there, or what you were planning to do?"

"He must have been listening when I talked to Mrs. Broderick." She told him how the door of the room across the passage had moved.

But Oliver was not paying much attention. Suddenly he said, "You told Mrs. Broderick everything, didn't you? I mean everything about the sugar?"

Rona nodded.

"Then she knows as much as you do. And she's the only witness to the fact that she drank some of the coffee. If the murderer was listening he must have realized that even if he had succeeded in killing you, he'd never have kept the truth from coming out unless—" His jaw very set, Oliver grabbed her arm. "Come on. We've got to get to her right away. Maybe there's time."

To Rona there was something unreal and dreamlike about that swift journey through corridors and up winding stairways to the Ives Wing. Neither she nor Oliver spoke. And yet she knew exactly what was in his mind, because she was thinking the same thing herself. She had left Mrs. Broderick alone in her room, Mrs. Broderick, who had it in her power not only to give the police a complete account of the murderer's blackmailing activities, but also to explode the cunningly devised trick of the coffee.

She, Rona Heath, had almost been murdered, and she was only half as much of a menace to the murderer as the Director's wife. There was real, terribly real danger for Caroline Broderick.

When at last they reached the Ives Wing they almost collided with Dr. Broderick coming down the passage from the direction of his wife's room.

Oliver asked sharply, "Have you been to see your wife? Is she all right?"

"All right?" A furrow of perplexity creased the Director's smooth forehead. "What do you mean? Yes, I—ah—did just put my head around the door. But the lights were out. I called her name, but she seemed to be asleep. I did not disturb her."

Rona said, "Stay here. I'll go and see if she's all right."

While the Director stared in astonished silence she hurried the short distance to Mrs. Broderick's room. She entered it. As Dr. Broderick had said, the room was in darkness. She could only just make out the dim figure on the bed. "Mrs. Broderick!" she whispered.

There was no reply. And the figure did not stir, The Director must be right. He had to be right. Mrs. Broderick must be only—asleep.

And yet, as she moved softly through the shadowy darkness of that small room, Rona felt her alarm mounting steadily. Less than an hour ago Mrs. Broderick had been so very much awake, so eagerly impatient to hear the results of Rona's expedition. Was it reasonable that, with so much hanging in the balance, she should be lying here in this dark room, sleeping peacefully?

Rona moved nearer the bed. A sudden, uncontrollable shiver passing through her, she turned to the bedside table, felt blindly for the light, and switched it on.

For one terrible moment she stared at the figure on the bed. Beneath the crumpled sheets, Caroline Broderick's body was sprawled limp and grotesque as a sawdust puppet. Her face was buried under a mound of pillows. One bare arm hung down over the side of the bed.

Rona stared at it, stared at its long white fingers, with their scarlet-nailed tips, tightly clenched. Then she screamed,

The next few minutes were a wild, fantastic kaleidoscope. The door behind her was thrown open. Someone was gripping her arm, steadying her—Oliver. Vaguely she was conscious of another figure, Dr. Broderick, hurrying to the bed, bending over it, lifting the pillows. She caught a glimpse of his face over Oliver's shoulder.

There was no need to look farther. The truth cried out from the ashen whiteness of his cheeks and the horror in his eyes. Then, dimly, his voice came through to her: "Caroline! Good God! She's dead. She's—she's been smothered under her own pillows...."

For Rona the period that followed was merged into a blurred, timeless nightmare where nothing seemed real except the appalling fact that Mrs. Broderick was dead.

The figures of Dr. Broderick and Oliver seemed to loom at her side through a mist. There was a vague memory of her brother striding into that small, constricted room, instantly taking over control, hustling them all out into the passage. Policemen seemed suddenly to be everywhere, talking, hurrying, crashing through the cloistered seclusion of a hospital at night.

Somehow she was giving replies to clipped, official questions. Then Jim's voice: "I'll want you again later, Rona. Go to the Director's office and wait for me."

For hours, it seemed, she was alone in that cold, impersonal room—waiting.

When at last the door swung open, it not Lieutenant Heath but Oliver Lord who came in. The young surgeon crossed to where she stood by the window, taking both her cold hands in his. "Rona, this is ghastly. And to think that—that it almost happened to you, too!"

Rona asked, "You've been talking to Jim?"

"Yes. He's interviewed everyone—Ellsworth, me, Venner, even poor old Broderick." He gave a harsh laugh. "At least the field of suspicion has widened. No one has any sort of alibi for the time it happened. Any of us could have slipped into that room without being seen by the night nurse. It's anybody's murder now."

"And she was—was smothered?"

He nodded. "Easy to see how it happened. He managed to overhear your talk with Mrs. Broderick and went in as soon as you left the room. Mrs. Broderick wouldn't have been alarmed because, as she told you, she had no idea who the murderer of her brother was. It wouldn't have been difficult to smother her before she had a chance to suspect anything or to call for help."

Rona gave a little shiver. "And—and as soon as he had killed her he went straight up to the theater after me!"

"Sure." Oliver's lips tightened. "You were as dangerous to him as Caroline, because she'd told you everything she knew. If he'd been able to kill you, too, I guess it might never have come out about the blackmail or about the poisoned coffee being a plant or …"

"Or about the sugar!" put in Rona. "If only I hadn't had that crazy idea of going to get the sugar myself, if only I'd stayed there with Mrs. Broderick, this would never have happened."

"You mustn't feel that way. You couldn't tell there was danger then." Oliver's hands slid to her arms, holding them tightly. "You went up to the operating room because—well, because you thought it would pull me out of a jam, didn't you?"

"I suppose I did." Rona smiled wanly; then her eyes clouded. "But you do think it will help, don't you? Now he knows the poisoned coffee was a frame-up, Jim can't suspect you anymore. The hyoscine must have been in the sugar. That must have been the way Dr. Knudsen was killed, mustn't it?"

As she spoke, the door opened, and Lieutenant Heath swung into the room. His face was very grim. "You were talking about that half-lump of sugar," he said tersely. "Maybe you'll be interested to hear that Peters' analysis report has just come in."

Both Rona and Oliver stared at him tensely.

Rona said, "It—it was poisoned?"

Lieutenant Heath gave a little shrug. "On the contrary. Peters says he found absolutely no trace of hyoscine."

"It wasn't poisoned? Then why …?"

"Don't expect me to answer any questions." Lieutenant Heath dropped into a chair and slung his leg over the arm. "I've put in a swell day. I had everything pinned on Lord, then I find out that was exactly what the murderer wanted me to do. Although I had the entire motive handed me on a silver platter, I haven't been able to pin the blackmail on anyone. I let Mrs. Broderick get killed right under my nose. I let my own sister come within an ace of being murdered. I haven't even figured out yet how Knudsen was killed!"

He glanced at Oliver with a slightly sardonic smile. "Maybe, as a smart young doctor, you can tell me a couple of things. First thing: Why should the murderer have tried to kill Rona just because she went searching for a perfectly ordinary lump of sugar? Second thing: How the hell was Knudsen killed by hyoscine when neither the coffee he drank nor the sugar he ate had any hyoscine in it?"

While the lieutenant had been speaking, a furrow of concentration had puckered Oliver's forehead. Now he looked up, his eyes suddenly bright. "I may be cuckoo, but I think I can give you a very good answer to both those questions."

"Are you being funny?"

"This is hardly the time for light comedy." There was a strange excitement in the intern's voice. "I'd never dreamed of it until this instant, but at last I see something that looks like daylight. It's that half-lump of sugar. You say it wasn't poisoned; but the murderer tried to keep Rona from getting it. There can be only one explanation for that. And it makes the sugar vitally, horribly important."

Oliver swung round to Rona: "Don't you see what I mean? No, I guess you don't. But"—he turned back to the lieutenant—"with any luck I could prove I'm right if you'd let us go up to Knudsen's office."

Jim rose to his feet. "Okay," he said. "I'll bite. Let's go."

Oliver did not speak on the long, eerie trek to the operating room floor. He waited impatiently as Jim produced the key to the outside door of Knudsen's office and let them into the room. Once inside, however, the young surgeon became very brisk and businesslike. He nodded at the clothes closet in the corner. "That's where Knudsen kept the white coats he used on his hospital rounds, isn't it, Rona? Maybe your brother would let you search through the pockets and see what you can find."

Jim grunted, "Anything goes." Bewildered but obedient, Rona went to the closet. She found a lump of sugar in each of the four white coats.

Oliver was smiling with grim satisfaction as she handed him the four pieces of sugar. "Excellent. We'll keep these as exhibits." He tossed them onto the desk and moved to the drug cabinet, asking Jim to unlock it. As he tugged open the door Rona saw that everything inside was just as it had been that afternoon when she had inspected it with Hugh Ellsworth—the rolls of adhesive, bandages, three hypodermic syringes, the stethoscope, iodine, adrenalin, morphine tablets, insulin ampules, alcohol, and digitalis.

"Now, if I'm right, I remember …" Oliver was scrutinizing the ranks of bottles and packages carefully. "Yes, there it is."

His fingers moved next to the hypodermic syringes lying on the bottom shelf. He picked one up, held it to the light, put it down, and took up another. Rona, watching at his elbow, saw that there were some remnants of colorless liquid inside. He placed it back in the cabinet and swung round to Jim, his eyes shining.

"You said you thought the method used to poison Knudsen was the most important point in the case. You're right. It strikes me we're up against the most ingenious damn ruse I ever heard of in my life. And it's something not one in a thousand policemen could be expected to stumble on, because it rests entirely upon a little problem in medicine."

His frank, attractive face under the mop of red hair wore an expression of grim self-assurance. He said, "I'm only a surgeon, Lieutenant, but I'm still fresh enough out of medical school to remember quite a bit of my medicine. I think if I give you a little lecture on 'Drugs and Their Uses,' you'll see what I'm driving at." His blue eyes glanced at Rona. "While I'm lecturing, there's a couple of things I'd like Rona to do for me. I'd prefer not to have her murdered doing them, so perhaps you've a nice, husky policeman you could send along with her, Lieutenant?"

Jim had been listening to him in uncommunicative silence. Still without commenting, he moved to the phone and gave rapid instructions. In a short time, a uniformed officer appeared.

"Okay. Now, here are the chores, Rona." Oliver took from the cabinet the hypodermic syringe which contained the dregs of liquid, and handed it to her. "Take this to Peters for analysis right away. Tell him to call me here the instant he starts getting an angle on the nature of its contents. Then rout out Venner, Ellsworth, and Dr. Broderick and tell them the lieutenant wants to talk to them up here—in quarter of an hour."

Rona's gaze flicked to Jim. A slight smile on his lips, the lieutenant said, "Maybe he's crazy and maybe he isn't. Go ahead, anyway."

Ten minutes later, her tasks fulfilled, Rona hurried back to Dr. Knudsen's office. Oliver and Jim were standing by the desk, staring down at the four lumps of sugar. The young surgeon still looked excited and rather flushed. But there was a marked change in Jim. All traces of baffled indecision had left him. "Well, Rona," he said, "your boyfriend here is pretty smart, after all. Did you get his message to those three people?"

Rona nodded.

"Fine. I'm going to try a little experiment. And I've got a couple of chores for you before they get here." He nodded to Oliver, who took one of the remaining two hypodermic syringes from the closet and handed it to him. He, in his turn, passed it to Rona. "Go into the scrub room and put a little water in this thing."

"Just about one c.c.," added Oliver.

Rona obeyed. When she brought the syringe back Jim replaced it in its former position on the shelf of the cabinet, the door of which he left open.

"They should be here any minute now," he said. "All the doors to the theater are locked except the one leading through this office, Rona. I want you to wait outside the passage and, when you see each person coming, tell him I want to talk to him in the theater. It doesn't matter who comes first, but it's your job to make sure each of them is alone when he goes through this office. Can you do that?"

"Of course, but why ...?"

"You'll know soon enough." Jim glanced once again at Oliver. "Everything's set, isn't it?"

"Sure." Oliver grinned. "The trap and the cheese."

"Okay. Then come on."

The two men moved to the door leading through the scrub room to the theater and disappeared. Rona, completely at sea, slipped out into the passage and moved to the head of the stairs by which the others would have to arrive.

In a very short time Hugh Ellsworth appeared, ascending the stairs. His dark eyes met hers, faintly amused. "Well, Rona, on sentry-go?"

She gave him the message and he strolled down the passage, disappearing through the door of Dr. Knudsen's office.

Gregory Venner came next, looking small and rather flustered. Rona sent him to the theater by the same route.

Finally Dr. Broderick himself appeared. The Director's face was still ashen-gray; he seemed to move in a daze. He acknowledged Rona's instructions by the slightest nod of his head and passed unseeingly down the corridor.

After a brief interval Rona followed him. She found Dr. Knudsen's office empty and heard the sound of voices coming from the theater. She moved to join the others, but, as she did so, they all came trooping back into the office, led by Jim.

"I guess it's better to be in here," he said. "Gentlemen, please be seated."

Lieutenant Heath's alert gray eyes moved from Venner to Ellsworth, resting finally on Dr. Broderick. "I've asked you all to come here because I want you to know exactly where we stand. I'm sorry, Dr. Broderick, to have to include you at a time like this but ..."

The Director waved the apology away. Very quietly he said, "You know there is nothing—nothing I would not do to have this terrible matter cleared up."

"I'm glad, Dr. Broderick, because I think it'll be cleared up very soon." Jim's lips were tight. "The whole setup of the two crimes is plain now, and a pretty dirty racket it's turned out to be. Someone here at the hospital had been extorting money out of Mrs. Broderick, using certain information about her daughter as a lever. Mrs. Broderick, herself, never knew that person's identity, but she confided in her brother, and Dr. Knudsen unearthed the blackmailer and threatened to expose him. He was murdered before he had a chance to do so."

He paused. "The murderer staked everything on the fact that the method he used for poisoning Dr. Knudsen would never come out. After the crime he put hyoscine in the remains of Knudsen's coffee, hoping to throw us off the right track and restrict suspicion to the people who had access to the lunch tray. That not only gave him a perfect alibi; it might easily have kept the truth from ever coming out. Even at autopsy, Lord says, it would have been almost impossible to tell that the hyoscine had not been administered in the coffee Knudsen drank."

Hugh Ellsworth had been listening intently. Rona thought he was going to break in, but he did not.

"Later in the evening," continued the lieutenant, "the murderer contrived to overhear a conversation between Rona and Mrs. Broderick. He learned that Mrs. Broderick had drunk some of the coffee. Since she had not been poisoned, both she and Rona were in a position to expose his poisoned coffee ruse. He also learned that Rona had stumbled on the idea of the sugar which, although it wasn't poisoned, was a damning piece of evidence. For those two reasons, he had to kill Mrs. Broderick, and he tried to kill Rona."

Jim glanced at Oliver. "I'm going to admit that I expected the half-lump of sugar to be poisoned, and, when we discovered it wasn't, the method of death had me completely stopped. Lord here, however, got a theory. I want you medical men to hear it—just the way he told it to me."

Oliver lit a cigarette. His strong hand, shielding the match, was very steady.

"First of all," he said, "I want to ask a question. We were all pretty close to Knudsen. Did any of you either know or suspect that he had anything the matter with him—a definite illness, I mean, that would require medication?"

Dr. Broderick looked up; his eyes showing surprise. Hugh Ellsworth, watching Oliver curiously, shook his head. It was Gregory Venner who spoke.

Emphatically he said, "But that's nonsense. Everyone knows that Knudsen was proud of the fact that he'd never had a day's illness in his life."

"I know he was proud of it," continued Oliver. "And it's logical to suppose that if ever he did have anything the matter with him, his pride would have made him terribly careful to keep anyone—even his closest associates—from guessing that he was ill. That, I believe, is exactly what happened. At the time of his death, and almost certainly for a considerable period before that, Dr. Knudsen was ill. And none of us ever so much as suspected it." He paused, adding very softly, "None of us, that is, except the man who murdered him."

A shade of Dr. Broderick's normal pompous manner returned as he leaned forward in his chair. "You appear to forget, Dr. Lord, that an autopsy has been performed. If Knudsen had been suffering, as you suggest, from some pathological condition, surely that would be revealed by the postmortem findings."

"Not necessarily, sir. The condition I refer to, if properly treated, need show no visible signs either during life or at autopsy. And there seems no question that Dr. Knudsen, in spite of his contempt for internal medication, had been using a standard specific to control his disease."

The moment of unrelieved silence that I followed was charged with tensity. Oliver continued suddenly, "It was that half-lump of sugar which gave me the clue. It put sugar way up front as an issue that was important to the murderer."

He stubbed his cigarette. "Rona happened to see Knudsen nibbling that sugar just a short time before the operation this afternoon. On several occasions in the past, too, she had seen him nibbling sugar. He had explained to her that he did it to get quick energy. That didn't sound particularly convincing to me. Knudsen always had plenty of energy of his own, and, even if he had needed an extra fillip, he would surely not have nibbled the sugar; he would have eaten the whole lump. The more I thought about it, the more certain it seemed that there was only one sound reason why Knudsen carried sugar around with him."

He leaned across the desk, pushing forward the four lumps of sugar which Rona had taken from the dead surgeon's coats. "I was sure I had the right idea when we found one of these in each of Knudsen's coats."

He glanced at Dr. Broderick. "It's not so long since I studied Diagnosis right here at the hospital. This problem turned out to be a lot easier than the ones we got in our year end quiz. Dr. Knudsen was by no means overweight, but he confined himself to a diet that was low in carbohydrates; he took no sugar with his meals; and yet, apparently, he always carried with him a lump of sugar which he occasionally nibbled."

He broke off and, getting up, moved to the drug cabinet. He took a small box from the top shelf and laid it down on the desk. Sliding open the lid, he revealed two rubber-stoppered ampules. "Here, I think, is the clinching evidence. This particular drug is practically never used in surgery. I can remember no occasion upon which we've needed it in the past six months. And yet there is always a package of it in this cabinet, and this particular one has been more than half used. There's only one possible conclusion to draw. Dr. Knudsen must have been using it on himself."

Dr. Broderick had been staring at the little glass vials with growing astonishment. "Insulin!" he exclaimed.

"Exactly. The rest is elementary. A patient who eliminated all sugar from his diet; a patient who took insulin; a patient who always carried a lump of sugar around with him." Oliver turned his keen gaze to Ellsworth. "Even a neurologist can figure out the answer to that one, can't he?"

Hugh Ellsworth was looking at him from impervious dark eyes. "I would say you've proved your point very ingeniously, Lord. You're implying, of course, that Knudsen was a diabetic?"

"Sure. That's the secret he tried so hard to conceal and which he succeeded in keeping from everyone—except the man who murdered him. Dr. Knudsen had diabetes!"

Oliver Lord, very sure of himself now, had risen and was standing, tall and broad-shouldered, behind the desk. His gaze fixed Lieutenant Heath.

"I didn't have much time just now to give you the lowdown on diabetes," he said. "In the first place, it's essential for all diabetics to take at least one injection of insulin a day. This keeps their blood sugar at the right level and prevents the danger of diabetic coma. But there is another danger, even after the insulin requirements of the individual have been thoroughly established. There is always the possibility of taking an overdose, which results in what is known as insulin shock. That's why every sensible diabetic carries a lump of sugar or its equivalent with him at all times. If he ever gets an abnormal reaction to his injection, it is the routine thing for him to nibble at the sugar—which modifies the effect of the insulin."

He ran a hand through his thick red hair. "The whole setup straightens itself out now, doesn't it? The man who had been extorting money from Mrs. Broderick knew Knudsen had diabetes." He turned to Ellsworth. "I don't know much about it, but I believe hyoscine is used almost exclusively in neurology, isn't it? Even so, it wouldn't have been difficult for any of us to get hold of some around the hospital, and a solution of hyoscine would be as colorless as insulin and just as easy to inject, wouldn't it?"

Hugh Ellsworth nodded. "That's absolutely true."

"And it wouldn't be difficult to take the rubber tops off some ampules and substitute a solution of hyoscine in place of the insulin. Once that was done, all the potential murderer had to do was to slip a poisoned ampule into Knudsen's current insulin supply."

He picked up the box. "As you see, this particular package has a slide top which opens only in one direction. That means that the patient would be more likely to use the ampules in the order they are in the box. Calculating on one ampule being used a day, it would have been possible for the murderer to plan ahead of time almost the exact moment when death would take place."

He shrugged. "Rona saw the Chief nibbling that lump of sugar before the operation. Obviously he'd just taken what he thought was his regular shot of insulin. He'd felt something was wrong, suspected an overdose, and, like all other diabetics, immediately took sugar. It was a most diabolically ingenious way to commit murder. Dr. Knudsen was tricked into poisoning himself while his murderer, if he'd wanted to, could have been in Timbuktu at the time when the crime was supposed to have been committed."

"Thank you, Dr. Lord." Jim's voice broke in, instantly deflecting all attention away from the intern. The lieutenant's gray eyes were gauging the various expressions of the men in front of him. "You've heard Dr. Lord's theory. In a very short time I hope to have evidence to prove it's the correct one." He paused, adding very quietly, "It may also interest you to know that I already have evidence to prove that the murderer of Dr. Knudsen and Mrs. Broderick is sitting in this room at this very moment."

Hugh Ellsworth propped his elbow on the back of the chair and stared straight ahead of him with slightly narrowed pupils; Gregory Venner clucked and threw a deprecatory glance at Dr. Broderick, who was gazing down at the polished black toes of his shoes. Rona, watching them, could feel the acute suspense in that small, bare room.

"The murderer," continued Heath levelly, "has two very definite attributes. In the first place, he was familiar with Linette Clint's medical history, which had been kept a closely guarded secret. Ellsworth, as the doctor who treated her, obviously had all the facts in his possession. But he is not the only one who could have known about the false epilepsy diagnosis. Mr. Venner, as the official record keeper, would have had the chance to see all the case reports on Miss Clint, and Dr. Broderick, as the girl's stepfather, might easily have heard about it from his wife. Theoretically, at least, any one of those three people had the necessary knowledge to blackmail Mrs. Broderick."

He picked up a pencil and tapped with it on the top of the desk. "The second attribute, however, applies to the murderer and the murderer alone. Only one of you people knew Dr. Knudsen had diabetes. That made it possible for the murderer to commit the crime. It has also, however, made it possible for us to solve it."

Beneath the short blond hair, the detective's face was very hard and uncompromising. "It's easy to figure out what the murderer did this afternoon when he managed to slip into the office alone after Dr. Knudsen had died. He realized, of course, that his remote control murder had been successful. His one remaining job was to conceal the true method of death. He had in his possession some extra hyoscine. He saw the half-drunk coffee on the lunch tray and realized that by putting the hyoscine in it, he could provide the perfect smoke screen."

He went on: "Next, probably, he searched through the scrap basket and got hold of the empty ampule which had contained the hyoscine dose. There was only one more thing for him to remove to make himself completely safe. The box of insulin ampules itself was no serious menace, because it was a reasonable thing for any surgeon to keep in his drug cabinet. But there was something else that was crucially important—the hypodermic syringe Knudsen had used to give himself the poisoned injection."

He broke off. Everyone in the room was watching him in taut, keyed-up silence.

"The murderer must have realized that Knudsen took the injection in a hurry before an important operation and probably would not have had the time to wash out the syringe. Almost certainly there would still be a residue in it, something which, if analyzed and proved to be hyoscine, would give the whole thing away. He had to remove it at all costs. But"—he shrugged—"there was the snag. Dr. Knudsen had put it back in its regular place in the drug cabinet, and the drug cabinet was locked. No one but Knudsen himself and Rona had a key. Knudsen's key was in his pocket—utterly inaccessible. Rona couldn't possibly be asked for hers without arousing suspicion. An elementary mischance like a locked cabinet had thrown a monkey wrench into the perfect murder setup."

Lieutenant Heath was still tapping with his pencil on the desk. The small, hollow sound echoed eerily in the stillness.

"Not to have provided against that beforehand was the murderer's first big mistake. But it was nowhere near as fatal as his second mistake." He paused and added softly, "And I might add that this second mistake has been made within the last few minutes."

He let the pencil drop. "I can imagine how all through the past hours the thought of that hypodermic syringe must have been preying on his mind. A combination of panic and a guilty conscience had forced him into killing Mrs. Broderick and trying to kill Rona in a desperate attempt to save the 'perfect murder.' But what good did that do him, when all the time the syringe with its vital evidence was here in the drug cabinet? Sometime this evening, we know, he was up here on this floor when he followed Rona. But at that time all the doors to this office were locked; there was a double barrier between him and the syringe."

Rona stiffened in her chair. She saw now exactly what her brother's little experiment had been.

"Just now," continued Lieutenant Heath, "each of you three men came through this office alone on your way to join me in the theater. The drug cabinet was open; the syringe was lying there for anyone to see. It seemed to the murderer like a heaven-sent opportunity at last to destroy the one really clinching piece of evidence. He went to the closet … and took the syringe. Look!"

He rose and crossed to the drug cabinet, pointing at the lower shelf. All the others were staring fixedly. Rona looked, too, although she had realized exactly what she would see. The hypodermic syringe which Jim had made her partly fill with water was no longer there.

"You can see now," Lieutenant Heath said, "just what a fatal mistake that was. The murderer didn't realize that things were playing into his hands a little too easily; he didn't realize he had fallen into a very simple trap. He did exactly what I hoped he would do. At the moment, he has that syringe in his pocket, and he might as well have a pair of handcuffs on his wrists too."

Oliver had risen now. He and Jim stood there by the cabinet, gazing fixedly at the three men in front of them. Hugh Ellsworth was still smiling his remote, faintly ironical smile. Dr. Broderick, very shaken and white, was playing abstractedly with his watch chain. Gregory Venner, his face a muddy gray, gave a little sniff and, thrusting his hand in his trouser pocket, pulled out a rolled-up handkerchief. With a swift, desperate movement, he jabbed the handkerchief against his wrist.

"I wouldn't bother to try any tricky business with that syringe, Mr. Venner." Jim's voice came sharp as a whiplash. "I'm afraid there's nothing in it but water. The original syringe Knudsen used is down in the analytical laboratory being tested for hyoscine. It'll be the State's Exhibit A against you."

Gregory Venner stared back at him from eyes that showed naked panic. There was a hard clatter as the handkerchief dropped from his fingers. Slipping out from its folds, a hypodermic syringe rolled across the floor.

Like a flash, Lieutenant Heath had sprung to pick it up. He stood by the anesthetist's chair, gazing at him from cold, steady eyes.

"This was almost too easy, wasn't it?" he said. "The fact that you took that syringe from the cabinet just now is damning enough on its own. But there are plenty of other things, too. You were very careful to establish an alibi for the time before Dr. Knudsen's death, but both Dr. Lord and my sister saw you go into the office as soon as the operation was over. You had just about time to pour the hyoscine in the coffee and remove the empty ampule. Rona met you on her way to Mrs. Broderick's room and told you Mrs. Broderick was going to give her some important information. I guess you were wondering just how much she did know. So you followed to the Ives Wing and did a bit of eavesdropping. You heard Rona talking about the sugar, which you knew might easily put us onto the track of the diabetes."

He continued relentlessly: "It was the diabetes that you really wanted to keep dark, wasn't it? Knudsen was your friend." His voice was edged with sarcasm. "You knew he'd never told his associates about it, but you had enough sense to realize that, if it did come out about the diabetes, suspicion would immediately point to you as the man who had gone mountain climbing with him. Around the hospital Knudsen was successful in concealing the fact that he took insulin, but it's inconceivable that he could have spent days and nights camping out with you and still have kept the secret of his daily injections from you."

He paused. "Lord has just told me about that time when Knudsen collapsed and you trekked so gallantly down the mountain to get him medical aid. It's a thousand-to-one shot that Knudsen collapsed from diabetic coma because his insulin either ran out or was lost, and that the medical aid you brought was—fresh insulin."

The little anesthetist had been staring at him speechless, his face a blank, dazed mask. Now, in the deep silence, while every atom of concentration in the room was fixed on him, he rose pointlessly to his feet. He looked pathetically small and helpless. "I—I saved his life," he said dully.

"You saved his life once," agreed Jim quietly. "And Dr. Knudsen showed his gratitude by giving you an opportunity to restore the money you'd blackmailed out of his sister. You used that opportunity to take the life you had previously saved."

"They were all getting money out of Mrs. Broderick. They had so much.... I had so little.... I never dreamed it would come to ..." Venner's voice trailed off. He looked around him wildly. Then suddenly he crumpled and fell to the floor.

They had taken him away.

For a while Rona was left alone in that austere, familiar room which had been the scene of so much tragedy and violence. She felt numb and tired—too tired to feel anything but a sense of relief that it was all over.

At some later, indeterminate stage, she was dimly aware that the door had opened. She looked up, to see the dark, impassive figure of Dr. Hugh Ellsworth.

"Well, Rona, we brought him around. When he heard Peters had found hyoscine in the hypodermic syringe, he made a full confession. He couldn't have done anything else. That trap your brother and Lord set caught him red-handed."

Rona shivered. "And they were friends! Poor little Venner, it seems incredible."

"It doesn't to me. People often get desperate when they grow old and feel their security slipping. He'd never felt his job was safe; he'd never had enough money; and he'd set his heart on going mountain climbing in Switzerland. When he had a chance to read Linette's case history in the record room, you can see what a hell of a temptation it must have been. A chance to get everything he wanted in life at a price Mrs. Broderick wouldn't even feel! And then Knudsen guessed, and accused him of the blackmail. Everything crashed—his new hopes and the few things he'd had to cling to in the past. He'd lost the respect of the one man who mattered to him; he'd lost the only influence which stood between him and Broderick's expressed intention of getting rid of him. There was nothing left to him except the money—and to preserve that he killed his best friend."

He shrugged. "You know the old adage: Once he'd put his hand to the plow of—murder …"

For a long moment they stood there without speaking. At length Ellsworth's lips moved in a slight smile. "Well, it's out of our hands now, and there's no use agonizing about it. At least, there's one piece of good news. Broderick's going to do everything in his power to put the grant through. That means a lot of expansion in the Neurological Clinic. I'll have some real work for you there if you feel like returning to the fold."

As he spoke, the door from the scrub room swung open and Oliver Lord came in. He crossed to Rona's side and put a possessive arm around her shoulders. Beneath the red hair his blue eyes stared belligerently at Ellsworth. "What's this about Rona going back to work for you?" he demanded. "She's staying right on with me."

Ellsworth did not speak. The wry smile was still on his mouth as he moved to the door. At the threshold he turned. "Rona will have to make up her own mind, of course. But, as a psychiatrist, I strongly advise the Neurological Clinic."

"Why?"

Ellsworth was grinning now. "Because I've always thought it is bad psychology for people to work together in the same department when they're—in love with each other."

He slipped out of the room, closing the door carefully behind him.

The End

THE GYPSY WARNED HIM
By Q. Patrick

Lew Warren, Gunner's Mate, Second Class, U. S. Navy, was high and happy. His white hat perched jauntily on the back of his curly black hair; he headed through the Manhattan dimout toward a blue neon sign which said: Eldorado Bar. He didn't know where he was. Somewhere in the Village. He didn't care. Eight hours of adventurous liberty stretched ahead before he had to rejoin his ship at the Brooklyn Navy Yard. He was young; he had the longest lashes, the quickest fists, the narrowest hips and the rowdiest appetite in B gun crew; and he was out to handle anything that came his way—preferably a blonde anything.

The sailor pushed through the swing doors into the Eldorado, snuffing appreciatively at the familiar aroma of beer and sawdust. A bar with a straggle of patrons stretched down one wall; couples sat together at tables. The warmth was good after the January outside. There was music too—the twang of a guitar and a girl's soprano singing a shrill "Rose Marie."

Lew's expert eye ran over the girl. She was a gypsy, colorfully out of place, with a scarlet blouse, a black swirling skirt and festoons of copper bracelets. Her dusky face stirred pleasant memories of a rough and Arabian night in Aden. Lew rolled to the bar, chose a spot where he could watch the girl and settled down with a beer.

By nature Lew was simple and amiable. He liked simple, amiable things. He liked the Eldorado Bar. He liked his beer and, as it seeped through him, he became sociably conscious of a plump little man in a camelhair coat who had just taken the stool next to him. Lew had never been to college but he had seen collegiate movies.

In spite of a pink bald head and a pink tuck of flesh under the chin, the newcomer reminded him of one of those minor characters who jump on the sidelines when the hero makes a touchdown.

The little man had ordered a straight rye and as he gulped it Lew grinned cheerfully, showing strong white teeth. The little man beamed back.

"Boy, that hits the spot." He put down the empty jigger. "Well, sailor, getting yourself a time in the Big City?"

"Sure."

"Jenkins is the name. Pleased to know you."

Lew took the pudgy, stretched-out hand. "Hiyah, Mr. Jenkins."

Mr. Jenkins' slightly piggy gaze moved around the bar and settled on the gypsy girl.

"Not bad, eh?" said Lew.

"Bad! Sailor, that gypsy's a genius. Sally, they call her. Best fortune teller in New York City. Told my cards the other night. Amazing. Didn't miss a thing—how many kids I've got, my wife's name, what line of business I'm in, everything."

"No fooling."

Mr. Jenkins leaned earnestly closer. "I'm not a guy that goes for that sort of thing as a rule. Fake, most of it. But this babe—well, she's uncanny. That's what she is—uncanny."

Lew watched with interest as the song stopped and Sally and her accompanist started through the tables, taking a collection. Mr. Jenkins consulted his watch with a wistful cluck.

"Well, I've got to be pushing along home or the little woman will have something to say." He winked. "But I've got to congratulate Sally first. Know what she did? Prophesied I'd land a big new contract today. And it came true. Yes, sir. Absolutely true. What d'you think of that?"

Lew's handsome young face was impressed. "Can any—I mean, does she charge a lot of dough?"

"Just a dollar." Mr. Jenkins beamed again and fumbled a loose wad of dollar bills out of his collegiate camelhair coat. He handed Lew one. "Here, boy, try your luck."

"Gee." Lew's large fingers folded over the bill. "Gee, thanks."

"Think nothing of it." Mr. Jenkins was in a grandiose mood. He tossed the barman another dollar. "Hey, Mac, see this sailor gets all the beer he wants." He slapped Lew's broad shoulder. "Good sailing, boy. Sink a couple of subs for me some time."

He bustled away through the tables. The barman shot Lew a beer. The sailor gulped it gratefully. Pretty decent guy for a civilian, that Mr. Jenkins. A buck's worth of free beer. And a buck fortune thrown in.

Although he didn't admit it, Lew, like most sailors, had a naïve confidence in fortune tellers. On his last convoy trip to England, an old Romany crone had read his cards in a dank, Liverpool pub. She had foretold a torpedo scare and, sure enough, it had come. Those gypsies had something.

Uncanny. He toyed pleasurably with Mr. Jenkins' word.

Mr. Jenkins had disappeared now. So had Sally. But in a few moments she reappeared, standing hand on hip at the back of the room. Lew beckoned and she came straight toward him. Lew liked the way she walked, proud and springy as a deer—just the way the babe in Aden had moved. She reached him. Her black gaze went up his tailor-made blues and settled on his face. She looked bored.

"Fortune, sailor?"

Lew grinned. "Sure."

"Okay. Come to a table."

She moved haughtily to an empty table near the door. Lew followed. She produced a grimy pack of cards scrawled with unfamiliar designs. Lew sat down opposite her.

Sally sniffed. "Fifty cent fortune or dollar fortune? The dollar fortune's better. More psychic."

"I'll take the buck fortune."

"Okay. Money first."

Lew passed her Mr. Jenkins' dollar which she stuffed swiftly into the pocket of her skirt.

"Take the cards. Make three packs. Pick a pack. Give it to me. Then give me your right hand."

Lew did what he was told. The gypsy dealt the cards in a circular pattern and poured over them, her dusky forehead puckering. She took Lew's palm, peering at the lines.

He said, "See any girls?"

"Quiet!" Sally's voice dropped to a professionally sepulchral level. "It is in your cards. It is in your palm. Tonight your whole life changes."

Lew's long lashes blinked. "Tonight?"

Sally fingered a card which seemed to represent a canopied bed. "I see a girl."

"Now you're talking."

"I see a beautiful girl. She is blonde. Yellow hair, I see it. Falling right down to her shoulders. She is very beautiful. I see her eyes—blue."

A parade of luscious blondes of the past moved through Lew's mind.

"Her name!" exclaimed Sally with mounting excitement. "I see it. No, it is gone. Instead what is it I see? A calendar. Yes, a calendar and on it all the months of the year."

"What about this girl—do I meet her?"

"Yes, yes. Tonight. There is trouble. I see that. She is pale and worried. You must help her. Whatever she says, do and ask no questions. Go with her anywhere. She will change your life. She will be the Big Romance of your life."

In spite of himself, Lew felt a tingle up his spine. He leaned across the table. "Give some more."

Sally rose, swept up the cards and shoveled them into her skirt pocket. "That is all."

Flashing him one black, disinterested glance, she moved away. In a few seconds she was back with the guitar man, giving to "A Pretty Girl Is Like a Melody."

Alone at the table, Lew scratched his head. *A beautiful blonde with blue eyes and hair to her shoulders.* Just his type. Meeting her tonight. He let his thoughts roam wishfully over the girl who was going to change his life. Then his dark face went sulky. That was the hokey sort of fortune you got for a penny in any weighing machine. Mr. Jenkins was a sucker to fall for stuff like that. Sally was a fake.

But he should worry. It hadn't been his buck.

Sally stopped singing about what pretty girls were like. The two gypsies disappeared. The barman brought Lew another free beer at the table. He started to drink it, but he felt foolish and uncomfortable now and the itch to move on stole over him.

His eyes, discontented behind their smudgy lashes, moved to the swing doors. The doors quivered as if some light pressure was pushing them from outside. They opened.

And a girl came in alone.

As she paused on the threshold, surveying the smoky interior, Lew glanced at her automatically. She wasn't the type that came to that sort of bar at that type of hour. He could tell partly from her expensively simple clothes but mostly from the indefinable something which stamped her as "class." He glanced again, more interested. She seemed to be looking for someone with a sort of tense anxiety. She was young, supple and built like a dream. She turned and he could see her face. It was beautiful as a spring meadow after rain.

Suddenly he stared, his pulses throbbing like a Diesel engine. For, as she moved, the light shone on her hair.

It was blonde. Honey blonde. Nothing to do with peroxide. The real thing.

And it fell in long soft sweeps around her shoulders.

For a moment she did not stir. Then her gaze met Lew's. Instantly her face lit up as if he was the one person in the world she needed. She hurried through the bar toward him. As he watched, dazzled, she came right to his table. She stopped there, a small gloved hand gripping the back of the empty chair. She was watching him urgently from eyes blue as the ocean off the Cape of Good Hope.

"You don't know me." Her voice sent a shiver of pleasure through him. "But I'm—I'm in trouble. I saw you. A sailor. You looked kind. I thought—" She smiled a tentative smile. "My name's April—April Osborne."

April. *A calendar with all the months of the year on it. Blonde hair to her shoulders—blue eyes—in trouble—April.*

Lew's head swam. It wasn't just the staggering coincidence of the gypsy's prophecy. It was the girl herself. Lew, who had taken women in his lusty young stride from Suez to San Francisco, had never really met this kind of a girl. He felt tongue-tied and abashed—exactly the way he'd felt at his first kid's party back in Short River, Ohio, when the Judge's daughter, devastating in pink organdie, had condescended to dance with him.

He half rose. "W-won't you sit down?"

The girl slipped into the chair opposite him. "I know it's awful speaking to you this way. But, you see, it's my brother Bob—Bob Osborne. Perhaps you know him. He's a sailor, too. He and his friend are in a house just down the block. I don't know what the matter is but they're in a little trouble. They need help. And Lanny—that's Bob friend—said that maybe another sailor would help, that sailors help each other out if they can. I came in here. I saw you. Oh, please, will you come with me?"

Suspicion stirred in Lew. Mr. Jenkins had said the gypsy was uncanny. But she couldn't be this uncanny. It must be a frame-up or—

"I know there's no reason why you should help me." April leaned over the table. "But, please—"

"What exactly do you want me to do?"

"Just come with me. You see, I talked to Lanny. Lanny's a cripple, poor thing. He can't help Bob himself. He said maybe there wouldn't be any trouble. Maybe we would just have to wait awhile and go away. But he also said there might be danger—a fight." A ghost of the smile came. "Can you fight?"

Lew looked down with frank pride at his bronzed right fist which had knocked him out of trouble in the toughest ports of three continents. Then he looked up at April. She was watching him, her blue, blue eyes pleading. She was even lovelier that close. She was all the things you dream about when you're a kid and your head's full of romantic ideas. Suddenly he was scared he might lose her.

Who cared if it was a frame-up? Caution never gets a sailor anywhere.

Lew got up, tilting the white hat even further back.

"Okay. Let's go."

"Oh, thank you." April's smile was shining. "I can't tell you how grateful I am."

She slipped her hand through his arm. As they moved toward the swing doors, Lew felt himself caught up in the wheels of Destiny.

The blonde who would change his life! Come on, baby. Change it!

Out in the murky darkness, April hurried Lew past closed stores and shrouded street lights. The Village with its twisting streets had a strangely un-American flavor. As they veered left and right down deserted sidewalks, Lew had the sensation of being in some foreign town. Marseilles, maybe. April was warm and close. A fragile perfume trailed around her. It reminded him of the daffodils on his grandfather's farm. She didn't speak and his diffidence with her kept him silent too.

At last they paused. They were halfway down a dark street at the mouth of a narrow, even darker alley.

"Here we are."

April drew him into it away from the feeble street light into pitch blackness. She didn't belong in this tawdry setting. Lew's suspicions flared again.

"Hey, where—"

"Shhh. Not so loud, please. This is the back way into the house. Lanny told me to come in this way."

April glided ahead. There was a squeak and her hand, finding his, drew him through a door she had opened into a little backyard. A path over straggly grass led to a rear door in a house. They moved to the door and April opened it quietly, guiding him into a nondescript hallway. A flight of uncarpeted stairs stretched upward. Somewhere close, canned music was playing—the dreamy music of a Viennese waltz.

April's honey hair glimmered in the pallid light. She turned to him gravely. "You'll trust me, won't you—whatever happens?"

Lew grinned a rather sheepish "Sure." Very alert, he followed her upstairs to a landing. At its end was a single door. She opened it and beckoned him inside into darkness that was even blacker than the darkness of the alley.

"We're to wait here," she whispered, "until Lanny comes for me."

Irrelevantly, Lew remembered another blonde in another bar in San Diego who had snuck him up backstairs into a dark room. That had been a very different proposition and, stupidly, in April's presence, the memory of it made him ashamed.

He said, "What about the light?"

"I'm afraid there isn't any. Wait a minute. There is a flashlight. I left it here somewhere."

She groped around and a beam of light sprouted, revealing a large, empty room. Paper was peeling off the walls. One solitary packing case loomed by the shaded window. On it stood a bottle of whiskey and glasses. April switched off the flashlight.

"We'd better stay in the dark."

"Where are we?"

"In the house where Bob and Lanny are."

"I know. But whose house is it?"

"I don't know."

"You don't know?"

"Please, please, don't ask questions." A heartbreaking catch came in her voice.

"But a guy's got to know something. You bring me here to—"

"All right." A note of irritation put an invisible wall between them. "Since you don't trust me, I'll tell you the truth. Bob made me promise not to unless it was really necessary, but—"

He said clumsily, "No you don't—"

Her hand found his, restoring contact. "This all seems as crazy to me as it does to you. But I've learned not to ask questions whatever Bob and Lanny do because they're—working for Naval Intelligence."

"Naval Intelligence?"

"Yes. It's terribly important—and dangerous. They brought me with them tonight because they thought I could help. And they sent me for you because they thought a sailor could help. We've got to trust them. We've got to do what they say."

Lew felt like a heel now for doubting her. "I'm sorry. Gee, you should have told me. Any sailor'd help them out if it's Naval Intelligence."

Her hand was still in his, warm and vibrant. There was a sweet smell of daffodils in the darkness. His feeling for her was so strong that it frightened him.

"Know something?" he blurted. "A gypsy told my fortune. Said I was gonna meet a beautiful blonde who was in trouble and that I was to help her."

April gave a quiet laugh. "She did?"

"She said something else too. His voice wabbled. "She said this girl was—was going to be the big thing in my life."

She moved a very little closer. If it had been any other girl in his brash young career, he would have gone into his routine then, pulling her into his arms and kissing her. But he couldn't treat her that way. Not April. His heart was thumping against his ribs. The dark, dreary room was caught up in magic.

Suddenly April stiffened. "Listen."

Lew listened tensely. Outside in the passage were shutting, irregular footsteps. "That's Lanny."

The footsteps came nearer. They were the dragging, obscurely sinister footsteps of a cripple. They reached the door and stopped. Five taps sounded.

"That's Lanny's signal." April slipped the flashlight into Lew's hand. "I'm to go with him. Wait till I come back. Please, however long I'm gone, wait." While his hand went out to her, she moved away. "If you want a drink, there's a bottle. Bob and Lanny brought it."

She tiptoed out of the room. Lew heard whispered conversation outside. Then her face, in shadowy silhouettes, reappeared around the door.

"You know where the whiskey is, don't you? On the packing case by the window."

She disappeared, shutting the door behind her. Then footsteps sounded again, going away—the tap of feminine heels and the clump of the unseen and crippled Lanny.

Without her in that dark, unidentified room, Lew began to feel uneasy. A healthy brawl with a bunch of roughnecks was one thing. But signal taps and secrets agents—he'd never run into anything like this before. As the minutes ticked by and nothing happened, his nerves, used to action, started to fray. April had the right idea about a drink. Turning on the flashlight, he crossed to the packing case, poured a generous slug of rye into a glass and carried it back to his post by the door.

He tilted the glass to his lips, gulping its contents into his mouth. He swallowed some. Then with a grunt of distaste he spat the rest out.

He had noticed only just in time the sweetish, alien taste in the rye. He sniffed at the dregs in the glass. They gave off a frail odor. Associations brought rushing back a waterfront dive in Port of Spain where a Creole tramp had tried to roll him by giving him beer doped with ether.

That's what it was. Ether.

The whiskey had been doped with ether.

Slowly, as his mind started to function, Lew saw his daffodil world of romance tumble around him. April had returned after her conversation with Lanny solely to make sure he would drink some of the whiskey. That could mean only one thing. The whole affair was a frame-up. Probably April and the gypsy had been in cahoots. All that talk about her sailor brother and secret government work was baloney.

She had lured him here to dope him.

For a moment he could not bring himself to believe that of April. Then, once again childish memories came of the Judge's daughter in her pink organdie. Later at the kids' party, she had offered Lew a coy, sticky kiss on the back porch. Afterwards she had run, sneaking on him, to her father in a flurry of tears and party frock, and Lew had received the first real thrashing of his life. The Judge's daughter, April—they were all the same, those classy dames. They'd double-cross you as soon as look at you. The old, deep-seated wound, merging with this fresh one, sent resentment boiling through Lew's body.

He was a very angry young sailor now. There was nothing to stop him walking right out of this mysterious house. But women who tried to make a sucker out of him did not get off that easy. Danger or no danger, he was going to find out April Osborne's dirty racket and put the skids under it.

A beautiful blonde in trouble. Do whatever she asks. She will change your life.

The gypsy had got it wrong. It was April's life that was going to be changed—quickly and for the worse.

Silent but in a roaring rage, he slid open the door and stepped out into the passage. He had no plan. To his right a flight of stairs led up to the next building. To his left sloped the stairs by which he had ascended. It was less risky to start his unofficial investigation downstairs where, if need be, he could escape by the yard door.

He reached the little hall on the ground floor. Apart from the back door, there were two others, one straight ahead, a second in the side wall. He chose the second.

There was no lock, only a metal catch. He loosened it and the door opened inward onto darkness. He stood still, straining his eyes and ears. The house was plunged in silence. A switch made a shadowy blur on the inside wall beyond the door. He turned it and springing light showed a spiral metal staircase going down.

It looked like a cellar. Probably nothing of interest there. He hesitated and, on an impulse, started down the steps until he reached the turn in them. He passed it.

As the cellar below came into view and he saw what was in it, he threw out a hand to support himself against the iron rail. Cold sweat beaded his forehead.

The cellar was small and neat. A furnace stood in one corner; covered pipes, like fat caterpillars, crawled around the walls; coal was piled in the rear.

But there was something else. It was sprawled at the foot of the stairs like a sack that had been tossed down from the door above. But it wasn't a sack. Definitely.

For the first wrenching seconds, Lew could not believe his eyes. But it was true.

Tumbled there, the legs grotesquely straddling the lower step, the arms flung backwards across the gray cement of the floor, lay the body of a sailor.

Lew had seen dead sailors before. On the Red Sea, he had seen his own buddies shot down around him by Stuka machine-guns. He knew there was no life in that limp, huddled body in front of him.

Dazedly he moved down one step. His legs were weak and nausea stirred deep in him. It must be the gulp of doped liquor he'd taken. Thoughts spun dizzily, like the hieroglyphics on the gypsy's cards.

Half stumbling over the last step, he staggered and dropped to his knees by the body. As he bent over it, he was dimly conscious that his handkerchief and liberty card had slid out of his breast pocket. But he did nothing about it—not yet.

The bald light from the ceiling splayed down on the dead sailor. He was young, dark as Lew and about Lew's build. In spite of the blind stare in his eyes and the half open mouth, his face was handsome.

From the rating on the sleeve of his jumper, he had been a Bosun's Mate, First Class.

Lew's gaze moved over the jumper. There were three thin slits in it above the left breast—slits that were wet and sticky with blood. The floppy black neckerchief was bloodstained too.

The unknown sailor had been stabbed through the heart.

Lew was catching on to his thoughts now, and the sense they made sent horror tingling through him. So this was April Osborne's racket. She lured sailors here, gave them doped whiskey and then, with her crippled associate, Lanny, she—murdered them. For what? For the handful of dollars they carried? In his most cynical moments about April, he had never dreamed of anything like this.

He felt in the sailor's breast pocket, hoping to find some identification. As he had expected, the pocket was empty. His fingers, recoiling from contact with the dead skin, pushed through the open neck of the jumper, groping for the inside pocket. There would be nothing there, either.

He touched something thick and rustling. He pulled out the contents of the pocket. His hand was folded over a wad of bills. Fifty-dollar bills. He counted them. Ten. Ten fifty-dollar bills.

Five hundred dollars.

Impossibly the dead sailor had five hundred dollars in his pocket, five hundred dollars which no one had bothered to take. The whole picture was blurring again. Lew stared at the cold, quiet corpse. He stared at the bills in his hand. He had never seen that much money in one place before. With rough clumsiness, he thrust it into the inner pocket of his own jumper. Whatever the sense of it, he could at least keep the money from April.

He made himself plan then. The police, of course. He had to lam out of this place at the double and get the police.

He jumped up, turning to the steps. Then another thought came. If he went for the police now, April and Lanny might return to the empty room upstairs, find him gone, put two and two together and escape before the police could catch them. Every consideration of personal safety or caution were engulfed now in his hatred for April, the beautiful blonde who had indeed changed his life, April, the fragile, aristocratic girl who murdered sailors. Lew was a stubborn young man. Once his teeth were in something, they stuck. He had forgotten all his hopes and plans for an eight-hour binge. He was not going to return to his ship until he had made April pay for this—and for her shining fake smile and her blue lying eyes.

As he stood in the bright, dreadful cellar, he saw with grim satisfaction, that the golden opportunity was his. Unless April had already returned to the empty room, she still thought of him as the sucker who had fallen so easily into her trap. She had lured him there, either to kill him too or to use him for some other mysterious purpose. Okay. He'd go back to the room, wait for her and pretend to be doped by the etherized whiskey. He'd let her do exactly what she was planning to do with him until he had her so deep in this murder that no court in the country would acquit her.

A formidable figure in his swaggering blues, he headed for the spiral steps. He remembered his liberty card and handkerchief and turned back for them. The handkerchief had bizarrely fallen over the dead sailor's hand. He picked it up, saw the shiny green of a liberty card beyond the body and stuffed it too into his breast pocket.

He left the cellar then, turning out the light and sliding the door back on its catch. Passing through the hall, he tiptoed upstairs to the gloomy landing. The door to the empty room was ajar at the exact angle it had taken when he left. He slipped inside into darkness and groped down for the flashlight. It too lay precisely where he had put it.

Almost certainly April had not yet returned for him.

He closed the door, found the whiskey bottle and poured some of the doped liquor on the floor to make it seem as if he had drunk a great deal. As he stood there, waiting, minute after minute, doubts began to stir. Perhaps he was playing into April's hands after all. Perhaps she had never intended to come back for him. Perhaps she and Lanny were already miles from the scene of their crime, calling the police to report that one sailor had murdered another in a brawl and that the murderer could be found in a drunken stupor upstairs in the empty room.

Maybe Lew's function in the drama had been to play scapegoat.

He thought with new uneasiness of the five hundred dollars in his pocket. Should he?— He went suddenly taut. From beyond the closed door came the faint sound of footsteps—the familiar tap-tap of feminine heels and the slithering shuffle of a cripple.

After Port of Spain, Lew knew what it felt and looked like to be dopey on ether. Clutching the whiskey bottle, he let himself slide to the floor so that he sat sprawled against the wall. His heart was thumping. He had no idea what he was letting himself in for, but he was going to turn the tables on April Osborne if it was the last thing he did.

The footsteps came nearer and stopped outside the door. Lew heard April's whisper. Then, squinting through half shut eyes, he saw a chink of light and two shadowy figures passing across it into the room. Darkness came again as the door closed behind them.

"Sailor—are you there?" It was April's lilting voice.

Lew did not answer.

A man's voice, reedy with anxiety, said, "He's gone."

"He can't have gone, Lanny. He promised to wait. He trusted me. I know he did." April was so close to Lew now that her toe almost trod on his hand. "There's a flashlight somewhere unless he moved it." Lew heard her fumbling. "Here it is."

Through closed lids he was conscious of a beam directed full on his face. April gave a stifled gasp. Lanny tittered a high laugh.

"So there's your sailor. Pretty picture. The whiskey did the trick a little too well."

"But what—what are we going to do with him?"

"Leave it to me." Lew felt a man's hand on his shoulder, shaking him. "Hey, sailor. Wake up."

Lew had to think trigger-quickly. Whatever their plan, they didn't want him to have completely passed out. Okay. He fluttered his lashes and opened one eye, peering with well-simulated stupidity. He mumbled something inaudible.

April dropped to her knees at his side. "Don't you remember me?" Her face was close to his, grave and lovely as ever, framed by the shining hair. "I asked you here to help my brother. He doesn't need help after all. Everything's all right. He's left and gone somewhere else. I'm terribly sorry to have given you all this trouble. Lanny and I are here to see you get home."

So her "brother," the sailor who was lying dead in the cellar, was "all right" now! He had left and gone somewhere else!

The blue eyes were still watching him. "Sailor, you know me, don't you? April?"

Lew muttered, "Sure, sure—April."

She slipped her soft arms around his shoulders. Lew let her help him to his feet while he dropped the whiskey bottle with a clatter. Her daffodil fragrance wafted to his nostrils. After the romantic way he'd felt about her once, it was horrible now to be touching her and hating her.

"Come on, Lanny. Let's get him out of here quickly."

The invisible Lanny had opened the door. As Lew staggered theatrically out into the passage, he took a cautious glance at April's associate. Lanny was indeed a cripple. She had not lied about that. The man's left arm was nothing but a shriveled claw hunched across his stomach; and his left leg dragged behind him, twisted at the knee and sheathed at the foot in a thick, built-up boot. That swift glance, however, warned Lew that Lanny was no lightweight adversary. Beneath a mane of sandy hair, his face was sharp as a fox's with quick, sliding eyes.

With Lanny limping ahead, April guided Lew down the stairs. Anxiety wabbled in him. It looked as if their plans had changed and that they were merely going to get him out of the house as quickly as possible. If that were so, something drastic had to be done.

It was when they reached the little hall that the idea came. Since they showed no signs of forcing the issue, he'd do it for them. With a convincing lurch, he broke away from April, muttering:

"Gotta get out of here."

He weaved across the hall and headed straight for the cellar door, pretending to have mistaken it for the other door which led to the yard. He was going to "discover" the corpse in their presence. That would put them on the spot. They would either have to play innocent and go with him for the police, or else they would have to show their hand—by trying to escape or by trying to kill him.

If there was any killing to be done, Lew was more than confident of his ability to protect himself.

He reached the cellar door and started fumbling with the catch.

April's voice sounded sharply, "No, no. That isn't the way."

"Sure it'sh the way." Lew threw the door open, teetered on the threshold and then leaned forward and snapped on the light.

"Hey, let me get him." Lanny's falsetto was hoarse.

"No, Lanny. I will."

April's footsteps clattered after Lew. He started down the spiral steps. She caught up with him, clutching at the sleeve of his blues.

"That's not the way, sailor. Come back."

He brushed her off, stumping on. The bend in the steps loomed. He felt throbbing excitement. Any second now, the corpse would come into view. April Osborne would have a hard time explaining away that little picture.

The girl was still clawing at the back of his jumper. He paid her no heed. He reached the bend. He threw out a hand to the iron railing just in case she tried to push him from behind.

She was right back of him. He could feel her warm breath on his neck.

He lifted his free hand to point.

"What—?" he began.

Then the words faded on his lips. His whole world seemed to have gone mad.

The neat bright little cellar was exactly the same. He could see into every corner of it, see the furnace, the coal pile, the pipes along the walls.

But the cement floor stretched blank and empty from the foot of the steps.

The body of the sailor was no longer there.

Lew stared dizzily. Somehow, while he was waiting upstairs, they had managed to remove the corpse—every trace of it. The situation had been violently changed—and for the worse. He had even lost his chance with the police now. He could never get them to believe his wild story unless he at least was able to produce the body. He had been thoroughly and humiliatingly outsmarted.

"You see, it wasn't the way, was it? This is just the cellar."

He swung round. April had spoken with the patronizing kindness with which one humors children and drunks. She was smiling as she watched him, a friendly, amused smile.

"You just leave everything to Lanny and me, sailor."

His strong right hand itched to take a sock at that lovely, smiling face. It was a real effort to control himself. But he saw that his only chance to expose April and to extricate himself from an impossible situation was to keep up his act and play along with them.

It was his wits now against April's.

He let her help him back up the cellar stairs. Lanny was waiting at their head, his face sharp as a greyhound's.

"Okay?" he asked.

"Okay," murmured April. "He lost his way. That's all."

She looped her arm through Lew's. Lanny closed in on the other side, his one good hand, overdeveloped and powerful, clamping down on the sailor's husky shoulder.

Lew was cat-tense behind the sodden front of drunkenness. They had run a big risk in luring him there. Surely, they must be planning to use him somehow. As they stood in the little hall, he became conscious again of the canned music he had heard when April first brought him. This time it was a pulsing rhumba.

"All right, sailor. Come with us."

Lanny limped forward. A twinge of excitement ran through Lew. They were guiding him not to the door opening onto the yard but to the third door which led deeper into the building. Something was going to happen.

April opened the door, revealing a long passage with another door at the end. The music was louder. They reached the last door and went through it. A tall screen blotted out what lay ahead. They moved around the screen.

They had come through a back entrance into a bar. It was a nondescript bar, much like the Eldorado. The lights were cloaked in pink shades and very dim. Cigarette smoke further misted the interior. There were wooden booths and a long bar. Music brayed from a florid red and silver juke box in the corner.

After the crazy horrors of the house, it was jolting to be thrown into an atmosphere where ordinary people were laughing and chatting and being humdrum over their beers.

Instinct warned Lew that the climax was approaching in this jumbled plot which still made no sense to him. They would never have brought him in here, rather than smuggling him out by the back way, unless they had some good use for him—right here in this bar.

They made a conspicuous threesome, a drunk sailor, a beautiful blonde and a cripple. As they appeared around the screen, there was a hush. Eyes flicked to them and stayed—curiously.

"Okay, April," muttered Lanny's thin voice. "Go get a taxi."

April shot Lew a doubtful glance. "You think you can take care of him in that condition?"

"Of course."

"All right."

The girl slipped away from them toward the exit door. Lew and Lanny followed more slowly, Lanny dragging his twisted leg, Lew playing drunk. The juke box stopped, scratched, hissed and then pounded into "Begin the Beguine." Although Lew did not dare watch too closely, he had the distinct impression that Lanny's eyes were scanning each dark booth, as if he was looking for someone.

They reached one of the middle booths. Out of the corner of his eye, Lew caught a glimpse of a blond soldier sitting there alone over a drink. As they passed through the smoky dimness, the soldier glanced up sharply and called:

"Hi, there you are, sailor."

Lanny brought Lew to an abrupt halt. By a deft maneuver, the cripple put his own body between Lew and the soldier so that they got only a vague impression of each other.

"Here's your friend, sailor," Lanny said that to Lew, his voice glossed with false amiability. "He's been waiting all this time for you."

Bits of the pattern slipped into place in Lew's mind. Was it for this then that April and Lanny had wanted him? Was he to understudy at this rendezvous for the murdered sailor who also had been dark and about Lew's build? That must be it. In the smoke-fogged light of the bar, Lanny and April could bank on the soldier's mistaking Lew for their victim. And Lew was supposed to be doped so that later he would remember nothing. And the money? How did that five hundred dollars come in?

The soldier said, "Thought you'd never show up again. Okay. Want it back now?"

"He's got your letter, sailor," Lanny said softly, dearly. "The soldier wants to give you back your letter."

"*Letter!*" Lew lurched and mumbled, "sure, sure. Letter—"

"Plastered, ain't he?" queried the soldier suspiciously. "He said it was important. Maybe I shouldn't give it to him in this—"

"Oh, that's all right." Lanny gave a shrill laugh. "We've just been having a little celebration back there. He's okay."

"Sure, sure," said Lew. "Gimme the letter."

The soldier scratched his head. "Okay. Maybe all this makes sense to you and that blonde dame. To me the whole thing's nuts." He produced a crumpled white envelope from his back pocket and, leaning across Lanny, stuck it into Lew's breast pocket. "There you are, sailor."

Lanny was smiling triumphantly. "He said he'd give you a couple more bucks for waiting, didn't he? Here you are." He flicked two dollars onto the booth table. "Thanks, soldier." Swiftly, he twisted Lew away from the booth and started to guide him toward the exit.

Lew was faced with a crucial decision. So the murdered sailor had entrusted that letter, whatever it was, to the soldier in the bar, offering him money to wait and return it to him at the right moment. The letter must be of vital importance to April and Lanny, otherwise they would never have gone to such dangerous lengths, involving kidnaping and doping a strange sailor, to retrieve it. Every instinct in Lew prompted him to bring things to a head right then; to go back for the soldier, tell him the whole story, grab Lanny and get the police.

But what of April? She was waiting outside with a taxi. The slightest hitch in their plans would send her skittering away to safety. Whatever happened, he wasn't going to let Miss April Osborne slip through his fingers.

Step by step, he and Lanny drew nearer and nearer the door. With sudden bravado, Lew decided he didn't need the help of any two-cent soldier or of any civilian police. This crazy murder with a vanishing corpse had developed into a private battle between him and the blonde who would change his life. He was getting somewhere now but he had a lot to find out still before the whole dirty business became clear. Okay. Go along with them for the next step. He had the letter and the money and therefore the whip hand. Go with them in the taxi—see what happened.

They were out now in the dark street. April was waiting by a taxi. She ran to them.

"All right?"

Lanny chuckled. "All right."

"Then come—quickly. We're late as it is."

April hurried into the cab and, leaning out, helped Lew in after her. "We're going to join my brother," she explained. "Then we'll see you get home." Lanny lumbered in, flanking Lew on the other side.

"Okay," he called to the driver. "Uptown and make it snappy."

As the taxi shot forward, Lew kept himself from looking at April. Even now the sight of her did things to his pulses. It was crazy that he could still feel that way when he hated and despised her. He tried to force her out of his mind by thinking of the letter sticking out of his breast pocket. Should he put it in a safer place? The only safer place was his inside pocket and he was scared that in doing so, he might reveal the presence there of the dead sailor's five hundred dollars.

He was still pondering this question when Lanny called to the driver, "Stop here."

The taxi ground to the curb. April stirred as if surprised. Lanny tugged open the door and stepped out onto the sidewalk.

"Okay, sailor. Here's the next stop."

He leaned in the cab, gripping Lew's arm. Lew let himself be supported to the sidewalk. For a brief second he and Lanny stood there. April didn't seem to be getting out. Lew's glance shifted from Lanny to the girl. In that instant, Lanny leaned forward with a fox-quick movement, snatched the letter from Lew's pocket, jostled him sideways and, dangling his dead leg, jumped back into the cab.

Lew lunged forward but the door slammed in his face.

"Quick, driver!" Lanny's voice sounded shrill. "The sailor's drunk. Shake him off."

Lew leaped for the running board but he was too late. The taxi swerved and, with a grinding of gears, hurtled away into the murky darkness and out of sight.

Lew looked around. There was no other taxi. There was no way of chasing them. For the second time that night, he had been outsmarted.

Hopelessly so this time. The corpse was gone. The letter was gone. April and Lanny were gone forever.

Bleakly he reviewed his own actions, thinking of a dozen different ways in which he might have behaved. Well, it was no use worrying about that now. This was the end. He would never know what was in that letter. Someone else would have to find out who the dead sailor was and why he had been murdered. April Osborne would be nothing but a maddening memory to haunt him on the long nights of the Atlantic Convoy.

In the flurry, he had forgotten the five hundred dollars. As he remembered them, tempting visions stirred. With five hundred bucks, his leaves could be the leaves of Reilly for months to come. But Lew's strict Ohio upbringing had made him scrupulous about money. He couldn't think of this fantastic windfall as legitimately his own. He would somehow have to get it back where it belonged. But where did it belong? The police? Shouldn't he in any case report his whole crazy story to the police?

His shuffling, "dopey" walk had stiffened him. He flexed the muscles of his broad back and surveyed the deserted street. A smudge of light on the opposite sidewalk showed a bar. A bar was a better place for figuring things out than this windy corner. He strode across the street and into the comfortable warmth of the beer joint.

The place was almost empty. He ordered a double rye and carried it to a table, sitting down facing into the interior of the room. The tang of the liquor braced him and brought back a little self-confidence. Perhaps he had given in too easily; perhaps, if he figured hard enough, there was still some way of catching up again with April Osborne.

The more he thought, however, the further the events of the evening slid from reality. The gypsy, April, that crazy house with its disappearing sailor's corpse, all seemed now like things out of a dream. Maybe it had been a dream. That happened to guys, he knew. They had some kind of a fit and lost their memories and when they came to they couldn't remember what had been real and what had been dream.

This disturbing thought brought sweat to his forehead. He pulled the handkerchief out of his breast pocket to wipe it away. As he did so, his green liberty card in its slippery celluloid case dropped onto the table in front of him. He picked it up, glancing at it.

His glance froze into a stare. Because the photograph pasted to the left-hand top corner was not his photograph. The face staring out of it was the face of the dead sailor in the cellar.

And the name printed below was:

ROBERT OSBORNE

The sight of that dead face gazing up from his own palm brought a kind of horror. Then everything somersaulted back into reality. There was no question now that it had all been real—April, the murder, everything. And it was obvious what had happened. When he stumbled over the corpse, his own liberty card had tumbled from his pocket. Later, in his hurried departure from the cellar, he had seen a liberty card on the cement floor and grabbed it, assuming it to be his own. But it hadn't been his. It had been the card which must have slipped from the breast pocket of the corpse when it had been so carelessly tossed down the cellar steps.

Thoughts rose and fell like white caps on a choppy sea. His own precious liberty card was gone. Under normal circumstances that in itself would have been a major tragedy. But now its loss was packed with dynamite. For certainly it would have been discovered in the cellar by April's associates when they removed the corpse. Soon April would know that he had seen the corpse. Not only that. She would know he probably had the murdered sailor's liberty card and that, with this tangible piece of evidence in his possession, he could at any minute get the entire New York police force out searching for Robert Osborne. Lew's position was incalculably strengthened. It was much, much more dangerous too. April Osborne wasn't likely to let a star witness against her walk the streets of New York unharmed.

A few minutes ago he had been desperate that he might have lost track of her forever. With a certain grim satisfaction he saw how wrong he had been to worry.

If he knew April Osborne, she would be figuring in his life again—very soon.

What should he do? Should he go to the police right now and, with the liberty card and the five hundred dollars, force them into immediate action? Or should he wait here on the chance that April, with murder in her heart, would show up again? He looked down at the photograph on the liberty card and the name printed beneath it. The dead sailor had been called Robert Osborne. April hadn't lied about that.

The chain of his thoughts was snapped by a woman's voice behind him, calling urgently:

"Bob—Bob—"

Footsteps clattered. Before he could turn, a hand clutched at his shoulder and the voice was panting:

"Oh, Bob, darling, I was so worried. I thought I'd never catch up with you. I followed in a taxi. I—"

He turned then. A girl was standing behind him, a small, dark, unknown girl with a face shaped like a heart and big brown eyes. She was dressed in a cute green tailored suit and her lips were half parted in something that had begun as a smile and had changed into a startled gasp.

"Oh, I thought you were Bob Osborne. I—" Then, as if a sudden truth had dawned, her expression changed to hot indignation. "Where is he? What have you and that blonde and that crippled man done with Bob Osborne?"

Lew was still dangling the dead sailor's liberty card. "Bob Osborne?"

"It's no good pretending." Anxiety and anger were warring on the girl's face. "I went with Bob to that bar. I saw that blonde and the cripple taking him inside. He told me that what he was going to do was terribly dangerous and that I was to wait for him." She grabbed Lew's husky arms just above the elbow and shook him. She was like a small and furious mother bird defying a hawk. "It's no use trying to fool me. You came out of that bar with them so's I would think you were Bob in the dimout and that I'd stop worrying and go away. Well, it didn't work. I followed in another taxi. And now I've found you. And you've got to tell me the truth."

She had bewildered Lew. He was suspicious of her. But in spite of that he liked her spirit. He liked her looks too—cute and pretty with no nonsense about her. She glared at him. He took her arm and pressed her into the other seat at the table.

"Okay. Now tell me who you are. And what's Bob Osborne to you?"

Her mahogany eyes smoldered behind lashes as thick and smudgy as Lew's. "I'm Dinah Lord. And I'm going to marry Bob Osborne next week."

"Marry him!"

"Yes, marry him." The girl must have read from his face the shocked confusion that was seething in him. Sharply she added, "What is it? What have you done with him?"

That was one of the most difficult moments in Lew's life. He stared at the girl and then at the liberty card in his hand. Dinah Lord had been going to marry Bob Osborne. Fate had unexpectedly sent him an ally. Did she have the courage to take the truth? He thought so. He tossed her the liberty card. She grabbed it up.

"Bob's liberty card! Why have you—"

"Listen—Dinah." Lew's distaste for what he had to tell showed itself in clumsy tenderness. "You've got me wrong. I'm on the level. I'm just a sailor like Bob. I didn't have anything to do with this crazy plot or whatever it is."

"Plot?"

The liberty card dropped from her fingers. He picked it up, putting it back in his pocket.

"Didn't you know these people were gunning for Bob Osborne?"

"I—I knew there was danger, that he was doing something important for Naval Intelligence."

"Naval Intelligence! So, April was right about that too."

Dinah's little hands clenched into fists. "Don't go on talking like this. I can't bear it. If you know, tell me what's happened to Bob."

Lew dropped his eyes because he didn't want to have to see her face. "This is tough, kid. But I guess you've got to know. Bob's dead—they murdered him. I saw his body down in the cellar of that house. Stabbed."

"Murdered!" The word, wrenched out of her, forced him to look up. Dinah Lord's face was white as a shroud, but her eyes still blazed with mahogany steadiness. "That's a lie."

"It's true, baby. It's tough, but it's true. Here, take a slug of my drink."

She shook her head, the dark hair swirling. "No, I'm—I'm all right. Tell me. I've got to know."

Lew had never known a girl show so much fortitude. As he told her everything that had happened since he entered the Eldorado Bar, she sat perfectly still, watching him. Only her fingers, digging into her palms, gave a hint to what was going on inside her.

"So you see," he wound up, "I was just a sucker, someone they dragged in to help them get that letter Bob had left with the soldier. Do you know anything about the letter?"

Dinah shook her head.

"And the dough—the five hundred bucks?"

Once again she shook her head. Every ounce of her control was concentrated on keeping her lower lip steady. Lew could tell that. He wanted to comfort her, but there was nothing he could do except to pretend not to notice, to go on talking.

"It all hangs around that letter," he said. "I had it and, like a dope I let Lanny and April get it back from me." A hauntingly vivid image came of April's flower-like face, her daffodil perfume. Absurdly, because he discovered he wanted to believe it more than anything in the world, he added, "A couple of things April told me were true. Maybe I've—I've got her wrong. Maybe somehow she's been framed too. Maybe she is Bob's sister and—"

"Sister!" Dinah threw out the word savagely. "How could she be Bob's sister when Bob didn't have any sister?"

That killed Lew's forlorn hope. He sat in a dejected slump, miserable in front of Dinah's tearless grief.

Suddenly, in a rasping voice, she said, "Only a week. We were going to be married in a week. Yesterday he—he bought the ring. He—"

The words faded. Her hands went up covering her face. Lew glanced around the empty bar. Except for the dozing barman there was no one left to see her suffering, and he was glad. He got up, putting his arms around her small shoulders, hating April more than he had ever hated her.

"Okay, kid, cry if you want to. Get it out of your system. But you and me, we've got a job to do. Lanny and April killed Bob. We know that. And we've got to make them pay for it, haven't we? I've been a dope. I thought I could figure this thing out by myself. But it's different now. You and me, we're going to take Bob's liberty card to the police right away and hand the whole business over to them."

"No." Dinah's hands fluttered from her stricken face. "No, we can't go to the police."

"But, baby—"

"That's the last thing Bob said. When he left me outside the bar, that's what he said. Whatever happened, I wasn't to call the police. Naval Intelligence have been making plans for months. Bringing in the police would ruin their plans. These people are terribly dangerous. They're spies or saboteurs. Oh, I don't know what. But the plans for rounding them up are more important than anything else—even Bob's life. That's what he said."

Oddly enough, that brought Lew a tingle of excitement. Dinah had vetoed the police. That put him in command again and, although it looked now as if his adversaries and the issues at stake were far more important than he had ever dreamed, that was exactly what he wanted. He knew he was just a common sailor and not any brighter than the next guy. He knew almost every card in the deck was stacked against him. But that only added to his exhilaration.

For Dinah's sake now as well as for his own, it had become for him an almost physical yearning to see that he personally gave April Osborne her comeuppance.

He grinned at Dinah, trying to steady her. "Okay. No police. Then you tell me everything you know and I'll figure out something. I'll go back to that dump. I'll break into it and—"

"No, no, please." Her hand took his in spontaneous anxiety for him. "They've left there anyway. And even if they've gone back they know now from your liberty card that you—you saw Bob. You're the only witness to the murder. They'll do anything to try to kill you. It's too dangerous, much too dangerous."

Lew grinned down at his fist. "Okay. I have a kind of feeling April will show up here any minute. We'll wait for her."

"Wait for her to come, with all her plans arranged? Whatever you did, you'd just be falling into a trap. No, I know what we must do. Listen to me. Bob didn't tell me anything. He couldn't, of course. But I know he's been seeing a lot of a man this week. I'm almost sure this man is his boss. He'd know what to do. His name's Clement Greene. I know where he lives. I—"

"No." Lew's dark young frown was against that. "No strange guys. That's too chancy." The frown smoothed out. "Of course! What a dope I've been. That gypsy girl's obviously in on it. She told me that phony fortune to make sure I'd be sucker enough to go with April. She's the gal we've got to see. You and me, we're going right back to the Eldorado and we're going to make Sally talk."

Dinah was doubtful. "But what could she tell us?"

"Whatever she knows." Lew was adamant now. "Bob was killed because of that letter. That means the letter's as important to Naval Intelligence as it is to April and Lanny. Since we can't go to the police, it's our job to get that letter back ourselves. That's the only way we can make sure that Bob didn't die for nothing. Right now, Sally's our best lead to April and the letter. Okay?"

"All right." Dinah got up. She watched him from brown, questioning eyes. "This isn't your affair. You'd be much safer out of it. Why are you doing this? Are you doing it for me?"

Lew smiled. "For you, baby, and for Bob Osborne, and for me, too. You see, I kind of don't go for blondes who run around bumping off sailors. I've just naturally got a dislike for them."

Her pretty face lightened. "You're kind of a swell sailor, aren't you?"

"Not swell, honey. Just mad as a hornet. Come on."

Lew was desperately conscious that time was short until his liberty expired, and precious time was wasted trying to locate the Eldorado Bar. But they found it at last and, with Dinah on his arm, he pushed through the swing doors into the familiar, smoky interior. Most of the customers had dwindled away and a glance around the tables showed no signs of Sally. They went up to the barman.

Lew said, "Say, feller, is that gypsy, Sally, still around?"

The barman looked up from a desultory job of glass polishing. "She'n her partner quit around one."

"Know where I can find her?"

"Not a chance. Gypsies don't hardly know where they lives themselves half the time. Always moving on."

"But we've got to—"

"Sorry, sailor."

The barman moved away. Lew turned to Dinah dejectedly. They had passed up the chance of waiting for April's possible return in the other bar. Now their last link with her had snapped.

Dinah said firmly, "We'll have to go to Clement Greene now. It's the only way."

"Exactly who is this Greene guy?"

"I just know that Bob's been calling him on the phone and meeting him ever since his ship docked last week. He hinted he was his boss in Naval Intelligence. Don't you see—?"

Lew's glance moved to the floor and suddenly kindled.

"Hey, wait a minute."

Lying with cigarette butts and dead matches at the foot of the bar was a pasteboard card. In bold letters across its middle, Lew could read:

MADAME SALLY JOHNSON

He stooped for it. The rest of the odd advertisement said:

FAMED GENUINE EGYPTIAN SEERESS DIRECT FROM EGYPT. I SEE ALL. BRING YOUR TROUBLES, LOVE AND OTHERWISE, TO ME FOR MODEST CHARGE.

In the bottom corner was an address on the lower East Side.

Dinah was reading over his elbow. "You think we'd find her there?"

"Not *we*, baby, *me*." Her small cute figure brought out all Lew's protective instincts. "Listen, it was okay for you to come here. Nothing much could happen while we were in this bar. But going to her hangout's something else again. There might be danger. I'm not getting you mixed up in this."

She stared straight back at him, her heart-shaped face set in an obstinate frown. "I let Bob go off and leave me and—and Bob was killed. Do you think I'd do the same thing twice?"

"But—"

"I'm coming with you." She put her hand on his arm. "I'm coming and no power on earth can stop me."

The warm pressure of her fingers on his sleeve made him feel surprisingly elated. Dinah Lord was a good thing to have around in danger—or out of danger for that matter.

For the first time on that eventful night, Lew had stopped thinking about April.

They took a taxi to the lower East Side address of Madame Sally Johnson. Shortness of time was still gnawing at Lew, and money meant nothing now with Bob's five hundred dollars. The taxi left them at a dark corner of a squalid street. It was a real slum section. The narrow sidewalks were littered with garbage cans and little areas seethed with stringy, suspicious cats. The houses were faded façades and shabby household goods sprawled on window sills. Only an occasional square of light hinted at the teeming life within.

As they made for Sally's house, the twang of guitars and the sound of shrill voices trailed through the darkness. They reached the house and the racket was deafening. It was coming from the basement apartment, and candlelight, streaming through its barred, uncurtained windows, revealed gypsies swirling around the rooms in un-American abandon.

Madame Johnson was not only at home. She was apparently receiving.

Lew and Dinah moved down an iron stairway to the basement door. Lew clattered the knocker against the blistered paneling, but nothing was audible above the uproar inside. He started thumping with his bare fists and finally the door opened a crack, revealing a little of a very large gypsy woman.

She launched a dusky moon of a face, topped by a scarlet bandanna, around the door edge. Black, clever eyes peered suspiciously from Lew's uniform to Dinah.

"Whatcha want?"

Lew said, "Madame Sally Johnson."

"Ain't no Sally Johnson lives here."

The gypsy's plump arms, festooned with copper bracelets, pushed at the door to slam it. But Lew thrust his foot into the crack and, shoving with his shoulder, forced the door inward, sending the gypsy's massive bulk staggering backward. He pulled Dinah into a cramped, candle-lit hall. A dilapidated blanket hanging over a side door muffled some of the raucous hilarity of the party.

"We know Sally Johnson lives here," said Lew. "So go get her."

The gypsy woman folded weighty arms over a blouse which blossomed with huge crimson peonies. Once again she surveyed Lew, her black gaze moving from his husky thighs past his broad shoulders to his face. This time she seemed to like what she saw. She beamed in shameless admiration and winked at Dinah.

"Good-lookin' boy, yeah?"

As Dinah shrunk from her, the gypsy's smile broadened. "I'm Rita. You come along with me and I'll get my husband—if he ain't too drunk."

She pushed through the blanket into the inner room. Putting his arm around Dinah, Lew followed.

He blinked at the sight in front of them. The room was small, but squeezed into it were at least forty or fifty gypsies, men, women and children, all dressed in carnival colors. There was no furniture except for a bundle of old mattresses folded in a corner. Threadbare blankets covered every inch of wall space so that the room looked like a weird kind of Arabian tent. The only illumination came from candles jammed into the mouths of empty gin bottles and balanced on anything that would hold them.

In one corner three women and a snake-supple boy were dancing in Oriental ecstasy while others clapped their hands and two men strummed tuneless rhythms from guitars. Everyone clutched a glass of something that looked like red wine; and everyone was shouting and laughing and shrieking.

With an unbridled leer at Lew, Rita waddled into the crowd, chattering shrilly in Romany. The other gypsies pressed around her, grabbing at her skirt, gazing at Lew and Dinah and jabbering questions.

Lew's arm was still protectively around Dinah. He wondered whether this was a typical quiet gypsy evening at home and stared into the dusky faces of the women in a vain attempt to pick out Sally. Soon Rita reappeared, her flamboyant peonied bosom shoving a path through the swirl of gypsies. She was shepherding in front of her a small, white-haired man.

Rita's husband was quite fantastic. Black eyes smiled slyly from a face brown and unshaven as coconut fiber. He strutted as he walked and his wiry body was clothed in tan riding breeches, tan riding boots, and a magenta pajama top, buttoned Russian-style high up the throat. In his hand he twirled an ebony cane with a silver head.

"My husband." Rita let a fat, caressing hand stray over Lew's uncomfortable back. "Tell him what you want, beauty."

With great dignity, the little man raised his cane and brought it sharply down on his wife's arm so that she let go of Lew's shoulder with a whimpering cry. Ignoring her utterly, his crafty gaze moved over Lew and Dinah. Then he bowed a grave, preposterous bow.

"Freddy Milanov," he announced. "Head King of all the gypsies in the United States. The Russian gypsies, the Serbian gypsies, the Rumanian gypsies—all the goldarned gypsies." He grinned a sudden, infectious grin. "Glad to know you, Mr. Osborne."

"Osborne!" Lew stared. "Why d'you think my name's—"

Rita spun round. With swift ferocity, she swooped on her husband's folded right hand. She forced back the fingers, revealing on his grimy palm a green liberty card. Storming in Romany, she snatched it and handed it to Lew.

"Every second of the day I have to watch him." She rolled her eyes, looking holy and shocked. "Just let him see a pocket and he picks it. One day those light fingers of his are gonna fly us all into jail for keeps."

Lew had taken the card dazedly. It was Robert Osborne's card all right. He felt in his pocket. Nothing there. By some magic legerdemain, Freddy bad managed to steal and read the card within the first seconds of meeting them.

The Head King seemed completely unabashed. In fact, he looked childishly proud of his exploit. He winked at Dinah and gestured toward the shouting, dancing and drinking which was working up to a mad crescendo. "Having a sorta party. *Patchiv*, we call it. Everyone drinks wine and gets drunk and is happy. Wanna join us?"

Lew had visions of more doped liquor. "We've just come to talk to Sally Johnson."

The Head King of the gypsies scratched his shaggy neck with the silver knob of his cane. "What you want her for?"

Lew shot Dinah a warning glance. "Me and my girl, we've just come to get our fortunes told. A guy told us Sally was the best fortune teller in the States. We've got plenty of money."

At the mention of money an avid gleam came into Freddy's eye. He looked at Rita who bobbed her head vigorously.

"Okay. Come with me."

Freddy Milanov started through the reveling gypsies who made a path for him as if he was indeed a king. With Rita stumping behind, Lew and Dinah followed to a door in the back wall which was also covered by a blanket. Freddy pushed it aside and conducted them into a small kitchen.

Even here there were no chairs. A huge cauldron of stew simmered on an old-fashioned range. Dirty dishes were strewn on a bare wooden table and on the floor. Freddy picked his way delicately through the dishes, shuffled a free space on the edge of the table and sat down. Rita quivered by the door.

The Head King stared brightly at Lew and Dinah. "Sally ain't here. But it don't matter because Rita, my wife, she's the best fortune teller in the world." He cocked his head craftily. "She's cheap, too."

"Sure." Rita's teeth flashed. "I'd tell the pretty sailor's fortune for—well, for almost nothing."

Lew shook his head. "We don't want anyone but Sally."

The thrum of the guitars and the shrill singing voices seeped through from the next room. Freddy seemed to be plunged in thought. Suddenly he said:

"You don't want Sally. I'll tell you frankly. Sally ain't so hot with sailors. She fakes." He grinned again, the sly, pixy grin. "Tonight even, at some bar, a guy pays her five bucks to fake a sailor's fortune."

Trying to keep his voice unconcerned, Lew said, "Why'd a guy want to have a sailor's fortune faked?"

"I dunno."

"Who was he? What sort of a guy?"

All the wrinkles on Freddy's face seemed to contract. He gave the impression of a turtle sliding back into its shell. "I don't know nothing."

Rita wriggled amply forward. "Okay, lovely sailor. Give Rita your palm, baby, and—"

Dinah broke in: "We want Sally. Where is she?"

Rita stopped. The Head King wagged his cane back and forth. He stared down at a wine stain on his magenta pajama top and dabbed at it. "Oh, Sally, she just kind of went out." He gestured to a door in the rear wall. "A couple of men just came. Hadda talk to her on business. She took 'em out into the alley."

"Into the alley!" Lew stiffened. "What men? What sort of men? What did they look like?"

"Oh, just a couple of *gapos*."

Dinah said hoarsely, "Was one of them a cripple?"

"Cripple?" Freddy's beady eyes weren't missing a trick. "I guess you kinda might call him a cripple. His arm all shriveled up and his leg kind of twisted and—"

Lew and Dinah exchanged glances. With sudden urgency Lew moved to the window, staring into the blackness of the alley outside. Dinah joined him. She panted:

"Lanny! Lanny's out there with her!"

Lew's mouth tightened. "I'm going out."

"No." Dinah caught his arm. "No, you can't. They'll have guns. They—"

But Lew shook her off. While Freddy and Rita stared in sphinxlike silence, he ran to the door, tugged it open and ran out into the darkness of the alley.

Dinah was right. Of course it was crazy to plunge headlong into danger that way. But Lew's angry desire to get at the sandy-haired cripple made him foolhardy.

The dim shaft of light from the open door designed a faint square on the rough cement. Lew slipped away from the light, heading deeper into the cavernous blackness of the alley. Somewhere in front of him, Sally was "doing business" with Lanny and some other man.

He strained his ears. They caught the inevitable sounds of a slum at night—a baby's thin wail, the yelp of a dog, the distant clatter of a street car. The festive music of the *patchiv* pulsed faintly too. But there was nothing else, no near, significant sound.

He tiptoed forward. Had Sally gone with the men to some other destination? If they were still in the alley, they were very quiet.

Suddenly he halted, catching his breath. Every nerve end in his body was taut. For he could hear a noise now—a faint noise that was growing fainter ahead.

It was the sound of mingled footsteps, one pair crunching and rhythmic, the other faltering and broken. Lew would have known that broken sound anywhere in the world.

It was the dragging clump of Lanny's twisted boot.

He started forward again at a quickened pace. Even now that his eyes were more accustomed to the darkness, he could see hardly more than an inch before his face. The footsteps ahead were fading rapidly. Whatever happened, he had to catch up with Lanny. His anxiety mounting, he broke into a trot.

He didn't care about making a noise now. His own footsteps clattered against the cement surface of the alley. He pressed on. Suddenly there was something in front of him. He stumbled against it, tried to regain his balance and half fell to his knees. He flung out an arm to support himself. His fingers made contact with the thing that had tripped him. It was soft and warm.

The feel of it sent a shudder of horror through him.

He staggered to his feet. His hand shaking, he pulled out a box of matches and lit a match. He raised its feeble flame, looking down at the thing he had touched. The horror welled up in him.

Lying on her back across the gray cement, her black skirt splayed like a wheel, her scarlet blouse vivid in the matchlight, was a gypsy woman.

The ground around her was spattered with blood. The scarlet blouse was stained too. And it was obvious where the blood came from.

Her throat had been savagely and murderously slit.

Blankly Lew gazed at the lolling head with its glassy eyes, its half-parted lips and the heavy copper earrings glimmering in the tangled black hair.

The gypsy was dead. There was no question about that.

And the gypsy was Sally—Madame Sally Johnson, Famous Genuine Egyptian Seeress Direct From Egypt.

There was no question about that either.

The match flame burnt down to his fingers, searing the skin. He dropped the match and darkness engulfed him again.

His thoughts moved clumsily. So Lanny had set a trap for Sally. They had lured her out here and—murdered her. She would never tell her story now.

In a dim, background way he was conscious that the ominous shuffle of Lanny's footsteps was no longer audible. He was conscious too of other sounds coming from the direction he himself had taken, running footsteps and a voice—Dinah's voice—calling:

"Where are you?"

He stood there in the darkness by the invisible body, torn two ways. Then people were jostling him. A hand caught his arm and Dinah was panting:

"I made Mr. Milanov come out with me and look for you. Thank heavens you're all right. Thank heavens—"

"Where's Sally?" Freddy Milanov's voice sounded. "Did you find Sally?"

In an odd, dry tone that didn't sound real, Lew said, "Sally's here. Sally's right here on the ground—with her throat cut. Dead."

"Dead!" Dinah gave a choked gasp. "They—they've murdered her, too."

"Dinah, Freddy, you take care of her." Lew was terrified now that he was letting Lanny slip through his fingers. "They were here a moment ago—Lanny and the other men. I'm going to get them."

"No, no." Dinah's cry was plaintive. "Come back."

Lew disregarded her. He clattered on down the alley until he stumbled out onto a street. He looked along its empty sidewalks. A couple of blocks away, the red rear light of a car twinkled in the darkness. As he stared, it vanished.

Once again he was too late. While he had stood there impotently by Sally's body, Lanny and his associate had escaped.

For the second time that evening, the slender thread that connected him with April had been ruthlessly slit.

As he turned back into the alley, he heard wailing cries from the darkness ahead. He reached the spot where Sally's body had been. It was a bedlam of scurrying, howling gypsies. Some of them were carrying the body, wrapped in a blanket. Others were jostling around them, brandishing gin bottle candlesticks like flambuoys. Glimpses of gaunt, foreign faces, scarlet blouses and glittering bronze made a weird pattern in the candlelight.

Somehow Dinah was back with him, a small, stubborn shadow. "When you ran off, when I thought they might be waiting there to kill you—"

"Too late," grunted Lew. "Saw their car drive away. Couldn't stop it."

Suddenly Dinah was trembling. She put her hands up onto his arms and buried her dark head against his chest. Her voice came husky and low:

"They killed Bob. They killed Sally. There must be dozens of them. They seem to be everywhere at once. Oh, what can we do? What can we ever do against them?"

Lew's pity for her overrode his own leaden disappointment. Poor kid, she'd taken more in one night than most girls have to take in a lifetime. And she'd taken it on the chin. He couldn't see her, but her face was so clear in his thoughts, defiantly steady and yet on the brink of tears. Almost before he realized it, he was stroking the dark silk of her hair.

"Bear up, honey. We'll make out somehow."

"But Bob's dead." The sobs came then, long, racking. "And we'll never, never get that letter back now. Bob'll have died for nothing. He—"

Lew's arms went around her. The wailing troop of gypsies was ahead, streaming back into the basement kitchen. He bent and kissed Dinah on the mouth. She made an uncertain movement to draw away and then her lips relaxed against his. It was a satisfactory kiss. Almost it banished the taunting image of April Osborne. For one wild moment Lew thought: *Dinah's the swellest girl I ever met. What if maybe Dinah and me—*

Then the picture of Bob Osborne rose up, Bob Osborne lying sprawled at the foot of the cellar steps, Bob Osborne whom Dinah had been going to marry in a week, Bob Osborne whose murder on his secret line of duty would always leave a scar. Lew knew he could not—should not try to compete with that memory.

Dinah's sobs had faded. She pulled herself gently away.

"I'm sorry. Seeing Sally lying there and then being scared for you—I'm afraid I haven't much courage."

"Baby, you've got all the courage in the world."

"You're so—so nice to me." Dinah gave a little cracked laugh. "And I don't even know your name."

"Lew."

"Lew." She said it gravely. "Lew. I'll never forget you. Whatever happens, I'll never forget you."

Her hand slipped into his. Together, in a silence that was exciting in a new way, they went after the gypsies back down the steps into the kitchen.

All the gypsies had crowded with Sally's body into the sitting room. Ignored, Lew and Dinah joined them. Sally, under the blanket, had been laid on a mattress which had been pulled into the center of the floor. All the candles in their gin bottles had been set in a circle around the corpse. And the gypsies themselves, like brilliant parrots, were clustered on their knees behind the candles, shouting, wailing and stretching their arms to the ceiling. Their shadows, scurrying over the wall blankets, hovered and swooped like giant bats.

No one seemed to think about calling the police. No one even seemed curious as to the cause of the tragedy. One of their group was dead and they were mourning. That was all.

Freddy, the Head King, was kneeling in the most conspicuous place at the top of the mattress. A few artificial looking tears glistened on his sly, wizened face. He stared ecstatically upward like a poet about to receive inspiration. Suddenly, in a high sing-song, he began a Romany speech, presumably listing the virtues of the departed Sally. His words grew in passion, and the gypsies started swaying to the rhythm of his voice. Their sobs merged into a chant-like humming. A man began to strum a guitar, softly at first and then rising in twangy fury. A gypsy woman rose and started to weave her arms back and forth. Imperceptibly her body writhed into a dance. And, imperceptibly, one here, one there, the others rose and joined her until the mattress was circled with dancing figures.

Lew gave this extraordinary spectacle only part of his attention. He was thinking about Freddy. The Head King had hinted he knew something of the man who had bribed Sally into faking Lew's fortune. That man must definitely be another of April's associates. He was the guy whom he and Dinah had to locate.

Rita, who had been invisible, was very much in evidence now, staggering into the throng of mourners with a huge flagon of red wine. Still howling and tearing their hair, everyone made a scramble for glasses. Soon they were swilling the wine with gusto.

Apart from the thing huddled under the blanket on the mattress, the wake was now indistinguishable from the *patchiv* which had preceded it.

Lew took Dinah's arm and pushed through the gypsies to Freddy's side. The Head King was brandishing a glass of blood red wine, looking proud, cutting a caper and crying all at the same time. When he saw Lew and Dinah, he beamed through the shiny, trickling tears.

"You see how they liked my speech? I guess I'm pretty much the best speechmaker in all the gypsies." He tilted the glass to his lips. "We started with a *patchiv*, and now we end up with a *pomana*. That is what we call parties for dead gypsies. *Pomanas*." The disarming, imp grin came again. "*Pomanas* are good. As good as *patchivs*. Everybody gets drunk."

Lew said, "Listen, we've got to talk to you."

Freddy's face fell. "But I gotta make another speech. I—"

"Are you nuts?" Lew watched him with a mixture of shock and bewilderment. "Don't you realize there's been a murder? Sally's had her throat cut. The police'll be here any minute. Make all the speeches you want to when they arrive. Right now, you're going to do some listening to me." He grabbed the King's magenta arm. "Come on—out of this madhouse."

Reluctantly Freddy Milanov let himself be drawn through the dance of death back into the kitchen. Lew pushed the Head King around so that he perched on the table. He had decided that the only way to treat these crazy people was to treat them tough.

"Okay." His broad young body loomed ominously. "Here's the setup. We came here tonight because we wanted to get certain dope out of Sally. She was murdered before we could get it. Understand?"

Freddy looked miserable. His heart was obviously with the *pomana* next door. "Sure, sure. Sally got herself bumped off. Sally was always a girl for getting in trouble anyways." He added irrelevantly, "She was my niece."

"I'll tell you who bumped her off. Those men who were here were friends of the guy who paid her five bucks to fake my fortune at the Eldorado Bar. Sally told you about him, didn't she? Miss Lord and me are trying to catch up with the guy. We want to know who he was."

The Head King of the gypsies looked at the great stew pot on the range and suddenly seemed to be hungry. He went to it, dipping in two fingers and pulling out a chunk of meat. At that moment the blanket was pushed aside and Rita came in. She was holding a glass of red wine and beamed affectionately at Lew. She seemed no more concerned than Freddy by the violent death of her niece. Freddy was eating his meat with relish. He paid no attention to his wife but watched Lew and Dinah from eyes that were crafty and, at the same time, rather stupid.

"I don't know nothing about what that guy looked like, nothing except what Sally told me when she come in and she had fifty bucks and she said she was gonna throw a party."

"Fifty bucks!" said Lew. "I thought you said he only gave her five bucks."

"Sure." Freddy wiped his greasy fingers on the front of his magenta pajama top. "That's all he gave her. But Sally figured since this *gajo* paid her to fake a fortune he was a crook anyways so she just—" he shrugged—"she just lifted his wallet. Next to me, Sally was the best pocket-picker in New York." He did look at his wife then, shooting her one, scathing glance. "She was much better than Rita. Rita's a lousy pocket-picker."

Rita sniffed and looked injured. Freddy went on:

"Fifty bucks Sally got in the wallet. That's why she threw the *patchiv*. Fifty bucks is big money for gypsies these days."

Lew was past wondering about the morals of gypsies. He said sharply, "The wallet—the guy's wallet. What'd she do with it?"

Freddy Milanov sent one wistful glance past Rita to the blanket which separated him from the *pomana*. "Oh, she knew her old uncle wanted a wallet. She just gave it to me. Wasn't any good to her."

From the lusty singing and shouting next door, the *pomana* seemed to be getting out of control.

"Show me the wallet."

Freddy's nail-bitten hand fumbled down the front of the pajamas and produced an expensive tan pigskin wallet. He handed it to Lew, who flicked it open. There were papers inside. Lew pulled them out, unfolding one and staring at it in bewilderment. It was a large sheet of paper covered with neatly typed blocks of figures. There were two other sheets similarly inscribed.

Dinah had been reading over his elbow. She clutched the papers eagerly. "Lew, they must be some sort of code. Maybe this is the real reason why they killed Sally, because she'd got hold of these papers. We must keep them."

As Dinah stuffed the papers into her pocketbook, Lew looked at the thing left in his hand. It was an orange card. He turned it over and gave an explosive grunt. The card was an air warden's license. There was no photograph but there was a name and an address.

The address was: Four Hundred and Fifty-six-A East Fifty-sixth Street.

And the name was—Clement Greene.

Lew handed Dinah the card. "Look, baby. That's the guy who got Sally to tell me that phony fortune. That's the guy who's working with April and Lanny. Your Clement Greene."

Dinah stared at the card. "Then he wasn't Bob's boss the way I thought. Lew, Clement Greene must be the brains, the person April and Lanny are working for, the man Bob was trying to get."

Lew watched her soberly. "Is that the address you knew?"

"Yes. Before we came out tonight, Bob told it to me. He told me if anything happened, I was to look for him there. I didn't realize. I thought he meant Clement Greene was his friend. But he meant that— that if he was killed, it was Clement Greene we had to look for. Of course."

Lew took the card back, pushed it in the wallet and slipped the wallet into his breast pocket. "Maybe you can have your wallet back later, Head King," he said to Freddy.

The gypsy was picking his teeth with a match. He didn't seem interested. Neither did Rita.

Lew glanced at his watch. By six he had to be back aboard ship. Nothing could change that. Time was getting terrifyingly short if he was ever going to settle his score with April. He had no real plan. There was nothing to plan on—only this meager piece of knowledge that a man called Clement Greene had some connection with April and that he lived at 456A East 56th Street.

He looked at Dinah. "Are you sure we can't go to the police?"

"Absolutely." She shook her head. "Bob said that over and over. Whatever happened, I wasn't to go to the police."

"Okay. Then I'm going to this place where Clement Greene lives. I know it's crazy. They'll probably be waiting for me with machine-guns. I don't even know what I'll do when I get there. But—" his jaw went grim—"it's just something I've got to do."

Dinah said simply, "If you go, I'm going too."

"But—"

"We've had this out before. I'm not going to leave you. And I'm not going to quit till we get that letter back."

Her little heart-shaped face was stubborn. Lew had learned that it was useless to argue with Dinah Lord.

"All right."

Dinah smiled.

Lew turned to Freddy. "Thanks, King. You've been a big help. You can get back to your *pomana* now. We're scramming."

Freddy grinned. "Are you and the lady going to the place where this guy is who killed Sally?"

"That's the idea."

"Then I'm coming too."

"You?"

"Sure. Gypsies can be plenty handy." He grinned. "Picking locks, maybe. I pick locks as good as I pick pockets."

Dinah said, "It'll be dangerous, Mr. Milanov. They want to kill Lew and me. They'll stop at nothing."

Freddy swaggered. "Ain't nobody can kill a gypsy that's got his wits about him."

Lew tried to figure him out. "D'you want to come because Sally was your niece?"

The Head King crossed to the range again and, fishing another hunk of meat from the stewpot, started to munch it. "No, it ain't exactly that." He glanced a little sheepishly at his wife. "You see, last month there was some trouble between Sally and I. She wouldn't come across with five bucks she owed me for dream books, so I beat her up. She hadda spend a couple of weeks in the *gajo* hospital and the cops gotta know about it. See what I mean? The cops are always picking on gypsies anyways. When they find her dead, they're just naturally goin' to arrest me." He wiped his nose on his sleeve. "That's something I don't want to have happen."

Rita nodded solemnly. "Freddy's right. He ain't kidding."

Lew stared from the fat gypsy woman to the shrimp of a gypsy man. Their pursuit of April, Lanny, Clement Greene and the letter was becoming progressively crazy anyway. They might as well make it that much crazier by taking with them the Head King of the gypsies.

"Okay," he said. "Come along. But we'll have to make it snappy."

Dinah had run to the door and was already out in the alley. While Lew waited impatiently, Freddy scrambled into a beetle-green overcoat which had been hanging on a peg on the wall. He threw one last, longing glance at the blanket which shut out the *pomana*.

"Too bad," he sighed. "I was gonna make such a good speech."

Twirling his cane, he strutted to the back door. Lew followed. Rita ran after them, her plump face wabbling with anxiety. She ignored her husband and threw her arms around Lew's neck.

"Be careful, my beauty. Don't trust Freddy. He ain't no good. Take care of yourself."

"Sure." Lew grinned. "I'll take care of myself."

The great arms slid from his neck. As they did so, Lew was conscious of fluttering fingers pausing a second over his breast pocket. He turned away from Rita and surreptitiously felt in the pocket. Sure enough, Clement Greene's shiny pigskin wallet was missing.

He glanced over his shoulder at Rita. She stared back from round black eyes that were far too innocent.

Freddy had belittled Rita's talent as a pocket-picker, and she had obviously stolen the wallet to restore her self-respect. Lew didn't have the heart to ask for it back.

"Goodbye, Rita," he said.

With its broad smile, Rita's face looked like a dusky Hallow'een pumpkin. "Goodbye, my sweetheart."

As he moved after Freddy through the door, Lew reflected that maybe it was just as well that Rita had the wallet. After all, they did not know what they were letting themselves in for. Perhaps—

There was no sign of Dinah in the alley. Lew felt sudden, sliding alarm. He called her name. She did not answer. He ran down the alley to the street. He saw her then, coming out of a dimly lit drugstore on the corner. Relief surged through him.

She hurried to his side. "I thought you and Freddy were following me. I got to the street before I realized I was alone." She smiled wryly. "I was afraid to stay in the dark by myself after what happened to Sally. I—I went into the drugstore."

She slipped her hand through Lew's arm as if his massiveness steadied her. "It's—pretty hopeless, isn't sit, Lew? We don't know that April and Lanny gave Clement Greene the letter. We don't know what the letter is. We don't even have a gun."

"You've got *me*." Freddy had caught up with them, grinning and swishing the air with his cane. "And I don't mind telling you that one smart gypsy's worth a half dozen *gajos*."

Lew looked at the Head King's little wrinkled face peeping out of the green overcoat. Judging from his experience with them tonight, gypsies were no more responsible than children. And yet there was a crying need for someone worth a half dozen *gajos*.

He only hoped that Freddy was not exaggerating.

It was past two o'clock by the time they scrambled out of a taxi on the corner of First Avenue and Fifty-sixth Street and started through the darkness into the elegant fringes of Sutton Place. Dinah hurried ahead, reading the house numbers. She paused before a building next to a yawning automobile runway.

"Here it is."

Lew and Freddy joined her. The house was in darkness and seemed deserted. On the first-floor plate glass windows, heavily draped with black-out curtains, indicated some sort of a showroom inside. There was an awning over the door. Lew strained his eyes, reading.

To his surprise, the legend on the awning announced:

GREENE'S FUNERAL PARLOR

"An undertaker!" breathed Dinah.

Freddy Milanov was sucking a match. "He kills guys and buries 'em too. A smart *gajo*."

Lew was thinking swiftly. So this mysterious Clement Greene owned a funeral parlor. Bob Osborne's body had been whisked away from the murder house to an unknown destination. There could be no safer place to conceal a body than a funeral parlor. Wasn't it probable that the murdered sailor had been brought here, that maybe even now his body was lying somewhere inside this gloomy building?

Lew made a private decision. Although Dinah was convinced that they should not enlist the aid of the police, it was surely better to have Greene and his associates arrested than to let them go scot free. If they could find Osborne's stabbed body there in the funeral parlor, he was ready to turn the whole thing over to the police.

And once they'd done that, Clement Greene's career, as a spy or whatever he was, would be effectively crippled.

Freddy was staring up at the building sagely. He scratched his head. "Looks like there's no one around. What's the good of bustin' into a place to find a guy to arrest him if he ain't there?"

"We're busting in anyway." Lew looked at Dinah who was standing pale and keyed-up at his side. Now there was a chance of finding her fiancé's body, Dinah was the last person in the world Lew wanted to have with them. He knew, however, that it would be a waste of breath to try to shake her off.

He turned back to Freddy. "Well, Head King, you said you could pick locks. Did you mean that?"

"Can I pick locks?" Freddy was insulted. "I'm the best lock picker in the gypsies. Once in San Antonio, Texas, I was hungry so I picked the lock on a delicatessen. The cops caught me and threw me in jail so I picked the jail lock and got out again. And I'd picked the sergeant's pocket too, so I didn't have to snitch no food. I bought it. Regular."

Slightly skeptical, Lew nodded to the opulent door beneath the awning. "Okay. See what you can do with this one."

Dinah glanced up and down the street. "It's awfully risky. Someone might come. Wait a minute."

Impulsively she slipped into the dark automobile runway. In a few moments she was back. "There's another door in there—a small door."

Freddy and Lew followed her into the runway. At its end large rolling doors showed a locked garage where the hearses must be housed. The door Dinah had found led into the building halfway down the side wall. It was small and raised over a few steps. Freddy shuffled to it and peered.

"Ain't nothing to this one. It's a cinch."

He fumbled into the beetle-green overcoat, produced some shadowy object and started scratching and poking at the lock. The Head King had not been vainglorious. In a short while, the door yielded to him, moving silently inward.

Freddy chuckled. "Didn't I say I was good?"

The three of them stepped into the corridor of the building. Dinah shut the door behind them. A corridor stretched ahead, lushly carpeted and lit by a spattering of blue shaded bulbs. Lew wondered whether the lights were kept on all night or whether they indicated the presence, somewhere, of Clement Greene. Halfway down the left wall, between two doors, a huge vase of calla lilies stood on an antique table. The whole mood was expensive and yet dejected—a professional tribute to grief.

Freddy glided ahead, his nostrils quivering. He looked like a shabby terrier on a scent. "Don't think there's no one around. Maybe though. You can't tell. Maybe there's a watchman." He glanced over his shoulder. "If this Greene guy ain't here, what do we look for?"

Lew didn't want to talk about Bob Osborne in front of Dinah. He said guardedly, "Oh, we just look around."

Freddy moved to the nearest door. He eased it open and peered inside.

"Gee!" His head came bobbing back.

"What is it?"

"Coffins." The Head King's black eyes blinked. "Nothin' but coffins."

Dinah and Lew pushed past him into the room. It was a medium-sized showroom decorated with lugubrious taste. The dim blue lights stared down on a series of period tables. On each table, presented with the elegance of a museum piece, stood an individual coffin. In front of each was propped a black-framed announcement.

Lew moved to the first one. The framed card, in flowery language, sang the praises of its specimen coffin, the craftsmanship, the lining, the type of wood. As Lew read this macabre sales talk, his thoughts raced. Maybe it was in here that Greene had concealed the body.

Cautiously he lifted the lid of the coffin and peered inside. It was empty. He moved to the next and the next, repeating the performance. Dinah, her face a strange gray in the blue illumination, watched him steadily.

"What are you doing?"

"Just looking."

The girl's eyes kindled with understanding. "You're—you're looking for Bob, aren't you? You think they brought his body here. That's what you're doing."

All the coffins were empty. Lew moved back to Dinah. "You've got to let me take over now. Don't ask questions. Just do what I tell you. Understand?"

"But, Lew—"

Freddy had disappeared. His crafty face appeared now around the door. He breathed, "Psst!" and beckoned.

Dinah and Lew joined him in the passage. The Head King had opened the door on the other side of the calla lilies. It led into another passage with closed doors branching off. Here, too, there was nothing to break the funereal silence. At the end of the passage, its pipes looming spectrally upward, stood an organ.

Dinah breathed, "These—these must be the parlors, the little chapels where they hold the services."

Lew went to the first door and opened it. Inside, illumined by a pallid blue light, was a small, square room. Against one wall stood a miniature altar. In front of it stretched a bare table on rollers. Wooden chairs were stacked forlornly in a corner. A door in the back wall indicated another room beyond.

Lew stepped back into the passage. Freddy, inquisitive as a magpie, was easing doors open on the other side. Lew moved past Dinah to his next door. He opened it, looked in and then, with pounding pulses, pulled it shut again.

"Freddy!" His whisper to the gypsy was urgent. He swung round to Dinah. "Get back down the corridor. Wait for us there."

The girl's face hardened. "What is it? Lew—?"

"Don't ask questions. Do as I say." He pushed her almost roughly backwards. "Keep away from here."

Dinah's hand fluttered out. Then, obediently, she turned and started away down the passage. Freddy was at Lew's side. Lew gave him one grim glance.

"Come on."

He turned back to the door he had just opened. He tugged it outward and moved with Freddy inside.

His first glimpse had prepared him for what they would find. The little room was exactly similar to the first one he had seen—the altar, the door in the side wall, the table and the wooden chairs.

But there was one difference, a difference which had set Lew's heart into high gear.

For this table was not bare. Stretched on it, under a chaste canopy of white carnations and roses, lay a coffin.

Lew moved toward it through the hollow silence with Freddy Milanov, bright-eyed, at his side. They reached the coffin. Beneath the blanket of flowers, the lower half of the lid was closed. But the upper part was slid open, revealing the face and shoulders of the body inside.

Lew stared down in mingled awe and excitement. The corpse's black hair had been neatly combed. A subtle touch of makeup had softened the dead stare of the dark eyes. Instead of the sailor's uniform, there was a gray jacket, a civilian shirt and tie.

But the body, lying there under the ironic tribute of flowers, was unmistakably the body of Robert Osborne.

Lew was staggered by the temerity of Clement Greene and his associates. Only a few hours before they had murdered this man. Now, his body was laid out here like any of the bodies which bereaved relatives entrusted to an undertaker's care. Almost certainly Clement Greene had among his hirelings a doctor who could fake a death certificate.

Under an assumed name, with a forged certificate and in civilian clothes, Bob Osborne could be buried without secrecy and with all the reverent pomp at the funeral parlor's command.

This was as brash and ingenious a method of disposing of corpses as any murdering gang had devised.

The Head King of the gypsies was staring from protuberant eyes while his fingers, automatically larcenous, twisted a white rose from one of the wreaths and slipped it into the lapel of the beetle-green overcoat.

"Gee," he breathed. "Another corpse."

Lew felt triumphant. He had Clement Greene exactly where he wanted him now. Greene may have managed a phony death certificate. But Lew knew that, under those sickeningly sweet flowers, Bob Osborne had been stabbed three times. Greene could not disguise that lethal fact.

Lew also had Bob Osborne's liberty card which could prove that, in spite of the civilian clothes, this was the corpse of a sailor.

Once they got out of this place and to the police, Clement Greene's doom was sealed.

And, with Clement Greene, Lanny and April too would come to the end of the road.

Lew would see to that.

The sailor stood for one moment in the deathly quiet, staring down at the coffin, savoring his own victory. There had been some bad moments. But that was all over. His stubborn pursuit of a will o' the wisp was going to end now in success.

He turned to Freddy. "Come on. Let's—"

He stopped there, the hairs at the back of his neck stirring.

For, from outside in the passage where Dinah was waiting, had come a shrill, frightened cry.

"Lew!"

It was Dinah's voice. Lew and Freddy swung round to face the door by which they had entered.

"Lew!" That urgent call for help came again.

Both of them made a spring for the door and then both froze. For a soft male voice behind them had said:

"Put up your hands and turn around. I'm afraid I have you both covered."

Slowly, in response to that voice which seemed to have come from nowhere, Lew turned back, raising his arms above his head. Freddy turned too.

The door in the wall beyond the coffin had opened and a small man in a dark suit stood on the threshold. One plump hand aimed a revolver. He was smiling.

"You must excuse the theatrical nature of my welcome," he said. "But now you are here I am most anxious for you to remain. I have been expecting you for some time."

Lew's anxiety for Dinah blurred everything else. He stared at the little man—not recognizing him for a second. Then realization dawned.

The little man in the dark suit was plump and bald. His round face exuded rosy affability. A tuck of flesh wabbled under his chin.

He was the man who had paid for Lew's fortune at the Eldorado, the man Lew had known as Mr. Jenkins.

Lew stared at the revolver and then, as a shuffling sounded behind him, glanced over his shoulder. The door from the passage had opened now. Standing in front of it, also aiming a revolver, was the gaunt, crippled figure of Lanny.

They were under a crossfire. They were very definitely trapped.

"So you've seen Bob Osborne's body for the second time this evening, Mr. Warren." "Mr. Jenkins" was still beaming amiably over his revolver. "You have a talent for seeing the wrong things at the wrong time. Permit me to introduce myself correctly. Not Jenkins. Greene. Clement Greene."

Lew glared at him. Dinah's cry for help still echoed in his ears. He blurted, "What have you done with Dinah?"

"Miss Lord is in good hands." Mr. Greene's piggy gaze shifted behind Lew's back to Lanny. "Isn't she, Lanny?"

The cripple laughed. "Sure. She'll be very comfortable."

The suddenness with which victory had been overturned into defeat had disorganized Lew. He managed to think: *I ought to have realized this little guy was back of it all. He came into the Eldorado looking for a sailor who could pass for Bob Osborne. He got me interested in having my fortune told and bought me free beers just to make sure he would keep me there until April could come in and pull her act.*

Desperately he said, "Miss Lord doesn't know anything." He jerked his thumb at the cowed Freddy. "Neither does he. They just came along with me. Let them go, and you and me can have this thing out."

Clement Greene chuckled. "A laudable gesture, Mr. Warren. But I'm afraid we know exactly how much both Miss Lord and Mr. Milanov know." He glanced at the coffin. "This is hardly the right setting for a discussion. Perhaps you would be good enough to accompany me to my office."

Still aiming the revolver, he started back through the door by which he had entered. Lanny hobbled forward and pressed his gun against Lew's ribs.

"Okay. Both of you. Move."

Their hands above their heads, Lew and Freddy walked through the door after the retreating figure of Clement Greene. They came into a luxurious office with gray drapes and chairs upholstered in scarlet leather. There was a large desk under the curtained window with a door at its side. Clement Greene moved around the desk and sat down. Lanny closed the door behind them and stood against it.

Clement Greene's revolver indicated two leather chairs near the desk. "Perhaps you and your friend would like to sit down, Mr. Warren."

Freddy, huddled in the beetle-green overcoat with its jaunty stolen boutonniere, slumped into one chair. Because there was nothing else to do, Lew dropped into the other.

Clement Greene produced a thin gold cigarette case. He offered it to Lew and Freddy. When they refused sullenly, he gave a cluck and lit one himself, puffing at it with little, plump puffs.

"Well, Mr. Warren, it is unfortunate for us and for you that you have developed this habit of—er—stumbling upon Bob Osborne's body. I admit it was clumsy of us to have left it for a minute or two in that unlocked cellar. We had planned to bring it here earlier, but there was an unavoidable delay. The—ah—hearse we sent for it had a little trouble." He smiled. "You were a trifle clumsy yourself, though, dropping your liberty card by the body and then expecting to break in here to rediscover the body—without our being prepared to receive you."

Lew scowled down at his bronzed fists, cursing himself for a fool. "Okay," he grunted. "You're scared of me because I know you killed Bob Osborne. What are you going to do?"

Clement Greene glanced at Lanny who still stood vigil, gun in hand, by the door. "There was another somewhat similar instance this evening. Our friend, Sally. I paid her well to tell you the most convenient fortune. With typical gypsy irresponsibility, she was foolish enough to steal my wallet during the transaction. In that wallet were certain very valuable papers listing in code the names and addresses of our associates in this country. When I discovered the theft, I sent two of my men—Lanny and another—to retrieve those papers. They had a little talk with Sally. She was most unreasonable, refused to say where the papers were and demanded more money." He shrugged. "We did not have to dispose of her body. Gypsies are always killing each other. We could rely on the police to find a suspect among her own friends. Isn't that so, Mr. Milanov?"

Freddy's face popped indignantly up from the overcoat. Clement Greene beamed at him.

"I am not concerned about those papers however. I have a feeling that in spite of Sally we shall retrieve them very shortly."

Lew thought of those folded, number-studded sheets which had turned out to be of such vital importance to Clement Greene's organization, whatever it was, and which were now in Dinah's pocketbook. Did Clement Greene, who seemed to know everything, know that Dinah had those papers? Alarm searing him like a brand, Lew wondered what they had done with Dinah—and what they were going to do.

He stared at Clement Greene. "So you murdered Sally and now you're figuring on murdering us. What makes you think you can get away with five murders in one night? This is New York. Not Nazi Germany."

"Unhappily." Clement Greene's eyes flamed with a sudden cold light. "This chaotic, labor-ruled country has a great deal to learn in efficiency and discipline from Nazi Germany. Perhaps, after the war, under the proper leadership—"

Lew sprang up. "So you are a dirty—"

But Clement Greene was all smiles again. "Come, Mr. Warren, this is not the moment for an ideological debate. You ask me how I can get away with five murders in one night. Having seen Mr. Osborne's body in the next room, you should realize how relatively simple the disposal of bodies can be. But I trust our relationship won't have to come to that. I was hoping you might understand our motives for killing Bob Osborne and—ah—sympathize."

"Sympathize! Bob Osborne was working for our Naval Intelligence. You and your Nazi stooges murdered him and you expect me—"

"One moment, Mr. Warren. I'm afraid you have a false picture of the truth. Bob Osborne was a sailor in the United States Navy, yes. But he was not working for your Naval Intelligence. He was working for me."

"You!"

"For me—and for the lady who is my superior."

Lew thought of April with a new surge of hatred. She wasn't just a hireling. April was Clement Greene's superior, the boss of this Nazi outfit.

He snapped, "Why should I believe what you say about Bob Osborne—or anything else?"

Clement Greene was watching him shrewdly. "For the simple reason that you are here as my—ah—guest and, under the circumstances, I have nothing to lose by being frank. It is most important for us to keep in constant communication with our associates in England. As a sailor on Atlantic Convoy, Bob Osborne was useful to us as a messenger. He could bring us all the information we needed, uncensored. When I hired him, I thought he was a realistic young man. I was mistaken. On this last trip, he was bringing us some information concerning convoy schedules. He knew it was valuable and he was rash enough to threaten to sell us out unless I raised his bonus. I do not choose to have men of that temperament in my employ." The plump shoulders shrugged again. "Bob Osborne hardly died a martyr's death, Mr. Warren."

So Bob Osborne had been a sailor in the U. S. Navy and in the pay of their enemies at the same time! The guy for whose memory Lew had been risking his life had been a traitor, far worse even than April and her admitted Nazi partner, Clement Greene.

The deadly importance of that "letter" which he had let slip from his grasp came home to Lew. Clement Greene and April had information on the convoy schedules—the convoy schedules of which he in his small way was a part. They had it in their power to send hundreds of Lew's own companions to their death.

He stared at the gun pointed toward him. If only Bob hadn't tricked Dinah into believing he worked for Naval Intelligence, they could have brought the police here with them and everything would have been all right. If things went the way he planned, there was still a chance that the police might come. But it was a very dim one and even dimmer that they should come—in time.

Clement Greene's eyes were twinkling. There was nothing benevolent in the twinkle. "Yes, Bob Osborne was not a trustworthy character. He was clever enough. Before he started to bargain with us, he was shrewd enough to slip the envelope containing the convoy information to someone in the bar downstairs at that house. It was a soldier, as it turned out. Lanny was with him at the time but he did not see the transaction since Bob Osborne carried it out in the—ah—Men's Room. Because Osborne alone knew to whom he had given the envelope, he thought we would never dare to kill him. He underestimated us. With your aid, it was easy enough to locate the soldier and retrieve the envelope from him."

Clement Greene cocked his head. "Earlier this evening when you discovered Bob Osborne's body, you appear to have abstracted five hundred dollars from his pocket. That was to have been his legitimate pay for bringing us our information across the Atlantic. Am I correct in assuming that you are interested in money?"

Lew flushed. "What d'you mean?"

"You are a sensible young man. So long as you remain hostile, we will be obliged to kill you and your associates. You realize, I'm sure, that we have no alternative." Clement Greene paused. "But since Bob Osborne's death, we have a vacancy. You are a sailor, too. In your attempts to outwit us tonight, you have shown resourcefulness and courage. In my employ I can assure you that you would be paid well for very little work."

Lew's indignation was tempered now by a faint breath of hope. As Clement Greene was ready to play ball, if he acted his role right, there was a slender chance. Trying to make his eyes look crafty, he blustered:

"You think I'd work against my own country?"

"Perhaps I can offer you sufficient financial recompense for your outraged sensibilities." Clement Greene beckoned. "Come here." He nodded to Freddy. "You, too. Come to the desk."

Lew and Freddy moved around the desk until they were standing at Clement Greene's side. Lanny, with his revolver, came closer, covering them both. Clement Greene opened a drawer and brought out a large roll of bills. He spread them in front of him—an impressive array of hundred-dollar and fifty-dollar bills. Freddy's grimy hands were twitching with almost uncontrollable desire. His heart thumping, Lew said in exactly the right tone of surliness:

"What's the deal?"

"A most generous one. If you cooperate, I will not only spare your life, I will see that you are paid seven hundred dollars for each message you bring us across the Atlantic. And, naturally, arrangements will be made, as they would have been made with Osborne, to give you and your particular ship—protection while on convoy duty."

Freddy, still hypnotized by the sight of the money, whistled. "Gee, I'm gonna join the Navy tomorrow."

Lew pretended indecision. "And what about Dinah and Freddy?"

"If you can persuade your friends to be reasonable, I assure you nothing will happen to them."

"I'm reasonable right now," said the Head King of the gypsies.

Lew stared Clement Greene in the face, yearning to take a sock at him. "Well, I guess a guy'd have to be plenty patriotic to turn down a deal like that."

Clement Greene smiled. "Then we understand each other?"

Lew tried to keep a dead pan. "Sure. We understand each other."

"Excellent." Clement Greene took a piece of paper from the open drawer. "I have everything ready. All you have to do is to sign this and you will be released pending further orders."

Lew took the paper suspiciously. "What is it?"

"You don't expect me to enter into an arrangement of this sort without adequate precaution."

Lew stared at the paper while Freddy hovered bright-eyed at Mr. Greene's side. The document began: *"I, Lew Warren, Gunner's Mate, Second Class—"* It continued as a clear-cut confession that Lew had perpetrated several specific acts of sabotage against the Navy and that he had been in the pay of the German government for two years.

Lew had a simple man's mistrust of the written word. As he read, he felt his confidence slipping. "If I sign this, I could be shot, as a traitor."

"Precisely, Mr. Warren." Clement Greene had picked up the revolver again. "I shall have this document with me constantly and shall be prepared to send it to the proper authorities at any moment. It should help to keep you from disappointing us the way Osborne did." He indicated a pen. "Sign, Mr. Warren, and we shall all be free to go about more important matters."

Lew had visions of himself trying to explain that document away before a Court Martial Committee. He could tell them that it had been signed under pressure in a single-handed attempt to round up a dangerous spy ring. But who was going to believe that an obscure and unauthorized Gunner's Mate either could or would attempt single-handedly to round up a spy ring? If he signed that paper, he could still put the skids under April and Clement Greene, but at the price of branding himself too as a traitor. If he signed that paper, his own future would be bound to Clement Greene's with bands of steel.

Lew was struggling with a problem too big for him. His own life—the lives of hundreds who might be killed if Clement Greene was able to act on the information in that "letter" of Bob's.

Out of the corner of his eye, he glanced at the revolver in Greene's puffy hand. He could just see Lanny, too, his gun aimed at the shrill green front of Freddy's overcoat. Every fiber in his lusty young body revolted from a mental solution and longed for a physical one.

If only the Head King was on the ball, there was one chance in a thousand—a dangerous chance but a far sweeter one than trickery and the signing away of his future.

His heart knocking, Lew suddenly shouted, "Freddy, get the cripple."

In the same instant he lunged forward, smashing Clement Greene's arm sideways so that the revolver clattered to the floor. With one spring, he hurled himself onto the little man and sent him tumbling backward out of his chair.

A sharp explosion sounded behind him, followed by a scuffle. With a stab of alarm, he glanced over his shoulder. The Head King of the gypsies had come through magnificently. Lanny's revolver, too, had been knocked from his hand. Like a mad artist's conception of a jockey, Freddy Milanov was riding the prostrate cripple and bumping his head with solid, rhythmic bumps against the hard floor.

"Nice going." For the first time that evening Lew was in his own element, where brawn ruled triumphant over subtlety and deceit. "Give him hell. By the time I'm through with this guy—"

His hands were around Clement Greene's throat. The little man's eyes were bulging with terror. It was the best moment in Lew's life. He stared down at Greene's gray, blotched face. He could not resist the hunger in him. His lips drawing tight against his teeth, he lifted his fist and brought it down into the flabby flesh of Greene's jaw.

Clement Greene screamed. And, at that instant, the door from the little chapel was flung open. Three men with guns strode in. Lew leaped off Greene, plunging for the gun which lay on the carpet. His fingers almost touched it and then felt crushing pain as one of the men, jumping forward, brought his foot stamping down. A second man was pulling Freddy off Lanny by the scruff of his coat. The third had swept up the cripple's gun from the floor.

The three men had five revolvers now. Dejectedly Lew realized his solution had been far too simple a one for an outfit like this. Freddy was standing, hands in air, facing the men. One of them barked: "Okay, sailor. Over here."

Lew got up and joined Freddy, letting his hands go up.

Lanny was limping unsteadily forward. One of the men slipped his revolver to the cripple and, moving to the desk, helped Clement Greene to rise.

Sweat was pouring from Greene's bald head. A smoldering red patch showed around his mouth. On the arm of his man, he tottered to the chair behind the desk and sat down. His gaze, glinting with spite, moved to Lew.

"That was very rash of you, Mr. Warren. I overestimated your intelligence."

He talked in rapid German to the man at his side who left the room and returned shortly with several lengths of thick cord. Clement Greene scrutinized them with satisfaction. His gaze moved back to Lew.

"I have some important business to attend to before I can deal with you and your friend. I am sure you won't mind remaining here as our guests for a little while longer." He gestured to his man.

Against five guns, Lew and Freddy were obviously helpless. While Lanny and one man took care of Freddy, the two others went to work on Lew. Within a few minutes, his hands were trussed behind his jumper, his ankles, under the bell-bottoms of his trousers, were securely tied together and a choking handkerchief gag stopped his mouth. He was rolled into a corner of the office. Freddy was flung down next to him.

Clement Greene had risen and, with a shaky hand, was pushing the money from the desk into his pocket. Surrounded by his retinue, he moved to the door into the funeral parlor. He paused on the threshold, glancing over his shoulder.

"Death rather than dishonor," he quoted sardonically. "Well, it's your own decision, Mr. Warren. I hope you won't regret it."

One of the men turned out the light. The party moved through the door. Lew could hear it close and lock behind them.

As he lay huddled in the darkness, he reviewed the dizzy shifts of the last half hour. He also contemplated the future. It was a gloomy prospect. Although he had battled the Nazis in more than one naval and air encounter, he had never been closer to the enemy nor closer to death than he was right here in this elegant Sutton Place Funeral Parlor. He could hear Freddy squirming against his bonds. A few jerks of his own body told him it was useless to struggle. In spite of the one remote chance of rescue which still remained, it was useless, too, to hope.

The war had taught Lew to face death with equanimity, even to expect it as the logical result of failure. And he had certainly failed miserably tonight. If he alone had been involved, he would have been able to take easily enough whatever Clement Greene was going to hand out.

But there were so many other things at stake. The security of his own country's ships as they plowed across the Atlantic. And Dinah, too. The girl's stubborn little dark face haunted him. He was racked with self-reproach. Why had he let her come with him into this danger? Clement Greene's parting words came back, *"I have some important business to attend to before I can deal with you."* Was that important business to be with Dinah? He felt slightly sick as he lay there, wondering what they might be doing to her.

And against his own will, Dinah's image merged with that of April. Dinah—April. It was odd meeting them both on one night, and tough that the meeting should end like this. Dinah, the girl any man would be lucky to get. April, the girl you long for in your craziest dreams—those dreams that are doomed by reality. April's blonde, spring-fresh face seemed to float in the darkness, mocking him.

With a futile effort, he managed to roll over on to his side. At that moment, a hand, coming out of the blackness, plucked at his arm. It fluttered up his jumper and then, incredibly, was loosening the gag from his bruised lips.

Lew took a deep breath and managed, "Who—?"

"Don't worry. It's only me." A faint chuckle sounded close to him. "Me, Freddy. Gettin' kind of rusty. Took me close on five minutes to get outta them cords."

"Out of—!"

"Nothing to it." The chuckle sounded again. "When I was a kid, my old man usta work all the State Fairs down South. That's the first job I had, gettin' tied up by him and wriggling out. Knew all the tricks. Kid Houdini, they called me. We had to do it, poppa an' me, on account of ma got tired of supporting us."

Expert fingers were slipping now over Lew's pinioned wrists and ankles. In a few seconds he, too, was free, and Freddy was helping him to his feet. Lew stretched the stiffness out of his limbs. The Head King's whisper came again.

"Hey! That thing you sailors have. What d'you call it? Pass? Liberty card? Don't you want it?"

"Want it!"

"I got it here." Even in the darkness, Lew could tell Freddy was strutting. "When the Greene guy called us over to the desk to see the dough—it was a chance I couldn't pass up. It was too risky to try for the money, but I picked his pocket. I got something I think's your liberty card. Some other junk, too." His hand found Lew's again and stuffed something into it. "Here. Wanna see?"

Lew lit a match and stared down at the things which the gypsy had put in his hand. One of the things, sure enough, was his own liberty card which he had lost at the scene of the first murder. The other thing was a crumpled white envelope, stuffed with papers. Lew pulled out the papers. They, like the other papers which Dinah had taken from Greene's wallet, were scrawled over by meaningless jumbles of figures.

As Lew stared at them, he could have kissed the Head King of the gypsies. For there in his hand was the envelope containing the convoy information—the "letter" which Bob had entrusted to the soldier, the "letter" Lanny had taken from Lew, the "letter" around which the whole night's activities had centered.

In the quivering matchlight, Freddy's face showed, wizened and rather dubious. "Any good—that junk?"

"Good! Head King, you said you were worth more than a half-dozen *gajos*. You weren't kidding. Right now you're worth more to this country than a half-dozen aircraft carriers."

Lew slipped the envelope and his liberty card into his jumper pocket. He felt an elation that seemed only half real. This crowning achievement in Freddy's career as a pickpocket and ex-contortionist had, once again, turned the tables. It had heightened the danger, too. Lew saw that. Any minute Clement Greene would discover his loss and come rushing back.

Somehow they had to find Dinah and get out of here—before that happened.

Almost certainly one of Greene's men would be on guard in the passage outside the chapel. Lew remembered the other door in the wall behind the desk. That was their best bet. "There's another door back here somewhere, Freddy. Let's try it."

With the gypsy hovering around him, Lew groped through the darkness. He found the desk and squeezed around it. He lit a match. The door was in front of him. He stretched for the handle.

He had no plan about Dinah. It was no use having a plan until he found out how the land lay.

He turned the door handle. It was not locked. The door opened outward and the flickering matchlight revealed the white-tiled walls of a washroom.

He stepped into it. The match showed a built-in shower and a washbasin. To his satisfaction, there was another door looming in the far wall.

He did not dare turn on the electric light. The match flame wobbling, he started toward the inner door. Then he came to an abrupt halt, his pulses pounding. For something dim and shadowy was sprawled across the white tiles in the corner, something that was unmistakably a human body.

And, in the brief instant before the match burned out, he had caught a glimpse of a girl's stockinged leg and a high-heeled shoe.

All his fears for Dinah, which he had tried to dam up, broke through him in a flood. He stumbled forward. Hoarsely he called her name:

"Dinah—"

To his infinite relief, a feeble answering tap of a heel sounded against the tiles. So she was alive. It was all right. By a miracle he had found her and she was alive.

"Dinah—!"

He reached the corner. His hand, moving down, touched soft, silky hair.

"Dinah, baby—"

He dropped to his knees, his hand moving across the invisible hair. Then suddenly his fingers froze because the quality of the darkness had changed.

Trailing through it, making it utterly different, was the faint fragrance of daffodils—April's fragrance which earlier that evening had meant all romance and which now had become the essence of danger.

Lew glanced around, expecting attack from he knew not where. Apart from that fragile scent, the little washroom was exactly the same. With a clumsy movement, he lit another match. He held it directly in front of the girl on the floor at his side.

He saw her, saw that her ankles were bound, her arms pinioned behind her, and that her mouth was crushed by a cloth gag. But as he stared, nothing made sense anymore.

Because the girl, gazing back at him from blue, pleading eyes, was not Dinah Lord.

She was April Osborne.

Stupefaction, suspicion and a kind of wild hope battled each other in Lew's mind. The sight of April's honey blonde hair and the soft skin of her face under the crushing gag stirred him beyond measure. Instinctively, long before he had figured out any "whys" or "whats", he was groping in the darkness to loosen the cords that bound her. Freddy Milanov was poised on the threshold of the washroom, but Lew had forgotten him. As he eased the knots from April's wrists, the daffodil perfume made a little circle of enchantment around him.

At last the girl was free. Lew helped her to her feet. Almost without his knowing it, he kept his arms around her to steady her. It was quite mad the way he felt—as if he had known her and loved her all his life, as if she was not the woman he hated, the woman who had tried to kill him, the leader of this desperate Nazi ring of saboteurs.

"April"—he said it huskily—"April."

"I'd almost given up hope." Her voice, with the same musical lilt, sent a tingle through him. "I knew they were going to bring you here to—to kill you. I've been praying that somehow you'd be able to save yourself, that you'd find me."

Lew was far too dazed to take in what she was saying. "But April—"

"I know you've been thinking I was one of them, that I—I deliberately lured you to that house, lied to you." She was so close to him in the darkness that he could feel the flutter of her heart. "I was a fool, a wretched fool. But everything I told you, I believed. I believed it because Bob was my brother and I trusted him. He told me he and Lanny were working for Naval Intelligence. I believed it. Until tonight I had never even heard of Clement Greene."

The wild hope leaping up, Lew blurted, "You mean you—you aren't part of this outfit?"

Her whisper was low, vibrant. "Oh, how can I make you understand? I know everything now. I know Bob sold himself to Greene, that he was a traitor, that he tried to hold them up for more money and was—was murdered. Once Clement Greene had me here as a prisoner, he took great pleasure in letting me know the truth." The little heart-breaking catch was back in her voice. "Bob was the only family I had. I loved him. I knew he'd always been shiftless, no good, really. But when he joined the Navy, I hoped so that he'd changed. Of course, I thought Lanny was a strange person for him to be seeing so often on his leaves. But all that seemed to make sense when Bob told me Lanny was his boss in Naval Intelligence."

There was nothing in the world now for Lew except his exultant desire to hear April say this and to be able to believe her.

"Yes, yes. Tell me. Tell me what happened tonight."

"It all seemed so simple. Bob told me he and Lanny were on a very important job, that he needed my help, that I was to ask no questions. We picked up Lanny and—and went with him to that house."

"Okay. You went in through the bar and Bob left you for a couple of minutes to go to the Men's Room?"

"That's right."

"There in the Men's Room he gave the envelope to the soldier." Lew was surprised at the ease with which he could piece everything together now. "Bob was planning to double-cross Greene. He figured that if he brought you along, an outsider, someone who didn't know anything, you'd be a protection for him. They wouldn't dare kill him while his sister was right there. That's what he figured."

In the darkness he could tell that April was quivering. "I suppose so.

It's awful to have to believe that of Bob. But—"

"Psst!" Freddy's voice came through the darkness in a sharp whisper. "If you two got any more to say to each other, save it. We got to get out of here."

In a half-real way, that brought back to Lew the dangers of the moment. With Clement Greene and his murdering henchmen ready to return for them at any second, they had indeed to get out—and get out quickly, He remembered the second door which led from the washroom. That was their one chance for escape. He moved toward it. As he left April's side, some of her spell went. The enormous responsibility of having those convoy papers in his pocket became once more the most important thing.

He turned the handle on the door. It was locked.

"Hey, Freddy. Get to work on this lock."

Lew heard a click. Then the Head King glided forward and stooped in the darkness over the lock.

"And quiet," warned Lew. "Some of them may be outside."

"Okay." Freddy's chuckle showed that he was still enjoying this most unenjoyable experience. "I locked the door we came into the washroom by—just in case they try busting into that office to get us again."

Lew moved back to April, drawn to her like a needle to a magnet. This miraculous thing that was happening had made him forget Dinah.

"Freddy, my friend, is working on the lock," he said. "Soon we'll have a fighting chance to get out of this place. Go on. Lanny and Bob took you to that house."

"We all went up to the empty room where I took you later. Bob told me to wait there, and he and Lanny went on upstairs."

"That house must be where Greene contacts his agents. Okay."

April's hand, moving through the darkness, found his as if she needed contact with him to steady her. The warmth of her fingers sent a tingle through him.

"After they'd gone, I just stayed in the empty room, waiting. At last Lanny came down. He told me Bob had sent him, that there was some trouble and that Bob wanted another sailor just in case there was a fight. Lanny explained that Bob still needed him, so I would have to go for the sailor. He told me about the back exit from the house and told me to go to the Eldorado. There were always sailors there, he said. It all seemed crazy. Of course, it did. But Bob had told me to trust Lanny and I expected everything to be crazy anyway. All I cared about was Bob's safety. Lanny had brought a bottle of whiskey down with him. He kidded and said that if I did get a sailor to help me, he'd at least expect a drink for his pains."

"So that's how he planned to use you to get me doped. Okay. You went to the Eldorado and found me. You hadn't any idea that Greene had been there first, prospecting, that he'd seen I was about Bob's build, that he'd bought me free beers and got Sally to fake my fortune to make sure I'd be all set to go with you."

A faint scratching told that Freddy was continuing his battle with the lock. Lew moved his hands to April's arms. He had lost all that awe of her which he had felt at first. She was no longer the glamorous, unapproachable girl—the Judge's daughter. She was just April Osborne—just someone like himself, a poor kid who had been made a dupe by a bunch of clever and unscrupulous crooks.

"Listen, baby. I see why they sent you for me. It was smart all right. They knew it was safe since you didn't suspect anything; they knew, too, a sailor's much readier to go places with a beautiful blonde than any other kind of stranger. But there was a much more important reason than that. They were crazy to get you out of the house. They'd already killed Bob by then, and Clement Greene told me his plans were all set to rush a hearse round there and bring the body here where it would be safe. The hearse was meant to arrive while you were getting me. But there was a delay. They must actually have been bringing the body down the stairs when we came back. That's why they had to dump it so quickly down into the cellar."

They stood together in the darkness. Lew breathed sharply, "Hey, Freddy, how's that lock coming along?"

Freddy's hoarse whisper came back. "It's tough. But I'm gettin' places with it."

It was grueling having to wait, completely impotent, completely dependent upon Freddy. To keep his own mind and April's from their extreme danger, Lew made himself carry the story through to its conclusion.

"Tell me, April. You took me to that house by the back door, the way you'd been told. You took me up to the empty room and then Lanny came for you. When he talked to you out there in the passage, he brought up the subject of the liquor again, didn't he? That's why you looked in to make sure I knew where to get it?"

"Yes. Yes."

"Okay. What happened then?"

"Lanny took me upstairs to an empty apartment. I was worried, of course, for Bob, and Lanny told me that everything had straightened itself out and Bob had gone on somewhere else. We were to wait there, he said, until Bob telephoned us where to meet him. We wouldn't be needing you, after all, he said."

"Sure. I get it. Lanny's job was to keep you safely upstairs while Greene's men got the body out of the cellar. And me, the poor dumb sailor, I was meant to wait there in the dark room, get bored and tank myself up with the doped liquor so's I'd be primed for the act with the soldier in the bar." He grunted. "I didn't play my part right. I found out the liquor was doped, got mad as hell with you, went raging around and saw the corpse before they'd come to take it away. Go on, baby."

"There—there wasn't much more. The phone rang. Lanny answered it. He told me it was Bob and that we had to go on and meet him somewhere else. It all seemed perfectly all right to me. I never dreamed poor Bob had been—been murdered."

"Sure. Of course, the phone call was really Greene saying they'd got Bob away and the coast was clear."

Behind his jubilation, Lew was on a razor edge of suspense. Surely Greene must have discovered by now that the convoy information had been stolen from his pocket. What the heck was Freddy doing with that lock? He peered through the darkness at the luminous dial of his watch. Four o'clock. It was over two hours since they had left the gypsies' house. He felt a chill of pessimism. Surely, if things had worked out there the way he hoped they would, something would have happened by now.

April was whispering, "That's when we came downstairs to get you. When we saw you there, lolled against the wall with the bottle in your hand, I didn't know anything about the dope or—or that you were pretending. I just thought you were drunk." There was the slightest trace of a laugh. "I—I had liked you so much up till then. And that—that shocked me, that you should have promised to help me and got yourself drunk."

"Of course, baby. I thought I was so smart when I tried to put you on the spot by 'discovering' the body again. And all the time you knew nothing. Even later in the bar, Lanny sent you ahead for a taxi. You never even knew about that business with the soldier and the letter."

"Even at the end, when we were all in the taxi, I never dreamed anything was wrong. I just thought we were going to meet Bob and drop you off somewhere where you wanted to be. When Lanny suddenly told the driver to stop and helped you out, I didn't know what was happening.

"Then he grabbed the envelope from you and pushed past you back to the taxi. Before I realized it, we had left you and were driving on. I tried to make him go back for you. He just laughed. I started to be suspicious then. I asked about the envelope, about where we were going. He said we were going to see Bob but I didn't believe him anymore. I tried to call out to the driver. Lanny put his hand over my mouth. I was terrified and—"

She gave a little shiver. "It was awful. Lanny brought me here, to that office. Clement Greene just sat, smiling, telling me how distressed he was at the prospect of having to dispose of me but that I had to pay for trusting my brother. And then he said he wasn't planning to kill me until he got you, too. He told me everything, how you'd dropped your liberty card by Bob's body and exactly how he was planning to lure you back here."

For the first time everything started to blur. "But how could Greene have known I was going to come here? I only got here because Sally, the gypsy, happened to steal Greene's wallet and she happened to give the wallet to Freddy and I happened to get in touch with Freddy. It was only one chance in a million that we got to his place."

April did not speak for a moment. Then, in a small voice, she said, "Haven't you guessed?"

"Guessed?"

"When Lanny had you in the taxi, he didn't know you'd seen Bob's body or he'd have brought you right here with me. But by the time we got here Greene's men had found your liberty card in the cellar. And she was with Greene. She found out from Lanny where we'd left you—and she went after you herself."

"She?" Lew was feeling dizzy.

"Yes, the girl who's the head of all these people, the girl who's more important even than Greene. She went after you—to see you got here where they could kill you."

Lew was completely unprepared for that. His thoughts staggered.

"Dinah! You mean Dinah's the boss of this outfit? She—but she was Bob's fiancée. She—"

"Fiancée? Oh, she must have been clever to make you trust her. Of course, she wasn't Bob's fiancée. I doubt whether she'd ever even seen him. She's far too important to—to have anything to do with Greene's agents."

In one spinning moment Lew realized the truth. It was Dinah who had insisted from the beginning that they were not to go to the police. It was Dinah who had tried time and time again to lure him to Clement Greene's. He remembered how Dinah had grabbed the code lists from Greene's stolen wallet; how Dinah had slipped ahead from the gypsies' house and how he had seen her coming out of the drugstore. She had, of course, telephoned Greene to let him know she had retrieved the lists and was bringing Lew to the Funeral Parlor.

While the blood flooded his cheeks, he also remembered Dinah's frightened call for help which had made him and Freddy swing round from the coffin and become an easy prey for Clement Greene stepping out with his revolver from the inner door behind them.

Dinah, "the girl any man would be lucky to get," had stood by him through thick and thin, not as a comrade, but as a—jailer.

Twice on that eventful night, his "male intuition" had played him hopelessly false. Dinah Lord, who had acted to perfection the role of the courageous bereaved fiancée, had fooled him as completely as he had fooled himself about April.

As he stood there tensely, his hand still on April's arm, Freddy's whisper came, "I'm gettin' it. Any second now the lock'll give. Never spent so much time in my life—"

The gypsy broke off. Lew swung round in the dark, his heart thumping, facing back toward the door which led to the office. Sounds had come from the room beyond—the sound of footsteps and then sharp, staccato voices. His stomach turned over. The inevitable had happened at last. Greene and his men had returned for them.

Lew ran to Freddy. "Quick. For heaven's sake, quick."

Freddy's chuckle was as unconcerned as ever. "Don't worry. I said I done it. I done it."

The gypsy turned the handle with a faint scraping. The door opened outward. Lew gripped April's arm and ran with her after Freddy out into the dim blue light of a passage. Behind, he could hear the noises, louder now and more confused. The far door rattled and someone called:

"It's locked. They must have got out this way."

The corridor was short. It led to another passage which stretched to the left and right. Freddy, an incongruously comic figure for such danger, stole ahead, his riding boots peeping out beneath the scarab green overcoat. There was pandemonium behind them in the office. Freddy glanced round. He saw April for the first time and blinked.

"Gee," he whispered, "we saved the wrong girl."

Lew pushed past him. He reached the end of the little passage and hesitated at the corner. He stiffened. From the corridor beyond he could hear voices talking in rapid German. One of the voices he recognized only too well. It was the voice of Dinah Lord.

Tensely he edged forward and peered around the corner. At the end of the corridor to the right, Dinah, Lanny and two other men had just come out of a room. They were standing with their backs to Lew. Dinah was talking. The men were listening in respectful silence.

Lew tried to gauge their very desperate predicament. Any second Greene and the men in the office would break down the washroom door and attack them from the rear. There was only one, pitifully uncertain course open to them. The corridor to the left was in full view of Dinah and her cohorts—but it was empty.

Lew turned to April and Freddy. "Our one chance is the passage to the left. Run like you've never run before. You first, Freddy. Then April. Then me."

The Head King gave a preposterous wink. With a flurry of overcoat and a clatter of riding boots he was off down the passage like a streak. April went tumbling after him. Obsessed with anxiety for her, Lew followed. He heard a crash behind them as the washroom door splintered open.

It was like some mad race in a dream. Dimly he was conscious of the shaded blue bulbs, the rich somber carpet of the corridor beneath his running feet. In the first seconds, there was no sound from behind.

Then all hell broke loose.

Lew heard Dinah's voice shouting. There was the sudden pounding of footsteps. A bullet, whistling past his ear, made a sharp report. There was another shot.

Ahead, the corridor twisted to the right. Freddy reached the bend and disappeared. Lew doubled his pace, caught up with April and dragged her around, too, into the safety that would remain safety only for a couple of seconds.

In their flight Lew had lost his bearings. But with a surge of hope he saw that the corridor ended in a door. And it wasn't just a door. It was the main door, leading out into the street.

The rush of footsteps sounded behind them. They stumbled on. Freddy reached the door. His quick, wizard hands were fluttering over the bolt. April and Lew joined him while two other shots echoed in the hollow corridor.

"Quick, Freddy. For God's sake, the door—quick."

"It's jammed," grunted the gypsy. "The bolt's kind of jammed."

The shooting had stopped now. Lew glanced over his shoulder. Dinah, Clement Greene, Lanny, the other men were all appearing around the bend.

"Don't shoot anymore," Dinah called. "We've got them anyway."

Freddy tugged wildly at the bolt. It gave. He started to swing the door inward. At that instant two of Dinah's men jumped on Lew. There was a cry from April as Lanny grabbed her.

Freddy had pulled the door completely open before Clement Greene leaped forward, knocking him sideways.

Lew shook off his two attackers. His fist, swinging, struck one of them squarely on the jaw. Then the world seemed to have turned upside down.

Because the door had not only opened. It had revealed two policemen and a plainclothesman who strode in from the street. Each of them had a gun.

Dinah gave a little shriek. Her henchmen stared blankly at the policemen and then down at their own revolvers. That instant of indecision deprived them of their chance. The plainclothesman shouted:

"Drop those guns. Put up your hands, all of you. The house is surrounded."

In a haze Lew put up his hands. April was next to him, her lovely face white and astounded. Dinah's gun clattered to the floor. Following her lead, Greene, Lanny and the men all lifted their arms above their heads. As they dropped their guns, the policemen picked them up.

"Okay," said the plainclothesman. "We've been here ten minutes getting every exit covered. We were just going to break in when the shooting started." He flashed a badge. "Inspector Lawson of the Homicide Squad. Anyone trying to make a getaway will be shot."

The shock was leaving Lew now, giving way to a giddy excitement. Other policemen were swarming in through the open and elegant door of Greene's Funeral Parlor. And, behind them, huge, flamboyant, plumply important, waddled the figure of Rita.

The inspector snapped, "Which of you's Freddy Milanov?" His glance rested on the disheveled Head King. "You, of course. We came here to get you, Milanov, as a material witness in the murder of Sally Johnson." His eyes moved around the group. "Looks like we've run into something else pretty murderous, too."

Rita, all scarlet bandanna and crimson peonies, had brushed majestically toward her husband, chattering in Romany. She came at Lew now, beaming with affection. Her bangled arm encircled his waist.

"Don't you worry, beauty. I told the cops you ain't had nothin' to do with it. It's just Freddy." Her eyes flashed. "The cops came and started pushing me around. They knew about the time Freddy beat up Sally and they just naturally figure he killed her. So—so I figured it would be kind of more comfortable for everyone if I bring 'em round here."

Lew was grinning broadly. Everything had come out the way he had hoped it would. His decision to let Rita get away with her pickpocketing experiment had, after all, saved their lives.

He said, "Rita, you're wonderful. If you hadn't brought the police, Freddy, all of us would be dead by now. Never say it doesn't pay to pick pockets. If you hadn't snitched that wallet from me and found Greene's address in it, you'd never have known where we were."

Rita lowered her lashes in coy admission. The Inspector was still staring around the motley assembly.

"Well, what's been going on here?"

Dinah, her face hard and calculating now, glanced at Greene. He began nervously, "Oh, it's nothing, Inspector. Just—"

"Just murder, Inspector," cut in Lew. "That's all." He strode forward, tugging jauntily at the narrow waistline of his blues. "You came to the right place and you came at the right time. These people are all Nazi agents. They murdered Sally and they murdered someone else too—a sailor. They were just getting around to murdering me and my friends when you bust in."

The Inspector stared as if Lew were a harmless lunatic.

"I'm not kidding." Lew was still grinning. By the time he'd produced all the evidence there was to produce, Dinah, Greene, Lanny and the rest of them would be put out of action forever. There was no question about that. "Here—" He pulled from his breast pocket the envelope containing the convoy information. He presented it to the Inspector. "This is code information about our convoys to England. They were going to turn it over to Germany. There's a code list, too, of all their Nazi boyfriends and girlfriends in this country." He jerked a contemptuous thumb at Dinah. "If you don't find it in this charming young lady's pocketbook, it'll be around here some place."

Inspector Lawson was gazing dizzily at the code papers in his hand.

Lew felt once again in his breast pocket and brought out Bob Osborne's liberty card. He tossed it to the Inspector. "This is the liberty card of the sailor they murdered. Just go down this passage, turn to the right and open the second door on the left. You'll find a fancy funeral parlor and in it you'll find a coffin all dressed up with flowers and in that coffin you'll find a body. Don't let the flowers and the civilian clothes fool you. Open the lid and you'll see the guy's been stabbed three times. Look at his face and you'll know he's that sailor." Lew found it pleasant to be the focus of so much staggered official attention. "When you've done that, come back and I'll tell you the rest. Make it snappy though. I've got to be back aboard ship in an hour."

The Inspector seemed to be the victim of some turbulent inner struggle. He glanced around him. He muttered orders to one of the policemen and then, taking another with him, strode down the hall. Soon he was back. He came to Lew, his face gray with shock.

"Looks—looks like you're telling the truth, sailor."

"Sure I am." Lew looked from the cold, defiant Dinah to the twittering Clement Greene. "Shoot those papers over to Naval Intelligence and they'll tell you how right I am. And if you take my advice, you'll handcuff this whole bunch right away. They're not the type to take chances with."

Trying to appear unruffled, the Inspector nodded to his men. In a minute, Dinah, Clement Greene, Lanny and their underlings were securely handcuffed.

"That's better," said Lew. "One thing more. This has been quite an evening for me. At one part of it I ran into five hundred bucks. It's the best Nazi money on the market. I guess I'll hand that over to you, too."

The Inspector scratched his head. "That will have to wait. But if you've done what I think you've done, sailor, you're going to be a national hero. Maybe they'll want you to hang on to that five hundred."

Lew's dark young face went stubborn. "I don't need any part of it. It's been burning a hole in my pocket ever since I knew where it came from. Here. You take it."

His hand moved toward the inside pocket of his jumper. As it did so, he noticed Freddy Milanov cast him one swift, uneasy glance. Lew pushed his fingers into the pocket.

It was empty.

The Head King of the gypsies was staring ingenuously up at the ceiling now. Lew strode to him.

"Freddy, give it back. You should be ashamed—stealing from a pal."

In an agony of reluctance, Freddy's hand fumbled into the green overcoat. He shook his tousled white head. "Guess I just naturally ain't no good," he moaned. "Five hundred bucks. I just couldn't resist it. Somehow I just had to—" He stopped. The hand came out of the coat, empty. He swirled round to Rita.

Rita Milanov was grinning a wide, toothy grin. With a flourish she fumbled down the peonied bosom and brought out a thick wad of bills. She handed it to the Inspector, but her black eyes, triumphantly, were on her husband.

"You!" she exclaimed. "You had the nerve to say I was a lousy pickpocket!"

This piece of light-fingered by-play seemed to tickle the gypsies immensely. Rita and Freddy both burst into gales of cackling laughter and started jabbering in Romany and slapping each other on the back.

It was then that Lew turned to April. He had deliberately kept himself from looking at her until everything was cleared up.

She stood there by his side, her lovely, flower-soft face watching him with admiration and wonder.

"You're—you're marvelous," she said. "All alone, you made things come out right."

"Not all alone, honey. There was Freddy. And you."

"Me!" The blue, blue eyes widened. "I almost got you killed. That's all I did."

"But you got me mad, too." Lew was smiling. Just seeing her there with him made everything gay. "If you hadn't got me mad, if I hadn't thought you'd played me the dirtiest trick any girl ever played me, this would never have happened."

Her lips parted. A faint smile came, spreading to her eyes with shining radiance.

Lew knew dimly that the Inspector was there, that the gypsies were there, that Dinah, Greene, Lanny and the policemen were there. But there was nothing that mattered except April's shining smile.

"The beautiful blonde who would change my life!"

His strong hands slid gently up her arms.

"Sally faked that fortune. But—baby, what a swell job of faking she did."

The End

THE CASE FOR LIZZIE
OR
A THEORETICAL RECONSTRUCTION OF THE BORDEN MURDERS

By Q. Patrick

I make no apology for advancing my theory on the Borden murders. It has occupied me for many years, and my only regret is that I never had the opportunity to discuss it with that Borden expert, the late Mr. Edmund Pearson. Some time ago I sent him a rough draft of my thesis and received a courteous and interested reply. He told me that, whereas many "solutions" had been offered, mine was a new and original one. He assured me that, so far as he knew, I had in no sense transgressed against facts, and he acknowledged the possibility and plausibility of my argument, while tacitly admitting that it did not agree with his own. Finally, to my delight, he invited me to come and see him in New York. The very week I had planned to go, I read the unhappy news that he was dead. And so the world lost a great criminologist, a fine prose writer, and the notable Lizzie Borden "Fan" of all time. In a forlorn hope that his mantle may descend, if but rustlingly, upon me, I humbly offer my own "solution" of the case.

On a swelteringly hot day, August 4, 1892, Mr. Andrew Jackson Borden (69) and his second wife Mrs. Abby L. Durfee Borden (62) were found dead in their home at No. 92 Second Street, Fall River, Mass. They were, in life, an unloved and an unlovely couple. In death, they presented an unlovely spectacle since, in both instances, their skulls had been battered by some "sharp cutting instrument, presumably an ax." Much blood had been spilled, but the wounds, though numerous, were "such as might have been made by a woman or relatively feeble person." Medical testimony showed that Abby Borden had been killed between 9 A.M. and 9:45 A.M. while tidying up the spare bedroom. Her husband met his death approximately an hour and a half later, somewhere around 11 o'clock, while resting on the living room couch after the heat of a morning walk.

In due course, and for many excellent reasons, Mr. Borden's younger daughter Lizzie (32) was arrested on a charge of willful double murder and, after various hearings and a period of incarceration, was tried by a jury of her peers. On June 20, 1893, she was—also for many excellent reasons—acquitted of both charges and went her way. But not rejoicing. Rich while comparatively young, she was destined to walk in loneliness and contumely for the remaining 34 years of her life. She died on June 1, 1927, and lies in the same vault as her murdered parents in Fall River cemetery.

So much for the stark facts. The circumstantial details are a source of constant fascination to all amateurs of crime.

The household, at the time of the tragedy, consisted of Mr. Borden, an unpleasant man whose very considerable wealth (accruing partly through the undertaking business, partly through skinning the widow's mite) had brought him neither the respect nor the affection of his neighbors. His picture shows a harsh face and a cruel, straight-line mouth, framed with unprepossessing chin whiskers. He grudged his wife's doctor bills, and gave up his seat in church because one of the warders raised his tax assessment. The only possible point I can make in his favor is that he showed a certain sense of financial responsibility towards his daughters.

In the favor of his wife, Abby, I can find nothing to say. Lizzie aptly described her as a "mean old thing." Even the defense counsel in the trial could find no word of praise for her. She was plain and monstrously fat, weighing over 200 pounds while only five feet in height. Sloppy in her personal appearance, she was an atrocious housekeeper (witness the warmed-over mutton and other gastronomical horrors served at that last grim breakfast) and a whining, possibly grasping woman. In short, she deserved her spouse, and while common decency prevents me from saying that she deserved her fate, I have always felt some surprise that she avoided the ax for 62 years—especially during the dog days.

Then there was Emma, the older daughter, a spinster of over forty, who is almost classic in her complete insipidity. Her infrequent flashes of character came out solely in her intense dislike of her stepmother and her valiant defense of Lizzie at the trial, which probably turned the scale finally in her sister's favor.

The work of the house was done by an Irish girl whose name was Bridget Sullivan but who was known to the family as Maggie, a sort of generic name inherited from a predecessor. Apparently she had none of the imagination or whimsy so common in her race. She was a plain, uninteresting girl whose dreams (if any) centered around work adequately finished, her morning "lie-down" or an occasional popping out for a dress length from a local emporium. Though occasionally obliged to chop wood, it is unlikely that ax-play formed any part of her recreation.

The whipping boy of the piece was a certain Mr. John Morse, brother of the first Mrs. Borden (deceased), and thus maternal uncle to Emma and Lizzie. He happened to be staying with the Bordens on a brief visit during which he transacted certain business deals for his brother-in-law. His historic interest lies in his sheer fortuitousness; the accident that he slept in the fatal spare bedroom the night before Abby was killed; and the fact that he was seized upon as the culprit by the indignant denizens of Fall River and almost mobbed. I hope to show that he wasn't such an accident as he seemed. Being an officious busybody, and interested in other people's property—especially their testaments—he was perhaps a catalytic agent; the spark that set off a ruddy conflagration.

Last, but certainly not least, there was our heroine, Lizzie. Lizzie Andrew Borden, the chaste delight of Reverends Jubb and Buck, the local ministers; Lizzie, the flower of the ladies flower guild; Lizzie, the 32-year-old spinster against whom no word of scandal had ever been breathed. Though many delicious fables have since sprung up round her name, in 1892 there was not one scintilla of real evidence to show that she was a woman of violence or stormy passions. Mrs. Belloc Lowndes endowed her with a mysterious lover whom she met during a trip to Europe. There is no evidence for this at all. John Colton and Carlton Miles, the authors of *Nine Pine Street*, plump for a clerical boyfriend; but both her clerical soulmates (Revs. Jubb and Buck) had perfectly good wives of their own, and loved Lizzie only for her hard and good works and for her subsequent notoriety. Psychologists have credited her with a mother complex, a raft of sex-perversions, and all sorts of Freudian fancies. There is no known justification for such charges.

Energetic she certainly was. Outspoken, too, with an almost male efficiency in the handling of money. Her friends were older women and her interests were—in common with countless other women who have lived and died—church work, clothes, and mild entertaining. It is my firm belief that she was a clear-headed, unmurderous young woman, with an intense respect for her pastors, her family name, and the good opinion of her neighbors. And she lived and died as such. As for marriage—it can only be stated that when she achieved notoriety and fortune she could have had her pick of countless males. But she chose to remain a spinster.

THE CASE FOR LIZZIE

So much for the *dramatis personae*. Now for the locale. Number 92 Second Street was—and still is—a rather ugly frame house like many thousands of others in Fall River and elsewhere in New England. It in no sense reflected the bank balance of its occupants. I stress the fact that it was a frame house, small and with relatively thin walls. This is important from the point of view of acoustics. It must be remembered that on that particular stifling August day two persons were hacked to death, and one of them was a heavy woman whose fall to the floor in an upstairs room must have shaken the house. It would have been heard from almost any of the normally lived-in rooms.

In that house, there had been for some time a terrific tension. The daughters disliked their stepmother. The father threw out dark hints, especially to his favorite daughter Lizzie, that mysterious enemies were plotting to take his life, and also the life of Abby. Following a problematical burglary in the house, he insisted that all the doors, both inside and out, should be kept locked and, if possible, double-locked.

There had been strange sicknesses too. To the frivolous, this does not seem odd, in view of Mrs. Borden's indigestible daily menus. But one particular bout of mass queasiness, two days before the murders, had all the appearance of a deliberate poison attempt.

On the very eve of the final catastrophe, Lizzie complained to a friend that there was a "doom" hanging over her home. This remark is readily understandable. It is not so understandable, however, why, on at least two occasions, she should have visited drugstores to inquire about the possibility of obtaining prussic acid. These visits, although not admitted into evidence at her trial, are established facts. To some, they are indications of her lethal intentions.

A short time before the fatal Fourth of August, Emma Borden had left this house of hatred to visit friends at Fairhaven, fifteen miles away. On August the Third, Uncle John Vinnicum Morse arrived at No. 92 Second Street.

The stage was now set for the most fascinating murder of all time.

On the historic morning of August 4th, Lizzie came downstairs about 9:00 A.M., and wisely refused the breakfast of warmed-over mutton and/or mutton soup in which her parents and uncle had indulged two hours before. Mr. Morse had already departed on a series of rural errands which were to establish him a bulletproof alibi. At some point between 9:15 and 9:30, Mr. Borden left the house to make some routine calls, and Lizzie, who was unwell, went down cellar where the toilet was situated.

Mrs. Borden, having issued various domestic instructions to the maid, trundled upstairs to take fresh pillow slips to the spare room bed. This was between 9:15 and 9:30. She was never seen alive again. Someone either followed her upstairs or was waiting for her in the spare room. That someone sprung on her unawares and struck her repeatedly with an ax or a hatchet until her head was hacked to ribbons.

Maggie, the maid, who might otherwise have heard her mistress' massive body crash to the floor, was engaged at this time in cleaning the windows on the outside of the house.

Neither she nor Lizzie seemed to have missed Mrs. Borden or to have suspected that anything might be wrong. Maggie continued to wash the windows. Lizzie, according to her own story, reappeared from the cellar, ironed a few dainty handkerchiefs in the dining room, and then sat a while in the kitchen browsing through an old copy of *Harper's Magazine*.

Sometime around 10:45, Mr. Borden returned home. He was observed to have some difficulty about opening the front door (and this for the first time in his life). He stumped around the house to the side door. He was finally admitted at the front door by Maggie.

Almost immediately after his admission, Lizzie was seen by Maggie at the head of the stairs, just outside the spare room where Mrs. Borden's murdered body lay. It was then that she was heard to utter a strange sound that seemed like a laugh. This utterance later made history as the famous "Lizzie Borden laugh."

Lizzie arrived downstairs. To Maggie's surprise, she greeted her father with this statement: "Mrs. Borden has gone out—she had a note from somebody who is sick." Mr. Borden made no recorded comment, took the key of his perennially locked bedroom from a shelf, and ascended the backstairs to his room. After a moment or two, he returned to the sitting room. Lizzie helped him to a couch and composed him there for a nap. With daughterly solicitude, she even suggested drawing the shades to temper the midsummer heat.

Leaving her father to rest, she followed Maggie to the kitchen and engaged her in a very curious conversation. She informed her that there was a cheap bargain sale of dress goods downtown, and suggested that the maid might like to "pop out" and inspect it. Maggie was not impressed by this information, but shortly before eleven o'clock—and most conveniently for someone—she stepped out of the picture by retiring to her attic bedroom for a "lie-down."

What happened while Maggie was lying down is the crux of the case. Lizzie claimed that during this period she never reentered the sitting room where her father was sleeping, but that she had gone out into an oppressively hot and dirty barn in the garden, there to eat some pears and to search for some pieces of lead. These pieces of lead, she maintained later, were needed by her as sinkers for fishing lines, although it was shown that she had not gone fishing for over five years. Subsequently she contradicted this statement, saying that she had wanted the metal to fix a screen.

In any event, to the barn she went—if she is to be believed. And an extraordinary place it was to put herself during those crucial fifteen minutes. It has puzzled all students of the Borden case.

Maggie, busy lying down at this time, had of course nothing to add to Lizzie's story. All she knew was that Lizzie's voice startled her out of her doze at about 11:10, calling, "Come down, Maggie. Father's dead; someone came in and killed him."

Someone had indeed killed Mr. Borden. He was lying on the sitting room couch, his head as terribly battered as his wife's had been.

It was these macabre events which later inspired the jingle so well-known even to this day:

> "Lizzie Borden took an ax
> And gave her mother forty whacks;
> And when she saw what she had done,
> She gave her father forty-one."

Actually there is poetic exaggeration in this lyric. The medical evidence showed that Mrs. Borden had received eighteen wounds in her head, whereas Mr. Borden himself got away with a mere ten.

After this, the fireworks started. The neighbors, including the friendly physician, Dr. Bowen, all came running in, and the gruesome remains of Mrs. Borden were soon discovered in the spare room. As it happened, the majority of the Fall River police force was off on an annual picnic, but those officers who were available put in an astonished appearance.

Lizzie proceeded to tell her story with a certain amount of fortitude and very little show of decent regret. There were discrepancies in her statements. But any good police officer will agree that when a serious crime has been committed, the innocent are more likely to be inaccurate than the guilty.

Numerous things happened subsequently. Sister Emma was sent for from Fairhaven where she was enjoying her perfect alibi. Uncle Morse wandered—fortuitously as usual—into a scene of carnage worthy of a Greek tragedy. Lizzie changed her blue dress for a pink wrapper. Dr. Bowen was seen burning a note in the stove, but explained to a police officer that it was nothing important. And through it all, Lizzie gave the authorities free access to herself and her closets. But she continued telling stories that did not quite jibe.

On August 7th, three days later, Lizzie was known to burn a dress in the stove at her home while police officers were in the house. She was seen to do this by a reliable witness who was also her friend, Miss Alice Russell. This fact, though not disclosed at the time, was one of the many damning pieces of evidence against Lizzie.

It must be remembered that, in the case of each murder, the rooms were a shambles, and it seems inevitable that anyone who had committed these two shocking crimes must have been drenched, especially about the lower portions of the clothing and body, with blood that had spurted from those many wounds. And yet everybody who saw Lizzie within the fatal few minutes after the crime, was convinced that there were no signs of blood about her clothing or her person. This was one of the major factors in her defense.

On August 11th, 1892, following the inquest, Lizzie Borden was arrested. And from then on until her final trial in June, 1893, she was the most notorious woman in America. Sides were taken all over the world with regard to her guilt, and the Reverends Buck and Jubb stirred up the Ladies Aid Societies and church organizations into a perfect frenzy over Lizzie's virgin innocence.

She was duly acquitted and, as already mentioned, disappeared into obscurity. In 1927, she died a marked and shunned woman.

The persecution of Lizzie was, in my opinion, undeserved; though here I differ from the great authority Edmund Pearson. I do not believe that the younger Miss Borden was guilty of murder or of being an accessory before the fact. I think that she committed an outrageous act and perpetrated a tremendous falsehood whose secret she carried with her to the grave. But her motive in doing these things was not altogether unadmirable.

Nor do I believe that any outsider was guilty. For it would have been virtually impossible to have remained unobserved in that house during the ninety odd minutes between the deaths of Abby Borden and her husband. And I am certainly not going to introduce any new characters such as the mythical "Lizzie's lover" or the Chinese boy from her church school.

Who then was the murderer? It was obviously a person of the household. It was obviously a person whose alibi could have been broken down. And it was obviously someone whom Lizzie lied to protect. I think, also, that she cleaned the lethal hatchet and lied about it to shield the murderer.

And here one must say a word about this hatchet. Another myth of the Lizzie Borden Case is that the hatchet disappeared after the crime. This is not necessarily the fact at all. The prosecution produced a perfectly good hatchet at the trial; one which fitted into the skull wounds; one which had been washed and scoured in ashes; one that had had its wooden head burned or broken off to destroy, perhaps, the signs of blood.

In order to show how this hatchet got into the Borden house, I am going to indulge in a purely imaginary conversation that might have taken place between Lizzie and her father at some date previous to the murders.

Mr. Borden, as we know, was a miser with money, and a hoarder of useless articles. He very seldom went for a walk without picking up some rubbish on the street. On the actual day of his death he had carried home an old rusty hatchet which was certainly not worth a nickel. Let us imagine that father and daughter met at the gate on this hypothetical day.

> Lizzie: Oh, Father, what have you picked up today?
> Mr. Borden: It's just an old rusty hatchet that I found down at the lumber yard.
> Lizzie: But we have a hatchet, Father—two, in fact.
> Mr. Borden: A penny saved is a penny gained, Daughter.
> Lizzie: But what could we use it for?
> Mr. Borden: I'll put it in the barn. It might come in handy someday to cut lead into sinkers so as not to blunt one of the good axes. Or if you wanted a bit of metal to mend a screen....

So there is the hatchet in the barn waiting for the final catastrophe. What hand was to raise it to take a human life?

The same hand that brought it into the house.

I believe that Andrew Jackson Borden deliberately and with malice aforethought murdered his own wife Abby Durfee Borden.

I believe that he himself died of a blow from the same hatchet. But not from a blow struck with murderous intent.

He had the means to murder Abby. Now let us come to the motive.

Mr. Borden had reached an age which is sometimes known as the male menopause, a period when even the staidest men are apt to go through a phase of emotional instability. Often this instability manifests itself as an antipathy to the wives of their bosom.

There were many things about Abby Borden that were antipathetic—her figure, for example, or her cooking. And then she had developed a habit of fussing Mr. Borden into making suitable disposition of his property. This would have been particularly galling to a miser whose heaven was on earth and in the bank and to an agnostic who had little expectations from the future life.

A cynical Frenchman once said: "Wherever there is marriage, there is a motive for murder."

This, it seems to me, is especially true of a ménage like the Bordens. And so I believe that for a considerable time Mr. Borden toyed with the idea of murdering his wife. It will be remembered that it was Mr. Borden who "discovered" the attempted burglary at Number 92. It was Mr. Borden who started the dark rumors—later repeated by Lizzie—of mysterious enemies plotting against his own life and his wife's. I see in this a sly plan to deflect suspicion from a crime he himself was contemplating.

It is also interesting to note that after the most violent bout of sickness which struck the house, Mrs. Borden was certain they had been poisoned. Mr. Borden categorically vetoed her suggestion of visiting a doctor.

Mr. Borden himself appears to have been equally sick at this time. Is not it possible however that he faked his nausea and vomiting? Is not it possible that this was his first, unsuccessful attempt to murder his wife?

We know that through this period Lizzie was very conscious of the "doom" hanging over the house. I believe she was actually conscious of attempted foul play but that her dislike of her stepmother prejudiced her into suspecting Mrs. Borden of trying to poison Mr. Borden— instead of the other way round.

This would explain her visits to the drugstores and her inquiries about poisons. A murderer—especially one who intends to use an ax—would hardly walk into drugstores where she is well known and ask for prussic acid. But a daughter, worried for her father's life, might well do a little detective work around town to find out whether her stepmother had been making poisonous purchases.

Let us assume this to have been the situation when Uncle Morse arrived. Uncle Morse, as we know, was interested in other people's property. Frequently in the past, he had brought up the subject of Mr. Borden's will. By now this subject had become dynamite. Imagine Abby seizing on Uncle Morse's remarks to drive home her own nagging pleas for a testament in favor of herself and her own family. Imagine the mounting exasperation of a man who had already attempted murder once—to spare himself from just such unpleasant reminders of his mortality. Thus Uncle Morse may well have been the innocent spark to the fuse.

I believe that Mr. Borden had made a decision before he went to bed that night. The time for such slow, uncertain weapons as poison was over. Tomorrow he would do the deed—and do it thoroughly.

Perhaps that morrow seemed to him a particularly auspicious day for a murder, since he must have known that most of the police force would be off on their yearly spree.

We have left the fatal hatchet in the barn. According to Maggie's testimony, she saw Mr. Borden go to the barn before his last breakfast; she also saw him return to the house, carrying a large basket of pears. The hatchet may well have been concealed beneath the fruit.

Mr. Borden was supposed to have left the Borden house around 9:15 that morning. Every movement he made from then on was suspiciously confirmed by witnesses. At one place downtown he was known to have inquired the time. At another, he remarked that a clock was wrong. Finally, when he returned home, he had conspicuous difficulty letting himself into the front door and even went around to the side door—an unusual act which attracted the attention of at least one neighbor.

In fact, this alibi was as carefully established as that of the most cunning murderers of detective fictions.

And yet, it was worthless, because he had no alibi for the moments when Abby was almost certainly killed.

As I said, he was assumed to have left Number 92 around 9:15. Possibly he pretended to do so. But no one actually saw him leave. A few moments earlier, Maggie, afflicted by a sudden and private attack of vomiting, had gone out into the backyard. When she came back, Mr. Borden was nowhere in sight and she imagined he had left. Lizzie herself, during this period, was down cellar.

How easy it would have been for Mr. Borden to have followed his wife upstairs to the spare room and to have hacked her to death with the hatchet. Blood must certainly have spattered his trousers, but they were dark and would show no obvious stains. There would have been time, at any rate, to change them and his shoes in his own room. The telltale clothes would have been safe there since no member of the household was permitted to enter his sanctum. How easy it would have been after that to slip downstairs unobserved and out by the front door—to hurry downtown to start manufacturing an alibi.

But ... here I believe something went wrong with Mr. Borden's plan. I believe Lizzie came up from the cellar earlier than he had anticipated and surprised him on the stairs when she thought he had left.

Imagine the conversation:

> Lizzie: I thought you'd gone downtown, Father.
> Mr. Borden: (agitated because he sees his alibi vanishing) So I did, Lizzie. But I came back because I met someone with a note for Mrs. Borden.
> Lizzie: A note for Mrs. Borden? Shall I give it to her?

Mr. Borden: (flustered into a terrible mistake) She's gone out.
Lizzie: (surprised) Gone out in her old work dress?
Mr. Borden: Yes, someone was sick. She was in a hurry.
Lizzie: Oh, who was sick?
Mr. Borden: I don't know. Someone at her sister's house, I guess. She didn't say …

After this, Mr. Borden went out to establish his alibi, feeling reasonably sure that his lie about the note would keep Lizzie from any immediate anxiety about her stepmother.

Now let us follow Lizzie. Her morning was a perfectly innocent one. She did a bit of ironing. Her flats got cold. She read a magazine in the kitchen. At some time between 10:00 and 10:45, she went up the front stairs to take the ironed clothes to her room. While she was still upstairs, she heard Maggie letting Mr. Borden in at the front door. She wanted to inquire if there was any mail for her. She started downstairs. But on the way downstairs she had to pass the spare room. Perhaps the door was open; perhaps she peeped in to see if the bed was made. At any rate she must have caught sight—and I believe for the first time—of her stepmother's terribly hacked body with the bloody ax at its side.

It was then that she uttered the involuntary sound which was later described by Maggie as a "laugh" and which has always been interpreted as a laugh of triumph at the sight of her second intended victim—Mr. Borden.

To me that exclamation was one of shock and horror. In a flash she would have realized the truth. Mrs. Borden had not gone out. Then Mr. Borden had lied about the note which was supposed to have called her forth. Mr. Borden—her own father, the only man for whom she had any real affection—must have committed this ghastly crime.

From now on, I see every one of Lizzie's actions as part of a desperate attempt to get Maggie out of the way so that she could confront her father in private with her awful suspicions. With amazing coolness she forestalled any damning remark Mr. Borden might have made, by repeating to him and to Maggie his own lie about the note.

(This explains why Lizzie had to bear the brunt of this lie later when it was proved that no note had been delivered.)

Still to keep Maggie unsuspicious, she made her father comfortable on the couch when he returned from his brief visit to his upstairs room (where, possibly, he changed back into his own bloody shoes and trousers, planning to "discover" his wife's body and thus provide a reasonable excuse for the stained clothing[1]). Lizzie then tried to tempt the maid out of the house by the bargain sale. She failed, but Maggie solved this problem herself by going up to the isolated attic for her "lie-down" shortly before eleven.

From now on it becomes increasingly difficult to reconstruct what passed through Lizzie's mind. There are no available facts. One can only imagine the reactions of this respectable, phlegmatic New England woman.

During the first moments of extreme shock, she had behaved with great coolness. Now however she was faced with the dreadful task of accusing her own father as a murderer. She may well have faltered. Was Mr. Borden's obvious lie about the note sufficient grounds for an accusation? Perhaps, as she was wavering, she remembered the bloody ax she had glimpsed by Abby's side. Where had that ax come from? If it was the old hatchet we are assuming Mr. Borden had brought back previously and put in the barn, then he must indeed be guilty, since only he and Lizzie knew of its existence.

I believe Lizzie did go to the barn—to search for the ax. It was not there, of course. And so, she returned to the house sure in her mind that she was the daughter of a murderer.

(Later, at the inquest, Lizzie claimed she had gone to the barn for some pieces of metal. All the evidence shows that she was not an imaginative liar and that her mind was literal. Obviously she could not have told the complete truth. Might she not have recollected and made use of the conversation she had had with her father on the problematical day when he brought home the hatchet? *Lead for sinkers; metal for fixing screens.* Might she not merely have been parroting Mr. Borden here—as she parroted him about the note? And then the ax itself was metal, a piece of metal. A curious half-truth of this sort, I'm sure, would have seemed less culpable to Lizzie than an outright lie.)

Lizzie, I believe, had steeled herself now. She went upstairs to the spare room, took up the telltale ax from beside the dead woman and tiptoed down into the sitting room where her father was lying either asleep or feigning sleep. What was in her mind? She had always disliked her stepmother and liked her father. Was the daughter in her prepared to discuss the dreadful deed and, perhaps, think out some scheme for shielding the culprit? Or was Miss Lizzie, the ardent church worker, the pet of Revs. Jubb and Buck, ready to sacrifice her father and her own family name on the altar of justice?

And what was in old Mr. Borden's mind as he lay there on the couch?

---

1 At this time blood typing was unknown as a science. It would have been interesting if Mr. Borden's trousers had been submitted to a blood typing test. Would blood of Mrs. Borden's type have been found there as well as blood of his own type?

Was he pretending to be asleep, planning to murder his younger daughter who, he must have realized, had it in her power to expose him?

It is useless to speculate. Personally, I think that Lizzie produced the ax as a tangible piece of evidence with which to confront her father. Personally, I am sure she had no intention of using it.

But something happened. Maybe, as she bent over him, Mr. Borden jumped up startled, knocking the ax from her hand and causing it to fall and strike him that first blow which gouged out his eyeball. Maybe he struggled for the ax, trying to kill his daughter, and she was obliged to administer that blow in self-defense.

At any rate, in those confused, unwitnessed moments, Mr. Andrew J. Borden received a fatal blow from the weapon he himself had wielded only a few hours before.

One can imagine Lizzie recoiling in horror from the couch as the blood spurted from her dying father. She had never anticipated so frightful a culmination as this. One can imagine the thoughts reeling through her normally pedestrian mind. She had killed her father—either accidentally or in self-defense. But she had killed him. The police would come. She would be questioned. And, worse still, she would have to blurt out the whole terrible story which would brand the head of the Borden family as a wife-murderer. Perhaps, as she stood there trembling, an even more poignant fear stabbed her. She thought of Mrs. Borden lying brutally hacked to death in the room above her.

What if the police did not believe her and suspected her of deliberate murder—not only of the murder of her father but also of the murder of the stepmother she had never loved? She tried to steady herself. No, Mrs. Borden had been struck so many, many times. Surely they would never believe that Miss Lizzie, the president of the Flower Guild, could have committed so bestial, so maniacal an act.

Maniacal. I can almost hear that word shouting in Lizzie's brain. For weeks Mr. Borden had been hinting at mysterious enemies who were after his life and Abby's. A mysterious enemy—a maniac.

It was then that Lizzie made a terrible resolve.

Perhaps it was possible, after all, not only to protect herself but also to shield the family name from dishonor. Could not she make it seem that both deaths were the work of some unknown, maniacal assassin?

But no one would believe that Mr. Borden, killed with a single blow, could have been the victim of the same frenzied killer who had struck and struck again at his wife.

Very well, that could be remedied.

I can see Lizzie, white but grimly determined, picking up the bloodstained ax and moving out through the door just behind the couch. Then—so that she need not see the dreadful thing she was doing—I can visualize her holding the door in front of her while, with her arm bare, she struck around the jam at the lifeless head of her father, struck and struck again until his skull was almost as shattered as that of the woman who lay upstairs.

This was a shocking act. Perhaps it was misguided. Certainly no person of imagination or sensibility could have committed it. But the practical Lizzie was not hampered by any imaginative sensibilities.

And revolting though it was, this attack on her father's dead body, motivated half by an impulse to protect herself, half to preserve her father's own good name, was more an error in taste than one in morals.

I see Lizzie guilty of no more than this.

Afterwards I can visualize her, almost calm again, taking the ax down cellar and washing it. A little water cleared her of the deed. Possibly she changed her dress.[2] She returned to the kitchen and called up the backstairs with classic ambiguity:

"Maggie, come down. Father's dead; someone came in and killed him."

Her subsequent actions are consistent. She sent for Emma immediately. I think she told her sister what had happened. Together they decided it would be fatal both for Lizzie and for the family if the truth became known.

The "mad assassin" was the only possible theory and they agreed to stick by it. I doubt whether either of the sisters dreamed that Lizzie herself would be arrested after all.

It is possible that Lizzie and Emma also confided in their good friend and family physician, Dr. Bowen. His behavior both at the trial and before it indicate that he was hiding something. In the Borden house he was seen by police officers to be burning a note on which the one word "Emma" was detected. Is it not possible that the sisters, realizing the embarrassing absence of the note supposed to have come for Mrs. Borden, made a clumsy attempt to forge one? And that the shrewder Dr. Bowen vetoed the idea and burnt the forgery?

Having started on her career of falsehood, Lizzie had to go on with it.

---

2 Probably there was no need to do this. If she acted as I think she did, she would not necessarily have been spattered with blood. But one can imagine that, after such an act, she would have felt a certain self-consciousness about her clothing. At the trial both Prosecution and Defense got nowhere on the subject of Lizzie's apparel on the fatal day. Personally, I feel that too much importance was attached to it. There is no doubt that Lizzie did burn a dress some days after the crime. Perhaps she did it because she feared bloodstains. Perhaps she did it because there were no stains on it such as a dutiful daughter must have incurred if she had shown decent solicitude for a dying father.

She was tripped up several times in interrogation, mostly because, as we have seen, she had repeated the mistakes of the real murderer. It is interesting to note, however, that in the record of the inquest, Lizzie only hesitated at one point, and that was when she was asked:

"Were your father and mother happily united?"

She hesitated because that lie was almost too big a one for a woman normally truthful, and she replied with remarkable, if somewhat ungrammatical, equivocation:

"Why, I don't know but that they were."

I am not suggesting that Lizzie would have allowed herself to be sent to the gallows without making some attempt to tell the true story. But I am sure both she and Emma felt convinced that she would never be convicted.

I make no pretense to omniscience. I cannot gauge the deviltries, the currents of murderous hatreds that crisscrossed the Borden household. My theory may not at all points hold water, though it nowhere violates known facts or the potential characteristics of the people involved.

Personally, I am convinced there is no other adequate solution.

The behavior I have ascribed to Lizzie may strain credulity somewhat. But any reconstruction of this case must sound incredible. It is the sheer incredibility of the events at No. 92 Second Street which gives them their imperishable fascination.

Surely, the picture of the Borden crimes, as painted here, is more plausible than one which presents Lizzie as a double murderess who hacked her stepmother to death, indulged in an hour's dainty ironing and housework, and then took a hatchet to her sleeping father.

The theory of Lizzie's guilt, however, is still universally held. This springs from some sadistic instinct, latent in almost everyone, which thrills to the thought of a respectable, churchgoing New England virgin bludgeoning her parents to death with an ax.

To me, however, it is grotesque that Lizzie should be held guilty simply because it has been fictionally fashionable to make villainesses out of virtuous spinsters. Except for certain inconsistencies of statement and behavior, there was no real evidence against her—as the Prosecution knew only too well. She has borne the burden of suspicion all these years chiefly because there seemed no one else to bear it.

This situation arose because no one, to my knowledge, ever thought of Mr. Borden as anything more than a murderee. To history he has always been a corpse—not a criminal.

History will never tell the exact truth about the Borden murders. I have done my imperfect best to apportion the blame where I believe it belongs. But the full secret of those few stormy hours is buried forever beneath that modest monument in the tree-shaded cemetery of Fall River.

There, Andrew and Abby and Lizzie Borden, united in death, must await a less imperfect judgment than my own.

■ ■ ■

The principal fictional versions of the Borden case or those referred to above by Mr. Patrick: Mrs. Belloc Lowndes' curious novel, Lizzie Borden: a Study in Conjecture *(Longmans, 1939), and the play* Nine Pine Street *by John Colton and Carlton Miles (French, 1934), which introduced Lizzie to Broadway in the person of Miss Lillian Gish. An interesting variant on the story is to be found in the play* Suspect *by Edward Percy and Reginald Denham (Dramatists' Play Service, 1940), which presented Miss Pauline Lord as an unconvicted ax murderess striving for anonymity some decades after the crime. A parallel case and a paraphrase of the great quatrain form part of the shenanigans in* The Man Who Came to Dinner *by Moss Hart and George Kaufman (Random, 1939). And Stuart Palmer's* The Puzzle of the Happy Hooligan *(Crime Club, 1941) contains some fine tomfoolery about a film treatment of Lizzie.* —A. B.

THE LAST OF MRS. MAYBRICK
by Patrick Quentin

On October 23rd, 1941, in a small, woodland shack between Gaylordsville and South Kent, Connecticut, a little old woman died. It was the lonely, inconspicuous death of an obscure eighty-year-old recluse, and her body might have lain long undiscovered had it not been for a kindly neighbor whose habit it was to supply her with the milk that she needed to feed her innumerable cats.

This neighbor, peering through the fly-spotted window pane, saw the crumpled little body lying dead amidst the filth and disarray with which, in life, she had chosen to surround herself. A cat or two, perhaps, nosing at one of the many grimy, milkless saucers, might have felt that life had changed for the worse. There was nothing or no one else to mourn the passing of this forlorn and eccentric character whom Gaylordsville and South Kent had known as Mrs. Florence Chandler.

"Mrs. Chandler," after a residence of twenty years, had become a familiar if somewhat shy figure in those parts, especially on the campus of the South Kent School where she was often seen, a dowdy, meagre little figure with a face wrinkled as a walnut, carrying over her spare shoulder a gunnysack stuffed with newspapers salvaged from academic ashcans. These newspapers comprised almost her only form of reading matter. Once she had written a book herself, but that was long ago and South Kent School knew nothing of her as a woman of letters. Now, too poor to buy books, she was too proud to borrow them. As intellectual nourishment for her, therefore, there was nothing but old copies of the *New York Times* and an occasional Bridgeport *Sunday Post*.

"Mrs. Chandler's" gunnysack served another less literary purpose. On outgoing journeys, it would often be filled with indeterminate scraps of food which were dumped at strategic points, usually on the school campus, for the delectation of the neighborhood cats. "Mrs. Chandler" had definite views on the care of cats. It was her belief that the summer folk went junketting off with the first fall of autumn leaves, leaving their cats to starve. Hence the amateur filling stations for orphaned pets.

This humanitarian impulse of "Mrs. Chandler's" was, on the whole, detrimental to the high seriousness of the South Kent students and a headache to certain members of the staff.

Headache! The word is pregnant. For when the kind neighbor discovered the pathetic body of "Mrs. Chandler" in the desolate New England shack, he had no idea that he was looking at all that remained of one of the world's greatest headaches. That tiny, disheveled creature had, in her day, caused more headaches possibly than any woman since Helen of Troy. She had been a headache to several American Presidents; to Secretaries of State; to their wives; to many famous journalists; and to a vast army of organized American women. She had been more than a headache to one celebrated English judge, in that she is reputed to have pushed him off the teetering brink of his sanity. Indeed, she had been a fifteen-year migraine to no less august a personage than the Queen-Empress Victoria.

And the name of that headache was Mrs. Florence Maybrick.

Mrs. Maybrick. To those in their carefree twenties, the name may ring a distant bell. To those in their thirties, it may conjure up dim memories of a murderess, an adulteress—or something interesting. To those over forty-five, Mrs. Maybrick will be remembered for what she actually was—an international incident.

She was born Florence Chandler in Mobile, Alabama, in 1862, and came from what is usually referred to as "good American stock," boasting among her forebears, direct and collateral, a Secretary of the Treasury, a Chief Justice, a bishop and two Episcopal rectors, co-authors of a work entitled: "Why We Believe The Bible." As an appendix to this illustrious list of ancestors, her mother had married, a second time, the Baron Adolph von Rogues, a distinguished German officer of the Eighth Cuirassier Regiment. Little Florence was educated, partly in America, partly abroad, by a succession of the most impeccable "masters and governesses." Nothing had been overlooked that might insure for her a cultivated and ladylike future.

As it happened, however, these fair beginnings did not help her much, for, from an early period, Florence Chandler was dogged by bad luck. At the age of eighteen, when the other Mobile maidens of her generation were fluttering toward good clean American romance, it is reliably reported that Florence, during a rough Atlantic crossing, stumbled on the sundeck of the liner carrying her to Europe. She stumbled and fell—literally and catastrophically—into the arms of a Cad, an English cad, at that. And, after all, the English invented the word.

The Cad was James Maybrick; he was old enough to be her father; and he married her. Probably it was the least caddish thing he ever did. But it was an ill day for Florence.

The April-October romantics lived for a while in Norfolk, Virginia. But

Florence's dark angel soon put a stop to that and, through difficulties concerning James Maybrick's business, shuttled them off to a suburb of Liverpool, England, a city where almost anything unpleasant is liable to happen.

The unpleasantness soon set in. James, reverting to Caddishness, started going merrily to hell with the belles and racehorses of Liverpool. And Florence, a young mother though still quite "unawakened," started herself to toy with the idea of the Primrose Path or, as the Victorians called it, "going her own way." It is even reported that she went her own way into a London hotel bedroom with an anonymous gentleman, but at this far date it would be rancorous to cast stones—particularly when one remembers James.

For James was going from bad to worse and from worse to worst. Eventually he reached a peak of Victorian depravity from which there was no going back and little going forward. He took to drugs. Not exclusively, however, to the conventional cocaine or the hackneyed hashish. James was too exotic for that. He favored the heavy metals. And his pet pick-me-up was arsenic. With increasing frequency he began to patronize the Liverpool chemist shop of a Mr. James Heaton where he would replenish his stock of *liquor arsenicalis*—an arsenic solution which he imbibed sometimes as often as five times a day. He found it just the thing for that morning-after queasiness.

Oddly enough, while Mr. Maybrick was guzzling arsenic to repair the ravages of his dissipations, Florence had decided that arsenic was just what she needed as a skin lotion to repair the facial ravages caused by her unhappy married life. To obtain this unusual cosmetic, she is reputed to have soaked arsenic out of flypapers (the old-fashioned sort), a rather messy procedure at which she was unfortunately observed by one of the maids, a certain Alice Yapp, who eventually became as loquacious on the subject as her name might indicate. Why Mrs. Maybrick needed to endure the sufferings of soaking flypapers *pour être belle* [to make herself beautiful] is a mystery since, at a later date, enough professionally prepared arsenic was found in the house to poison a whole Panzer Division.

The Maybricks were distinctly an arsenic-conscious family.

In May, 1889, James, a gay dog to the end, went to the Wirrall Races, got wet and returned home next morning feeling very sick to the stomach. For religious reasons and for the sake of the two young children, the Maybricks had manfully tried to gloss over the shortcomings of their marriage and were still living in technical harmony. James was put to bed, visited by a doctor and, in due course, provided with a day nurse and a night nurse, Nurse Gore and Nurse

Gallery. Florence, however, guided by a stern sense of duty, was not willing to leave her ailing husband to the care of strangers. She herself was a frequent visitor to the sick room. According to the nurses, she was too frequent a visitor. While James went on feeling sicker and sicker to the stomach, she would try to tempt him with little delicacies of her own contriving, much to the disgust of the dietetic Nurse Gallery. Also she developed a nervous habit of shuffling bottles and medicaments around on the patient's bedtable. Her sickroom manner was later described as "both suspicious and surreptitious." And she does seem to have behaved in a rather silly fashion. One of the silliest things she seemed to have done was to bring together a bottle of Valentine's Meat Juice and a pinch of some white powder, believed by many to have been arsenic.

It is hardly startling that, in spite of the ministrations of Nurse Gore and Nurse Gallery, in spite of his wife's tender solicitude, James Maybrick did not improve. On the 11th of May, 1889, he finally passed away.

Since he had shown symptoms suggesting irritant poisoning, officious busybodies insisted upon an autopsy, and arsenic was found—not surprisingly, perhaps—in his body. Actually, the amount discovered was merely one tenth of a grain, a dose not sufficient to kill a normal respectable citizen, let alone James. But people feeling the way they do about arsenic in stomachs, Mrs. Maybrick was arrested and charged with the murder of her husband. Immediately all the silly things she had done around the bedside came to light. Alice Yapp remembered the flypapers. And, before long, the anonymous gentleman and the London hotel bedrooms were dusted off too.

Florence's bad luck again.

To make matters worse—a sorry fact due perhaps less to bad luck than bad management—Mrs. Maybrick began to discover that nobody liked her. Her husband's two brothers had never been able to abide her. Now they acted in a most high-handed and spiteful manner, whisking off her children and branding her even before she was accused. Also, Alice Yapp, her fellow servant, Mrs. Briggs, Nurse Gore and Nurse Gallery showed the most unfriendly symptoms. They had nothing to say in Mrs. Maybrick's favor and seemed to take savage delight in bringing out evidence to her discredit.

Later, when she was brought to trial, the English public didn't like her either. There was something about her. Perhaps her American blood had a little to do with it. In the Golden Jubilee years of Victoria, American women were frowned upon in England. And the Queen consistently snubbed them when they came to court. Perhaps they dressed better, looked smarter and managed to be more amusing than their more stolid

English sisters. Even the most impeccable Victorian male was not above rolling an appreciative eye at them, so long as they stayed out of trouble. But once they were in the soup, the men were as ready as the women to trace the scarlet A blazing forth beneath the chic American camisoles.

As if this weren't bad luck enough, Mrs. Maybrick had bad luck with her jury and terrible luck with one aspect of her defense.

The jury, consisting mostly of simple-natured men, were not the type accustomed to think for themselves on nice points of law. Their professions, perhaps, speak for them. There were three plumbers (three of them!), two farmers, one milliner, one woodturner, one provision dealer, one grocer, one ironmonger, one housepainter (at that time no ominous trade), and one baker.

In preparing her defense against this literal-minded group of her peers, Mrs. Maybrick was advised not to bring forward any evidence as to the true character, the immorality, the dissipation, the general caddishness of her husband. Sentimentalists have held this as a virtue in Florence Maybrick that she adhered so rigidly to the principles of *de mortuis nil nisi bonum* (of saying nothing bad about the dead). Actually, it was the smart, but not smart enough, idea of her solicitors that the less James was discredited, the less apparent motive there would seem for his wife's having wanted to murder him.

In consequence of this blunder in psychology, Mrs. Maybrick faced trial as an American hussy who had mistreated and deceived a perfectly good English husband, a man, as far as the jury knew, without a blemish on his character. To add to her troubles, her star witness, Mr. James Heaton, the chemist from whom Mr. Maybrick had so constantly purchased his swig of *liquor arsenicalis*, was so sick when he came to court that his vital evidence was all but inaudible. Even the brilliant rhetoric of her attorney, Charles Russell, later Lord Chief Justice Russell, could not soar above these obstacles.

And, as a final disaster, Mrs. Maybrick was not merely facing trial, she was facing Mr. Justice Stephen on the bench. In the light of his future career, which ended one year later in the madhouse, Mr. Justice Stephen was a little more than even the most callous of murderesses deserved. This once illustrious personage was already losing grip on his sanity before the trial started; all he needed to complete the process was Florence Maybrick. From the beginning he liked her no better than anyone else had. As the trial limped along with no one exactly knowing who did what, his dislike for her swelled within him until it reached almost psychopathic proportion. This manifested itself finally, in his summing up, as a two-day harangue of impassioned malignity and misogyny. In one of the most biased speeches ever to come from the English bench, he referred to poor Mrs. Maybrick as "that horrible woman" and branded her as the epitome of all that was vile. Startling even the prosecution, he vindictively maneuvered the Valentine's Meat Juice and a certain bottle of glycerin around until he left no loophole for the unlucky woman's innocence.

As obedient Britons, the jury did not hesitate in following the guidance of a Social Superior. As a man, the three plumbers, the two farmers, the milliner, the woodturner, the grocer, the ironmonger, the housepainter and the baker brought in a verdict of guilty. Judge Stephen—with a certain rather lunatic satisfaction, perhaps?—donned the black cap and pronounced that Florence Maybrick should be hanged by the neck until she was dead.

A short time later he was himself pronounced insane.

The verdict, coming after a trial in which nothing seemed to have been proved one way or the other, staggered England. It staggered the world. In a few weeks hundreds of thousands of people had signed petitions for Mrs. Maybrick's reprieve. Public opinion, in the face of what seemed like gross injustice, swung round to her side. Florence was popular at last.

For two or three weeks she lived (to use her own ill phrase) "in the shadow of the gallows." Finally, a little intimidated perhaps by the general clamor, Mr. Matthews, the home secretary—for there was no Supreme Court of Criminal Appeal at that time—retried the case *in camera* and commuted Mrs. Maybrick's sentence to one of penal servitude for life. His reasons for this clemency were that:

> "inasmuch as, although the evidence leads to the conclusion that the prisoner administered and attempted to administer arsenic to her husband with intent to murder him, yet it does not wholly exclude a reasonable doubt whether his (James Maybrick's) death was in fact caused by the administration of arsenic."

In other words, Mr. Matthews was of the opinion that Mrs. Maybrick had been guilty of attempting to kill her husband with arsenic although it wasn't certain that he had died from arsenical poisoning. This charge was something Mrs. Maybrick had not even been tried for during a court procedure at which nothing had been proved beyond the fact that James was dead—a sad eventuality which had been common knowledge before ever the slow-moving wheels of the law had got underway. If that wasn't bad luck—what is?

Whether or not Mrs. Maybrick was guilty, and of how much, is no longer calculable. That she was grievously wronged is beyond doubt. The English bench has never been noted for its chivalry or its leniency toward women accused of murder, particularly where there is also a whiff of adultery. Mrs. Thompson, of the haunting love letters, and other sisters in misfortune reached the gallows as adulteresses rather than murderesses. Mrs. Rattenbury alone, that poor darling with her fatal attachment to the boy chauffeur, had a fair deal in this respect. But prudish public opinion soon snuffed her out as efficiently as the hangman's rope.

If Mrs. Maybrick learned one thing from her dismal experience, it was that virtue pays dividends when a lady happens to get mixed up in an English murder trial.

That London hotel bedroom turned out to be very expensive.

Mrs. Maybrick proceeded from one squalid penal institution to another, suffering all the hardships of a habitual and vicious criminal, conspicuous among which was a period of nine months' solitary confinement. But though her memory had been rinsed off the disdainful hands of British justice, she was not forgotten. Soon a tornado broke from the other side of the Atlantic. American Woman was just beginning to realize herself as a Cosmic Force in 1890. American journalism was making itself felt in Europe. And American public opinion was beginning to mean something. Petitions thick as fleas started to pester various, successive Home Secretaries. In England, Lord Russell himself was active on her behalf, stalwartly proclaiming her innocence. From this side, Presidents, ambassadors and their wives, notables in all walks of life signed formidable statements, one of which, penned by no less a figure than the Honorable James G. Blaine, is worthy of quotation since, with magnificent daring, it snatches the garland of "snobisme" from its traditional resting place on the coronetted British heads and hurls it back like a boomerang across the Atlantic. Mrs. Maybrick, writes James G. Blaine, was guilty of no crime other than that:

> "she may have been influenced by the foolish ambition of too many American girls for a foreign marriage, and have descended from her own rank to that of her husband's family, which seems to have been somewhat vulgar...."

This blast at the Maybricks' social position was paralleled in the *North American Review* by the famous American newspaper woman "Gail Hamilton" who addressed an open letter to Queen Victoria protesting Mrs. Maybrick's innocence, inveighing against her unfair treatment and begging for her release. But Gail Hamilton and the Honorable James G. Blaine received like treatment. The Queen was neither amused nor interested.

Finally, however, one Home Secretary, Lord Salisbury, goaded beyond endurance by these transatlantic stabs at British justice, parried with a nettled and emphatic statement which might have been penned by the Queen herself. It read in part:

> "Taking the most lenient view … the case of this convict was that of an adulteress attempting to poison her husband under the most cruel circumstances while she was pretending to be nursing him on his sick bed. The Secretary of State regrets that he has been unable to find any grounds for recommending to the Queen any further act of clemency towards the prisoner...."

The women of America continued their losing battle with the stubborn little woman who ruled England. Mrs. Maybrick's mother, the Baroness de Rogues, is reputed to have spent a fortune in an attempt to have her daughter freed.

All to no purpose, however. Florence served out her sentence, penal servitude for life usually being taken to mean twenty years with three months off a year for good behavior.

She was finally released in July, 1904. On August 23rd, shaking the dust of England off her skirts forever, she arrived in New York.

Life held little for her. Both her children, whom she had not seen since the day of her husband's death, had died themselves. Her mother died penniless shortly afterwards. In sore need of money Florence Maybrick wrote a book—*Mrs. Maybrick's Own Story*, published by Funk and Wagnalls in 1905. In this she sang a dismal ballad of atrocities in English gaols and amassed formidable evidence of her own innocence. It is a lugubrious work, filled with lamentable clichés and poignantly trying to arouse interest in something which once had been a headache but was now only a bore. People read it for its possible sensationalism. They were no longer interested in Mrs. Maybrick's misfortunes *per se*. For a while she tried to lecture, largely about conditions in English prisons, but it did not go so well. After a while she began to realize (as Lizzie Borden, settled with her squirrels at "Maplecroft," had already realized for many years) that people do not take kindly to women who have faced a capital charge, even if they have been shockingly wronged.

Poor Florence. They were back not liking her again.

For several years, in Florida and Highland Park, Illinois, she stubbornly retained her married and now infamous name. But about twenty years before her death, she gave up an unequal struggle. Destroying all records of her past and reverting to her maiden name of Florence Chandler, she withdrew to a life of virtual solitude in the tiny three-room shack she had built for herself in the Berkshire Foothills.

There, unknown to her neighbors, she lived on, accepted by the community and, with the years, acquiring from successive generations of South Kent boys the harmless nicknames of "Lady Florence" and "The Cat Woman."

South Kent and Gaylordsville have none but kindly memories of her. There were rumors, at times, of course, as there must be about any lonely little old lady who lives a secluded life, rumors that someone had left her a vast fortune; that a lawyer in a limousine with a liveried chauffeur appeared at regular intervals to bring her checks. But these were rumors without malice and, unhappily, without foundation in fact, for she died penniless save for an old-age pension finally wooed out of the government.

South Kent and Gaylordsville remember her as the little scurrying woman with the walnut face, the gunnysack and one loyal and indestructible brown straw hat. To them, she was eccentric, yes. It was eccentric in her that she would let no one enter her house; that, at night, there was always a single light twinkling from her window till morning—to exorcise what demons?—and that with age she had let slip in her squalid little home the niceties of hygiene. But to her neighbors, Mrs. Chandler's eccentricities bore no sinister stamp. It was cute rather than grotesque when, fighting against the loss of one of her few remaining teeth, she tied it to its nearest partner with a piece of string. She did no harm, except perhaps to leave a little too many scraps in the wrong places for the campus cats. The South Kent boys liked her.

And they never knew, until the day she died, that the woman they were liking was that most magnificently unliked of women—Mrs. Florence Maybrick.

Which leads to the only really comforting feature of this long and uncomfortable life. There in the little village of South Kent and Gaylordsville, Mrs. Florence Maybrick found good luck at last—good luck of so sensational a nature that in a way perhaps it neutralized all the tough breaks she had endured earlier.

Mrs. Maybrick was able to spend the last twenty years of her life unpersecuted. And yet, had things gone other than the way they did, this lengthy stretch of tranquility might never have been granted her.

Shortly after her arrival, a neighbor, a Mrs. Austin, was kind to Mrs. Maybrick and, to show her gratitude, Mrs. Maybrick gave her a dress which was trimmed with really good lace. It was undoubtedly the dress in the famous "wedding" photograph and to the cynical will perhaps give further proof that there is a real affinity between old lace and arsenic.

When Mrs. Austin shook the padding which stuffed the shoulders of this dress, there dropped out a cleaner's card reading: Mrs. Florence Maybrick, Highland Park, Ill. The name struck a chord in Mrs. Austin's memory. She consulted a sister who in turn consulted a female probation officer in the district. Before long these three women and the two married ladies' husbands all knew the unhappy tale of Mrs. Florence Maybrick. A family council was called; the evidence was weighed; and it was decided that she had suffered more than enough already. The Austins and their in-laws thereupon made a vow never to show by word or hint that they knew the real identity of the new arrival.

And so, from the start, "Mrs. Chandler's" future was in the hands of this small group of people. Miraculously, those people kept their vow for twenty years. Never once, at church socials, at whist drives or quilting parties or at the grocery store, did one of those three ladies succumb to the almost irresistible temptation of launching the juiciest piece of gossip in ten counties.

More power to these gallant ladies of Gaylordsville, so very, very different in character from Alice Yapp, Mrs. Briggs, Nurse Gore and Nurse Gallery! More power to these gallant ladies of Gaylordsville who refrained from giving a bad name to a forlorn stray who once had been almost hanged for it!

This was the astounding piece of good luck which came at last and enabled Mrs. Maybrick to reach the grave, unwept, perhaps, unhonored, but at least—unstoned.

On Saturday, October 25, 1941, "Mrs. Chandler" was soberly buried on the South Kent Campus. It had been her own request. Five of the students, boys of "good stock"—shades of Florence's own beginnings!—were her pallbearers. These boys, whom a local newspaper with misprinted enthusiasm termed "Socialists from the swank South Kent School," carried her to her last resting place. And there, as if a final hand from the grave beckoned her back to respectability, her coffin lies next to that of Miss Doylan, an old friend and beloved South Kent Housemother.

R.I.P. Mrs. Florence Chandler Maybrick.

And good luck to you—wherever you are!

THE ORDEAL OF FLORENCE MAYBRICK
By Patrick Quentin

For many years I, as a crime writer, have been fascinated by Mrs. Florence Maybrick. Of all the women famously convicted of murder, she has seemed to me the most probably innocent and certainly the most cruelly wronged. She intrigues me far more than any fictional lady in distress that I have created myself. I would love to have met her.

It is ironic, therefore, that once I actually offered her a ride in my car without having the faintest idea who she was.

It happened in July, 1940, fifty-one long years after the trial at which Florence Maybrick was sentenced to hang, by a mad judge, for the murder of her husband. I was driving to visit some friends in South Kent, Connecticut. As I passed the campus of the South Kent School for Boys, I noticed a little old woman trudging along the street. She was shabbily dressed, almost a hobo; her grizzled head was bare; and over her shoulder she was carrying a bulging burlap sack which seemed to be stuffed with newspapers.

As I drew the car up alongside of her, she turned to look at me. Her face was wrinkled as a walnut and her eyes gazed with sunken vagueness. Her lips parted as if she were going to speak and I noticed that two of her few remaining teeth were bizarrely tied together with a piece of string.

"Want a ride?" I asked.

Slowly she shook her head, turned away, and started plodding forward again along the road.

When I reached my destination, I mentioned the little old woman to my hostess.

"Oh, that must have been Mrs. Chandler," she said. "She's been living here for years in a tumbledown shack with dozens of cats. She hangs around the school campus. She's quite an institution there. The boys call her The Cat Woman. She's perfectly harmless, but, of course ..." She put a finger significantly to her head.

I forgot the old woman until, just over a year later, I read in the paper that a South Kent milkman had found the little 79-year-old recluse, Mrs. Chandler, dead in her bed, surrounded by hungry, wailing cats. From documents discovered in the squalid shack, Mrs. Chandler was disclosed to have been Mrs. Florence Maybrick.

Mrs. Florence Maybrick, that name which once had been familiar to millions of people all over the world! Mrs. Florence Maybrick, the bent little woman with the burlap sack who had refused to ride with me!

I put down the newspaper, looking back to one of the most bitterly lost opportunities of my life....

Florence Maybrick was the victim of a disastrous marriage. At 18, the pretty, convent-raised daughter of a wealthy and aristocratic Alabama family, she met James Maybrick on a transatlantic liner. He was a coarse, new-rich cotton merchant from Liverpool, England, and was old enough to be her father. It is impossible at this late date to know what attracted her to him or why her charming, worldly mother, married for a second time to a German baron, allowed so obvious a misalliance. But Florence married James Maybrick, and after a brief stay in Norfolk, Virginia, the couple went to live in Battlecrease House, Garston (a suburb of Liverpool).

At that time "Society" in English provincial manufacturing towns was extremely narrow and insular. Immediately, Florence was eyed with suspicion as a foreigner. Her husband's two brothers were hostile to her. The dowdy neighboring ladies, envious of her youth and her smart clothes, looked down their noses. Even the servants, snobbishly aping their "betters," made it plain that they despised their imported American mistress.

To make it worse for Florence, her husband, once back in his own setting, showed himself in his true colors. He both tyrannized her and neglected her, and soon reverted to his old bachelor habits of drinking parties, race meets, and affairs with the local tarts.

And that was not all. He had yet another and secret vice. He was not only a hypochondriac; he also took dope. His unusual tastes ran to strychnine and arsenic. Arsenic, he claimed, "picked him up" after his many debauches.

For eight years, in which she bore her husband two children, Florence Maybrick endured this lonely, humiliating existence without complaint or rebellion. But she never became absorbed in the Liverpool way of life. She remained the outsider, a predestined victim for mass hysteria, if ever an opportunity came to arouse it.

The opportunity came. Early in 1889 Mrs. Maybrick met a young Texas cotton dealer named Alfred Brierly. Little is known of this relationship except that at one time they were both registered at the same hotel in London. Her accusers twisted this fact into proof of a sordid affair. This may or may not have been true. It is certainly true that some sort of "indiscretion" must have occurred between them and that Florence Maybrick felt she had at last found a friend, a chivalrous champion.

It must also be true that this new friendship brought the strained Maybrick domestic drama to some kind of a crisis.

On March 29, 1889, a few days after Mrs. Maybrick's return from London, the Maybricks attended the Grand National Steeplechase at Aintree. Brierly too, it was claimed, was there. The Maybricks had their first public quarrel. Later, when they had returned home, James, in front of witnesses, struck Florence in the eye. Florence went immediately to pack her bags. She would have left the house forever if Maybrick's relatives and friends had not dissuaded her "for the sake of the children."

From that moment on Florence Maybrick was lost. Accident and malice conspired together to destroy her. She herself struck the first nail into her own coffin. On April 24 she bought a dozen arsenic-coated flypapers from a local chemist. On April 26 one of the familiar packages of "medicine" arrived for James from his London dealers. He took some and next morning became violently ill. He blamed the attack on the "strychnine" in his medicine but was well enough to go to the races at Wirral. That evening, however, he felt worse and summoned the family physician, Dr. Humphreys, who confirmed his patient's diagnosis and put him to bed. On April 29 Florence Maybrick bought two dozen more flypapers from another chemist. On April 30 Alice Yapp, the children's nursemaid, saw the flypapers soaking in a basin of water.

These flypapers virtually convicted Mrs. Maybrick of murder. But she had her own innocent explanation for their purchase. Arsenic, in those days, was universally used as a beauty aid. She claimed she had bought the flypapers as an ingredient for a face lotion she wanted to prepare because she had to attend a charity ball with her husband's brother, Edwin, on April 30.

In any case, she went to the ball with her brother-in-law. James improved and returned to work on May 1. On the 3rd, however, he had another attack, suffering from pains in the legs and severe thirst. Dr. Humphreys put him back to bed.

A trained day nurse was hired, but for the next five days Mrs. Maybrick helped attend her husband, bringing him the many prescribed medicines and invalid's foods and, for all we know, surreptitiously providing him with his private "white powders" which, unknown to her, were strychnine and arsenic. James Maybrick did not improve, and slowly, the hostile, excitement-hungry servants smelled Murder. On May 8 Alice Yapp told two neighbors, Mrs. Briggs and Mrs. Hughes, about the soaked flypapers. That was enough. "Mrs. Maybrick is poisoning her husband." The news spread like wildfire. The older Maybrick brother, Michael (composer, as "Stephen Adams," of such song successes as the still popular "The Holy City"), was summoned from London. Edwin Maybrick hired a second nurse and expressly forbade Florence to enter the sickroom.

It must then have been clear to Florence that she was under suspicion. She lost her head. She wrote a hysterical letter to Brierly and handed it to Alice Yapp, who, instead of mailing it, passed it on to Edwin Maybrick. At its most damning, this letter only showed guilty fears at some past indiscretion and the need for someone to cling to, but it contained the words "M. is sick unto death." This was all Edwin Maybrick needed.

When his brother arrived, they both confided their suspicions to Dr. Humphreys and to another family doctor. Immediately every sickroom bottle that Florence had touched was analyzed. Nothing was found except a faint, unlethal trace of arsenic in a bottle of Valentine's meat-extract. Later, Michael Maybrick saw Florence pouring the contents of one bottle into another. He snatched the bottles from her for analysis. The result, once again, was negative.

Meanwhile, James Maybrick grew steadily sicker and, on the evening of May 11, he died.

Naturally enough after her ordeal, Florence Maybrick collapsed. Instantly, every member of the household started a hysterical search of her room. They hit the jackpot. Alice Yapp found a sealed package, marked "Arsenic—Poison for Cats," and a candy box containing two bottles. The next morning Mrs. Briggs found two hatboxes. In one of them was a wooden box containing three bottles and, beside the box, a bottle of meat juice. In the second box was a glass of milk and a rag. Analysis showed that there was enough arsenic in all these items to kill at least 50 people.

Since James Maybrick had been a steady and furtive arsenic addict, these caches might well have been secreted by him or by his unsuspecting wife at his own request. But even if the arsenic had belonged to Florence Maybrick, arsenic turned out to have nothing to do with the case. For the postmortem showed no more than a tenth of a grain of arsenic in the dead man's organs. Such a small amount could not possibly have killed anyone, let alone the arsenic-habituated James Maybrick.

But the lynching was on and there was no turning back. On May 14

Superintendent Isaac Bryning of the Liverpool police arrived to arrest Florence. She was too ill to be moved. Frightened and half out of her wits, Florence moaned that she had no money, no one to turn to. The neighboring Mrs. Briggs, who was with her, sarcastically remarked, "What about your friend Brierly?" With pitiful naiveté, Florence wrote him a second note. "Your last letter is in the hands of the police. Appearances may be against me, but before God I swear that I am innocent."

This letter, too, was given to the police, and as soon as possible Florence was taken to the Liverpool jail. In spite of the medical evidence, the coroner's jury found that James Maybrick had died from an irritant poison administered by his wife. She was charged before a Grand Jury on July 26 and brought to trial five days later.

She never had a chance. The prosecutor's Victorian thunder against the woman taken in adultery was shockingly abetted by the judge, Mr. Justice Stephen, who constantly referred to Florence from the bench as "that horrible woman, the epitome of all that is loathsome and evil." One year later Justice Stephen was shut up in a lunatic asylum. But that was too late for Florence Maybrick. After a mere 45 minutes, the jury found her guilty as charged. Mr. Justice Stephen put on the Black Cap and sentenced her to be hanged.

The verdict became a public scandal. Many people believed that James Maybrick had died of gastroenteritis and had never been murdered at all. Public protest grew so strong that the Home Secretary had finally to commute the sentence to life imprisonment.

But there the matter stood. In spite of worldwide indignation, appeals to the Home Secretary and to Queen Victoria herself, in spite of the efforts of Florence's mother, who spent her entire fortune on a fruitless attempt for a pardon, Florence served her 20-year term, including a nine-month period of solitary confinement.

In 1905 she was released and, still courageously using her married name, returned to the States where she lived for a while in Highland Park, Illinois, and in Florida. Her mother had died. She had no friends. Except for a small pension, she was penniless. Notoriety dogged her wherever she went.

Finally, in 1920, she started a new life, under her maiden name of Chandler, in South Kent where she became the little shack-dwelling recluse with her cats and her shy appearances on the South Kent campus.

I hope, after all she had suffered, that she found some peace in those last 20 years. I know that I wish her well. And, beyond anything, I wish she hadn't walked away from my car, so that I could have taken her

hand and said:
"Good luck to you, Mrs. Maybrick."

THE END

Q. Patrick/Patrick Quentin/ Jonathan Stagge Bibliography

As Q. Patrick

Novels by Rickie Webb and Patsy Kelley

Cottage Sinister (1931; abridged in *Triple Detective*, Winter 1948)
Murder at the Women's City Club (1932; published in the UK as *Death in the Dovecot*)

Novels by Rickie Webb

Murder at Cambridge (1933; published in UK as *Murder at the 'Varsity*)
The Grindle Nightmare (1935; published in UK as *Darker Grows the Valley*; abridged in *Detective Novel Magazine*, May 1947)
Death Goes to School (1936)
The Girl on the Gallows (1954)

Novels by Rickie Webb and Mary Lou Aswell

S.S. Murder (1933)

Novels by Rickie Webb and Hugh Wheeler

Death for Dear Clara (1937; Inspector Trant)
The File on Fenton and Farr (1938)
The File on Claudia Cragge (1938; Inspector Trant)
Death and the Maiden (1939; Inspector Trant)
Return to the Scene (1941; published in UK as *Death in Bermuda*)
Danger Next Door (1952; UK only; U.S. version, *Detective Story Magazine*, May 1937)

Short fiction by Rickie Webb and Hugh Wheeler

Darker Grows the Valley (*Mystery*, May 1935)
Killed by Time (*Street & Smith's Detective Story Magazine*, Oct 1935)
The Dogs Do Bark (*Street & Smith's Detective Story Magazine*, Nov 1935)
The Frightened Landlady (*Street & Smith's Detective Story Magazine*, Dec 1935)
Call the Heart Home (*Sketch*, Dec 18 1935)
The Scarlet Circle (*Street & Smith's Detective Story Magazine*, Jan 1936)
The Hated Woman (*Street & Smith's Detective Story Magazine*, Feb 1936)
Murder or Mercy (*Street & Smith's Detective Story Magazine*, June 1936)
The Jack of Diamonds (*The American Magazine*, Nov 1936)
Death Goes to School (Smith & Haas, 1936)
Danger Next Door (*Street & Smith's Detective Story Magazine*, May 1937)
The Lady Had Nine Lives (*The American Magazine*, Aug 1937; Inspector Trant)
Exit Before Midnight (*The American Magazine*, Oct 1937; reprinted as "Murder on New Year's Eve," *Ellery Queen's Mystery Magazine*, Jan 1950, as by Patrick Quentin)
Death and the Maiden (*American Weekly*, Jan 22 & 29, 1939)

Death for Dear Clara (*Five-in-One Detective Magazine*, June/July 1939)
Another Man's Poison (*The American Magazine*, Jan 1940)
Death Rides the Ski-Tow (*The American Magazine*, April 1941; UK serial as "Death Rides the Ski Trail," *Woman Magazine*, March 6-20 1943; Peter Duluth)
Ordeal (*Woman Magazine*, Oct 18, 1941)
Murder with Flowers (*The American Magazine*, Dec 1941; Peter Duluth)
Portrait of a Murderer (*Harper's Magazine*, April 1942)
Humphrey (*This Week*, May 24, 1942. Reprinted as "Cat's Cradle," *Woman Magazine*, Sept 26, 1942)
Lest We Forget (*Woman Magazine*, June 27, 1942)
The Gypsy Warned Him (*Short Stories*, October 25 1943)
The Woman Who Waited (*The Shadow*, Jan 1945)

Short fiction by Hugh Wheeler

White Carnations (*Collier's*, Feb 10, 1945; Inspector Trant)
The Plaster Cat (*Mystery Book Magazine*, July 1946; Inspector Trant)
Murder at Cambridge (*Thrilling Mystery Novel Magazine*, Jan 1947)
The Corpse in the Closet (*This Week*, Feb 16, 1947; reprinted in *Ellery Queen's Mystery Magazine*, January 1948; Inspector Trant)
This Way Out (*Mystery Book Magazine*, March 1947)
Love Comes to Miss Lucy (*Ellery Queen's Mystery Magazine*, April 1947)
Footlights and Murder (*This Week*, May 11, 1947; Inspector Trantglamoou)
Little Boy Lost (*Ellery Queen's Mystery Magazine*, Oct 1947)
Murder in One Scene (*This Week*, May 2, 1948; Inspector Trant)
Mother, May I Go Out to Swim? (*Ellery Queen's Mystery Magazine*, July 1948)
Farewell Performance (*Ellery Queen's Mystery Magazine*, Sept 1948; Inspector Trant)
The Wrong Envelope (*Mystery Book Magazine*, Winter 1948; Inspector Trant)
Murder in the Alps (*This Week*, Feb 20, 1949; re-write of "Girl Overboard"; Inspector Trant)
Death and the Maiden (*Detective Novel Magazine*, Spring 1949; reprinted in *This Week*, May 26, 1949)
Who Killed the Mermaid? (*This Week*, May 26, 1949; Inspector Trant)
Thou Lord See'st Me (*Ellery Queen's Mystery Magazine*, July 1949)
The Case of the Plaster Cat (*This Week*, Sept 3, 1949)
Town Blonde, Country Blonde (*This Week*, Oct 16, 1949; Inspector Trant)
Woman of Ice (*This Week*, Oct 30, 1949; Inspector Trant)
This Looks Like Murder (*This Week*, April 30, 1950; Inspector Trant)
A Boy's Will (*Ellery Queen's Mystery Magazine*, June 1950)
Death on the Riviera (*This Week*, July 30, 1950; Inspector Trant)
Death and Canasta (*This Week*, Oct 15, 1950; Inspector Trant)
Death on Saturday Night (*This Week,* Nov 26, 1950; Inspector Trant)
This Will Kill You (*Ellery Queen's Mystery Magazine*, Nov 1950)
Girl Overboard (*Four-&-Twenty Bloodhounds*, 1950; Inspector Trant)
All the Way to the Moon (*Ellery Queen's Mystery Magazine*, Sept 1951)

Death before Breakfast (*This Week*, March 11, 1951; Inspector Trant)
Glamorous Opening (*This Week*, June 3, 1951; Inspector Trant)
Death at the Fair (*London Evening Standard*, Nov 9, 1951; Inspector Trant)
The Pigeon Woman (*Ellery Queen's Mystery Magazine*, July 1952)
Revolvers and Roses (*This Week*, Dec 7, 1952; Inspector Trant)
The 'Laughing Man' Murders (*The American Magazine*, March 1953)
Death on a First Night (*Mackill's Mystery Magazine*, May 1953)
On the Day of the Rose Show (*Ellery Queen's Mystery Magazine*, March 1956; reprinted as "Revolvers and Roses, *This Week,* Dec 7, 1952; Inspector Trant)
Going...Going...Gone! (*This Week*, May 10, 1953; Inspector Trant)
Two Deadly Females (*This Week*, April 3, 1955; reprinted as "Lioness vs. Panther'; Inspector Trant)
Lioness vs. Panther (*Ellery Queen's Mystery Magazine,* July 1958; Inspector Trant)
The Fat Cat (*Suspense*, March 1959; reprinted as "The Fat Cat Which Sat on the Mat," *Aberdeen Evening Express*, October 18 & 19, 1961)

Short fiction by Rickie Webb

The Predestined (*Britannia & Eve*, Aug 1, 1953; *Weird Tales*, May 1954)
The Red Balloon (*Weird Tales*, Nov 1953)

As Dick Callingham

Short fiction by Rickie Webb and Hugh Wheeler

"Striking Silence" (*Street & Smith's Detective Story Magazine*, Feb 1936)
"Terror Keepers" (*Street & Smith's Detective Story Magazine*, March 1936)
"Frightened Killer" (*Street & Smith's Detective Story Magazine*, May 1937)

As Patrick Quentin

Novels by Rickie Webb and Hugh Wheeler

A Puzzle for Fools (1936; originally "Terror Keepers" by Dick Callingham; Peter Duluth)
Puzzle for Players (1938; Peter Duluth)
Puzzle for Puppets (1944; serialized as "Ring around the Roses" as by Q. Patrick, *Woman Magazine*, April 18 - May 9, 1942; Peter Duluth)
Puzzle for Wantons (1945; reprinted as *Slay the Loose Ladies,* 1948; originally serialized in the UK as "Puzzle for Frauds," *Woman Magazine*, January 20 - March 10, 1945; Peter Duluth)
Puzzle for Fiends (1946; reprinted as *Love Is a Deadly Weapon*, 1949; originally *Mystery Book Magazine*, May 1946; serialized in the UK, *Answers Magazine*, August 24, 1946 - Feb 8, 1947; Peter Duluth)

Novels by Hugh Wheeler

Puzzle for Pilgrims (1947; reprinted as *The Fate of the Immodest Blonde*, 1950; Peter Duluth)
Run to Death (1948; originally *Mystery Book Magazine*, 1948; Peter Duluth)
The Follower (1950)
Black Widow (1952; published in UK as *Fatal Woman*, 1953; originally *Cosmopolitan*, July 1952; Inspector Trant, Peter Duluth)
My Son, the Murderer (1954; published in UK as *The Wife of Ronald Sheldon*; originally

BIBLIOGRAPHY

Cosmopolitan, May 1954; Peter Duluth/Inspector Trant)
The Man with Two Wives (1955; serialized in *Woman's Own Weekly* from June 16, 1955 - Aug 4, 1955; Inspector Trant)
The Man in the Net (1956; originally *Cosmopolitan*, Sept 1955)
Suspicious Circumstances (1957)
Shadow of Guilt (1959; originally *Cosmopolitan*, April 1959; Inspector Trant)
The Green-Eyed Monster (1960; originally *Cosmopolitan*, Feb 1960)
Family Skeletons (1965; originally *Cosmopolitan*, Dec 1964; Inspector Trant)

Short Story Collections by Rickie Webb and Hugh Wheeler

The Ordeal of Mrs. Snow (1962)
The Puzzles of Peter Duluth (2016)
The Cases of Lieutenant Trant (2020)
Hunt in the Dark and Other Fatal Pursuits (2021)
Exit Before Midnight: A Final Collection of Murder Tales (2023)

Short Story Collections by Hugh Wheeler

Death Freight and Other Murderous Excursions (2022)

Short fiction by Rickie Webb and Hugh Wheeler

Honor the Valiant (*This Week*, Oct 20, 1940)
She Wrote Finis (*Maclean's Magazine*, Dec 1940 - Jan 1941; Inspector Trant)
Puzzle for Frauds (*Mystery Book Magazine*, Sept 1945; Peter Duluth)
Witness for the Prosecution (*Ellery Queen's Mystery Magazine*, July 1946)
Puzzle for Poppy (*Ellery Queen's Mystery Magazine*, Feb 1946; Peter Duluth)
Murder on New Year's Eve (*Ellery Queen's Mystery Magazine*, Jan 1950)

Short fiction by Hugh Wheeler

Passport for Murder (*The American Magazine*, March 1950; reprinted as "Mrs. B.'s Black Sheep," *Ellery Queen's Mystery Magazine*, Sept 1967)
Death Freight (*The American Magazine*, Jan 1951)
The Scarlet Box (*The American Magazine*, Dec 1951)
The Laughing Man (*The American Magazine*, March 1953; reprinted as "The Laughing Man Murders," *Ellery Queen's Mystery Magazine*, Aug 1963)
Death and the Rising Star (*Better Living*, June 1955; Peter Duluth)

Short non-fiction by Rickie Webb

The Naughty Child of Fiction (*The Writer*, 1942)
A Theoretical Reconstruction of the Borden Murders (*The Pocket Book of True Crime Stories*, 1943)
Who'd Do It? (*Chimera*, Sept 1947)

Short non-fiction by Hugh Wheeler

The Last of Mrs. Maybrick (*The Pocket Book of True Crime Stories*, 1943)
Unlucky Lady (*American Weekly*, May 10, 1953)
The Ordeal of Florence Maybrick (*The Quality of Murder: Three Hundred Years of True Crime Compiled by Members of the Mystery Writers of America*, 1962)

As Jonathan Stagge

Novels by Rickie Webb and Hugh Wheeler

Murder Gone to Earth (1936; published in U.S. as *The Dogs Do Bark,* 1937; Dr. Hugh Westlake)
Murder or Mercy? (1937; published in U.S. as *Murder by Prescription*, 1938; Dr. Hugh Westlake)
The Stars Spell Death (1939; published in UK as *Murder in the Stars*; Dr. Hugh Westlake)
Turn of the Table (1940; published in UK as *Funeral for Five*; serialized in US newspapers as *The Table Talks*; Dr. Hugh Westlake)
The Yellow Taxi (1942; published in UK as *Call a Hearse*; serialized in US newspapers as *Riddle in Red*; Dr. Hugh Westlake)
The Scarlet Circle (1943; published in UK as *Light from a Lantern*; Dr. Hugh Westlake)
Death, My Darling Daughters (1945; published in UK as *Death and the Dear Girls*)
Death's Old Sweet Song (1946)

Novels by Hugh Wheeler

The Three Fears (1949)

Short Fiction by Jonathan Stagge (all featuring Dr. Hugh Westlake)

Death, My Darling Daughters (*Mystery Book Magazine*, Jan 1946)
Death's Old Sweet Song (*The San Francisco Dramatic Chronicle*, 1946; *Thrilling Mystery Novel Magazine*, May 1947)
The Dogs Do Bark (*Street & Smith's Detective Story Magazine,* Nov 1935, as by Q. Patrick; *Triple Detective*, Fall 1947)
The Stars Spell Death (*Argosy*, Oct 28, 1939; *Triple Detective*, Fall 1952)
The Three Fears (*Two Complete Detective Books* #61, March 1950)
The Yellow Taxi (*Triple Detective*, Winter 1950)

Works by Hugh Wheeler

The Crippled Muse (1951; novel)
Big Fish, Little Fish (1961; play)
Look: We've Come Through (1961; play)
Five Miles to Midnight (1962; film script)
Rich Little Rich Girl (1964; play)
We Have Always Lived in the Castle (1966; play)
Something For Everyone (1970; film script)
Travels with My Aunt (1972; film script; WGA nomination, Edgar nomination)
The Snoop Sisters (1972; TV film)
Cabaret (1972; revised film script, uncredited; Oscar nomination)
A Little Night Music (1973; musical book; Tony award)
Irene (1973; musical book)
Candide (1974; musical book; Tony award)
The Queen's Cage (1975; book for an aborted English stage version of *La Cage aux Folles*)
Truckload (1975; musical book)
Pacific Overtures (1976; revisions to musical book)
Sweeney Todd (1979; musical book; Tony award)
Nijinsky (1980; film script)
The Little Prince and the Aviator (1982; musical book)
Meet Me in St. Louis (1989; musical book, posthumously performed; Tony nomination)

Novel by Mary Louise Aswell

Far to Go (1957)